THE FAE CHRONICLES

Embracing Destiny

AMELIA HUTCHINS

Dedication

This book is for those who have been with me since book one. For the new fan's that took a chance, and waded through some of the errors or cringe-worthy writing of my humble beginning into publishing. To my team who helps endlessly, day and night to get these books ready for publishing.

To Cups, Texas, and Sky-bunny. Thank you for always being there, and from beings fans who became friends, and now are family.

To my family who shares me with the fans without questioning my sanity. Yes, without you I would have had this series finished a lot sooner, but I wouldn't trade for anything. Well, maybe a margarita. Yeah, probably.

To those people who are having a hard time with the world falling apart around them, we got this. We've been training for this moment our entire lives! We're introverted book nerds who know how to vanish within the pages of a story. I hope you all enjoy this story and their ending as much as I have enjoyed writing it.

This story was supposed to be finished in one large book, but unfortunately, it was too long of an ending to accommodate that option. The need for paperbacks made it impossible to put it out in one book. As an Indie author, my options are limited and I refused to take away from Ryder and Synthia's ending to make it fit into one book. I hope you understand, and enjoy the story.

ALSO BY

Amelia Hutchins

Legacy of the Nine Realms

Flames of Chaos
Ashes of Chaos *Spring 2020*

The Fae Chronicles

Fighting Destiny
Taunting Destiny
Escaping Destiny
Seducing Destiny
Unraveling Destiny
Embracing Destiny
Crowning Destiny May/June 2020

The Elite Guards

A Demon's Dark Embrace
Claiming the Dragon King
A Demon's Plaything
The Winter Court

A Guardian's Diary

Darkest Before Dawn
Death before Dawn
Midnight Rising TBA

ALSO BY

Amelia Hutchins

Playing with Monsters series

(Part of the Fae Chronicles)

Playing with Monsters
Sleeping with Monsters
Becoming his Monster
Last Monster Book *TBA 2020*

Wicked Knights series

Oh, Holy Knight
If She's Wicked
Book Three, *TBA*

Midnight Coven Books

Forever Immortal
Immortal Hexes
Wicked Hexes

Finished Serial Series

Tempted by Fae *May 2020*

E.V.I.E. 13 Days of Slaying October 2020

READING ORDER

If you're following the series for the Fae Chronicles, Elite Guards, and Monsters, reading order is as follows.

Fighting Destiny
Taunting Destiny
Escaping Destiny
Seducing Destiny
A Demon's Dark Embrace
Playing with Monsters
Unraveling Destiny
Sleeping with Monsters
Claiming the Dragon King
Oh, Holy Knight
Becoming his Monster
A Demon's Plaything
The Winter Court
If She's Wicked
Embracing Destiny
Crowning Destiny

WARNING

Warning: This book is **dark**. It's **sexy**, hot, and **intense**. The author is human, as you are. Is the book perfect? It's as perfect as I could make it. Are there mistakes? Probably, then again, even **New York Times top published** books have minimal mistakes because, like me, they have **human editors**. There are words in this book that won't be found in the standard dictionary because they were created to set the stage for a paranormal-urban fantasy world. Words in this novel are common in paranormal books and give better descriptions to the action in the story than can be found in standard dictionaries. They are intentional and not mistakes.

About the hero: chances are you may **not** fall instantly in **love** with him, that's because **I don't write men you instantly love**; you grow to love them. I don't believe in **instant love**. I write flawed, raw, caveman-like **assholes** that eventually let you see their redeeming qualities. They are **aggressive**, **assholes**, one step above a caveman when we meet them. You may *not* even like him by the time you finish this book, but I promise you will **love** him by the end of this **series**.

About the heroine: There is a chance that you might think she's a bit naïve or weak, but then again, who starts out as a badass? Badass women are a product of growth, and I am going to put her through **hell**, and you get to watch **her** come up **swinging** every time I knock her on her ass. That's just how I do things. How she reacts to the set of circumstances she is put through may not be how you as the reader, or I, as the author would react to that same situation. Everyone reacts differently to circumstances and how Synthia responds to her challenges, is how I see her as a character and as a person.

I don't write love stories: I write fast-paced, knock you on your ass, *make you sit on the edge of your seat wondering what is going to happen next* books. If you're looking for cookie-cutter romance, this isn't for you. If you can't handle the ride, ***unbuckle your seatbelt and get out of the roller-coaster car now*. If not, you've been warned.** If nothing outlined above bothers you, carry on and **enjoy the ride!**

Embracing Destiny

Here's the thing about family: It isn't who is born into it by blood or birthright. It is about those who come when you need them most, those who stand beside you as you fall, and when you're down, they help you back up. I've watched lives twisted and traumatized by those who sought to ruin us. I've seen my friends dying in front of me, and I've found a love that will withstand anything that comes at us. I've faced death and made a sacrifice no one should ever have to make. Even knowing the mages are marching towards us and we won't all make it out of this alive, I wouldn't change a thing. Life isn't about planning where to go; it's about where you go when you stop allowing everything else to plot your course. How do I know that we won't all make it out of this alive? Because the God of Death is standing right beside us as we prepare for war, waiting for the warriors to fall.

Synthia Raine McKenna

Chapter
ONE

An eerie, deafening silence had fallen over Faery since Ryder and I returned home. It was like the entire world was holding its breath as war made its way toward our doors. The fairy glens were vacant of the life that once flourished within them. Meadows that had once fought off intruders or stray humans were barren of flowers and devoid of life, long since crunched beneath the heavy feet of those who marched into battle. The horde stronghold was now teeming with warriors, all honed and created for battle, and we all held our breath to see who would make the first move.

Fires from the many encampments around the fortress spread miles out in each direction, burning brightly throughout the long, cold nights. Battle cries filled the air, inciting the need to fight as more and more refugees came by the early morning light to join the horde against the invaders who wanted to destroy our home, ruining our way of life.

I should have felt safe, but I didn't. I'd never known war, and yet I knew the cost of losing this one would be too high a price to pay. If we lost and Faery fell, we, along with all its inhabitants, would be forced into a world that would never accept us for what we were. I knew that much after having been one of the enforcers who had hunted the fae down, punishing them whether they'd committed the accused crime or not.

My children were being protected by my father in the Blood Kingdom when not here with us. More and more, I brought them home to remind them why we were fighting. To understand what was at risk if we lost. It was selfish, but soon enough, they'd go with Destiny, safeguarded in a place they couldn't be reached. Ryder and I had taken extra measures to protect them and to ensure the safety of their innocent hearts. Yet I still felt a deep foreboding within me that twisted my stomach, making me feel ill as drums pounded with the impending reality of what we faced. War had come to Faery, and it came with an ugliness that would touch every corner of this world.

I was neither blind nor stupid enough to think there wouldn't be heavy losses on both sides. We wouldn't make it through this war unscathed; to assume otherwise would, well, it would be a colossal mistake, one I wouldn't dare make. War was messy; it was brutal and unforgiving. It tore worlds apart, turning children into orphans, leveling villages, and leaving destruction in its wake.

I slowly moved my gaze away from the remarkable spread of tents, warriors, and campfires below to peer into the shadows of the balcony. A dark figure silently surveyed me. A soft snort escaped my lips while my stare swung back to the commotion happening around my new home. It was beautiful chaos that showed courage and strength in the face of insurmountable odds.

I felt the turmoil of the world around me. The endless pain that was ripping Faery and me apart as the mages made their way toward us, leaving a trail of bodies behind them. Even now, Faery screamed so loudly with the need to be avenged, it sounded as if war drums were pounding in my ears, deafening me. Slowly, I pushed my long, platinum-blonde hair off my naked shoulders, lifting my head to the stars sparkling in the midnight skies. I prayed silently to the gods to forgive me for what I was about to do.

"Is it done?" I asked, sensing the shadow's unease.

"It has already begun. I fear what you are doing and that the path you've taken will destroy you, goddess. If you continue down this road, there is no undoing it. What once was can never be again if you do this. Do you understand that? If you proceed, I cannot help you, nor can anyone undo what might happen," the shadow warned, concern lacing her words as a current of unease and apprehension shivered through me.

I shook off the uneasy feeling, knowing that if I backed out now, it would all be for naught. "I'd die for Ryder. I'd also destroy worlds to find him, and I won't chance it happening. That creature is my entire universe, and without him, I'm willing to slay them all; happily, more than eager to do so," I replied firmly.

"But would he die for you?" the shadow asked carefully, aware should she speak out of turn, I'd take her life. "Men are wishy-washy creatures controlled by their baser needs. You are certain he is worth this?"

"It doesn't matter if he would or wouldn't. I wouldn't want Ryder to die for me. I want him to live." I turned, staring at the figure concealed by shadows that swayed around her lithe frame. "The God of Death is here, and he will not take that man from me. I have tasted life without him, and I would always choose a life with him. Do you understand what I am saying? You offered me a way to avoid that cost, and now you question if I should take it? I chose to walk the road you proposed, and I'm moving forward. I will not change my mind after the fact, if that's what you fear."

"What if the God of Death isn't here for just your

husband? What if he is here for all of you? Your mother is gone, and without her, this world is nothing. What if this is the end of Faery?"

"Then we will die fighting to prevent that from happening," I returned bitterly. "Do you hear me, Death?" I demanded of the second shadow that had appeared on the balcony, scrutinizing me from behind the first. "If you think to take those I love, know this: I will fight you with my dying breath to keep them alive. I will do everything within my power to protect my family."

I didn't back down as blue flames peered at me from beneath a black hood. The wind howled, matching the turmoil in my soul as if sensing my unease at Death's presence and what it meant. My anger fueled the world, creating gusts of wind that whipped my hair against my face as my white gown ruffled, lashing harshly against my skin while I stared Death straight in the eye, promising a fight.

"If you are thinking of taking my family, Thanatos, I suggest you change your plans quickly. I will rip you apart and enjoy every cut you endure at my hands. I've not gone through hell to lose them now. I will fight you, even at the cost of my soul."

Thanatos exhaled as the blue flames burned brighter against the midnight, regarding me carefully as he stepped out of the shadows, strolling leisurely toward me. "War is coming, Goddess. No one is guaranteed to survive. Both sides will carry the heavy burden of loss. Pray to your gods I don't get carried away reaping the souls of immortals. Hell is empty, and immortals are always collected to rebuild the walls once broken. You're about to wage war, and in war, the only certainty is death.

"You want to know why I am here and have brought the reapers with me? I've come to reclaim souls that have escaped or trespassed against the laws of this world. You and your kind have thrown the laws of death out the window too many times to be ignored. I am owed souls, including yours, which Danu denied me. It's not personal, Synthia; death is never personal. Death is part of living, and when one soul is given and then taken, it creates an echo. You have made such an echo, and it's still heard throughout Faery. Your God of Death is no longer here to give the souls of Faery peace, but I am."

"I'm aware that we caused a stir when I refused to die. I don't want this war, either. Faery never asked for this war, but we will fight to secure peace. We're not the bad guys here. My family is fighting to survive. The fae are fighting to live so our children and their children will know peace within this world. If we fail, you'll be rather busy since there will be nowhere else to flee than the human world. I am trying to prevent the humans from paying that price, as I'm sure you're already aware of the chaos unfolding there."

"To wage war against the mages, you will lose people," he stated softly. The fire burning in his depths intensified as he spoke, and shadows swayed around him, catching and merging into his robe. "Hold tight to the ones you love and keep them close. Tell them you love them today, for tomorrow is never promised to anyone, not even the gods. Send your children to the City of Gods for safekeeping, where no one can reach them. You can weep the loss of their childhood, but if you don't make that sacrifice, you will lose them; this is the only warning I can or will give you. Consider it a debt repaid for the favor your mother granted me long ago. Anything else, and I jeopardize doing more harm than good.

"I'm not here as your enemy, nor am I here to hurt you. I am here to take those you lose in this fight from the agony they will undoubtedly know without my ability to end their needless suffering when they fall. I'm merely here to ease their passing to the Otherworld and ensure they're not cursed to walk endlessly through the shadows of Faery and the dead. Good luck, Daughter of Danu, Queen of the Horde, and Goddess of the Fae. May you survive this war to prosper and create many more pretty little girls, like the little one with eyes the color of fresh honey, sparkling from within. She is a rare beauty, sweet goddess, hold her tightly." Thanatos vanished into a plume of smoke that billowed into the air the moment he spoke the last of his chilling words.

I swallowed down anger at his parting words. He'd seen my daughter, and that bothered me. Thanatos was one of the gods of death in mythology, so what the fuck was he doing here? Faery wasn't his playground or where he belonged. It wasn't his monkeys or his circus, yet he'd been right beside me. How was that even possible, and how was he allowed to intervene with this world? There were rules, and if he broke them, that meant he could be removed from Faery.

"He cannot stay away for long. Thanatos will be drawn to this world once souls begin weeping to be harvested. What are your orders, Synthia?"

"I will prepare my children to go with you. First, I want you to do what you offered. If I die, I must know my family will go on. I need you to go to the Fates and be certain they can see their future with this path, should we choose to follow it. *All of them.* Make sure they see my babes and my husband's futures, even if I am no longer in them." Turning, I peered into the bedroom, where Ryder and my children awaited me. I could hear the happiness in their laughter, which was music to my soul. "Once you have completed your task, return for my kids, and I will poison Ryder myself."

"If he turns, and you don't tell him? He may never forgive you, and may even hate you for doing this to him." Her warning was clear. "Can you live without him?"

"No, and that's the point, isn't it? Hate, I can endure. His death would make me into a monster. I would never return from that, and we both know it. Destiny has already told me the Fates have yet to see my future. I'm not scared to die or frightened of the unknown. I am afraid of living without that man at my side. I have not walked through the fires of Hell to lose him. If it's a choice between Ryder hating me or dying, there's only one option with which I could live. His sense of betrayal will lessen in time. We are endless. We have all the time in the world. After this war is over, we will deal with the consequences of what I've done. Now go, do as I have asked, creature. I'll have the children ready to leave with you when you return."

She nodded, and I studied as her slim form vanished into a heavy mist that a powerful gust carried through the air allowing her to disappear into the dark skies above the stronghold. Her ominous warning echoed in my ears for a long moment. I made my way into the bedroom, stopping to gaze lovingly at the family we'd created as my gentle beast played with his little beasties.

Smiling softly, I watched as Ryder tickled Kahleena while she squealed with laughter, pointing at Zander, demanding her father get her brothers instead.

Cade silently observed them from where he rested against the pillows, peering down at them with large violet irises as his black curls curved around his chubby cheeks. Cade was more intense than his siblings.

His pensive stare missed nothing, and he reminded me of Zahruk, always ready for battle, should the need arise. He'd traded places with Zander, who was no longer the somber and carefree one of the triplets. My brother Liam had a lot to do with it, and that was something I'd never be able to thank him enough over.

"Daddy," Kahleena panted out of breath, snorting as she pointed her tiny finger at Zander, who had crawled up behind Ryder to attack him. Her golden eyes sparkled with a multitude of galaxies within their amber depths as she laughed loudly.

"I got you!" he shouted, jumping on his father's back to save his sister from the tickles her father loved to give. It had become Ryder's favorite sound, the laughter of the wee beasties as he tortured them playfully. This was the light in our darkest hour. Their giggles and sounds of their happiness were everything good in the world. They would drive us through the upcoming war, reminding us of what we fought to protect.

"Is that so, my little princeling?" Ryder growled, flipping Zander upside down beside his sister to tickle him.

"Cade! Save us," Kahleena pleaded urgently, her giggles enough to work the corners of my mouth as I slowly made my way to where they played.

"Momma," Cade whispered softly, his voice barely audible. "Is the man in the shadows going to take you from us?"

Ryder's golden eyes were slowly swallowed by the obsidian beauty of the beast's stare, peering into the darkened corners of the room, searching for unknown enemies. He pulled up from where he played with the children, staring at me over his shoulder, watching while I slowly walked toward him. "Is something wrong, Pet?"

"No, he was just an old friend come to check on us and make sure we were okay," I assured him gently as I settled on the bed, stroking Ryder's sharp jawline with the tips of my fingers. He leaned over, nipping my ear as the kids studied us. "It seems our bed is rather full of little beasties tonight, Fairy," I murmured huskily. Already our babes were children, and time within the City of Gods would take whatever childhood they had left away from them—and us. It wasn't a choice any longer, not when war marched toward us by the minute. Not with the message Thanatos had given before dissolving into shadows, vanishing without causing a disturbance in the air.

"I think we should add a few more," Ryder countered as a wicked glint filled his dark stare. He leaned closer, a devilish smile curving his sinfully full mouth. "How about we get started on that right now?"

"Eww, he's going to kiss mommy!" Zander warned as he scrunched up his face in disgust. Blue depths the color of freshly polished sapphires examined Ryder as if he were about to do precisely what he'd suggested. "Get him!" he shouted, and I laughed at the look of panic that flashed over Ryder's face as Cade and Kahleena moved to do as their brother had ordered.

"Gods," Ryder chuckled, holding one on each arm while Zander held onto his neck. "They're attacking me, shouldn't you be helping?"

I stared into Ryder's golden eyes before moving my gaze to Kahleena, who squealed with laughter as hers sparkled with merriment. I leaned over, taking advantage of their conquering the mighty King of the Horde by kissing him gently, brushing my lips over his before pulling back as the children made gagging sounds.

"Didn't you just say you wanted to make more?" I crossed my arms to stare at him pointedly with a wide grin I couldn't hold back.

"Can't we just practice making them?" His eyes glowed while his eyebrows wiggled playfully.

"I love you, Fairy," I whispered huskily. I smiled before leaning over, kissing his lips again as our children cringed. Ryder pulled me down onto the bed and then leaned over me, smirking roguishly as the kids laughed and attacked us both. I'd just let out a hoot of laughter when the alarm screamed out a warning.

"Our kids," I said, sitting up.

"Take them to the tower," he ordered through clenched teeth, standing to release the beast that had been observing us play from within Ryder's form. I stood abruptly, collecting the children as Zahruk entered the room with Sevrin and Savlian.

"Come, my darling little monsters." I grabbed hands, collecting them as we moved out into the hallway, finding Olivia and Ciara there waiting beside their mates. They stood on tiptoes to deliver soft kisses to their men before falling into step behind me. Both women were heavy with child, and we expected deliveries to come any day now. Cade and Kahleena each took a hand while Zander latched onto Ciara's, gazing up at her in wonder.

"Oh, my," Olivia whispered, grasping onto the wall with one hand as the other rubbed her swollen belly.

"Olivia?" I asked softly, noting the way her eyes pinched together in pain.

"I'm fine." It was a lie; her face lost color, but she slowly gained her footing and started forward.

My stare moved to Ristan, who examined her slow progression from the bedroom where Ryder was glamouring on armor. Something had him worried. He studied her form with a look of horror and fear while she held the wall moving away from him.

"Protect her, Synthia." Ristan shook his head, his gaze swirling as a frown tugged at his mouth. "I cannot lose her."

"Ciara, no babe without me," Blane warned, studying the overly pregnant female beside me while Zander glared at Blane, crushing on his auntie something fierce. "I love you, my world." Eventually, I'd have to break it to Zander that he couldn't marry his very married auntie.

"No. No one says goodbye today. Do you hear me? No one says goodbye before going to battle; it is bad luck. Let's go, ladies. Darynda, help Olivia. Mira, help Zander with Ciara." I took Fury from his mother and tucked him into my arm. "Kahleena and Cade, with me now," I instructed firmly, straightening my spine against the worry forming in the hallway. "Everyone hold hands and follow mommy, just like we practiced."

I turned back a moment, staring into golden depths that smiled at me with pride burning within them. "I love you, Fairy. See you soon."

"I'll always come back to you, Pet."

I swallowed past the lump that formed in my throat. My heart hammered against my ears, deafening the sound of the drums in the courtyard as Ryder sifted from the room, vanishing from sight.

Death stepped from the shadows, watching me before his eyes lowered to my children and the women moving with us down the hallway. He bowed his blond head, turning to disappear back into the darkness without a word.

Chapter TWO

I was good under pressure. I was amazing in chaos, but the fact that my babes were in danger horrified me. The idea that Ryder was heading out to face an unknown enemy left me feeling numb. All because some ancient law forbade the queen and king from riding into battle together.

It was medieval bullshit that needed to be rewritten immediately, but the impending war was putting a kibosh on those details at the moment. One of us had to remain in residence, or one of our heirs if they were of age to rule. Sure, before Ryder had taken his throne, Lachlan played his placeholder, but since taking our vows, the law was in play. I hated it. It all but had me ringing the dinner bell, wearing mom jeans and an apron.

I stopped at the door, counting heads as the women entered the room one by one. Turning, I peered down the hallway as the sound of footfalls echoed from the other end. Lilith and Icelyn appeared with their arms full of little ones.

"Darynda, with me," I said urgently, moving toward the women who had dirty children behind them. Mixed fae orphans were being dropped off daily at castles throughout the many kingdoms as a result of the mage war currently ravaging the countryside. Ours had been overrun with little babes, changelings, and other creatures' offspring lately. It looked like we were building an army of filthy but cute tiny urchins.

Once I reached Icelyn, I took the tiny bundle from her arms as her hand moved to her swollen belly. Her face scrunched up, and a frown tugged at my lips. Darynda picked up a small changeling and held him to her hip before catching my eyes over Icelyn's ice-blonde head. Glancing at Icelyn's belly, Darynda's mouth flattened into a straight line, and she absently worried her bottom lip as we ushered everyone into the protection of the tower.

When we reached the door, I spun on my heel, tilting my head to the right while I used my inhuman hearing to see if anyone else was rushing toward us. Leaning forward, I peered into the room, gazing at the multitude of little ones along with the few heavily pregnant women getting settled inside.

I silently stepped inside the room and placed my hands against the wall, waiting as the glowing blue runes sealed us into the safety of the heavily warded tower. It was Ryder's version of a safe room. We had ample supplies and multiple rooms and nooks that could be filled with people.

It was also his idea of a pretty prison to hold us, so when the big bad warriors went to war, us damsels could sit around drinking tea and eating biscuits. As proof, Darynda was taking coffee and tea orders. Ryder was one stage above a caveman, and yet I loved him all the more for it.

The main room was big enough to fit a large

assembly, but with the babes and children huddled together, it still felt confined.

I exhaled, regaining my composure, then noticed Olivia rubbing the small of her back, which bothered me.

Ciara, on the other hand, was bouncing Fury on her ample, protruding belly while he giggled.

Icelyn stood away from them with Lilith at her side; they'd bonded over the similarities of their former lives. They both came from the lesser courts, and as such, had given us a wide berth. We were trying to close that gap, wanting them to realize sooner rather than later, that they were family.

"Keely, Meriel, and Faelyn, we need food placed on the tables in the other room. See that it is prepared and set out so the little beasties can eat before they start gnawing our legs or something else. Darynda, make sure the other handmaidens prepare the bedrooms for our guests; worry about tea and biscuits later," I instructed low but clearly. Clapping my hands, I plastered a smile on my face, hoping to reassure everyone that everything was going to be okay.

My chest rose and fell as my gaze flitted around the room, never settling on a person or object too long. I worried about what was happening outside the walls of the fortress. We had no way to communicate outside the barrier of the stronghold to learn what was going on, which was a huge design flaw. We only had cell reception within the castle walls. I did better in battle than I did being locked in some tower like a damsel in distress. It wasn't sitting well with me. I needed to know Ryder was okay, and I wasn't good at waiting idly by while he fought our battles without me.

Silently, Ristan's mom, Alannah, slipped in beside Olivia, scrutinizing her through a silver glare that matched her son's. For a petite demon, Alannah sure loved to stir up shit. Ryder's mother, Kiera, played similar games, forcing him to move her to the Dark Kingdom.

She still spoke of dark omens and refused to keep her distance from the children and me. It didn't matter that I loved her son. She only spoke of how, together, we would destroy the world. Not to mention, she had an affinity for randomly attacking me, as well as Ryder, who she called Alazander, accidentally mistaking the two.

It concerned me that so many of the women here were heavy with child. There was a good chance that eventually, each would need to shelter-in-place when the alarm sounded. Judging by their size and slow running due to their pregnant bellies, we had to find a better way for them to get here. While having the women shelter-in-place wasn't ideal, it was the best we could do, considering their delicate situations.

I poked my head into one of the rooms and saw Kahleena holding court like she'd been born to be queen. The orphans sat dutifully around her, gaping as they hung on her every word while she leisurely sipped her tea.

I leaned against the wall, taking in all the kids who were abandoned on our steps. Zander leered while he watched the boys with a furrowed brow, his tiny fists balled at his sides. Cade mirrored his stance, one brow lifted to his hairline as his sister described where they'd hidden, the Blood Kingdom, in vivid detail to all the children surrounding her, hanging on her every word.

"Uncle Liam, while scarred by my grandfather, fights like a knight," Kahleena explained, swinging her arms like she held a sword as her tea spilled on the skirt of her dress. "I plan to be a fighter one day, just like my momma."

"Aren't you a girl?" one of the young boys asked.

"Girls can fight, too," Kahleena huffed, rolling her eyes toward the heavens for patience. She turned to me silently, waiting for a response, and when my lips turned up in the corners, she pointed at me. "My mom rips the throats out of her enemies, and she's a girl."

Oh, shit. I hadn't been ready for that to come out of her lips.

"She's not normal," the boy exclaimed.

"Take it back!" Zander's face reddened, and his

nostrils flared as he gripped his tiny fists so hard that his knuckles were turning white.

"Children," I muttered, exhaling slowly as I rubbed my temples. "There is enough fighting in our world, let us not add to it, sweet ones. Who is hungry?" I asked, changing the subject before the children ended up brawling with a horde of orphans. At their nodded replies, I heard a deep chuckle, and my attention turned to Alannah.

"Follow me, wee ones. Let's see what the king and queen have placed upon our table, shall we?" Alannah's pretty eyes swung to Olivia, brow raised in question. "Would you like a heart from one of the orphans? My grandchild must be half-starved with your inability to feast on flesh."

"There is no need for that. Ristan feeds me well, Alannah." With a saccharine smile, Olivia pushed her red curls away from her face. "He blends the hearts with fruit to remove the bitterness. In fact, I had one just this morning."

I shivered at the thought of eating hearts and

moved to my children. Hunching down to their level, I stared at Kahleena, who frowned, causing my mouth to mirror hers.

"Not everyone is like us, daughter of mine. Women were not created to fight as men, and while some of us do it, not everyone will agree that we should, and that is okay. It's an opinion. Everyone has their views regarding what is expected of women. Even if you don't agree, they are entitled to their point of view. It's important for people's opinions to be heard. Even though I am your mother and queen, not everyone agrees with what I have done, Zander," I whispered, a smile lifting across my mouth.

"I am the only one who can be hurt by their words if I decide they are valid, which I don't. I am not normal, and I am perfectly okay with it. I love you all, but keep in mind that they look to us to lead them. You must be kind and decide what you allow to bother you. Words cannot hurt us unless we let them. Now, go eat and make friends." I ruffled his hair and then kissed Kahleena on the cheek. "One day, you will lead, and you will need to do so while being able to see the world through the eyes of others. Hearing their comments and opinions and not being offended is very important. Kindness is a better quality in a leader than anger; that's important to remember."

I stood up, taking in Icelyn's posture as she winced, running her hand over her belly while Lilith stood beside her, rocking an infant in her arms. They remained at a distance from the other women, indicating as newly joined members of the horde, they still felt like outsiders. As I moved toward them, Icelyn cried out and bent at the waist, her hand gripping the small of her back. I gazed at the floor, watching the fluid that rushed down the inside of her legs.

"I think I wet myself," she admitted as pink colored her cheeks.

"Darynda," I murmured, knowing my trusted handmaiden would be close by, waiting for me to direct her. "I need my bedroom emptied of people, and towels and clean water brought in immediately." Her eyes followed mine before growing round and wide as they settled on Icelyn. I produced a towel, lowering it to the floor, silently cleaning the fluid that continued to trickle down Icelyn's legs.

"Oh, don't do that. You're the queen," Icelyn muttered with tears filling her icy-blue eyes. "I think I wet myself, but the babes keep shifting, and my body isn't my own anymore," her tone was filled with embarrassment and horror. "I can do that." Icelyn bent toward the towel, but the pain stopped her. "Something isn't right."

"You're in labor," I announced, standing as the cloth vanished. "I may be queen, but I am never above helping my family, no matter what title I hold."

"No, I can't be in labor. I'm not due for two more months." Icelyn's face suddenly turned ashen, and her body began to tremble.

"Your water just broke, which means the babes are coming whether we are ready for them or not. Come with me, so we don't worry the other children as we bring yours into the world." I extended my hand to her while Lilith gave the infant she'd been fawning over to Keely. "I had my chamber prepared for you."

"But I will soil your bed," she complained.

"It's just a bed, and it's the only room where you can have privacy. It's also soundproofed, so your screams will not upset the little ones. I am queen, remember? You have to do as I say." I smiled tightly like an idiot as she laughed, but it was empty from the pain she was enduring. "You will come to my bedroom, where we will assist you through the beginning of your labor. I am sure the men will return shortly, then the wards on the tower will cease, and Eliran will be able to come up from the infirmary to deliver your children. Until that happens, we need to get you laid down and comfortable."

"I'm not ready, though, Sinjinn isn't here." Icelyn's eyes widened in horror as the reality of the situation hit her.

"He will be here before your babes arrive. You can't worry about what is happening outside the doors, Icelyn. Your children are coming, and what is happening right now is all that matters. Ciara, assist me," I whispered, watching as Ciara handed Fury to

Meera, the newest handmaiden.

Worried violet eyes held mine as we helped Icelyn into the room and disrobed her before settling her onto the bed. Blood coated her thighs along with mucus from the membranes of her cervix. We were both thinking the same thing: Icelyn's children were coming too early, and complications of an early birth could be bad, very bad. Once she was stripped naked, I removed the blankets from the bed, laying her down and pulling the sheet up to cover her the moment she was in a prone position.

Standing back, I nodded to her, terrified that we were locked inside the tower, and no one could reach us until the men finished handling whatever was occurring outside the fortress. I withdrew the phone from my pocket, dialing Eliran as I stepped outside the bedroom door and stood in the narrow hallway. I silently prayed the reception would work well enough to reach him in the infirmary.

"Syn? Everything okay?" his deep, soothing voice came through the receiver.

"Icelyn is in labor," I answered, somehow keeping the fear from my tone.

"She isn't due for two more months."

"I'm very aware of that, but her water broke, and we're locked in the tower. I don't know how long it will be before Ryder opens the door, and from the way she is wincing, her contractions aren't that far apart. What do we do?"

"This isn't good," he muttered worriedly. I could hear him moving around in his medical ward through the phone. "Is there a lot of blood?"

"Just a little, but it looks thin. There's no gushing or anything like that."

"That's good," Eliran sighed in relief. "It's Icelyn's first pregnancy, so it won't be a quick labor. The fact that she is having twins is going to complicate the situation, which isn't good news. I'll get the staff ready to meet me outside the tower door, so we can get to her as soon as it opens. I'll get a message to Ryder stating we have a precarious medical condition in the tower. Keep her rested and be sure she drinks enough fluids. I need to prepare the incubator since the babes are premature; they will need help. If I'm not there when they come, you need to be ready to deliver them."

"Let's just plan on you doing that part." I expelled a breath, listening to the women, who were keeping the conversation lighthearted in the room behind me.

"Was the fluid clear?" he asked gently.

"Yeah, it looked like water on the floor, but there were some traces of blood. I have Icelyn resting on my bed, but she's not happy about her children being born early."

"That's good; that's really good. Just keep her calm and rested. If it comes down to it, and she feels as if she needs to push, don't stop her. Trying to stop her labor would do more harm than good at this point. Thousands of babes are born every day. It's natural, and her body will do what it's supposed to do. Just be there to clean out the babies' mouths and find something to clamp the cords if they do come quickly.

I'm here, too; if anything changes, call me and I'll walk you through it."

"If the babes are born this early, do you think they'll survive?" I asked, hating to pose the question that no one else would.

"No. The odds are against them," he stated honestly. "If the twins are born this early, they may be stillborn. I need not point out the other complications of having children in this world since you know it better than most."

"Thanks for being honest," I snapped.

"I can't lie; besides that, you need to prepare for the reality of what is happening. Keep her hopeful because if she gives up, we may lose her too."

"Eliran, I can't do this. What if I mess it up, and they suffer because of it, or something worse happens?" I whispered, voice trembling as a tear rolled down my cheek.

"You can because you must. You are one of the fiercest women I have ever had the pleasure of meeting, Synthia. If anyone can do this, it is you."

I hung up the call, entering the bedroom with a smile in place, wincing as Icelyn released a pain-filled shriek. Darynda lifted the thin sheet, peering between Icelyn's legs, and frowned, shaking her head. Righting the material back over Icelyn for modesty's sake, she walked to me, urgency filling her stride.

"Something is wrong. The babies are coming faster than they should be."

"They're tiny and very early," I admitted. "Get water for her to drink, please. Check on my babes. Make sure Olivia and Alannah are keeping them occupied and not killing each other in the process. Let Olivia know that if she feels the need, she is welcome to help us here. I know she is closer to Icelyn than we are."

Babes, my children were far from babies, and yet it was hard to admit that only a few weeks ago, they'd been crawling. My attention moved back to Icelyn, and I positioned myself next to the bed, studying the strain on her face as I took her hand in mine.

"You said hours, but I don't think we have hours." She swallowed a cry, raising an icy-blue stare to lock with mine. "It's too early for them to survive."

"It is early, but sometimes babes are born before their time, especially when they are twins," I replied lamely, smiling even though it probably made me look clinically insane. "We got this." I patted her hand, hoping to reassure her as my stomach flipped with the lie. The reality of what was coming hit me. "If you feel the need to push, we need to know. Eliran said it might take a few hours, but if you feel the need to push, you push." She nodded while the others sat around, offering helpful advice when needed. Before an hour had passed, they had Icelyn laughing and telling lame jokes to fill the silence of the room.

An hour later, the contractions were closer, and Icelyn cried as pain racked her delicate frame. Olivia held one hand while Ciara held the other. The sheet had been removed, and the first babe's head was trying to push free from his mother's body.

Over an hour of labor occurred, and Icelyn

weakened more and more with each contraction. Tears slipped down her cheeks, forming drops of ice that fell to the bed.

The room was freezing, so Darynda brought baby Fury in and handed him to Keely. His presence brought the temperature up to where we could withstand the chilling cold Icelyn's pain was sending through the room. Every contraction she had lowered the temperature. Then, Fury would giggle, and it would rise again. Thank the goddess for the little dragon babe, because everyone was already covered in blankets to bear the cold.

I paced aimlessly, fighting against the rising panic that held the room in its clutches. I cursed the men for being slow against the monsters that had set off the alarms and then cursed myself for doing so.

Icelyn screamed again, and Darynda looked over her shoulder to where I paced, shaking her head in worry. I could sense the men fighting, knew they were doing everything they could to get back to us, and yet I knew they wouldn't make it in time.

I moved closer, peering down between Icelyn's legs at the dark hair that finally crowned, but refused to come out any further. I worried my lip with my teeth, noting the others who looked at me with anxiety while Icelyn sobbed in pain. Every moment the babe remained stuck in the birthing canal, the chances of survival decreased.

Icelyn bore down, her body covered in sweat from the effort to bring her babe into the world. Exhaustion marred her face, and her scream filled the room as she continued to push while blood covered the mattress beneath her bottom.

I ground my teeth together in frustration, redialing Eliran, the call going straight to voicemail. Tossing the phone aside, I crawled onto the bed, straddling my legs beside Icelyn's frame as I sat behind her. The women moved into place, switching from chairs to the bed.

My skin touched hers, and I tried to take away her pain. Thankfully, I'd learned that was part of my gift, and the skill had come in handy a lot lately. It did little, though, to help the woman sobbing while her body contorted. Something was wrong, and no one knew what to do. I didn't know how to save her or the babies.

"Icelyn, you need to listen to me. The baby is not coming fast enough." I wrapped my arms around her. "We're here to help you and your babies, do you understand?" She nodded, and I continued speaking low and clearly. "When you feel the urge to push, push, and we will do our part. On the next contraction, give it everything you have."

Olivia grabbed one leg, and Ciara grabbed the other while I held Icelyn's belly. I sent a silent prayer to the gods. Not that those fuckers cared, but we needed any help we could get. Icelyn shook her head, begging us to get help for the babe. The problem was, no one was coming to help us. We were alone.

The moment we felt the contraction, we all helped Icelyn. She screamed while we helped push her knees against her chest. My hand pushed down gently on her swollen belly while Darynda watched the babe trying to be born. Her gaze lifted to mine in apprehension while the contraction abated. I exhaled slowly, uncertain what else we could try.

Another contraction occurred, and still, no babe. I closed my emotions down to prepare for the worst to happen, praying we wouldn't lose this child before it even had a chance to fight. Icelyn screamed when the next contraction hit harder than the last, and I massaged her stomach while she cursed the fates that were punishing her. Water exploded from her body as the first babe finally pushed through.

"Oh no," Darynda muttered, holding up the lifeless, blue body. Silence filled the room with her words, and my heart stopped beating.

Icelyn wailed while Olivia and Ciara both held her, pushing her face into their chest while I stared at the lifeless form we'd just fought to bring into this world. I slipped from behind Icelyn, rushing to the babe.

"No, no, no. Don't do this to us," I cried, rubbing my hand over the child's chest before I took him from

Darynda. My mouth touched his, feeling for breath before I blew over his mouth and nose, and checked it for anything blocking his airway.

"My baby," Icelyn sobbed, the anguish in it hitting me hard as tears burned my eyes.

"I forbid you from dying," I snapped. "Do you hear me? I forbid it!" My hands glowed amber as silence filled the room. The glow spread throughout my body, and my skin looked as if someone had sprinkled glitter all over me.

The door burst open, and men flooded through the doorway, yet I didn't stop. My hair floated around me as my hands held on to the tiny being, refusing to allow him to leave his parents. "You will not die, do you hear me? I said I forbid it! You are loved, and you are our family. Stay," I pleaded with tears running down my face.

"Holy Goddess," Icelyn whispered as a tiny scream filled the room. Relief washed through me violently as small ice-blue eyes opened and held mine, little lips parted, and the baby wailed his displeasure.

"You blessed him, Synthia."

My eyes slid from the child to his mother and back. My hands trembled with emotion as I moved, handing Icelyn the wailing babe. I stepped back, taking in the worried gazes watching me and my every move as I glowed like Danu had often done. I spun around, rushing from the room and the anxious glances, not bothering to stop until I was in the hallway.

"Destiny!" I shouted, hugging my stomach.

"Synthia?" Ryder demanded, Zahruk and Ristan beside him.

Ryder's armor was covered in blood, proof of why they'd been delayed. Eliran rushed past us, not stopping to see what had transpired as he made his way to the room with the incubator. Power erupted around us, and I turned, staring at Destiny.

"Tell me I didn't intervene. Tell me my children will not pay for what I just did!" I demanded.

Her eyes bulged and moved to Ryder and then back to my glowing body. "What happened?"

"I forbid a babe from dying. He wasn't breathing, and I forbid it from happening, and then I began to glow with power. Tell me my children are safe. I didn't mean to use my powers."

"Oh, Synthia. You did what you're meant to do. You saved a child of Faery. No one can intervene with whom you save when being born. Your children will not pay for you forbidding a life from ending before it has even begun. You are Goddess of the Fae, and therefore the only one who can forbid death from occurring in the first stages of life. You saved a babe. It's part of the job you perform for your people. The only thing you cannot do is bring life back from death. Although he never breathed, he wasn't dead. He just needed your help to take his first breath."

Relief slammed into me, and I sagged. Wiping away the tears of fear, I doubled over, placing my hands on my knees, exhaling a ragged breath. I nodded to Destiny, knowing she needed to be elsewhere. "Thank you."

"Don't thank me. Your mother knew this world

needed you. I voted to end your life," she said with a shrug. "Now, go enjoy the happiness of his birth. You've earned it."

Inside the room, Eliran was checking the babe's stats. He lifted his gaze and nodded to me. "It's a boy," he announced.

"I'm very aware. He peed on me."

Arms wrapped around me while the room became chaotic. "You saved my nephew, Pet."

"No, I just wouldn't allow him to go before his parents knew him. It terrified me to lose the baby before Icelyn and Sinjinn had gotten a chance to love him, or even hold him."

"I know, I felt it," Ryder growled at my ear. "We all did. I knew you could do this. You're the bravest woman I know."

"I have a son." Sinjinn smiled proudly through tears swimming in his vision as Sevrin peered down at the tiny red infant. "I have a son blessed by the Goddess of the Fae."

"You have a beautiful son, but he had a tough birth. Icelyn did amazing, but everyone needs to give Eliran room to deliver the other babe. Anyone who doesn't need to be here should leave," I ordered, expelling a shaky breath. "He is perfect, Sinjinn."

"Thank you. Thank you for saving my son."

"He's family. We don't give up on family around here," I uttered thickly, leaving the bedroom to check on my children. At the door, Sinjinn called out to me.

"His name is Finn."

Chapter
THREE

Outside the protection of the tower, I surveyed the horde partying below the balcony as Ryder held me tightly against his body. He hadn't let me go since the moment I'd stepped outside, as if he feared I would vanish. He could sense my anxiety and the anger that hummed through me with the helplessness I'd known in that room. I never wanted to feel that powerless again so long as I lived.

I wanted to argue his stupid policy and evacuation plan, and yet I understood it now more than before. If Icelyn had been in labor while we were under attack and the mages got inside these walls, we'd have lost all three of them. I hated that his plan made sense. Admitting it to this man was like eating crow.

It didn't change the fact that Ryder had put me in the tower, and I'd been blind to what was happening with him and his men. My emotions had risen, and when the surrounding women had looked for me to lead them, I had nothing to give. War, I could handle.

Childbirth?

Apparently, that wasn't my strong suit. Luckily, Eliran had delivered Fiona, Icelyn's second babe, without any problems.

I experienced a sense of desperation in that tower, and it burned. I hadn't been able to call to Ryder, and that had terrified me in a way I couldn't express. The wind howled in the distance, and I watched as the trees swayed and cowered against it while flames from fires below danced to its seductive force.

"Spit it out, Synthia," Ryder murmured huskily, rubbing the shell of my ear with his nose. His hands held me firmly, calming the storm of emotions that continued to rage inside of me.

"You put me in a fucking tower like I'm some

damsel in distress." He kissed my neck, pushing his fingers through my hair to expose more of it to his hungry mouth.

"No, I did not. I put the biggest, most powerful warrior in my arsenal between our enemies and our kids. I placed you there because I know no one else will protect our children as well as their mother. I didn't put my sweet, impish pet into the tower to shield her. I put her there to safeguard the ones that needed it the most."

I exhaled slowly, the truth of his words calming the storm inside of me. He pushed my body against the railing, and my hands tightened around it. His warm mouth kissed along my bare shoulder, sending a wave of butterflies dancing through my belly. Soft, velvety lips danced over my flesh while men and women moved about below, unaware of our presence as they celebrated their victory.

Ryder's boots nudged my feet apart until my legs spread wide enough apart for him to gain access to the part of me that always yearned for his touch. He chuckled darkly as his hands slipped up the back of my thighs, slowly trailing his fingertips along my skin, causing goosebumps to appear all over my body. At the curve of my ass, he paused, pushing his fingers against my clenching sex.

"Ryder, what are you doing?" I stared down at the tents and campfires that stretched farther than the eye could see along the walls of the fortress. Music played loudly, and cries of victory continued as warriors drank and brawled playfully below, unaware their king and queen were watching them.

"I'm about to fuck the Goddess of the Fae in the presence of the entire horde, so they know she belongs to me. You're mine and only mine, woman." His hands lifted the skirt of my dress, bunching it up over my hips and forcing me to lean over the railing precariously, my ass lifting to his touch with violent need.

"Someone will see us."

"That's the fucking point. I'm going to fuck the Queen of the Horde while they celebrate the slaughtering of mages. You're my fucking victory trophy, woman," he laughed darkly, ripping the panties from my body as I gasped.

Ryder's fingers pushed through my wet folds, and he growled hungrily against my ear. He stepped back, going down on one knee as he lowered his head. Slick fingers entered me again, and his other hand opened my flesh as he began licking and flicking my clit with his tongue until a soft moan exploded from my lips.

"Quiet, Syn. Do not make a fucking sound, or I'll spread your legs and stretch your tight pussy painfully as I fuck you. I won't stop until you're screaming my name. Then every person inside this kingdom will know exactly how you scream for your king as he destroys his pretty queen's tight cunt. On second thought, fucking scream, because I like the idea of them hearing how you sound as I destroy you, woman," he warned in a guttural tone. "I have ten minutes before I have to be inside the war room, so let's make every one of them count."

"Then stand up and fuck your queen, My King,"

I demanded.

"My queen is a greedy little girl who enjoys my mouth on her needy pussy, and I'm a greedy king who likes to eat that pussy and watch her squirm for me. Now stop fighting me and come so I can taste you on my tongue while I plan for war."

His fingers pushed into my body again while his tongue ran around them. I fought the whimper that built in my throat as he lapped greedily between my legs. Moving his fingers faster, I gripped the bars tightly, leaning over them, giving him more access. Ryder chuckled, uncaring that people below could see my naked breasts or body at any moment while he ravaged my pussy. His laughter vibrated against my flesh, and my lips trembled in response.

His tongue flicked and lapped gluttonously against my clit while his fingers went deeper into my core. My body clenched against them, needing more as he moved them slowly. The deep rumble of his growl shuddered through me while he stoked the fire building within to a raging inferno. The orgasm grew while he tortured me. Another digit stretched inside me, and I pushed against it, wanting him deeper in my wet flesh.

Ryder's mouth eased away, and he stood behind me, pulling my body against his. I heard the buttons of his pants and listened as he slid them down, kicking them off as his hands pulled my hips back against him. Fingers danced down my stomach, finding my thigh and lifting it to the railing, exposing even more of me than before so that any onlookers below could see.

"This pussy is drenched, you dirty girl. You like the idea of being caught fucking me?"

"Ryder, there's nothing you've done to me I didn't like or want. There's also nothing hotter than getting fucked by my king. Now fuck me," I hissed, rubbing myself against his fingers.

I was needy; my body buzzed with adrenaline as he teased playfully against my opening, knowingly driving me to a crazed state of need. When he finally pushed his cock into me, I cried out, and he chuckled, running his nose over the shell of my ear.

"I warned you, didn't I?"

"I'm game, fuck it. Just do it now, please. I need you, Ryder," I whimpered as he laughed, kissing my neck. He moved my leg to the ground, nipping against my shoulder.

"Hold on to the railing, and try not to scream too loudly, at least not yet. I'd hate to kill my army because they watched my pretty queen coming for me."

"You wanted this, Fairy."

"For them to hear you, not see what belongs to me."

One hand snaked around me, pinching a nipple before it slipped over my mouth as he entered me again, hard and fast, smothering the scream that tore from my throat as he laughed darkly. My eyes moved to the scene below us. People celebrated war, and here we were, fucking beneath the stars.

"You're so tight, Pet. You feel me against your womb, right where I fucking belong?" he asked, withdrawing to the tip, then lunging forward, causing a scream to escape, only to be smothered again by his hand.

Ryder chuckled darkly, releasing my mouth and turning me around before reaching down and lifting me. Parting my legs with his hands, he hoisted my body up to his as I held tightly to the railing, exposed to the world.

Anyone could look up to the balcony and see him taking me. It terrified me, and yet it was highly erotic. "Watch the sky," he ordered, increasing his speed as he pounded into my naked pussy with no mercy. I exploded without warning, watching lightning crash against the mountains in the distance. The sky lit up beautiful colors that would shame the aurora borealis as the orgasm continued to vibrate through my body.

The sky turned violet, blue, and red while the men and women below noted the changes. "That's what happens when I fuck the Goddess of the Fae, and she comes with her pussy stretched around my cock. You come apart for me, and the entire world sees it while you stare into my eyes, caring only for the galaxies within them."

"Harder," I demanded, enjoying his deep, rumbling growl of approval. Setting me down, he turned me around and bent me over the railing again before he let loose. His cock grew painfully large, stretching my body while he fucked me. I moaned loudly, uncaring who heard or saw us.

"Good girl," he growled huskily.

My hands tightened against the railing as another orgasm tore through me while the storm intensified around us. "Ryder!" He tensed behind me, jerking as he came within me. I exploded again without warning, and the entire sky filled with shooting stars, continually turning a mixture of vibrant colors. "Good gods."

"Beautiful, isn't it?" Ryder asked, and then someone below whistled, and he peered over my shoulder, pulling me to the floor of the balcony with him as he laughed silently.

"Someone saw us," I whispered.

"They did." Ryder laughed harder. "I should go kill them."

"Ryder!"

He let loose, laughing until it became contagious as I laughed as I lay above him, naked. I stared down at him, his smile brightening as his eyes glowed with happiness. I leaned over, kissing him softly until his hands lifted, holding the back of my head as he devoured my mouth. Then, he slowly stood, carrying me into our bedroom. On the bed, he pulled me close, holding me in his arms and kissing my forehead.

"I love you, Pet," he murmured, tightening his hold on me. "I didn't put you in that tower to shield you. I did it to protect everyone else, allowing the men to focus on the battle at hand. Having you there makes the women and children feel safe. It also ensures that my men stay focused on their duties, knowing that their families are protected from harm while we handle everything outside the stronghold. I need their heads in this war, and because of you, Sinjinn has a son."

"I almost lost that baby today," I admitted, tracing my fingers over his shoulder, studying him carefully. "I want to bring in more doctors."

"I told you Eliran could handle it," he argued, and I adjusted in his hold. Standing up slowly, I glamoured on a sheer, ice-blue nightgown with a long, flowing skirt and V-line neck that stretched across my cleavage.

"I know, but I need reassurance that if something happens outside of the tower, you have our best doctor with you. Eliran can't be in two places at once. Olivia is overdue, and Ciara can have her babe any day now. I didn't know what to do, and it terrified me. There was no one inside that room that had any idea how to deliver a child."

"Fine," he stated.

"I was terrified that I would kill the babes or Icelyn. Why are you arguing this? Wait, did you just agree with me?" I paused, studying his face.

"I did," Ryder chuckled with a shrug. "You

shouldn't be forced into that situation. I know it frightened you because I sensed it here," he said, pointing at his heart. "Faery felt it and trembled. Your emotions are tied to the world now. When I fuck you, it is magical. When you cry, it rains. When you're afraid, the entire world holds its breath until you release that fear, and then it breathes again with you. I'd hate to know what happens when you are angry."

I laughed nervously and rolled my eyes. "I'd probably burn down the forest, or worse."

"Mmm, you set fire to my soul, woman. I don't like outsiders coming to our home, but I understand your concern, and I'll allow it for you."

"What's the catch?" I studied him closely as I ran my hand over the muscles of his chest.

"I get that needy pussy whenever I want it. And if these new doctors betray us, I will rip their spines out through their mouths and fuck you on their corpses."

"Mmm. Is it bad that I hope they betray us?" I asked innocently, continuing my leisurely perusal of his body as my hand dipped low to stroke his cock once before smiling at him.

"Naughty little thing, aren't you?" he countered. "I have it on good authority that the entire horde trembles at the mention of your name."

"Good, it was my intention when I ripped their self-appointed leaders' throats out," I said, gripping his cock in my hand, beginning to stroke him slowly. "You taught me that you control the horde by fear, so let them fear me. The first moment you were gone, your people planned to replace you. They wanted to rape me on your throne." My grip tightened as my hand began to move faster. "I showed them that it could not be done. No one fucks me except my king, and Ryder, you are my fucking Fairy King."

"I'm glad you understand that," he whispered huskily. "Now, ride my cock, Queen of the Horde. I find I cannot get enough of you lately, especially when you glow while I fuck you, my delicate, dainty little damsel."

"I've got your delicate right here, Fairy."

Squeezing his cock for emphasis, I licked the tip and sat up. Removing my nightgown, I tossed it aside as he leaned back against the bed, crossing his arms behind his head. "And for the record, I don't glow when you fuck me."

"You do, and it's the most beautiful thing in the world, Synthia."

Chapter
FOUR

Ristan walked up and down the main hall continuously. He was on edge, and I couldn't figure out how to ease the turbulence within him. Olivia wasn't just overdue; she was two months past her due date. By human standards, she was in her eleventh month of pregnancy. Nothing we did could lessen her pain or stopped the soon-to-be new father from making sure everyone knew his child wasn't coming out.

To say it frustrated Ristan would be the understatement of the century. The man paced endlessly day-in and day-out, and if you interrupted him, you got to hear his opinion of Olivia's selfish womb, preventing that little dangle baby from escaping.

"This is insane, right? It makes little sense. Demons birth their children similar to the fae, and yet she isn't even having contractions. She's craving hearts, gulping them down like some fucking delicacy, and she hasn't given birth to my daughter yet."

"Who says it is a girl?" I asked, crossing my arms and eyeing him curiously.

"I do," he countered, stopping mid-pace, staring at me like I'd grown a second head with my question. "I want a daughter; therefore, I am having one."

"Oh, is that how it works? I assumed you created a babe, and whatever the gods gifted would be born." Turning, I smiled and faced Ryder. "I'd like to order another daughter. Please tell your sperm that unless it's female in gender, it ain't getting into my womb."

Ristan stared at me before slowly turning his silver gaze to Ryder, snorting loudly. "I want a girl," he shrugged his broad shoulders. "I will love my child no matter what it is, understandably, but I'd prefer a daughter."

"You mean if the child has a penis, you'll still take him?" I questioned, smoothing the smile behind my hand. Both sets of eyes turned to stare at me. "If it is a boy, it will have a penis."

"Obviously," Ristan harrumphed as he paced to the other side of the room, dismissing me.

"Hey, who knows how long it takes to bake a dangle? I mean, we know next to nothing about the breed or child you two created, or if it is actually overdue."

Rubbing the back of his neck, Ristan turned and his gaze bounced between Ryder to me, moving his hands animatedly as he spoke. "Have you seen Olivia lately? She's miserable. Not to mention that we have not had sex in weeks!"

"So what's the actual problem? That you are not getting any sex or that you're worried about the babe being overcooked? Eliran said everything looked great, and even though he can't see the child perfectly, he knows it is healthy."

"Something isn't right, I can feel it," he said, pushing his fingers through his hair before he resumed pacing.

"Demon, we've asked everyone. No one knows how long it takes when an angel and a demon of your breed—mixed with fae, at that—comes together to make a person. No, I take that back," I said, trying to ease some of Ristan's tension. "There was that one guy who said it took nine hours on high, and to add rosemary before consuming it." The narrowing of his eyes told me that he didn't appreciate my joke. "That's beside the point. It will be okay. Everything will work out as it is supposed to in the end. Eliran has his people looking into it, and Olivia's good. She is strong, and while she might not want sex, it may induce labor. Put on your thinking cap and get those demon moves into gear."

"It hurts her!" he snapped, and my eyes narrowed on him. "I'm sorry, Flower. It's fucking killing me. What happens if we're not meant to breed? What happens if our child dies?"

"You can't think like that. Think about it this way. Danu fixed you to create this life. Your child is supposed to live."

"That's not reassuring. Danu fucked me over every way she could before the bitch bailed and left me to deal with what she did."

"Ristan," Ryder warned.

"It is okay, Ryder, let him speak."

"I'm scared," Ristan admitted.

"I'm aware you're scared, we all are." I took Ristan's hand and squeezed it reassuringly. "I don't believe Danu gave you a child to take it away, demon. I know you two had a chaotic past, and you don't want to share how fucked up it was, which is fine. I get that it's your business, but she was trying to fix things in the end. I don't think her last days were filled with shit she wanted to mess up. She gave her life for me, and she fixed you so you could create life." Dropping his hand, I turned to look at Ryder, then back to Ristan. "I'll check at the guild to see if there's anything in the libraries or archives that includes the gestation period of children born of demons or angels. All the details on Olivia's mother are there also; I'll pull it too. Alden may have more information."

"I'll go with you," Ristan offered.

I shook my head. "I need you to stay with Ryder. New recruits are gathering at the guild. I don't want them bailing before they've signed a contract."

"Be careful, Pet," Ryder warned.

"I'm always careful." I smiled as I crossed the room and lifted on my toes to kiss him. "I love you. I'll be back shortly. Liam has the triplets at the Blood Castle, so keep our spies outside of its borders. I know their tower that matches ours is supposed to be foolproof, but it's not one hundred percent."

"You have them checking in every hour, on the hour. They think you're the most overprotective mother in all the lands." Ryder snorted, watching me.

"I am," I shrugged. I wasn't ashamed about it, not when we had enemies marching toward us, and traitorous allies looking for any weakness to exploit. "I make no apologies for being overprotective; I grew those little monsters from scratch. They're our world, and our enemies are very aware of it. Better to have spies watching the spies and be certain of who is on our side and who isn't. You taught me that too, Fairy. Now kiss me like you fucking mean it, big boy."

"Sassy witch," Ryder chuckled as his hand threaded through my hair, pulling my head back to bare my mouth for his heated kiss. His tongue pushed past my lips, claiming me as a moan built in my throat. Coughing sounded behind us, and he pulled away slowly. "To be continued when you get back."

"Are you two done tongue-fucking each other?" Zahruk asked.

"For now," Ryder snorted, looking over his shoulder to where his second stood.

Zahruk was decked out in armor. His freshly polished swords slung low on his hips, and his hair was pulled back into a leather strap, away from his face. His sapphire gaze observed me, a slight smirk lifting his full mouth into a slant. He was perpetually ready for war, or to stroke his swords. I wasn't sure which one he preferred, but that was his business.

"There have been some skirmishes from within the shifter camps. I guess not all of them agree with aiding our war. Some went into the Unforgiving Forest and have not been seen since. The camps on the other side have yet to send word that they made it through alive."

"Unfortunate, but if they were fleeing rather than helping, I fail to see where it's our fucking problem."

"My brother, Fang, was in the group that fled," Zahruk admitted.

"Wait, you have a brother? Well, I mean besides the ones here?" How did I not know this?

"My mother had a life before she became a concubine. My father murdered her entire pack while he forced her to watch. When Alazander asked what my mother would give to spare the lives of her sons, she offered herself if he would allow them to live.

Fang isn't much for the horde or my help. He's rather reclusive and has his pack to protect. I'm guessing the thought of war wasn't appealing to them."

"I didn't know you had family outside the horde." I looked to Ryder, and he nodded, indicating the truth of Zahruk's words.

"I don't. To Fang, I am nothing. He doesn't like or want my help, but he gets it regardless. I promised my mother that I would endure Alazander's wrath to protect him. I look after him from afar, and the horde leaves his pack alone, so they don't get a visit from me."

Turning, Zahruk tilted his head and made direct eye contact with Ryder, his brows drawn together slightly. "I need to send scouts out to make sure he didn't end up dead from foolishly running. I'm asking you for this, Ryder, not as the second-in-command, but brother to brother. I need to know he made it through alive."

"Do it, send the scouts with a war party." Ryder's amber eyes locked with mine, and I nodded in agreement. It was foolish to send any of our forces through the forest, but it was for Zahruk. He had never asked for anything himself, expecting nothing in return for his never-ending service. "Make sure the scouts are aware this is an escort detail. They are not to be seen unless they cannot avoid it."

"Thank you," Zahruk said, nodding to Ryder before he sifted out of the room.

"You think they're already dead." Ryder brought his hand up, rubbing the bridge of his nose with his thumb and pointer finger. The scent of sandalwood and masculinity assaulted my senses with his subtle movement.

"I think they ran, and if they did, then yes, they are likely dead. I gave the order to slaughter anyone who ran. I was trying to prevent our forces from abandoning us."

"Why, Ryder? Tell me you didn't give that order to everyone. Tell me you didn't issue that order against those who had yet to swear allegiance to the horde," I demanded. My stomach twisted with anger and fear.

"These are our people."

"They're your people. I am the King of the Horde, not of Faery."

It felt as if he'd slapped me across the face with his words. "You're my husband."

"Which makes you the Queen of the Horde," he growled, lifting his chin in challenge. "There is no place for weakness or pity for those who flee our kingdom amidst a war that will decide the fate of Faery."

"You get that I am the Goddess of the Fae, right?" Taking a deep breath, I began speaking through gritted teeth, trying to hold back my temper. "I cannot select with whom I wish to give a fuck. We need allies, not enemies. You have the horde. You have them all on their knees, fighting for you and beside you because you rule them ruthlessly. Do you know what happens when your people fear you?"

"They obey me."

"No, they do not!" I pounded my fist against the

table beside me, and Ryder glared at me. "The horde looks for the first fucking chance to be rid of you. They may follow you, but they do so with a dagger ready to stick in your back. Take your father, for instance, Ryder. He ruled with absolute terror instilled in his people. What the fuck did you do to him?"

"I'm not my father," he snapped.

"Thank the gods for that, Fairy," I laughed mockingly. "Retract the order."

"I will not," he seethed.

"Why?"

"Because now is not the time to appear weak!" Ryder slapped his hands down on the table that separated us, narrowing his eyes, daring me to continue challenging him.

I stiffened and shook my head angrily. "You ordered anyone murdered who chose to flee from war! You ordered *my* people and *our* people to be put down like dogs with rabies because they're running scared?" My fingernails began to bite into my palms as

I clenched my hands into fists, trying to force myself to calm down. "Everyone is scared, Ryder. *Everyone!* The war drums beat every night, and each night we all pray it isn't our last. Be their king, be the man I married. The one who didn't make mandates of his people without just cause."

"It's not that easy."

"It is that easy. You're the fucking king. They fear you, but they won't respect you if you kill their families or friends who run from this war. If they have no family left, what is their reason to fight? We're fighting for our family. Don't be the king who slaughters innocent lives because the people who fight with us are scared. Not when we're terrified too. It doesn't make them weak to want to protect their families from what is coming by running with them from the danger. It makes them worth having on our side." Sighing, I dropped my shoulders and relaxed my stance, offering a small smile as I reached out to touch Ryder's hand. "If they have something to protect, they will fight harder."

His amber eyes narrowed on me as he pulled his hand from mine. "I'll run my kingdom with or without you at my side, woman. I want you here, but this is the horde. If you show an ounce of weakness, they will descend on us, and we will have a war on two fronts instead of one." Leaning across the small table, Ryder bared his teeth and glared at me as he spit out his next words. "I cannot allow that to happen, not now, not ever! You knew who I was when you married me, keep that in mind."

My eyes widened, and I swallowed hard. "Understood." I turned to look at Ristan, then back to Ryder as a cold resolve filled me. I drew myself up to full height, lifted my chin, and cocked an eyebrow. "I may be longer than I had planned at the guild. Don't wait up for me."

"What the hell is that supposed to mean?" Ryder demanded.

"What's it to you? You will run this kingdom as you see fit, so fucking run it." I walked away from Ryder and Ristan with a purposeful stride. "I have other commitments that need and want my opinion." I vanished the moment the words were out, appearing at the guild. "Fucking fairy," I snapped into the darkness that filled the street in front of the guild.

"Problems at home, kid?" Alden asked gently.

I turned, staring at him, his grey eyes softening as I moved up the steps to where he stood. "Hey, old man," I smirked, hugging him tightly. "I hate war."

"No one likes war," he replied, wrapping his arms around me.

"That's not true," I said, pulling back to stare at him. "Why are you outside? What happened?"

"Getting some air," he chuckled awkwardly. "Come, let me show you what you've missed, Syn."

Chapter FIVE

The guild was filled with hunters from other guilds around the globe, some from different branches of the military. With the newly redecorated world of brimstone and angels falling daily from the skies, it was all hands on deck, and yet not one other organization dared to set up amidst the chaos, except us.

"I'm glad you could make it, but you probably should be at home, all things considered."

"Alden, we're opening, and this is my plan. I am the one who wanted to do this, and now you're stuck doing everything. I asked Adrian and Adam to help you since Ryder and I are preparing for war. Now Adam is doing the same in the Dark Kingdom, and Adrian is dealing with the demon infestation in this world while doing what he and Vlad can to protect humans." Alden nodded, silently agreeing with the reason for Adrian and Adam's absence as he began walking me through the halls of the guild. "That has left you to do everything yourself, but tonight we are here to celebrate your kicking ass on this place." I waved my hand in the direction of the main gathering hall as evidence. "So, tell me what's new, how many recruits did we end up with, and what do you need that I can provide to make this easier on you?"

"Three more hunters showed up last night. We've got the dormitories set up for species." Passing a door on the left, I peeked inside to see rows of beds and makeshift closets against the walls between each bunk. "So far, it's mostly witches and a few wayward creatures that are tired of being kicked around by demons. Headcount as of last night was sixty people. Not bad for our first week open, huh?" Alden's eyes sparkled with renewed life. I also noticed the old pep in his step that he'd lost months ago, which made my insides warm with happiness that he was filled with purpose once more.

"You're in your element, Alden." I took in the men and women moving about and winced at how scrawny and undernourished they were. "You need food?"

"No, you guys supply enough to keep them fed. They just need time to recover. A lot of them come from towns that had little left. Some came from as far as California when rumors of a new hunters' guild reached them. Others are from guilds that went down when Seattle fell. It's not like they could go out and just grab some food.

"Most of the enforcers hid. It's been weeks since the walls fell, and even with Lucian and his men keeping the streets clean, they can't get all the demons. By the time they clear one town, another fills with those nasty creatures. Lucian and Vlad have been rather helpful, but there's only so much they can do, all things considered. Now, Erie, she's enjoying hunting demons, and most of the ones around here are now under her control, somehow. I choose not to ask since she smiles, and it freaks me out a little. She's using the demons in her influence to fight against the others."

"Erie is? I would think she would be too busy running from Callaghan to be useful."

"He's around too," Alden muttered. "It's a fucking mess out there. Vlad has sent some humans here, and he's housing a few below his bar. My guess is he doesn't plan to run out of food anytime soon, so they're safe enough there." Wrapping one arm around my shoulders, Alden pulled me into him in a side hug. "Why are you really here, kid?"

"I need to go through the archives."

Coming to a stop, Alden dropped his arm and took a step back. "You could've just asked me to bring the files you needed." Rubbing his chin, he arched his brow, studying me before he cleared his throat. "What else is going on?"

"Ryder gave the order to slaughter anyone who fled the Horde Kingdom and the war."

"That's expected in the middle of a war, kid." Nodding at my angered expression, he smirked, crossing his arms, willing me to argue against what he'd just said.

"It's not, though, Alden. Think about it." I began walking again, my feet falling heavy on the stone floor as my previous anger started to build again. "I'm the Goddess of the Fae, and those are my people. Ryder didn't even ask me what I thought. He just gave the order," I said, my voice raised enough that it echoed slightly through the hall, and I winced apologetically at my outburst. "These people just want to protect their families, and if we're the ones killing them, then how can we expect them to fight with us?"

"Ryder's the King of the Horde, kid, not the fae." Sad, understanding eyes met mine, and I knew Alden was about to impart his wisdom on me, and I wasn't going to like it. "His job is to rule the horde, and the only way to do that is if they fear him. That puts him in a position where he must do the hard shit no one else wants to do. One of which, it seems, is to slaughter those who run from their responsibility in the impending war. It's coming one way or another; they can't run from it."

"Why? Why is it the only way? They're scared, but so am I! It's a war that no one thought would happen, and while we saw it coming, no one listened. The mages are fucking changelings, for fuck's sake."

Alden snorted, and we continued to walk. "Yeah, but they're changelings with a god on their side. Are you pissed off because Ryder didn't ask your permission first?"

"No. Maybe. I don't know. I'm pissed off because when the fae die, I *feel* it. I'm attached to them and the land that my mother created. It's too much, and yet last night I saved a babe's life. I glowed like Danu. I forbid the babe from dying, and he didn't die." I looked at Alden and took a step back. His eyes widened, and his mouth fell open and then closed quickly. "It was insane. I have never been so terrified in my entire life. I held their babe's life in my hands, and I panicked."

"And did you have to pay a price for that?" His voice trembled slightly, and I could sense his fear.

"No, because they are my people," I admitted, frowning as he exhaled the breath he was holding while he studied me. "I'm allowed to save them, but not if they die before I reach them. He wasn't dead; he just hadn't taken a breath. It was Sinjinn and Icelyn's child. Their son was born early with premature lungs, according to Eliran, but he's alive. Speaking of babes, I need Olivia's files."

"You won't find anything in the files. Besides that, Olivia and Ristan took them," he shrugged. "They're being kept in the basement of the Shadowlands. Our information on angels is less than two pages in a manila envelope. Demons, there's over nineteen rooms on demonology, and yet nothing on Ristan's breed. Ryder and Ristan asked me to look through the files a while back. Did you know harpies can reproduce offspring in a matter of weeks or that a demon's child can take anywhere from five days to two years to be born?"

"Ouch," I winced at that news. "Olivia is eleven months pregnant. I doubt Ristan will survive much longer. No one we've talked to has any idea what happens when an angel and demon create a child."

"You could kill the mother, and the child before

it's born," a deep timbre offered from behind me.

I turned around slowly, taking in the male who had spoken. "That little baby dangle is my family."

"Demons are evil, in case you're not aware of the current situation, sweetheart." He shrugged from where he leaned against the wall, carving a piece of wood with a wicked-looking blade. He had a swimmer's body with dark black hair and smoky-colored eyes that surveyed me carefully. He had thick tattoos, visible through the AC/DC t-shirt he wore, and his arms crossed over his chest as he glared at me. "And you'd be?" His gaze slid down my body, stopping at my breasts before slowly perusing my frame down to the high-heeled, leather knee-high boots that hugged my slender calves.

"Synthia, Queen of the Horde and Goddess of the Fae, and you?" I returned pointedly, studying his kind eyes.

He smirked as if he thought it was cute. "I'm Lucifer. If you're the Goddess of the Fae, I'm motherfucking Lucifer, baby."

"No, he's a lot taller than you and better-looking too. Even though Lucifer's got a crushed skull at the moment, he's still better-looking and built for sin." I cringed at the memory of what Lena had done to his head. "But, to be honest, he deserved that one."

"I'm Stanislav," he snorted. "Is she for real? Sweet ass comes on in here claiming to be a goddess and shit. I'd hire her for the balls of that claim alone." He snickered, turning to study Alden, then dropped his smile and frowned at Alden's lifted a brow and crossed arms.

"Adrik Stanislav, meet Synthia McKenna, Goddess of the Fae, Queen of the Horde, and my niece," Alden chuckled as he watched the color drained from Stanislav's face.

"Fuck me," he muttered, scrubbing his hand over his mouth, taking me in once more.

"Well, Stanislav, at least we know you got some balls on you. What breed are you?"

"Hybrid wolf, born from a long line of hybrids

in Russia," he announced, rubbing the back of his neck nervously. "I don't know how to address you correctly. Should I bow?"

"Hell, no," I laughed outright. "I'm here as one of your potential bosses. Basically, if you prove worthy, you work for me, Alden, Adam, and Adrian. I will be behind the scenes, and Alden will work beside you." I spit out all the 'A' names and considered changing a few to something cool, like a codename.

"And if we get into trouble, we're just fucked and left on our own?" a feminine voice asked. I observed the young woman as she strolled out in front of me, twirling cherry colored hair around her dainty finger. She popped a bubble between her matching red lips as I took in her appearance, noting the multitude of weapons she concealed. Slowly, I peered up into her glowing blue eyes that watched me with the gaze of a predator.

"Then you get your fucking ass out of it," I shrugged nonchalantly. "I'm not your crutch. We're hiring warriors, not damsels in need of saving. Be the dragon that eats the prick and leaves nothing but bones when she's finished. If you can't do that, then get the fuck out because this world will eat you up, strawberry lips and all, sweetheart." I was brutally honest, but we didn't have time to hold anyone's hands. The world needed people out hunting for demons now. Not tomorrow. Not next week.

The young woman chuckled before tilting her pretty head to the left. "So, you're nothing but a threat that we whisper to our enemies? We get in trouble, and they take our fucking heads before we can spit out your name."

"I cannot intervene, but I have friends in every dark corner and every shadow that can rain down hell on whoever thinks to fuck with my people. Make no mistake; you will be my people if you make the cut. I will protect you to the best of my ability. The thing is, if you're good enough, I shouldn't fucking have to save your asses. I never needed to be saved when I worked here as a witch. Strive to do the same...?" I raised my brow in question, allowing the young woman the opportunity to share her name.

"Ivory Henderson. I'm a born witch and bitten shifter," she shrugged nonchalantly, mimicking me. "I'm in it to kill creatures that piss me off. Don't piss me off, and you won't be on my list, sugar."

Smiling wickedly, I disappeared and reappeared behind her, watching her search the room before I whispered into her ear. "Do better, so you live longer, little girl." Picking her up, I sifted us to the level that housed my new office, high above the stairs and only obtainable through sifting. I spoke against her ear as I held her securely against me. "Too easy. Even with weapons, you're an easy fucking kill. Get smarter, Ivory. Learn to listen to the wind; it speaks to you." I sifted again, placing her right back where we'd started.

"How the fuck?" Ivory demanded.

Pushing her forward and away from me, I narrowed my eyes. "Shut your mouth, stop chewing gum, and listen to the room. Sifting, materializing, and displacing air all make a sound. Learn it, and you'll live longer. Drop the attitude; you're not untouchable. Being sassy works, being cocky? That shit will get you murdered just for the simple fact that they'll need to teach you a lesson. Let our enemies be cocky, and then when they're flapping their lips, cut their fucking heads off and show them why they don't fuck with women."

"I think I'm wet," Ivory swallowed audibly.

"My dick just got hard," Stanislav said, chuckling.

"Someone is up on the roof, Syn. Why don't you go say hello," Alden interrupted, scrubbing his hand down his face at Ivory and Stanislav's choice of words.

"Really?" I asked. "Need a lift, old man?" I offered softly.

"I'll meet you up there in a few minutes. I need to make sure all the doors are locked."

Nodding to Alden, I took one last look at Stanislav and Ivory before I materialized on the roof. I studied the dark silhouette that stared out over the ruins of the city with his arms crossed and legs spread apart. He'd dressed in low-hung jeans and a black button-down shirt with new tattoos covering his arms. I slowly closed the distance between us, silently watching as his dark head lifted, inhaling my scent.

"Fancy meeting you here, Synthia," Adrian said without turning to look at me.

I stopped beside him, leaning my head against his shoulder while I surveyed what used to be our city. It was beautiful, chaotic destruction that wouldn't be easy to fix. Garbage littered the streets, debris thick enough to wade through marring some of them. Flames danced from trashcans, billowing smoke into the night. The entire city was lit by the stars as if darkness had descended and swallowed the light.

"We could have stopped this from happening if we'd all been here together," I said thickly, fighting my emotions while staring at the remains of a once beautiful city.

"No, we couldn't," he returned, wrapping his arm around me. "We'd just end up another dead creature they destroyed."

"We could've fucking tried," Adam growled,

forcing our gazes in the direction where he'd materialized without causing a disturbance. Adam's arm wrapped around my waist, too, and together we stood in silence, staring out over the destruction of the city. "It wouldn't have been this bad. Not if we'd been here to fight the demons when they first came through."

"You're wrong." Adrian shook his head. "Vlad had people out battling the demons, and they never returned. Vampires just vanished, and you think we could have stopped this? No, we'd have died trying to prevent what was inevitable because we would have refused to stop fighting, even if we were losing. It's who we are: fighters who continue to fight for the underdogs."

"I could have…"

"Could've, would've, should've. It doesn't matter anymore, Syn. You had shit going on, hell, we all did. Lucifer did this by setting a trap for Lena to walk into Hell. He opened the Hell gates to escape his prison. Now we take it all back. We push them back into Hell from where they escaped, and we close those fucking doors for good."

"Look at you three. Would you look at you three assholes," Alden stated, watching us as he came through the one door that led to the roof. "Out of all the enforcers in this guild, who would have thought you would be the last three standing?"

"We did," I stated offhandedly, and when Adrian and Adam snorted, I swatted them. "I knew we would survive. I knew we would because you taught us that losing was never an option and giving up isn't something we carry in our blood. We had a damn good teacher." I laughed and looked at the three men on the roof with me. "A fairy, a vampire, and a goddess walk into a bar…"

"Sounds like a horror show in the making," Adrian snorted.

"Yeah, there goes the fucking bar." I turned, staring at the sadness in Adam's eyes that had also entered his tone. He felt it, but more than that, we all felt Larissa's absence at the moment.

"Eventually, we need to speak about the body you took," I muttered, turning sad eyes to Adam.

"Not today, we don't. Today we celebrate reopening this guild's doors. Today is for the living, not the dead. I can't believe you did it." Adam smiled, changing the subject.

"We did it; we all did it." I hugged them all tightly, staring back out over the city that had raised us. "Today marks the first day of the new guild of hunters, and the day we take Spokane back and make it a haven for those in need of a safe place to go."

"That's why I'm here," Adrian snorted, pulling out a hundred-and-fifty-year-old bottle of scotch. Alden pushed aside a broken cabinet door, withdrawing four dirty, soot-covered glasses. I whispered a spell, adding fae magic, and smiled as the glasses came clean. "Here's to a new adventure and old friends. To the ones who gave their all, and to the ones out there fighting to get home, may they all find peace and feel no more pain." He smiled at me, kissing the top of my head as we exhaled.

"That was a good toast," I admitted.

"He must be getting smarter in his old age," Adrian snorted, patting Adam on the back. "I cannot believe this place is operational again. I'm proud of us; we've come pretty far from the mouthy punk kids that thought we could run it one day."

"Yes, you did, and I'm thankful you guys are at my side today. I couldn't think of a better makeshift coven to open the new guild, even if you're no longer witches. I'm proud of you all, and of whom you have become. You never lost sight of who we were forging you to become, even though you changed into what we feared at the time. You taught me more than a lifetime of learning could, and good fucking lord, you taught me patience while trying mine to the limits. You put me through hell and showed me that rules could be broken. You ready to help me run this guild correctly?"

"That's why we're here," I said, watching the liquid amber as it filled my glass. "That's why we're all here again."

Chapter SIX

Back at the castle, I paused inside the throne room as the men came into view. Ryder and his brothers were arguing about where to place troops and where to reinforce against attacks. I hiccupped and snorted simultaneously, knowing I was gone entirely too long since time moved differently between worlds. A dark head lifted from the table, and I watched as narrowed amber eyes settled on me.

"Where the hell have you been?" Ryder demanded as power erupted inside the room.

I didn't respond, not when he was oozing anger mixed with power, creating a palpable force that fought to smother and intimidate me. It slithered over my flesh, pulsing through me with the intensity of everything that made him the King of the Horde.

"Fucking answer me, woman." Ryder slammed his hand down on the table, never taking his eyes from me. "You were gone for days, Synthia. I told you that you could only have a few minutes at the guild because you were needed here. You do realize your obligation is to this kingdom now, right? Do you understand me?" Everyone around Ryder looked away, pretending to be engrossed in the map at the center of the table as they listened to every word he growled at me.

"And what is my obligation?" Tilting my head, I crossed my arms over my chest and smirked, not backing down even though we had an audience.

"You're supposed to be my queen and help me run this kingdom, or did you forget that already?" Lifting his head in the air, Ryder inhaled deeply and glared at me. "Tell me, how is Adrian? I can smell him on you."

"He's great," I snorted, swaying on my feet.

"Are you drunk?" His power intensified inside the

room at his sudden spike of fresh anger.

"A little." I shrugged my shoulders and smiled. Okay, so it was probably more than just a little. But hey, I was with my coven. We were celebrating the reopening of what had once been our home, and I'd earned a fucking break. I'd been cooped up in this place since the day Erie took Hell's army and marched off with it.

"You're supposed to be here helping me run this castle and prepare for war, Synthia. You were gone for *days*."

"Last I heard, you didn't need or want my help running *your* kingdom." Shifting on my feet, I uncrossed my arms and studied my fingernails, noting they could use a new coat of polish. "It's not like you would listen to me anyway, so does it really matter if I'm gone? Besides, the guild is reopening, and we were celebrating." I smiled, then hiccupped again.

"How fucking cute." The brands on his arms ignited and pulsed with his anger as he moved closer to where I stood. "Your obligation is to this world now, not theirs."

"On the contrary, Fairy. That is my world too, or have you forgotten who I am? How easy it is for you to forget where I came from." Suddenly, I didn't seem as drunk as before as my anger ignited. "The entire world is on fire, and humans are being hunted down like dogs. Spokane is covered in ashes and brimstone. The guild is the only one fighting for that world, and if me being there for a few hours is a crime, then fuck it, charge me." Pushing my shoulders back, I straightened and took a step closer to Ryder as I gritted my teeth. "You told me you would run this kingdom with or without me, and now you want to get angry that I wasn't here?"

Ryder's hand snaked through my hair before his mouth lowered to mine. "You're my fucking wife, or have you forgotten?" His face reddened, and his nostrils flared as he pointed his finger at me. "You'll fucking do as I say, understand?"

"Am I? Because you promised your *wife* you wouldn't become a tyrant, and we would win this war together as a *team*." I pulled back slightly and glared at him, shaking my head. "You haven't included me in the team part. You don't get to pick and choose what you tell me. You sent out a fucking kill order! Do you know how many fae died in the last three hours since I've been away from here? Over three thousand, Ryder," my voice cracked, and tears blurred my vision as I began to shake from the anger and grief rolling through me. His golden eyes watched me angrily while his hold tightened on my hair. "I feel every one of their lives slipping away. Did you even think about me, your wife, the Goddess of the Fae, when you gave those orders? I'm the one cursed to feel every life you have taken with that order."

"We are in a fucking war, Synthia."

"Let me go," I demanded, and when he didn't, I ignited my brands with the eerie silver hue that had been glowing on and off since I'd saved Finn's life.

Black gossamer wings exploded from Ryder's back as he continued to hold my hair with his lips brushing across mine. "Never." Pressing his forehead against mine, he met my eyes with a promise. "I will never let you go as long as I live."

"Now," I growled, creasing my brow.

"I have to be the King of the Horde right now, Synthia. I must rule them with an iron fist, or they will rise against us. You may have placed fear into their hearts, but they're the indomitable horde. You are their queen, and I am their king. You are needed here. Alden can handle the guild. You know he can run it without you, and that pisses you off, and I don't fucking care if it does. I need you; he doesn't anymore. Faery needs its goddess to get her pretty head out of her perky ass. I can't win this war without you by my side."

"By your side or locked in a damn tower, so you know where I am at all times?" I pushed him away from me. "Wrong fucking damsel, Fairy," hissing, I stared him down coldly.

All the men remained silent, watching and waiting to see what would happen. I exhaled the anger before peering around the room. Ristan watched me with a guarded look in his eyes, and Zahruk had his hand on his weapon. I snorted, noting that we'd come full circle.

"Place your troops where you think they should be. I have things to do." I started to walk away when Ryder grabbed my arm, forcing me to turn around and face him.

"You're leaving?"

"I'm going hunting." Pulling away from his grip, I stared at him with calm determination. "There's a Stag that hasn't been seen in months, and he promised me he'd be here when the war reached Faery. War is here; he isn't."

"You're drunk," Ryder pointed out icily.

"And?"

"And we're at war."

"I'm tipsy, not plowed. I am very aware of the fact that we are at war. Remember, unlike you, I sense every death that occurs inside this realm. I also understand why my mother wasn't completely sane. There's no off-switch. I don't think I could even get drunk enough to drown out the pain within me because of your fucking orders and the mages endlessly slaughtering the fae. So, I will find the Stag and ask for his advice with the upcoming war. Do you want to come with me?" I bat my eyelashes and feigned innocence, then laughed sarcastically. "Oh, that's right, horde laws state that the queen and king must not leave the palace simultaneously during times of war and unrest. No wonder your father had thirty wives and over one hundred concubines in residence. He could leave whenever he liked, couldn't he?"

"I chose to have one wife, Pet. You."

I studied his liquid amber gaze intently. "I bet you regret that choice."

"No, I don't."

I exhaled slowly, frowning before I moved to a bench to sit. Ryder followed me, ignoring the heavy stares of the others as he sat beside me. His fingers threaded through mine, and he pulled my hand to his mouth, kissing it.

"You're my world," he breathed. "But I am the King of the Horde, taken from my own fucking wedding by the witches. It made me look weak, and I am not. My people are testing me, and if you can't understand that, I will do this alone."

He dropped my hand, standing to his full height before walking away from me without a backward glance. I studied his stiff back, ignoring the worried looks from the men as he sifted mid-step, vanishing.

"Flower," Ristan said, starting toward where I sat.

I vanished, disappearing before he could say a word or ask a question. I understood he wanted answers, but the thing was, Ristan had taken the guild's files. He or someone else had destroyed the entire archive on demonology. My guess was that Ristan had already gone through them, and hadn't found what he was looking for, but it also meant I couldn't help him. We had no reports on angels that were useful to him, so he had taken Olivia's file with Alden's permission. The guild was starting over from ground zero, and anything it once held was gone. I needed to find information to help me manage the pain that worsened with every fae death, or I'd be useless in this war.

Chapter
SEVEN

Days went by without sight or trace of the Stag, and yet every day, I hunted him. I passed villages that were nothing more than ashes, corpses scattered around in different stages of decay. Today, I was in the Deadly Forest, studying the troops we'd sent to track Zahruk's brother, Fang. Following rumors of the White Stag, I ended up deep in the woods.

Off in the distance, I could see soldiers blending in with the foliage, and yet they didn't approach the shifters who trekked deeper into the Deadly Forest of Faery. I observed as a blond-haired male turned, staring directly where our troops had stood. He lifted his nose, sniffing the air before whispering orders to the surrounding wolves. Slowly, I moved closer, remaining just behind my shield of invisibility, observing. The man's sapphire-colored gaze slid back to the horde's soldiers who watched them, secretly protecting him if the need arose.

I sifted, standing silently between the soldiers and wolves as the blond-haired male removed his shirt, intending to shift to his wolf form. He smelled of sandalwood and spices from faraway lands that danced through my senses. His body was covered in thick, black tattoos he'd found worthy enough to carry for eternity. He stepped forward, running smack into my frame.

"Show yourself to me, monster," he sneered, reaching for his weapons.

It would really suck to kick Zahruk's brother's ass today, but Zahruk had stabbed me once upon a time, so it might not be so bad after all. I materialized so Fang could see me, and he stalled with his hands on his weapons. A wide-eyed stare slowly slipped down my frame. Silently, he took in my tight jeans and the tank top that said *Bang a Fae Bae Today*. Finally, he lifted his gaze to my face.

"Give me one reason I shouldn't kill you, right here, right now, woman?" Fang demanded, unimpressed with me.

Ouch! Obviously, being married wasn't helping my sex appeal, and my ego felt that to my bones.

"Let me start with, you can't," I offered, shrugging. "You're in a bad area. One you chose over war, why?"

"Fuck you," he hissed.

"Hmm, so much anger."

He drew his swords, swung, and would have removed my head if I hadn't known it was coming. I snapped my fingers, turning his blades into roses, and watched the shock spread over his face. I shared his horror at the destruction of the beautiful blades I'd just destroyed.

"Mmm, pity those were pretty swords. Now, if you're ready to listen to me, we can talk." He balled up his fists, and I lifted one brow in warning. "Okay, your fucking brother already stabbed me once and almost killed me, and if you punch me, I have no problem turning you into a fucking daisy. I'll even pluck you and take you home to stick in a vase. This is the only warning I'm giving you, Fang," I said, daring him to try me.

"That asshole sent you? Tell him to leave me the fuck alone. I don't need his help." Fang took a step back and huffed.

"No, you don't. But you've almost been a snack to a dragon, sexually assaulted by sirens, which may not have been a terrible thing unless they'd decided you were worth taking home with them. Then there were the redcaps we threatened to eat, and the water sprites who wanted to use your body as fertilizer for the…"

"Do you have a fucking point?" he snapped, folding his arms across his chest.

"You're an accident waiting to happen, and Zahruk is trying to save you. Why do you hate him?"

"That's between the goddess and me, not you,

lady." Turning his back on me, Fang began to walk away.

"Hmm, funny, because I happen to be the goddess you'd talk to." He stopped and faced me with a sarcastic grin on his face. I shrugged. "I know, I don't look the part, but I assure you, I am."

"Yeah, and I'm a fucking dragon." His snort pissed me off.

"No, you're not. You're a shape-shifter just like your brother, only you're pretending to be a werewolf. Your mother was a shape-shifter, and she thought herself a wolf because it spoke to her. But that isn't your wolf, it's your mind communicating with the creatures you've pretended to be. You're pissed because you feel like Zahruk has had a better life, and you've had to fight for everything you have. I get it, but it's not his fault. Life's fucking hard, but it forges us into what we are supposed to be. Look at me." Extending my hands out at my sides, I smiled at Fang. "First, I was a witch, then an assassin enforcer of the fae, then one of the creatures I hunted, now I am the fae, and I'm the freaking Goddess of the Fae."

"You're not the fucking Goddess of the Fae," he chuckled. "I've heard she has tits the size of melons, hips made to hold while she's ridden from behind, hair the color of the moons when they reach their zeniths, and the beauty of a maiden. You are nothing like they describe of her in ballads."

"Wow, really? Damn, so basically, I'm a blow-up sex doll? I'm guessing a man came up with that description."

"As I just stated," Fang snorted coldly. "You're not the goddess."

I glowed, my presence lighting the surrounding woods. "Holy shit," I murmured, looking at my arms in awe of my essence. "That's new."

"Synthia," Zahruk growled, strolling up beside me, facing off with his brother in silence. "You're needed at the stronghold. You're fucking glowing, woman," he hissed into my ear.

"Yeah, we just discovered that."

"*Why* are you glowing?" Zahruk eyed his brother before focusing on me.

"Fang said the Goddess of the Fae had huge tits and looked more like a blow-up doll, so I was proving him wrong."

"Turn it off," Zahruk muttered.

"I can't," I admitted, laughing.

"What do you mean, you can't?" Cocking his head to the side, he stared at me disbelievingly.

"What the fuck are you doing here?" Fang demanded, staring at Zahruk through hate-filled eyes. His hands clenched into fists, and I lifted a brow in a silent warning, causing Fang to drop his hands.

"I'm searching for the Queen of the Horde," Zahruk grumbled, and I snorted. Of course, Ryder had dispatched his best tracker to find me.

"She isn't here," Fang snapped.

"Yes, she is, asshole."

"I have no business with the horde, and I sure as fuck would know if she was in my camp."

"She's right in fucking front of you." Zahruk motioned to me and then looked at his brother as if he were the dumbest fae in Fairy. "Fang, meet Synthia, Queen of the Horde and the Goddess of the Fae. Syn, meet my asshole brother."

"We've met, he's cool," I said offhandedly, trying to take some of the tension away from the brothers. "Anywho, have you seen the White Stag? He can either be a Stag, a beautiful man, or pretty much anything he wants to be. It's a toss-up as to what he wants to appear as, I guess."

"No, I've never seen him." Fang shook his head.

"Okay, take me back to my prison, Zahruk," I mumbled, turning to stare at him. It filled his cold, unforgiving eyes with an expression I'd never seen, one that looked like regret. Slowly, he grabbed my hand, and we vanished together, reappearing just outside the war room.

"Why would you seek him out?" Zahruk demanded the moment we were back.

"I wasn't looking for Fang. A sprite said the Stag is known for being in the forest, so I thought I'd check it out. I watched him for a bit when I stumbled upon our guards. He almost discovered their presence, so I intervened. "Why were you there?" I countered.

"Ryder asked me to bring you back so you two could talk," he admitted, rubbing the back of his neck. "Go easy on him, Syn. He isn't wrong. People think he is vulnerable and that you make him weak. He has to show the horde that isn't true, and that he is their king. If they smell blood, they will attack us. That can't happen with the mages moving their forces closer to us every day. You love him, and he loves you. That's a fucking problem. The horde doesn't understand love, and they don't understand Ryder's changes. They see it as something to exploit. Also, glow bug, we're about to head into battle, and he can't do that if his head is here and not there."

"When do you guys leave?" I asked, hating that,

once again, Ryder and I would be separated at two different battlefronts.

"In a few days," Zahruk admitted, a frown deepening and creasing his brow. "I know you hate being here, but the guys fight better without women in battle. Ryder can't fight while worrying if you're okay. You're the queen, one who the people respect. I'm not saying you won't be fighting with us soon, but while we set up the troops where they're needed, stay home. You're the biggest fucking piece in place, and Ryder trusts you to hold his throne while he's doing what is necessary. You are right where you are supposed to be. Now, turn that shit off because you're killing my fucking eyes."

"Sorry," I said, closing my eyes until he chuckled. Opening them, I smirked, happy to have finally stopped glowing. "Take me to him, and I'll hear him out."

"He's in the throne room, poring over maps with his counsel."

Chapter
EIGHT

Ryder watched me approach with Zahruk by my side as we entered the throne room. His dark head lifted from the map on the large wooden table. Slowly moving across the room, I noted him, taking in the tight jeans that hugged my legs and the thigh-high boots. My heels clicking against the smooth, marble floor was the only sound in the entire room, even though it was filled with men planning for war.

"Decided to apologize?" I asked, hitching one brow before crossing my arms, waiting for him to do just that. He shook his dark head, letting power slither over my flesh while he remained cold and distant. Golden eyes lifted, locking with mine in a silent battle.

"I have nothing to apologize for, Synthia," he

muttered, studying my narrowed gaze. "You've wasted enough time hunting the Stag. It's time you helped around here and stopped wasting your fucking time pouting about stupid shit." I studied the faces around the table who observed me carefully, while those who knew me refused to meet my confused stare.

My spine stiffened as I pondered his words, wondering what I'd failed to do for the prick. I'd held court, ate nasty food with creatures that made my skin crawl while somehow keeping a smile plastered onto my face during the entire process. Ciara had helped order food, sending it out to the fae who needed it, and still storing a more substantial portion in the cellars that lined the dungeons in case we endured a siege.

I'd spent entire days preparing the castle in the event it was attacked and making sure that, if the villages of the horde had to evacuate, they could find shelter here with us. I'd worked endlessly, and in my spare time, which wasn't much, I'd hunted the Stag.

Today had been the only day I'd gone out early, and I'd checked my schedule, which was filled with mundane tasks anyone could have done. I breathed deeply and exhaled slowly through my mouth while noting the heads of the horde clans were here today, and while I wanted to slap the smug look off Ryder's face, I wouldn't.

"What do you need, My King?" I asked in a saccharine sweet tone. The words dripped over honey, so no one heard the barb buried within them.

"For you to do your fucking job as queen, and tend to your fucking people," he snorted. "Stop acting like a child for a little while and realize there's a lot more at stake here than your wounded fucking pride." Still glaring at me, Ryder pointed to the room next door. "There is an entire room of creatures waiting to be heard. I can't run battle strategies and listen to the grievances of our people. Go change your clothes into something that isn't so fucking human, Synthia. Act like you're the Queen of the Horde for once," Ryder hissed, raking his angry glare slowly down my body.

"As you wish," I hissed back, holding his angry stare until he swallowed hard. "I'll change immediately and do my duties." It felt like he'd backhanded me with his words, and swallowing my reply burned my throat as I took it without argument.

Turning on my heel, I left the room in long, angry strides that took me as far away from him and the heads of the horde houses as quickly as possible before I shoved my four-inch heels down his throat. Of all the things he could have said, that wasn't what I expected. Maybe I'd asked for it by blurting out what I had upon entry before I'd noted who was around the table. But between learning to handle the never-ending pain that rushed through me in waves and the war breathing down my neck, I didn't think much before I acted. I was scared and hurting, and it wasn't a good combination.

I could see his point of view. Hell, I had been in his place and knew the horde was full of treacherous, unfaithful fuck-faces. However, he didn't get to treat me like I was nothing. Ryder didn't get to argue about my clothes; you simply did not hunt shit down in a fucking dress. What the hell did he want? Me on my knees, sucking him off as the horde watched? Fuck that noise.

I had done everything he'd asked without question, even though most of those tasks had been things the servants were already doing. Like make sure they had fed the horses. We had a fucking stable full of horses, and stable-hands tended them! He was in battle mode, fine, whatever.

I didn't deserve to be treated like his slave, and I sure as fuck wouldn't stand for that kind of treatment in front of his counsel. He'd changed them, too, in the last few days, another thing he'd failed to inform me. I wasn't on his team. He was a war party of one, and I was the odd man out by his choice.

I paused as Darynda came into view. "Where are the other women?"

"In the women's parlor, drinking tea," she replied softly, noting the way my eyebrows pinched together. "Most are unhappy, so basically, it's a bitch session, as you refer to it. The men have been issuing orders and doing so in a manner in which we're not very pleased. We didn't want to bother you." Seeing my expression, she frowned. "Is everything okay? You seem tense, Synthia."

"I am dealing with the King of Assholes treating me like I should lick his boots clean." Exhaling my resolve, I began marching down the hall. "Let's go. Call the other handmaidens to the parlor, please."

"Would you like me to have the kitchen send up refreshments?" She pushed her red curls away from her face, waiting for my reply.

"No, but have some drinks sent to the council in the throne room. Make sure it's the horde's best liquor." A wicked thought came to me, and I smirked, "Actually, Ryder had some stashed away for a special celebration, so use that. Have some sandwiches delivered as well. They must be so hungry with all their manly war planning. Also, make sure they are all comfortable. Take them some pillows for their pompous asses to sit upon. We can't have them getting overstressed, now can we?" I hesitated, watching her frown deepen. "Is there a problem with my orders, Darynda?"

"It's just that the head of the horde houses are down there, and Ryder asked rather explicitly to not be disturbed."

"Then make sure the king is made aware that as the queen's duty, I am making sure that he and the men are well-fed and supplied with drinks. We are ensuring they're happy and in good health. If he doesn't like it, he can suck on a fucking fairy cow's farting ass."

"Okay, but I don't have to say the last part, right?" Her stare widened with fear, and it gave me pause enough to exhale, shaking my head.

Watching Darynda walk away with her shoulders slumped, I silently counted to ten, tightening my hands into fists at my sides as I let my anger deflate. Ryder had been saving that alcohol for some time now, hiding it from everyone to drink during a celebration. It would piss him off, and that made me happy. I smirked, imagining the look on his face when he realized his secret stash was being dished out to people he didn't even like.

Instead of sifting into the parlor, I walked the rest of the way, enjoying the clicking sound of the heels I'd chosen, even if Ryder didn't like them. I entered the room in a swirl of frustrated anger, and everyone stopped talking. The moment I arrived, they all went silent, and that irked me, too.

"Continue, don't stop bitching on my account," I stated, taking a seat in the high-back chair I'd brought from my old apartment. I hadn't been able to walk back into that apartment after what had happened, but Alden had gotten it for me. No one spoke, and I chuckled darkly. "Please, tell me what your asshole mates have been up to, so I don't feel so bad when I tell you what my king has been telling me," I insisted, fighting to keep my power within me, instead of acting like Ryder when he wanted to intimidate me.

"Blane argued that I should be moved into the tower until this child is born," Ciara seethed. "Can you imagine being in that place for weeks? Like, I'm not a fucking damsel. I'm the mother of fucking dragons!" She swung one arm through the air while still bouncing Fury, though a little faster in her anger.

Not that he minded at all. He waved his arms happily, making bubbles with his lips, staring at the women with an innocent smile.

"Well, as long as winter isn't coming, you can be the mother of dragons," I muttered, holding up my hands in mock surrender, and Icelyn coughed, choking on her tea. We all turned to look at her, and my lips tightened with the smile I tried to restrain.

"Oh, I'm not coming anytime soon. My body is healing slowly, and the goddess knows that we don't need me to have an orgasm and bring a winter storm. So, rest assured, winter is *not* coming." Icelyn shivered then smiled sheepishly.

We laughed, which seemed to lighten everyone's spirits in the room. Thanks to binge-watching *Game of Thrones* last month, we all had jokes about winter, and what happened when it came. Icelyn also affected the weather when she experienced mood swings, so the catchphrase was a big hit. At least that wasn't one element I could control with my moods.

"Sinjinn also thinks the babes and I should be held

in the tower until it is safe to roam the stronghold. I don't enjoy the idea. We're up there the majority of the time as is, with all the alarms going off nonstop lately." Icelyn frowned as she bounced Fiona in her arms, and I smiled sadly. Fiona had silver hair that, while different, was beautiful. Wide, green eyes like her fathers were alert. She peered at the woman who had carried her and Finn with an expression of love.

My gaze strayed to Lilith, who had been silent, and she huffed out a sigh before standing and pacing in the middle of the room. "Asrian is an asshole. He told me today that if I couldn't be useful, I should just go to my room. I mean, I get that they're stressed out because of everything happening, but since when do they get to lock us up or order us about?"

"Nobody puts Baby in the corner," I muttered.

"What?" Lilith countered.

"Who is Baby?" Ciara asked, confusion playing across her face.

"Never mind, it's from a movie. Anyone else?" I

turned to Olivia, who smirked, knowing exactly what I was asking. She would know since she had Fae-Per-View on hand, with Demon-on-Demand.

"Zahruk used me and fed, and then he left without so much as a goodbye less than an hour ago," Darynda grumbled from where she'd entered the room. "Like hey, I just fed you with my vagina, you're welcome! He didn't even pretend to care who fed him."

"I thought we decided to ignore Zahruk when he was hungry?" I asked softly without judgment.

"Handmaidens don't get a choice in the matter, Synthia. We're here to serve, which means if he wants to fuck me, I bend over and take it. Not that it's so bad. He's a generous lover and hung like a horse." The women laughed as Darynda blushed to her pretty auburn-colored roots. "It's just that there are feelings involved, and not on his end. I want more than to be used for food, or being bent over a table in his bedroom, fucked for hours, and then told to leave." Darynda's sad eyes looked down to the floor in front of her. "This last time, he was rougher than usual.

He used my hair to hold me, and then instead of only using my uh, well, using that, he used my mouth. He's never done that." She looked at me as a tear ran down her cheek. "Zahruk is normally gentle with me, and yet lately, he's been darker."

We all stared at her, and no one said anything. "Well, I mean, darker isn't always bad, right?" I offered to end the awkward silence.

"Ristan won't even have sex with me. Since he doesn't feed from sex, he says it isn't good for our daughter. We don't even know if we're having a daughter. I can't help but feel he will be let down if it is a boy. I mean, yeah, sex hurts sometimes, but I miss it! I miss him being the kinky bastard he used to be." Olivia huffed and looked at us matter-of-factly.

"Ryder just shouted at me in front of the entire council. He told me to act and dress like the Queen of the Horde." I sighed and leaned back in my chair, crossing one leg over the other. "I've been busting my ass until I'm exhausted. However, I still search for the Stag to understand how to control this endless pain ripping me apart from the inside out, which he doesn't even notice. I get it, I do. I know he's under a lot of strain, and that war is coming. I know that to run the horde, you have to lead by fear and strength. I don't need to know everything, but being kept in the dark isn't helping me help him.

"He replaced the entire war council without even mentioning it to me, and we're supposed to be a team? How can I help if he keeps me in the dark? I've been standing around with my thumb up my ass for weeks while he flitters about, fairy fucking around while I wait." I looked at Olivia and met her eyes because I knew she would understand. "He doesn't touch me the way he used to, and it feels like we're being ripped apart."

Oliva nodded silently, and I continued. "The most I have gotten lately is a quickie on the balcony or bent over whatever was closest to us to be fucked. I can't reach through to the man I love, and I'm losing him to this war." I put my elbow on the arm of the chair, resting my forehead in the palm of my hand as I rubbed my temples. "I miss our children, and soon they'll be leaving my father's kingdom to go to the City of Gods." I looked up, taking in all the women. "When they return, my kids could be old people! And what does it even mean to dress less human? Humans raised me, and he hasn't cared about how I dress since forever."

Everyone was silent, staring at me with expressions of horror or disbelief, totally at a loss for words. We were all lost in thought on how the men were behaving for several moments, and I smiled. I plotted, taking in the faces of the women who looked beaten, brow-ridden, and outright defeated with how they had been treated. Standing, I frowned before considering our options as I started pacing.

"We can take it and wait for them to realize the error of their ways, or we can remind them we're women and we don't fucking heel like dogs just because they demand it. I don't know about you, but I'm dead fucking tired of being beaten down by the men."

"Personally, I want to know how you plan to do

the second option," Ciara asked, pointing at her belly while Fury held onto her fingers.

"Like this," I said, snapping my fingers and changing the entire room of women into slinky dresses. Ciara's dress was red, representing dragons, and the bottom was a dark orange, resembling a flame. Icelyn's dress was ice-blue with a darker blue bodice, drawing the eye to her milk-filled breasts, which had grown two cup sizes. I decked Darynda out in silver, while Olivia wore white, with a flowing skirt and sapphire blue streaks winding up to her waist to hide the fact that she was overly pregnant. Lilith wore nothing but shadows that slithered around her in the form of a dress, exposing just the right places to the eye when she moved.

My dress was black, with a deep V-neck that stopped at my pelvic bone, leaving the back exposed to the arch of my spine. My arms held silver torques, marking me a goddess and royalty. Upon my hair, which was decorated in war braids, sat obsidian crystals resembling a crown. My feet were covered in strappy heels that left my freshly painted *Good Girl*

Gone Plaid—amethyst-colored, and a new favorite polish—showing. I painted my lips blood-red, and the smirk I wore told the ladies everything they needed to know.

"Okay, ladies. Listen closely to the plan, and by the time they leave for battle, we'll all either be divorced or delighted women," I said conspiratorially. "Keely, Maryam, and Meera, please take the babes to the tower. We will be there shortly after we've finished reminding the men who make their worlds go round." Smiling, I headed for the door. "Shall we, ladies?"

Chapter
NINE

We entered the throne room unannounced, throwing open the doors with magic. The men paused, turning to look as we stormed the room silently, the only sound coming from the clicking of our heels. My gaze brushed over Ryder, then dismissed him, fully aware he'd noted the outfit I wore and wasn't happy about the amount of flesh shown. The dress exposed my sides, my slender hips, and a lot of other things. Releasing power, my brands pulsed, dancing over my skin in delicate silvery-blue hues, and I smirked, knowing every male present felt my power, raw and unchecked, as I moved further into the room.

I walked right by Ryder, moving toward the raised dais without stopping as every eye in the room inspected us. Once there, I spun around to show the slim waist the dress exposed. I silently watched as the women moved into their places in the empty chairs reserved for the family during ceremonies. It was a place of honor and was heavily warded against enemies, offering them more protection should shit hit the fan. Once they were seated, I turned to the guard and nodded.

Sitting upon the throne, I stared straight ahead as Ryder approached me. He lifted a dark brow while I glared at the door, not bothering to acknowledge he was there. I felt the heat of his gaze as it slid hungrily down my body, noting my dress exposed a lot of skin; skin he wouldn't be touching anytime soon.

"A word, Synthia?" Ryder growled.

"If you'd like to schedule time with Her Majesty, Synthia, Queen of the Horde and Goddess of the Fae, I can see if she has time next week, My King," Ciara snapped angrily. "Otherwise, Her Majesty is about to hear grievances from the people of the horde and has no time for petty nonsense or small talk, Your Grace."

She bowed her dark head before glaring at him, daring her brother to argue.

"The fuck, Ciara?" he snapped.

"I am the Queen of Dragons and Princess of the Horde, Your Grace. Respect the titles I wear, as I am respecting yours," she said fiercely, her violet glare boring into his, once again daring him to argue. "Would you like to be scheduled?"

"She's my *wife!*"

"Mmm, yeah, but she has a duty to fulfill, does she not?" Ciara clapped her hands at the guards near the back of the room. "Run along and play your war games, brother. Let the people in; the queen will hear their grievances now." Dismissing Ryder, Ciara moved back to her seat.

I stared ahead, observing Ryder's angry glare while I surveyed the people filing into the room. I sat back, materializing the staff that mirrored Ryder's. He used the staff when holding court and listening to complaints and disputes happening around the palace and throughout the kingdom.

He opened his mouth to speak, and I pounded the staff against the floor three times to signal the first citizen to be heard, dismissing Ryder before he could say more. The crowd was filled with couples who stared up at the throne, frowning, expecting it to be the king who would listen to their protests and pass judgment.

Ryder stepped back, narrowing his burning amber eyes on me before turning on his heel and heading back to where the men now openly securitized us. Blane's mouth had yet to shut. Ristan's eyes were acting like lasers, as if he could stare hard enough to see through the dress Olivia wore.

Sinjinn's mouth was tight, probably because his wife's ample cleavage was exposed, and her figure was back, thanks to her inhuman healing. Zahruk stared at me cautiously, which was disheartening.

I was positive he felt that at any moment, the entire palace would implode because of the tension filling the room, and I was the only one who could hurt the king, whom he protected. Asrian, on the other hand, appeared to be considering ways to hide the perfected body of his wife, who wore nothing more than a dress created of shadows.

We were fucking hot, and everyone was fully aware of it. Even the males entering the room took notice, staring at me and then the entire row of women dressed scantily, oozing sex from our pores.

I sat up straighter as the guard brought forth a chubby man who hadn't even bothered brushing his hair before coming to court. His wife fidgeted with her torn, work-worn dress. Looking them over, I noted her hands were calloused, while his were soft. Her skin was red from burning beneath the sun's unforgiving heat; his wasn't. In fact, his skin looked as if it hadn't ever seen the sun, he was so pasty.

"My Queen, this is Dothan, and his wife, Clara," the clerk said. "His wife has not fed him properly and is charged with neglecting her husband."

My eyes moved from the couple to the clerk and then back to the couple. "You're not feeding your husband?"

"He refuses to provide shelter for our children and me. We have twelve mouths to feed, and the roof hasn't been patched in months. He expects me to take care of the children, fix the house, and tend the fields while he watches. I am also supposed to care for the animals we sell to live off year-round."

"Is this true?" I asked Dothan.

"No," he sneered and waited.

"No? That's it?" I tapped my finger on the arm of the throne impatiently.

"Clara was gifted to me and is mine to feed from whenever I want."

"And does Clara tend to the children, the fields, the livestock, *and* your house?"

"She was gifted."

"And?" I demanded, losing my patience.

"And she is my wife. She does what I want her

to do, and she feeds me when I want to be fed! Clara refuses to suck my cock when I demand it from her, saying she is too tired from working in the fields. She smells like horse shit most days, and should be happy I even allow her into our bedroom after she's tended the livestock! How is a man supposed to be able to get his cock sucked when the stupid bitch does nothing but complain?" Dothan looked to the men around him for support, and they nodded their heads in agreement.

"So you want to get your cock sucked, is that it?" I asked carefully.

"Exactly," he smiled, licking his lips, regarding me with a beady glare.

I snapped my fingers, and the sound of Dothan's spine cracking and breaking echoed throughout the room as those around him gasped. I glared coldly at him with amusement as a horrified look of pain tore through him. He hunched awkwardly in a painful position, and several pops sounded as his bones fused, preventing them from being healed. I inspected my handiwork with a satisfying smirk on my lips.

"What the hell did you do to my back?" Dothan demanded from his newly hunched form.

"I removed a portion of your spine so that you may suck your own cock. That way, your wife can continue to do everything while you enjoy sitting around on your ass, pleasuring yourself." I smiled at his wife and dismissed them, tapping the staff on the floor again. "Next." The entire room was eerily silent as Clara helped her husband out of the room, snickering on her way to the doors.

"My Queen, this is Darrion. His wife drinks potions to prevent breeding with him and is emotionless during the feeding process."

"Is this true?" I asked the wife, Darrion growling deep in his chest until his wife cowered in his presence. Her face was covered in bruises, probably from his brutish fist. She had marks around her throat and arms that bespoke of recent abuse.

"It is, My Queen," Darrion answered for his wife.

"I wasn't speaking to you, Darrion. If I had

addressed you, you'd damn well know it," I countered coldly, looking at his wife. "Is this true? Do you refuse to breed with your husband?"

"I don't enjoy him or what he does to my body, Your Grace. He forces himself on me and allows his drunken friends to use me after he is done. I use a potion once a month to prevent pregnancy. I fear I will have someone else's child and be tossed out because of it, even though it isn't my choice to take other lovers. I don't like being used by all the men in our town, or hated by their wives. My husband makes me available by tying me up to the post outback at night, freeing me in the morning to wash before I am given to the men again."

"Did you choose to marry him willingly?" I inquired carefully, nausea swirling in my stomach from the pain in her voice.

"No. Darrion killed my parents when he raided my village and took me as a trophy when I had barely had my first breeding cycle. I have been with him ever since. When the king took you as his wife,

Darrion turned it into a joke, forcing me to marry him naked before the entire town. He fucked me in front of everyone and allowed any man who wanted to do so fuck me as well. I was raped by every man that attended the marriage, some more than once. I was left hanging there overnight because Darrion forgot I was there when he passed out drunk."

"Is this true?" Darrion nodded dismissively, beady eyes smiling as if he assumed I couldn't do anything about it. "And now that she refuses to breed, you bring it before me? Tell me, was it my face you saw when you fucked your bride on her wedding night, or when you stood back and let any male who wanted to fuck her take their turn?"

"Does it matter?" he laughed huskily before letting his lecherous stare trail over my thighs, exposed from the slits in my skirt.

"I assure you, it does."

"Fine, I imagined it was you I was with, and then you who the entire town took turns fucking as I watched."

"And what is it you want from me? To force the poor girl to breed with you," I laughed emotionlessly. "And if she breeds with one of the many men who you allow to rape her, you would probably murder her babe, or what? If it is a daughter, would she also end up on a pole to be used for your entertainment?"

"Do your fucking job," Darrion hissed, and Ryder stood, staring at me as if he would intervene.

"You want a pussy you can share with your friends, one that's submissive, allowing you to breed and use it however and whenever you want?"

"Exactly!"

I snapped my fingers, and Darrion screamed, looking down at his hand in horror. "What did you *do*?"

"I gave you a pussy that you can share with the town, but I'm afraid it's only good for fucking, not breeding. A man like you shouldn't be allowed to procreate. You," I said, turning to Darrion's wife. "You're divorced. You can begin working in the kitchen of the castle effective immediately. If you need an escort to retrieve the items from your village and ex-husband's home, we will appoint someone to assist you. Hopefully, he argues with them or stands in their way and loses his head in the process. You're dismissed, enjoy it!"

Darrion's face grew red, and he seethed, spittle flying from his mouth as he spoke. "My hand is a pussy! What the fuck am I supposed to do with this?" He waved his hand in the air for all to see.

Regarding him through a smiling gaze, I touched the tips of my fingers to my thumb and inserted the index finger of my other hand through the center of the opening they created, making a rude hand gesture. "You can use it alone or share it with a crowd, big boy. You're a pussy for abusing women, and I thought you should have one to remind you of that fact, lest you forget. I contemplated turning your mouth into a pussy as an added crowd-pleaser, but I decided to be majestic and shit." I waved my hand nonchalantly and winked at the women.

Smiling, I watched his mouth opening and closing before I spoke again. "And honestly, I wanted to hear your thoughts on your new appendage, and that couldn't happen with a pussy for a mouth, now could it? I suggest you get out of my throne room now, while I'm being kind enough to allow you to do so. I took into consideration how you allowed an entire town to rape your new bride while picturing my face on her. Somehow, I decided to be lenient with you. I should rip your fucking throat out, but I'm still feeling regal, so shoo, Darrion, before I change my mind and have the flesh whipped from your back until your spine is exposed enough for me to rip it out without fucking up my manicure. *Next*!"

The silence in the room was deafening, and a few people exited between Darrion and his ex-wife as they departed from separate doorways. I stared at the next couple that approached before lifting my gaze, searching the audience, and finding a common theme. Almost everyone seeking an audience with the queen was couples, except for a few single men.

"My Queen," the clerk said, not meeting my gaze

but instead, staring off to the side where Ryder sat, drinking his whiskey. "This is Geoffrey and Genevieve. Geoffrey states…" the clerk paused, looking at me, then back to Ryder, who watched silently, leaning his lengthy frame against the table with his arms folded. "Geoffrey is rather upset about his wife, and her lack of interest in the bedroom. He states she just lays there and doesn't enjoy it. She doesn't come, which makes it hard for him to feed."

"Seriously?"

"Yes," Geoffrey said, studying me carefully, looking like he was ready to bolt at a moment's notice. "She finds no pleasure in my touch."

"Have you tried to get her off, or do you just jump on up and two-pump chump it?"

"I don't understand, Your Grace," he said nervously.

"Have you asked your wife what she likes?"

"Why would I?" Geoffrey looked around, confused.

"Because it is her vagina that you're trying to please, is it not? You can't just poke it and think it will rejoice that you figured out where your cock fits. Find out what she likes and use your words. Communicate with her, and I'm sure you will figure out how to please her. It is your job to please her, Geoffrey. Fuck, lie on the bed, and let *her* ride *you,* at least."

"I'm supposed to be able to mount her wet hole, and she is expected to feed me for it," Geoffrey said in frustration.

My mouth opened and closed as my eyes swung to Ryder's burning gaze as he watched me. His lips tipped up in a smirk as his gaze dropped to my chest, and then lifted, anger pulsing within him at the amount of skin exposed. I tore my eyes from his and frowned at the problem before me.

"Is that what you think it is? A wet hole that is supposed to get pounded and boom, you get fed? You poor, poor woman," I laughed sympathetically, noting her blush. "I assure you it is not just a hole in which to aim and poke. Try playing with it, arousing it until she's at least making sounds of pleasure. Explore a little and see what turns her on. If you think you can just aim and shoot, you will starve to death, Geoffrey." I frowned, moving my gaze to his wife. "Do you enjoy your husband, Genevieve?"

"I like my husband, but he doesn't stimulate me. He climbs above me and ruts quickly, and before I can even feel much pleasure, he's finished. If he could maybe take more time with me, I could feed him properly, as I would like." Genevieve worried her hands in front of her and smiled slightly.

"Well, tell him that. Use communication in the bedroom and see what happens. If it still isn't working, come back before poor Geoffrey starves to death. Next," I said, pounding the floor three times with my staff.

"My Queen, this is Lance. He wants to exile his wife to the human world. He found a mistress that suits his needs better, but his wife's family owns the property, and the only way to be rid of her is through banishment."

"Is this true? You want to throw your wife out of Faery for your mistress?"

"It is, it is my right by status and station to toss her aside."

"Right, so listen, jerk. I hereby banish you and your mistress to the human realm. Have a nice time with the apocalypse they've got going on there. May I suggest you stay on the East Coast so that your chances of survival are a little greater than they would be on the West Coast? Wife, you may remarry anyone you wish, so long as he will swear allegiance to My King and the horde. Next."

Lance gasped, and his mistress howled, slapping him repeatedly as they were dragged from the room by force. I smirked, lifting my hand for Darynda to bring me some water as I spun the staff in place beside me. Once I'd drunk deeply from the cup, I slammed the staff against the floor three times.

The clerk began to speak, and I held my hand up. "How many are here because they're unsatisfied with their wife? Please answer by raising your hand." Most of the audience held up their hand. "How many are dissatisfied with her due to a lack of sex?" I counted hands. "How many have a stupid fucking reason for this?" Everyone lifted their hand. I smiled at their stupidity. I snapped my fingers, surveying the crowd, waiting, and then someone broke the silence of the room.

"I have no dick!" one male shouted.

"You stole my balls?" a man in the front row cried.

"I did, and when you figure out how to stop being selfish pricks, you may have them back. Wives are more important than just satisfying what lies between your thighs. You have grievances that you brought before us because you're all fucking dicks. So, *I* took your *dicks* to show you that if you can waste my time, I can waste yours, and when I do it, it's on a much grander scale.

"When you've earned your dicks back, which I suggest you do rather quickly, your wives will give them back by drawing a cross on your pelvic region. If I catch so much as a whisper that any of you have assaulted, threatened, or harmed your wife in any way, I will be there to take it off with a dagger permanently. Are we understood?" When no one responded, I stood up, glaring down at the men. "I asked you a question."

All the men nodded, and I slid my eyes over the audience as they exited, leaving one male scrutinizing the others flooding out of the room. He was shorter than most fae and had tri-colored eyes.

I silently observed the man as he approached me, waiting for him to be announced. The clerk turned, staring at the staff I held. I turned to the women, waving my fingers over at their section before slowly moving my attention back to the male, slamming the staff on the ground three more times.

"Jensen Carlson," the clerk said. "He claims the dragons are eating his family's livestock and leaving corpses in the wake of their eternal hunger. He also claims one of the dragons has been burning his fields for fun."

"Is this true?" I asked, noting that Blane and Ciara stood. I held my hand up, stalling Ciara from arguing the accusation.

"It is," he said. "I am fae. I cannot lie. I saw the dragons do it myself." I glowered into his tri-colored gaze and snorted.

"Hmm, and which village was this?" I countered. Jenson's gaze searched mine, and I noticed the sweat beading at his brow. He fidgeted as his nostrils flared. His gaze swung to the ladies, and I narrowed mine on him. My hand came up just as he revealed a detonation device.

I sifted, appearing in front of him as time stopped around us. Slowly, I opened his shirt, discovering containers of iron, along with a long, wicked-looking blade etched in a substance that pulsed with power. I sent the blade sailing toward Zahruk's feet, then I emptied the iron cylinders and sifted back to my chair, returning time.

Jenson's hand clamped down on the device, and he stared down at his chest. I smirked coldly, watching the horror of his predicament sinking in. I stood slowly, stepping closer to him while the men came to attention. They saw the situation and began closing in around us as they took in the scene. I waved my hand, sealing Jenson and me inside a protective bubble.

"Are you aware of the consequences of your actions, *mage*?" I asked, somehow keeping my tone calm and collected.

"We will destroy you, whore."

"You can try, but you will fail. I have no intention of giving this world to you or your kind since you seem hell-bent on destroying what my mother built." Jenson attacked me, and I deflected it, grabbing his arms and crossing them over his chest, holding him from behind. "My men will torture you for information, but do you know what you'll no longer need?" I whispered huskily against Jenson's ear as Ryder glared at me from the other side of the barrier.

"We are murdering your people, Goddess of the Fae, and that weakens you, doesn't it? You feel them dying, and it opens you to pain. We're just getting started, and already you're losing strength, aren't you?"

"Oh, sweet boy, I am never weak enough to be taken down by the likes of you," I said, ripping his arms from the sockets, blood coating my face and the barrier. I released the protective bubble, watching as Ryder walked toward me, staring, his breathing labored in anger. "The mage is all yours, husband. I'm finished and famished. Toodle-oo, dick," I said, waving my fingers at Ryder as I nodded for the women to follow me. "I hope the cook made the honey cakes we requested."

"I want chocolate-covered hearts. It's so gross, but I can't help myself," Olivia chuckled.

"Let's get you a heart then, shall we?" I offered, feeling Ryder's heated gaze on my back. We exited the throne room the same way that we'd arrived, ignoring that the men existed, which, besides being obtuse assholes, was how they were treating us.

Chapter TEN

We'd filled the kitchen full of women, and we were in our element. Finger foods and cake bites were covering the counters while the cooks watched us like we'd gone insane in the pantry. Apparently, royalty didn't eat in the kitchens of the stronghold. Champagne was flowing, and everyone was laughing. Olivia burped and then blanched as she held her hand over her mouth in horror. I shook my head, grinning.

"I am so sorry; it's as if my body isn't mine anymore."

"You're pregnant; it's like a tiny mutant is now in full control of your body. I remember how it felt to have my three little monsters within me. I miss it, ya know?"

"Yeah, agreed," Ciara snorted. She shoved a cake pop in her mouth and then slammed her hand down, sending flour sailing into the air. "Oh, this is so good. I think I just came."

"Well, at least someone is coming today," Lilith chuckled before her dark gaze rounded, shocked at what she'd said, causing everyone to laugh.

"Did you see Ryder's face? How are you not terrified?" Icelyn asked softly.

"What's he going to do? Spank me? As if," I frowned before sliding another cake pop between my lips and moaning. "These are superb. Maybe these can replace sex. You think we can order the staff to make them by the platter?" I turned, smiling around a mouthful as the cook shook his head.

"Blane didn't look away from me the entire time," Ciara admitted, a saucy smile playing on her full lips. "I felt powerful for the first time since he knocked me up with Fury. I was sexy tonight."

"I felt like a sexy house," Olivia said, causing

everyone to laugh even more. "Ristan, though, he wanted me. The heat in that demon's stare was hot. I miss that look like I'm a sex goddess he can't stop staring at."

"Sinjinn, too, like he realized that I was a woman again. Not just a mother, or his wife, but that I was a woman. It was freeing, so thank you for that, Synthia."

"Zahruk didn't even acknowledge that I existed," Darynda frowned, and then looked horrified when everyone began to hug her. "It's for the best. I felt like I did when I first came here. I felt like heads turned and saw me, not as a source of food either. It was like they finally realized I'm a woman and not simply a nursemaid, but that I am from a good family."

"And what the hell was up with the couples' sessions? *My dick can't hit her sweet spot. It must be her fault because it certainly isn't mine,*" Ciara groaned. "Like seriously, how many men are actually that dumb?"

"And why would any women marry those men?" I frowned, popping another piece of cake into my mouth. "It makes little sense to wed someone who gives you no pleasure. I mean, I can understand the miscommunication, but why would they want to stay in that situation?"

"You took their dicks," Olivia laughed and snorted, shaking her head as she held her belly.

"Oh, my goddess, you totally took their dicks away! Do you have any idea how hard it was not to laugh?" Lilith announced, and the room burst into peals of uncontrollable laughter.

"Those men deserved their punishment," I snorted, picking up a handful of flour and sending it soaring through the air, gasping as it landed on all the women. "Oh, oops," I winced.

Ciara picked up a cake pop and sent it flying at my head, and the room silenced, waiting for me to explode at what she'd done. I gazed at everyone, and Ciara gasped, covering her mouth with her hand, staring wide-eyed in horror as an evil smile curved my lips. I grabbed a bottle of honey and pointed it at her.

"You wouldn't, Synthia," she hissed and then squealed when I squeezed the plastic bottle, shooting honey all over her dress. "Oh!"

Darynda surveyed everyone in shock as food began soaring through the air, hitting each of us. "Synthia!" I turned, staring at Darynda as a cake pop hit the side of my face. I squirted honey on her too, and grinned, watching her emerald eyes as they grew large and round. She picked up a cake pop and held it, looking at me. I smiled, and then laughed as she half-heartedly threw it at me, hitting me in the shoulder.

"You can do better than that," I teased, picking up a bottle of sparkling cider before shaking it up and turning, intending to send it shooting into the air behind me. The cap popped and shot fizz into the air, right into Ryder's face.

The room hushed, and we paused, covered from head to toe in food and drink. He stared at me while I reached behind me, sensing the men sifting into the room, hesitating as they took in the mess. My fingers lifted, wiping honey over his face before he caught my hand, staring at me in disbelief.

"What the hell are you doing, woman?" he demanded, and right then, Ciara bent over and groaned loudly. Our heads turned toward her, watching as her water broke.

"Baby time," I stated, clapping my hands to clear the food mess off everything but Ryder. "Darynda, fetch Eliran. Olivia, go rest, sweetheart. The rest of you, come with me," I ordered, offering Ciara my arm. "I got you."

We slowly moved through the castle, knowing that it was too dangerous to sift while Ciara was in pain. The fact that her babe was a dragon instead of fae put a kibosh on that option. Every few minutes, Ciara would slow down and bend over, gradually breathing through each contraction while an army of apprehensive men followed behind us.

"In through your nose, out through your mouth slowly," I instructed. "When the contraction is over, we'll walk again."

"Let me pick her up," Ryder offered.

"No, we're women. We're not helpless beings that need your fucking assistance in delivering what you've all planted within us. We can handle it ourselves. Plus, walking will help hurry the labor along. Let her be; if she needs help, she will say so," I replied softly.

"I want to walk," Ciara announced as Blane moved in beside her. "I don't want to walk with you!"

"What the hell did I do?" Blane asked crossly.

"You want to lock me in a tower like some weak-ass bitch. I am not weak. I am not Baby, and no one puts Baby in the corner." She groaned as another contraction started.

"Who the fuck is Baby, and who the hell said anything about putting you in a corner? It's for your protection and that of our children who need their mother." Blane ducked when Ciara spun around on him, and everyone paused in the hallway as they argued.

"No, it's so you can push me into hiding, just

like my brothers did. I am not weak!" Ciara growled through the contraction, making her sound demon-possessed. Her grip on my arm tightened, and we stopped walking as Eliran ran down the hall to catch up with us.

"How far apart are the contractions?" he asked in a calming tone.

"Three minutes, if that." Eliran took Ciara's other hand, helping her down the long hallway. "Her water broke, clear and clean like Icelyn's. Pain is manageable, and I'm only adding a little power to numb it for her, so we're aware of when she is contracting."

"Good, that's great, Synthia. What were you doing when it broke?" he asked, and Ciara snorted and started giggling. Laughter sounded in a line down the hallway, and I flinched, smiling at Eliran as he glanced at the other women, and then back at me.

"Oh, you know, having a food fight?" I offered hesitantly.

"Only you girls could induce labor with a food

fight. Gods, I would have paid to have seen that. Good to know you're all holding it together instead of falling apart up here."

"We're stronger together," I stated, turning to glare scathingly at Ryder, who watched silently as we made our way to the room Ciara shared with Blane. "Darynda?" I called over my shoulder, noting Zahruk's gaze as he studied me. When she answered, she looked sheepish. "Take baby Fury to the tower with you for the night. Blane will come for him once the babe is born."

"Yes, My Queen."

An hour later, Phoenix was born. She was smaller than her brother had been at birth, and a little more wrinkled. She was quick to wail her displeasure at being evicted from her mother's womb. Thick, tiny, midnight curls covered her head, and her violet eyes, lined with a deep electric-blue, surveyed the room warily.

"She's absolutely perfect, Ciara," I muttered with thickness clouding my words. Unshed tears burned my eyes as I took in the child Eliran had forced me to deliver and bring into the world. My fingers reached up, stroking the babe's forehead as I pushed her tiny curls aside. A glowing blue trail covered the skin I had touched. "Blessed be, little firebird. You will give your uncles grey hair, along with your daddy, won't you?" I asked, and her tiny hand curled around mine, causing her long, slender fingers to glow blue.

"You blessed our daughter," Ciara whispered from where she leaned against Blane for strength.

"Of course, I did, she's my niece. Plus, us girls need to stick together," I smirked. Carefully handing Phoenix back to her mother, I turned to find Ryder leaning against the wall, regarding me silently. "Rest, you will be moved to the tower on my orders," I said to Ciara, holding up my hand as she began to argue. "You need rest, and your daughter needs to feed. Fury is already there, and I'm sure he is in a hurry to meet his sweet baby sister. It's not because we want you hidden or think you're weak. I am moving into the tower myself, considering the current situation, and I wish to be with the women. We're better together."

"Okay," Ciara agreed, nodding through the exhaustion of labor she'd just endured.

I stepped back, turning on my heel as I left the newborn babe with her parents to announce her arrival to the palace. Outside the room, there were couples lined up, waiting to learn if Ciara had given birth to a boy or girl.

"It's a beautiful baby girl they've named Phoenix. She's perfect, and if I didn't know any better, I'd say she's an exact replica of her mother."

Fyra smiled and nodded her approval. Remy hooted and slammed Fyra on the back, sending her sailing into Zahruk, who stared down at her, then pushed her back toward Remy. It didn't seem to bother Fyra, and I hid a smirk at the fire that burned in her gaze.

"I heard a rumor about an epic food fight," Fyra snapped, and I lifted my eyes to hers. "Next time, remember that I have a vagina too, please. Also, way to go in court. Men think they run the world, but we have the one thing that they don't. The one thing they crave and want most of all: a pussy. So, don't forget about me. Plus, I'm good with a blade, and I like cake."

"If we have another food fight, you're welcome to join us. I'll make a note that you're a woman, too," I said, smiling. "Us girls, we need to stick together, with the men playing war games. Us weak beings with tits and ass, well, we'll find purpose in solidarity."

"Our bedroom, now," Ryder said, sifting without waiting to see if I followed him.

"Hmm, he forgot to schedule an appointment," I announced, shrugging. "Doesn't he know how this king and queen thing works? Men," I huffed, while the women agreed, and the men snorted.

Chapter
ELEVEN

Silent tears slipped from my eyes as I took in the darkening skies from the garden pool. Vivid purple and orange hues streaked the horizon as the sun began to set in the distance. Agony, caused by the ongoing deaths of the fae, rippled through me while I studied the utter perfection of the world Danu had created me to save. Now, I wondered if I'd actually be able to do it with the pain worsening every day. It was one thing to want to save Faery, but the mage from last night had been right. I was weakening with the deaths of so many fae targeted at once.

Flower petals floated on the water's surface, glowing with the small pearls of lavender I'd dropped onto each one to calm my nerves. Rubbing the back of my neck, I slowly expelled a shuddering breath, releasing some of the tension. Music drifted up from the camp below the pool in the raised gardens. I leaned my head back and closed my eyes, letting the melody of the song soothe the aches of my soul.

Power rippled through the small area, and I sensed Ryder before he'd finished sifting into the garden. I didn't acknowledge his presence, knowing that it would piss him off to be ignored, but still recognizing his anger. I missed him in our bed, but more than that, I missed Ryder trusting me enough to tell me what he was planning. Instead, he'd turned cold and distant, ignoring our bond as partners, acting only as the formidable Horde King. I knew that's who he needed to be right now, but that didn't require him to shut me out or treat me any differently.

Slowly turning, I peered at the dark figure who watched me from the shadows. Ryder's golden gaze glowed with an intensity that lit a fire within my core. Slowly, he stepped from the darkness, smirking wickedly while removing his shirt over his head. Sinewy muscles rippled as he tossed the garment onto the ground.

Never taking his eyes from mine, he held me paralyzed in their amber depths, lost within the galaxies of their glittering stars. The brands on his body pulsed, slithering over his skin as he lowered his hands, unfastened the button of his pants, and stepped out of them.

I inhaled his earthy scent of rich sandalwood paired with the aroma of masculinity that was uniquely Ryder, making my core clench with an aching need. I studied the naked perfection of the male who slowly walked into the water, stalking me.

He was a lethal predator in this moment, and once again, I knew I was the prey he hunted. I was lost in the intense stare that held me prisoner, breathlessly waiting for him to devour me. He growled low in his throat the instant my sanity returned, and I stepped back.

"If you run from me, I will show you why that isn't a good idea."

"You don't scare me."

"Don't I?" he chuckled darkly. "I can smell your fear and excitement, little one." His features were sharper than usual, his body pulsing with a power that sent a raw current kissing along my heated core, stroking it to a burning desire. "I can smell your delicate flesh aching for me to fill it. Is that naughty pussy ready to be destroyed?" His head tilted to one side, illuminating his large, black pupils, leaving only a galaxy of gold to peek through smoldering depths. "You're a very wicked girl. Did you dress up like that to get my attention? I'm paying attention now," he hissed. I turned around, intending to run, only for him to sift and appear in front of me, blocking my retreat.

He captured me, sending power rushing over me as his hand fisted through my hair, yanking my head back as his mouth crushed against my lips. Ryder demanded entrance, pushing his tongue past my lips to dominate mine. A moan escaped my mouth, swallowed by his own as he picked my body up with his free hand, holding me against him.

One minute we were standing beneath the stars, the next, I was slammed onto a bed. I sat up in my wet bathing suit, peering around the room. Searching for Ryder, I cried out as he grabbed my arms, yanking my wrists into cuffs that were connected to chains. Clicking them into place, he vanished again. Lifting a brow, I stared at my arm that was stretched and fastened to the bedframe.

"I'm still mad at you!" I snapped crossly, and then yelped as my ankle was captured and secured too, before he vanished once more. "Ryder!" I demanded hoarsely, then screamed as I stared down at my naked breasts, feeling them burn as the remainder of my swimsuit disappeared. "You didn't schedule *this*!" Deep, dark guttural laughter sounded from beside the bed. I glared up at Ryder and swallowed hard when I found him stroking his massive cock inches away from my mouth as he smiled darkly. Absently, I wet my lips, holding his burning glare.

"The day I schedule destroying your cunt is the day I die. Besides, I doubt Ciara actually wants to put that description on your calendar, and I assure you, those are the words I would use. If you think I wouldn't tell her to mark the king down for an afternoon of destroying his pretty queen's cunt, you're wrong. I would, and I'd love hearing her tell you and your court what was on your schedule for that day.

"Now, if you ever wear a dress like that again outside of this bedroom, I won't be held responsible when I bend your ass over and fuck you in front of everyone. Your little act of defiance made my dick hard. Very fucking hard, and it hasn't gone down since the moment you entered that room with fire in your pretty blue eyes. My fucking cock was rock hard with a need to ravish your flesh while you fought an assassin, Synthia. I want to throttle you while I fuck you, so subduing you will have to appease me for now. Tell me to destroy your pussy, woman."

"Suck it, Fairy."

"Oh, you will suck my cock, Synthia. I intend to be sure that when I leave this room tonight, you will know exactly to whom that pretty pussy belongs. I may have neglected it lately, causing *you* to forget who makes you scream, but *I* have not forgotten," he announced darkly, materializing a chair and slowly sitting down.

I studied him, noting the dark smile on his face and the pearl of precum on the tip of his cock. His thumb rubbed across the thick, rounded head while I gazed, transfixed, watching every slow, methodical stroke he made with hunger.

"I don't even like you right now, you know that, right?" I offered, trying to sound bored, playing it cool because I was mad at him, so mad.

My body jerked as a scream ripped through my lungs. Ryder filled me with magic, forcing my core to stretch painfully before subsiding. I inhaled, gasping for air as he watched me, his hiss the only indication that he had felt it too. He couldn't use sex magic on me without feeling as if he was the one fucking me, and I smiled, watching as more precum gathered, glistening over the tip of his massive cock.

"I don't know about you, woman, but my schedule is clear all night. I told Zahruk to inform everyone that I was not to be disturbed for at least twenty-four hours. I have a pussy to destroy and a naughty wife to remind who is in charge of this kingdom." Ryder's magic entered me again, filling my ass and my heated core until I was moaning.

My eyes rolled back in my head as my spine arched, and then I was slammed against the bed as his magic filled my body. I sensed him pushing against my mouth, rubbing his thumb over my cheek, encouraging me to accept what he offered.

My jaw opened, and he lunged forward with a bellowing growl that exploded throughout the room. Ryder filled my throat, threading his hand into my hair, using my head to guide himself in and out of my throat. His deep moan echoed through my body, sending shivers racing up my spine as he increased his speed, watching me through dark, smoldering hooded eyes.

"You're so beautiful with that dirty mouth of yours fucking my cock," Ryder hissed and then growled as my teeth skimmed his shaft, purposely. "Mmm, careful, sweet wife." His deep, seductive chuckle sent a shiver of anticipation through me. "You like my cock, and it likes you. Play nice, or I'll play rough," he warned.

He pushed my unbound leg against my chest, and his cock slipped from the grip of my throat.

"Look at that mess," he murmured, releasing my leg to sift to the foot of the bed.

Power erupted in the room until pressure pushed against every inch of me. Ryder slipped my legs into padded straps and then hoisted me up while watching from where he stood. My gaze followed his magic as it moved the straps, raising my cuffed arms and spreading my legs wide, exposing my neglected sex. My eyes slid hungrily back to his cock, which jerked as though it knew I was staring at the proud beast.

Ryder sifted in front of me, dropping his head between my legs. He began kissing the inside of my knee, up the sensitive skin of my thigh, and finally toward my ravenous flesh. I clenched with desire, ready to beg him to touch me where I wanted him most. I knew he wouldn't, not when he had yet to make me crazed with the need to be owned. He repeated the action on my other leg and then pushed his fingers through my heated arousal.

I moaned, lifting my pussy toward his face, begging him to ravish me. I didn't care if I was pissed at him. He was the fucking God of Sex, his touch was a drug, and I was the proverbial addict that would suck his cock to get my fix. His fingers pushed into my body again, deeper, and he chuckled, watching me ride them with a need so violent and dark that it shocked me to my core.

"Fuck, you're the prettiest thing in this world when you need to come. Look at you, all lit up for me," Ryder groaned, lowering his hungry mouth, licking me once then allowing his tongue to flick several times over my sensitive nub. "Look at you, so fucking needy, you're riding my fingers to sate the desire of that greedy pussy," he purred, removing his fingers to savage my flesh with his mouth.

I groaned through swollen lips that craved his hungry kiss. "Ryder, please," I hissed when his tongue swelled within me, fucking me with it until I was riding his face instead of his fingers. His hands held my ass, trapping me against him as his magic stretched through me, driving my mind to a shattering bliss of ecstasy that he controlled.

Ryder slurped and growled against my flesh, sending a violent tremor racing up my spine. I arched my back and felt him pushing against my ass, whimpering the moment pain pushed through me. He pulled away, staring at what he'd just done.

"Such a tight, pretty ass." He pushed against the plug he'd just inserted, smiling as he watched me fighting against the discomfort.

Ryder lifted his body, rubbing his massive cock against my opening. He released my arms, straps tied around both hands as he held me up before he reached for my hair, forcing me to look at his cock.

"No," I whimpered, shaking my head, taking in the thickness of his erection. "That won't fit, Ryder."

"Maybe not like this," he admitted, reaching up to tweak my nipples. "You're my good girl, though, aren't you, Syn? If I tell you to take it, you'll take it all for me. All of it, right to the base of my thick cock." He leaned over, licking one nipple before his teeth scraped over it. He continued to the next, slowly kissing his way up to my neck. His mouth sucked against my pulse as he pushed the thickened tip of his cock into me, growling at the low, desperate moan that exploded from my lips. "See, such a good girl for me, Synthia," he whispered seductively. He pushed forward, and I howled at the burning pain as my body clenched around his.

Ryder continued sucking my pulse, growling while his cock held still, nestled in the cradle of my body. His fingers danced between our bodies, his thumb working slow, calculated circles over my clit. He wanted me to come, but I wouldn't give it to him yet. I fought against it, ignoring the aching fullness he created. I refused to give in or succumb to his touch, though sweat beaded on my brow. I knew he had figured out my game when his deep, rumbling laughter vibrated through me.

Leaning back slightly, Ryder stared down at where our bodies were joined, then to my clenched hands against the red silk sheets that stuck to my sweat-covered body. My hair pooled out beneath me, still decorated in war braids even though it no longer held the crown of obsidian. I whimpered, fighting the need to come and stop the stretching pain that ached between my legs, turning into a burning sensation.

Ryder withdrew an inch, studying my face before pulling out of me completely, hissing at the sight of my flesh that was no doubt red and swollen from being stretched. Removing my restraints, Ryder picked me up and rolled me onto my stomach, placing a pillow beneath my head. Pushing my legs slightly apart, Ryder put the straps around my knees, instantly yanking my legs open wide, giving him full access to my ravenous core.

"Perfect," he mused, pushing his fingers through the slick mess of my pussy. "I know you want to punish me. I get it. I'm a fucking asshole. I've treated you indifferently, and shown the horde I bow to no queen, not even the one I love. I'm a dick, but you knew that already. It's time you figured out where you belong, Synthia. You can't straddle both worlds, or we will lose this one, and our children need Faery."

"Shut up and fuck me, asshole," I snapped, wiggling my ass with urgency.

He growled, and I yelped as his hand landed against the tender skin of my ass cheek before slowly rubbing it. He repeated the action several times until I was mewling, the need to be fucked more pressing than getting air into my lungs. Fingers pushed into my body, and I took them willingly, fucking them, uncaring of how it looked. When they withdrew, I whimpered from the loss of the fullness they'd created and then moaned as magic filled me, fucking me with a slow, steady rhythm that pissed me off.

His mouth lowered, fanning his heated breath over my hungry pussy before his nose pushed against the plug in my ass. His tongue licked the slit of my sex, cleaning the arousal that pooled between my legs from his merciless teasing.

Ryder rose, pushing his cock against my opening before thrusting into my body. He stretched me until it ached, knowingly forcing more into my core than I could take. I took it all, working my pussy against his cock, greedily wanting everything he could give me. I sensed the manipulation of more power stirring, ready to be wielded against me.

The kiss of the electrical current that wrapped around me pinched against my nipples as wings displaced the air, sending my hair rising with the immense power of the beast who had just taken control.

"Naughty mate," the beast hissed, pulling out until only his engorged tip remained sheathed inside my body.

I felt the plug being removed and whimpered against the foreign pain before he lunged, filling me until I was screaming and trying to escape the massive cock that was destroying me with quick, hard thrusts into my core.

He didn't slow down, violently fucking me until I was one endless orgasm. His power rushed through my body, hitting every nerve ending in my sex and anything attached to it. "Mmm, I enjoy you like this, helpless to do anything but take me as I am," he growled thickly, pushing his magic into my ass as tears blurred my vision. His hand traced up my spine, dancing over it as if to remember every single vertebra before gripping my hair.

The beast pulled my head back, his onyx eyes staring into my gaze, searching my soul. Enormous gossamer wings stood proudly behind him, while Ryder's black brands hummed and glowed like his eyes when he held control.

"Who do you belong to, little one?" he asked softly.

"You," I whispered through tears while his magic continued to fuck me painfully. It was beautiful pain, meant to destroy and claim, but tonight he was more forceful than ever before. He was testing my limits, punishing me for fighting them. It worried me that he wasn't taking into account that he could rip me open if he wasn't careful. As if he realized my concern, he pulled some magic back and began fucking me slowly. My ass burned, and he smiled, enjoying the pain.

"Then why do you fight me?" he snapped, pushing into my body, causing a moan to escape my throat. His hand released my hair and removed the straps from beneath my legs. Carefully he picked me up, turning me around until I was on his lap, facing him as he continued using magic to punish me.

The beast pushed me down on his cock, filling me as his mouth crushed against mine, demanding I open to him. Arms wrapped around me, claws brushing over my hips as the beast used them to control my body. Pleasure erupted within me, and I exploded around him, glowing with the release that caused a multitude of colors to explode outside of the window, lighting the room with their beauty.

"I am yours, but I am the Goddess of the Fae. I have a duty to you and my people, beast," I whispered as he pulled away.

"You fight me when you fight him. You are ours only."

"I am. I belong to both of you forever." My body trembled as tears swam in my vision. The room began to spin around us in a kaleidoscope of colors as if something else was happening, and I held no control over it.

"Do it," the beast growled.

"I'm afraid."

"You were made for this, woman. I tire of sharing a body. Do what you were created to do," he demanded, and I swallowed the scream as the beast tightened his hold, demanding I obey.

"Ryder," I whispered through tears as the room faded to black around me.

"Pet." Ryder kissed my forehead as he held me up, cradling my face in his hands. Slowly, he released his magic, watching me as he continued rocking his hips. His hand found mine, clasping on to me through the talons of the beast that had yet to recede. His other hand mirrored the action while holding me on his lap, watching as I lifted my head, staring into his golden eyes.

"I love you," I whispered through trembling lips.

"I love you, too."

My body began to glow with power, igniting his brands in a pulsing thrum of magic that filled the room until it became deafening. Ryder thrust into me feverously, watching me with his mouth wide open as I fed him magic, changing him, making him more powerful.

Blue and violet streams of power pushed through my hands into him, transforming his black brands into a golden color that slithered over his flesh. When he jerked with his release, I whispered his name, igniting more than a blessing of power.

I pushed a part of my soul into his, binding us closer than we'd ever been.

He growled, staring into my eyes, unseeing, as I gave the power of his beast to his fae form, just as the beast had commanded. My head rolled back, and he called my name as everything went dark.

Chapter
TWELVE

I awoke to Ryder cradling my body, glaring at me through darkened eyes burning with flecks of gold as his wings concealed us. I touched the back of my head and winced against the pain. Although I could tell he was concerned, he didn't look happy. I lifted my head, moaning before I rested against his shoulder, continuing to stare at him in confusion. My body trembled violently, hating that I didn't know what happened because nobody could fall asleep on this man's dick. My guess was that I'd passed out from too much pain.

"Your wings are out," I uttered through chattering teeth.

"Yeah, about that," he replied angrily. "What the

hell did you do?"

"What, what do you mean?"

"You pushed power into me, but then it changed to something else, something violent. I felt like I was on fire and being ripped apart into a million fucking little pieces, and I told you to stop, but you looked right through me and kept fucking pushing more magic into me, Synthia."

"I didn't do that to you." Confused, I blinked at the dark wings, noting the sharp, pointed talons along the outside edges, resembling serrated teeth. They unfurled, spreading wide, then snapped closed to reveal a room full of men, all glaring at me accusingly. "I didn't…" My mind replayed the magic at the end of the sex, wanting to do whatever it took to protect Ryder from our enemies. I'd wished him strong enough to live through what was coming, so had I done this to him? "I don't know what I did. I just remember pushing power into you, willing you to survive the war. I felt something inside of me shift, and then it entered you."

"The beast within me has yet to speak, Synthia. Is that what you wanted? For him to no longer be a part of me?" Ryder demanded, tossing me onto the bed, staring at me through narrowed eyes full of hurt and betrayal.

"No, never," I whispered carefully. "Ryder, whatever I did, I did to protect you. I would never want to change who and what you are. You're everything to me, and the beast is a part of you. I love him, too."

Cold, angry eyes narrowed on me, surveying the tears that rolled down my cheeks as I sat up, studying him. I wasn't sure what I'd done, only that I'd been unable to stop it from happening. I may not always enjoy the beast, and yeah, he could hurt me, but he never meant to. He wasn't of this world, and his thoughts were more focused on fucking, owning, or worse, breeding my womb, but I loved him.

"Undo it!" Ryder demanded harshly.

"I don't even know what I did. I'll call Destiny."

"Call her now!" The harsh tone of his voice

wrapped around my heart and squeezed it tightly.

I whispered Destiny's name, sensing the moment she entered the room, and turned to see her gaping at Ryder's form. Her head moved from Ryder to me, and her gaze narrowed. It was as if she sensed the change in him immediately and wasn't surprised by it at all.

"I see you finally figured out how to combine them. How did you do it?" Destiny stared at Ryder, examining in his wicked-looking wings before turning to look at the men who growled their disapproval at her words.

"I don't want them combined. I don't even know how it happened!"

"I'm guessing you were mid-fuck, and you tried to feed him?" I nodded, and she laughed outright at me.

"Feeding straight from a goddess has consequences, especially if she loves her mate. Your mother always tried to combine the beast to the man and failed. Danu fed Alazander gluttonously, and he took and took from her, and yet he never did become one with the beast he carried. How did you manage it?"

"I—uh," I paused, horrified, then looked at Ryder before glancing back to the half-naked goddess. "I wanted to protect him, and then I pushed power into him the same way I do when I feed him. My thoughts were of the war, and that I could lose him. Suddenly, everything changed, and it was as if we were one being, and Ryder was staring through me like he didn't see me. I felt him fucking me, but I no longer saw him. After a few moments, the room began to spin with a rainbow of colors, and then everything faded to black."

"Amazing," Destiny said, still looking at Ryder. "You gave him a piece of your soul, Synthia. You combined man and beast by giving him a part of yourself. You love him enough to sacrifice that piece of yourself to protect him. Apparently, that's the one thing your mother was unwilling to do when she tried to merge the beast with Alazander."

"How do I undo it?" She snorted in response, throwing her hands up in the air. "Ryder doesn't want this, and neither do I."

"Are you sure? You've succeeded in transforming Ryder into what your mother always meant him to become. As Horde King, Ryder was forced to carry the beast which appeared as the part of him you were created to soothe—you know, so that he wouldn't go insane like his father. Do you know why Alazander went mad? He wasn't strong enough to be both beast and man, because no one is.

"Unfortunately, Danu hadn't seen that complication of her creation. The beast she created had to choose a host with enough strength and power to hold him. Once inside the host, they would slowly lose control because the beast is an animal, hungering for more without ever fully satisfying that hunger. Your mother searched endlessly for a way to combine man and beast. She even offered herself to Alazander in the guise of his newest concubine and endured his brutality in her efforts to find a way to save him.

"When Ryder took his beast, Danu created you to quench his hunger. She knew his need to fuck would be insatiable and would drive him mad unless he fucked and fed from a goddess or demi-goddess, and Danu was unwilling to feed another beast herself. She spent thousands of years trying to fix the flaw in her creation and failed. She thought it was impossible, but you succeeded through love. It is truly amazing." Reaching out, Destiny ran her hand over Ryder's wings while we all stared at her.

"Yeah, I don't think Ryder agrees with you. He's sorta pissed off, in case you didn't notice from the glares he is giving us."

"He is unused to it, but he'll get over it in time."

"The beast isn't speaking to me anymore," Ryder snapped.

"Of course, he's not. The beast is no longer a separate part of you. You've merged, and now you're what the Horde King was always supposed to be: the Beast of Men. You no longer hold him; you've become one with him. You still have all the abilities of the beast, but you don't have to fight him for control. He allowed Synthia to merge you into one being. You are the perfect killing machine now, as Danu had always intended. You can't hear the beast because his thoughts are now yours. Danu created each breed of the horde to house their monster on the outside, Ryder. Yours, however, was flawed until now."

Closing his eyes, Ryder growled as he shook his head and lowered it. "I didn't ask for this."

"No, but here's the reality of what would happen, Ryder," Destiny shot back at him. "Synthia was created to be your balance, and your anchor to keep the beast sated, but eventually he would've wanted more. His sole purpose was to breed and kill, and yours was to survive so that he could live. Why do you think Alazander had thousands of children? It wasn't because he craved them. It was because his beast would never stop.

"I'm not saying Alazander wasn't a murderous bastard, but he also was maddened by the beast within him. So, he killed and he fucked, but now man controls the beast and his urges. Luckily, Alazander died before he could give Danu a child of her own, and she created you instead. It may take you time to come to terms with the changes, Ryder, but consider this: Had your beast not accepted Synthia's magic or wanted to be one with its host, it wouldn't have happened, no matter how hard she tried. He'd have torn Synthia apart to prevent the transformation, and she doesn't have a scratch on her. The beast didn't fight your wife, so why are you?"

Ryder looked at Destiny, then to me, his face red with anger as he clenched his jaw. "I'm preparing for war, and I don't have time to figure out how to control the beast again."

"Put your wings away, Ryder. Just like you would the beast," Destiny instructed, and he glared at me, damning me for something I had little control over. His wings twitched before they vanished, only to reappear again. He did it several times before narrowing his eyes on Destiny. "*You* are the beast. You have nothing to learn. You've spent every moment since he was gifted to you learning to control him. You need to stop thinking that Synthia cursed you, because she didn't.

"She anchored your fucking beast to your soul, and by adding a sliver of hers, she gave you what Danu would never give to Alazander. Synthia," she said, turning to look at me, forcing my gaze away from Ryder's anger. "Don't be ashamed of what you did for Ryder. You had no more control over it than he did. Your love for him, pure and untainted, offered him what no one else could. Your soul chose him and found him worthy of housing a piece of you. That type of love is endless."

"Like what Erie gave to Callaghan? Because that didn't work out well for them," Ryder countered, still glaring at me.

"Yes, just like that, so if either of you dies, when your souls are reborn, you would find one another again, and love each other. Erie, however, was brought back differently, by force, creating an entirely different situation. I don't think you should use Erie as an example because she's psychotic. There's nothing normal about her."

"Thank you," I said, watching her aura shimmer before she vanished.

"Out, now!" Ryder snapped, and I stood to leave the room. "Not you, Synthia."

I turned, staring at him through pain-filled eyes. He stood from the bed, unfolding his wings and growing taller, power emanating from him with every move he made. The men paused, eyeing Ryder, then me, before leaving the room, deciding I was on my own.

I sat on the bed, staring up at him through unshed tears. I'd wanted to protect him, and in doing so, I'd changed him into something else. I didn't blame him for being upset. Hell, I was pissed at myself for what I'd done.

"Ryder, I didn't mean for this to happen."

"Strip," he growled, balling his fists up at his sides. "Now, because I need to be inside of you, Pet. You created a monster, and the only thing I can think of at the moment is fucking your warm sheath until I come deep within it."

I blinked and nodded. In ways of punishment, I was pretty much on board with this one. "I'm good with that," I stated, watching a dark, sinful smile spread across his lips.

"Keep that thought close," he warned, observing my slow movements as I began to remove the gown he had glamoured onto me. His stare narrowed, observing everything I did with interest as I stood, letting the fabric pool at my feet. "Now, bend over and don't fucking move."

Chapter
THIRTEEN

Ryder

Synthia fucked up, plain and simple. She'd made me insatiable when she combined me with the beast. I already held secrets she didn't know about. It wasn't as if she didn't have secrets of her own lately either— yet she wanted trust. She'd been keeping company with gods and shit that didn't even belong in my world. Her entire existence was flawed with her need to protect shit on her own, and that didn't fucking work for me. Synthia was mine by right. I'd claimed her, fucking her until she didn't want off of my dick. I'd bred her womb, filling it with our babes, and then she'd gone and died to bring them into this world.

Now she'd started keeping company with the wrong people more and more, and not doing what I needed her to be doing. Did she think I didn't know who had walked into my home? Synthia did nothing the easy way, stubborn as fuck. She grasped on to everything, holding it close with fear that once it was gone, it could never be gotten back.

She sunk her claws in, dug her tiny heels deep, and held on with everything she was and had. I couldn't reach her once she'd dug in, and while I'd supported her half-assed efforts to accept this world, I was done fucking around with her. The war was at our doors, and she was sulking over stupid shit.

I reached down, running my fingertips over the wet cunt that clenched in fear. Red and swollen, it dripped with arousal from the magic steadily fucking her tight sheath endlessly—and I watched her take it. I was punishing her, and she was aware that it wasn't ending soon.

It was make-it or break-it time, and she'd rather break than reach for the world that needed her. She'd run off to her world and the guild, spending time there while I crunched numbers. I made plans and hard decisions that might win or lose this war, and then she bitched about not being included. She hadn't even been here when I needed her. She'd fled to help rebuild the guild. I couldn't have her helping me only to leave when I needed her at my side.

Then she went and changed what I was because she was afraid for me? I was indestructible. I wouldn't die here, not in this war. I'd go on with her, but my family wouldn't. I wouldn't lose them, not after everything I have done to protect them. Not after what I did to myself to be strong enough to murder the bastard who terrorized us, and then hold the beast within me. I evolved, changing myself into the one thing Danu couldn't sense. I buried that power so fucking deep that not even the gods knew what I was or what I did.

Synthia thought she had evolved, but she hadn't fully become what she was born to be, or I'd have felt it. Fuck, the entire world would have sensed it. Synthia thought I needed to change to survive, and yet she was the one unwilling to change. She'd been playing house and hadn't even unpacked her bags that were still sitting by our bedroom door. Her shit from the guild was in our closet, still packed. When she spoke of home, she referred to that world, and I needed her tight, sexy ass here in Faery, fighting beside me instead of against me.

Her tender flesh beckoned me to abuse it more, and I leaned over, dragging my tongue through the mess as she whimpered for me. I devoured it, pulling her legs apart until I was sure they burned, sliding my mouth over every inch of her needy cunt until she started quivering and exploded in my mouth.

"Not enough, you need to do better. I don't remember saying you could come yet, either," I taunted, my magic stretching her for coming without permission. I stared as her head lifted, and her lips parted on a scream escaping her tight throat. "Quiet, or I'll fuck that warm mouth of your next, Pet."

I surveyed Synthia as she rocked against my magic, fucking her greedy slick flesh as it tightened around my cock. Sex magic was heady, and I was its master. I could feel her as if I was in her pussy, deliciously wrecking that tight hole. My magic fucked her ass hard too, and it took everything within me to be gentle.

Her humanity was stopping me from taking her ass myself, and I craved it. I wanted to watch those pretty eyes grow languid, coming undone on my cock, buried in that tight little ass up to my ball-sack.

Pulling the magic back, I watched as she sagged against the bed in relief. "What's the matter, Synthia? Not happy with the change you forced on me?" I asked, gazing at the electric-blue eyes that locked with mine. Fire banked within them, and then sadness slipped in as her head shook with her reply.

I'd done shit her way for as long as I could, keeping secrets from her that could destroy the tenacious, precarious relationship we had together. She knew who I was, just not what I was. How did I tell this beautiful woman that I was the one who wrecked her life, setting everything into motion that had happened to her? Worse, I was about to do something so horrendous she'd leave me without question if she found out. It would break her into a million pieces, ruining everything we'd built in the last year together.

Synthia took away the beast. The one constant thing I knew could never change. She fucked him right out of me, and he had allowed her to do it. It burned, pissing me off until I wanted to hurt her, viscerally and so profoundly that she would know the betrayal I felt.

I'd heard her plotting to change me, knew she was holding court with creatures I'd forbidden from entering my kingdom, and now I was expected to pay the price? Fuck that, and fuck waiting around for her to get her shit together. This war didn't have an endless amount of time before it would be pounding on our gates and knocking down our doors.

We'd all helped her, taught her how to wield her powers and fight. The one fucking thing she had to do alone, and she's refused to accept it. The power of Faery is hers, and it was right there, waiting. I'd fucked her in front of the horde, shown her she was more than just a part of this world. I'd pounded into her tight pussy as the skies changed, and she'd fallen apart, stretched painfully on my cock, coming so hard the world shattered with her. She still didn't reach for that power.

Standing up, I moved to the bed, turning her onto her back, staring at her sleeping face. Her chest rose and fell with her breathing, and I snorted. If she accepted what Faery offered, she wouldn't tire. Gods didn't sleep. Synthia needed sleep, which should have told her the transformation from human to goddess was incomplete.

She ignored everything we said, tuning us out as she accepted us and not the world around her. She had to wake the hell up before we lost the war, and our children paid the price. I'd been gentle, loving, and nothing came from it.

I had tried to make her realize that she wasn't accepting Faery. Dristan point-blank told Synthia that she needed to take what Faery was offering her. She'd looked at him with a soft smile curving her beautiful mouth as I'd studied her from the shadows. Her response? *Is that so?* Not *how*, or *help* me, just lame-ass replies to the one thing that could help us win this war before it started.

The fucked up thing was, Synthia had to want the power Faery was offering. It couldn't be forced upon her or taught. One had to want it with everything within them and grab the power the moment it entered them, tethering it to their soul. Synthia was too busy shoving her soul into me, and yeah, that was also a fucking problem.

She'd taught me love, unwavering, undying love. She was the stars in my eyes that she loved so much. Synthia ignited a fire within me, and yet she still held herself at arm's length while demanding I give her every part of me. She didn't even realize she was doing it, or that when she spoke of her home, it wasn't here with her children or me. She was fighting for us, but she sure as shit was not fighting with us, not yet.

I parted her thighs, enjoying the look of her pretty, sleepy eyes slipping open as I rubbed my cock against her hungry cunt. Inserting my thick tip into her haven, she clenched invitingly around me as a groan escaped her lips. I lunged deep without warning, pushing into her tight body until her greedy flesh took me all the way to my aching balls, swallowing me entirely.

"I'm not finished with you, woman. Wake up and fuck me," I hissed, a growl escaping my throat. Those pretty electric-blue eyes turned to violet and back again as she came alive for me. "Move, ride my cock, Synthia," I chuckled. Pushing her knees against her shoulders, I added more length and width until her eyes went wide, and her pretty mouth opened on a scream. I stretched every inch of her until I knew she ached.

"Ryder, it hurts," she complained, and I leaned down, claiming her lips hungrily to stifle her complaints. Her body moved, her argument turning into a moan as I slowly rocked against her.

"Good, it's supposed to hurt. You're a naughty girl," I growled, turning us until I was on my back, and I filled her pretty pussy with as much as she could safely take, clenching against me with the need to come. "Ride me, or I'll add more length and watch you struggle to get off of it."

Tiny hands moved to my chest, going flat as she lifted onto her knees, staring down at my engorged cock, so large she could hardly move on it. I was willing to bet, right about now, she was regretting that she transformed me. I had no plans to help her. If anyone could take my cock, it was her. My gaze dropped to where she stretched around me, her greedy cunt milking my dick until it fucking ached.

"Look at your tight, messy pussy. Make it come for me. I want to watch you fuck me, Pet." I noted those angry eyes lifting to mine, burning with rage and anger. "You pissed off? Good, take it out on my dick, woman. It's your only option right now."

I barely contained the groan as she placed her feet on the bed and stood, gripping every inch of my cock enveloped in her body as she slipped it from her swollen flesh. The popping noise of her body as she freed herself from me sounded throughout the room.

My arms moved, resting behind my head, staring at the angry red flesh of her sex. I expected her to move from the bed; she didn't.

Synthia slammed down, taking every fucking inch of my cock, repeating it over and over until I exploded into her cunt, trembling. Throwing her head back, Synthia roared her release as magic filled the room. I moved, rolling her onto the bed, stalling her orgasm long enough to own that shit. I pumped my hips hard and fast, wrecking her flesh until she whimpered, trying to escape me as we both came until completely drained and gasping for air.

"Woman, you undo me," I chuckled against her perky tits, nipping one and then the other as her head lifted and fell back without words. I bucked my hips, and her head shook, unwilling to take more of the monster she'd created. "Tired? Too fucking bad, Pet. I'm still hard and not finished ruining this pussy yet."

Hours passed, and I continued to wreck her until we were both depleted and satisfied, and even then, I didn't want to be out of her body. I felt like the beast with his insatiable hunger to fuck and claim her in the most basic primal way.

I wanted her womb filled, her body drenched with my come, and I wanted her swollen with my babe growing within her. It took everything I had inside of me not to release the reigns I held on that part of me. I could knock her up, and all it would take was me wanting to do it.

Once this war ended, she would give me more babes, and we'd live in peace as I watched her belly swell with them. Fuck, I wanted this woman and the life we could have together, but I needed her to wake up first. I needed the warrior within her to see what awaited her, but rose-colored glasses prevented that from happening.

I was out of time and patience, waiting for her to grow the hell up and take what was rightfully hers. She wasn't my equal, not yet. I would force her to become it, though, because this world depended on both of us to ensure it survived.

"Ryder, go to sleep," she uttered hoarsely, her

voice long gone from screaming.

I smiled harshly, withdrawing from her. I glamoured a nightgown onto Synthia's naked body and some simple clothes onto mine, fully aware of the eyes watching me from the shadows. I turned, leaving the room to join Zahruk, who waited for me in the hallway. We didn't speak, not until I sifted out of the stronghold and appeared next to the Fairy Pools in Scotland, far away from my mischievous wife and those she'd allowed into my home.

"Was she there?" Zahruk asked, palming his blades while watching my face.

"Synthia brokered a deal with her. What she agreed to, I have no idea."

"Synthia betrayed us." Zahruk frowned, unhappy with her choices.

"She changed me, and yes, she's betrayed me. I don't know what she has planned or what she has done. Until we know, I don't want her to realize we're aware of her secrets. She loves us and wants to keep us safe, and I fear someone else, a god or goddess perhaps, is playing on those emotions to get to her. I'd rather be certain of her reasoning before assuming she has committed treason against us out of malice. Have we moved the children and warned Liam of our concerns?"

"Yes, they're hidden where no one will find them."

"If we do this, I want guards posted everywhere. I don't want her to walk in while it's happening. Synthia would react before she knew the truth."

"Maybe if you piss her off enough, she'll wake the fuck up and take the powers from Faery that we need to end this war." Zahruk's sapphire eyes studied me intensely.

"I told her we issued a kill order on the fae, and she went to the human world. Synthia didn't move to protect the people of Faery from me. She ran back to Alden and the guild. I don't know what to do with her, other than force her into that tower and fight this war on our own."

"She invited creatures into our home. Synthia refuses to become part of this world, straddling the line between both. She has to be forced to choose one, Ryder. The human world doesn't want her or need her anymore. Faery is screaming for her the only way it can, with the blood of the fae drenching the soil. That pain she feels? It will go away the moment she finally accepts this world as her home and stops grasping on to the one that refuses to let her go."

"Do it, set the trap and bait the pest. Don't get fucking caught. I don't need to tell you what a shit show it will be if that happens."

"And if I get caught?"

"Then we handle it, nothing changes. It can't. Too much depends on ending the threat within our walls."

"It's your funeral."

Chapter
FOURTEEN

Synthia

The shadows swirled, becoming the silhouette of a goddess. I surveyed her warily, allowing my gaze to slowly dip to the dress she wore, brushing over her delicate ankles. Midnight ringlets bounced over her shoulders as she stepped out of the shadows and entered my private bedchambers.

Ryder was somewhere else in the stronghold, occupied with the coming war. Her long, slender hands pushed the shadows away from her frame as her blood-red painted fingertips dusted off the stubborn shadows remaining on her bare shoulders that refused to release her.

"You were supposed to be here days ago." I spoke low and clear, anger lacing my words.

"It wasn't easy to get the potion without the other gods noticing me. I'm here now," she said in a bored, breathy voice.

Between her fingers was a vial of glowing blue liquid. The bottle was small, easily pinched between her fingertips. I didn't reach for it, studying her face silently, and she watched me for any signs of weakness. After a few moments, she snorted.

"I thought you wanted it?"

"I do," I admitted, carefully. "You were supposed to be here to take my children to the City of the Gods. Yet you have not asked where they are, why?" I scrutinized the woman before me as I waited for her to respond.

"I cannot take them yet," she confessed, frowning. "I need to arrange a secure place to hold them where they can thrive instead of being smothered. I'm sure you understand the need for secrecy, and I don't think you want the other gods and goddesses to know your offspring are within their world." At my silence and continued glare, she went on, "I will take them, but I need a little more time. They're safe for now."

"And the potion, it will turn Ryder into a god?" I asked, watching for any sign that she was lying.

"It will, Synthia. I promise you it will make him into a god, but of what, I cannot be certain. You should administer it as soon as possible. He will head south within a matter of days to cut off the mages and troops marching toward us, and you'll want him here as he goes through the change. Have your children here tomorrow morning. I will be back for them."

"That's rather short notice," I mused, tapping my chin with my finger. "I need four days to hide the fact that it will be you picking them up instead of Destiny. Ryder will also be in transition, and won't be present for the handoff. I need your assurance this potion won't harm Ryder, and that you will protect my children with your life."

"I've given you my word," she mumbled. "I will

do everything I have promised. I will ensure your children are within the City of the Gods, and your beast changes into what you wish him to be, like you. Synthia, you need to know that once you do this, it cannot ever be undone. Be sure you can live with your choices, because you may lose him."

"I can live without him. I cannot live without him in this world. Thanatos is here, and we both know what that means. There are only a few people within this realm whose soul is strong enough to rebuild the walls of Hell. My husband is one of them. So I will do this to protect him."

"Put it in a glass of ambrosia, and it will hide the bitter taste," she offered, handing me the bottle.

I stared at it, noting the way the tiny bubbles fizzled against the plastic stopper. My fingers cradled the vial, and my eyes closed against what its contents meant for Ryder. Slipping it into my dress pocket, I wiped away tears blurring my vision.

"Four days, and then return for my children," I whispered thickly.

"I promise that you will make it through this, Synthia. You will feel it, but you will survive. Life is chaos in motion, and that motion is beautiful waves of destruction that shape us into what the universe intended for us to become. Good luck," she said, vanishing into a mass of shadows slithering out of the bedroom window.

I exhaled deeply, staring at the window long after she'd left. It took me time to come to terms with the path I'd chosen. Treachery was everywhere. No one was safe from Thanatos, and we all knew it.

I reached into my pocket, holding the bottle before I looked around the room slowly, noting the vanity Ryder had created for me. I moved to it, opening the drawer. Reaching in, I withdrew a thin velvet pouch used to hold the crown for ceremonies. I wrapped the vial in the soft material and closed the drawer, locking the potion inside.

I left the bedroom and asked a passing servant where I could find Ryder since they all seemed to know where the king was at all times.

"He's in the feeding room, My Queen." The servant bowed low at the waist as my heartstrings tugged.

"Why would he be in there?" I asked carefully.

"The king said he was preparing to feed and didn't wish to be disturbed," he admitted, albeit sheepishly while his fingers rubbed the back of his neck.

My stomach clenched as unshed tears swam in my eyes, blurring my vision. I opened my mouth to speak but couldn't get words past the tightness in my throat. I shook my head, uncertain if the servant had misunderstood Ryder's orders, or if maybe he was wrong. I continued down the hallway with shaky legs, threatening to deposit me onto the floor.

The moment I came into view of the guards standing before the feeding lounge doors, I paused. This was the room where the men and soldiers fed from willing women and where orgies occurred, playing out in gluttonous debauchery. Mere feet from the door, the guards stepped in front of me, blocking my entrance.

"My Queen," one said, scrutinizing me. "You're not allowed to enter the feeding room."

"Is the king inside?" I hated the weakness in my voice. When they refused to answer and looked at each other before looking back at me, I asked again. "Is Ryder within the feeding room?"

"You may not enter," the guard repeated. I brought my hand up, snapping my fingers, catching both guards before they toppled to the floor.

I could feel my heart beating in my throat, and a sick sensation churned through my stomach as I opened the door and stepped inside. It was dark. Candles held in sconces along the walls lit the room in soothing, muted shades of light. The smell of sex and alcohol filled my senses as I moved further inside. Flesh meeting flesh in a passionate rhythm was the only noise other than the lusty moans and groans echoing within.

Slowly, I moved forward, peering into each room I passed until I reached the end. Relief took hold as I saw nameless guards in sinful feeding frenzies, fucking whoever offered their services. Standing in front of the last room, I whispered a silent prayer before opening the door.

Ryder's back was to me, his arms filled with a nameless feeder screaming for him to fuck her harder. My stomach dropped to the floor as the world fell from beneath my feet, a viselike grip squeezing my heart painfully. Golden brands pulsed with untold power as he vigorously pounded his cock into a woman, his wings concealing her face. Tears slipped free of the hold I'd had on them, and I covered my mouth with my hand as the other held my stomach.

"Yes, My King! Fuck me harder!" the woman screamed.

"You dirty whore. You like that, don't you? Being fucked by your king," Ryder purred. "Come for me, you filthy little slut."

I stood there in shock, a silent scream held in my throat while he continued to fuck her. The sound of his flesh meeting hers in ecstasy echoed in my ears as her screaming turned into incoherent babbling. She cried out her release, and he chuckled darkly, turning her in his arms before he sat in a chair, staring into my horrified gaze.

"Synthia," he whispered with a wide, panicked look as guilt covered his face.

I turned, running from the room with tears streamed down my cheeks. I could hear Ryder bellowing my name, but I ran blindly. Everything inside of me screamed in denial, trying to convince my heart that my eyes had been wrong. The sob exploded in my chest as I rounded a corner and slid down the wall. This wasn't happening. It couldn't be, not when everything depended on us working together to end the war.

How could he do this? How could the man I loved more than I loved myself be in there with another woman? I held my hand over my mouth, pushing myself up the wall to make it to my room. People stared at me, whispering as I moved through the stronghold. Tears blurred my vision, and I ignored those who called out my name as I passed them.

Ristan stepped out of a room, staring at me before he moved to walk with me.

"Flower, what is it? What happened?" he asked, studying me while I shook my head. When I didn't speak or answer him, he grabbed my arm. "Are you okay?"

"How long?"

"How long what?" he countered carefully.

"How long has he been fucking other women?" I shouted, causing everyone around us to stop and peer in our direction.

"What?" he asked with concern burning in his gaze. "Synthia, Ryder wouldn't do that."

"No? I just came from the feeding rooms where I watched him fucking some whore! I saw it with my own eyes, Ristan." A sob racked through me as wind gushed through the hallway. Outside, thunder rumbled, and lightning crashed close to the stronghold. "Tell me you didn't know that he was in that room."

"Ryder wouldn't cheat on you, Synthia. He

wouldn't."

"Tell me he isn't fucking that whore!"

"You need to calm down," he countered.

"I need to leave," I replied, moving to do so when Ryder rounded the corner, dressed in all black, staring at me through an angry glare.

"You're not leaving," Ryder snapped.

"No? You think you can stop me?"

"I think you're my wife, and you are staying."

"I don't think so, bastard."

"I've had our children moved from the Blood Kingdom. If you wish to see them again, you will stay here."

Bile pushed against my throat as I peered into eyes that watched me with something dark swimming within them. I stepped back, turning on my heel as the entire Elite Guard stood around me, blocking my path.

"Move," I demanded, watching as they peered over my head for Ryder's approval. Whatever they saw made them step back, letting me pass through their ranks, surveying me carefully, as if I'd attack Ryder in retribution.

At the opposite end of the hallway stood the female that had been with Ryder. Her hair was dripping with sweat, and a smile covered her mouth as she watched me approaching her.

"You didn't think you'd get to keep him all to yourself forever, did you?" she chuckled.

I grabbed a handful of her hair, slamming her head into the wall as Ryder watched me. She slid to the floor slowly, and I followed her to the ground. There, I smirked through the tears that filled my gaze.

"You can have him, because I don't fucking want him anymore," I whispered thickly. Standing, I glared at Ryder. "You and me, we're done, asshole."

"We're done when I say we are done, Synthia. Go to your room and don't leave it unless I say otherwise."

Chapter
FIFTEEN

I surveyed the guard collecting supplies to add to the war wagons. The stronghold was silent tonight. Not a single sound reached me in the tower. I'd warded my room to keep Ryder from entering, or anyone else for that matter. He'd fucked another woman, and that ruined us. Moving the children and hiding them from me had destroyed anything I might have felt for him. He'd tried to enter my room several times this evening, and yet all he'd accomplished was tearing down the entire wall, still unable to gain entrance. I was safely sheltered within the wards, never facing him or acknowledging his presence.

My stomach churned with the uncertainty of my future. The betrayal stung like nothing I had ever felt before, leaving a foul taste in my mouth that hung on the tip of my tongue. Currently, Ryder paced outside of the wards, demanding entrance into the room we'd once shared as I continued to ignore him.

Memories flooded my mind, replaying all the times he'd shown me how much I'd meant to him. Had I missed it? Had there been signs of his cheating that I'd failed to see? There were several nights he hadn't come to bed, but I'd trusted him. We didn't have issues with our sex life, none.

The war and the endless planning had made it difficult at times to find a spare moment alone, forcing us to get in a few quick bouts of sex when the opportunity for it arose. I'd always made sure to feed him well, filling him with power so that he was at his strongest. He shouldn't have needed a feeder.

"Pet, let me in," he snapped.

"Go to Hell," I whispered brokenly. Ryder sifted in front of me on the balcony, and I stepped back, moving far enough away that he couldn't reach me.

"Let me in the room," he growled, studying me carefully. His hands pushed against the wards, and I watched as he pulled them away, covered in blood. He exhaled, lifting star-filled onyx eyes to mine. "We need to talk."

"I have nothing to say to you. Go tell your dirty little slut whatever urgent matter you need to get off your chest. I'm certain she'll be a good little whore for her king and listen to whatever you want to say. Me? I don't care. There's nothing you can say or do that will fix this situation. I deserved better from you, so did the children.

"You were supposed to be my forever, and now it's gone. We're done. The only way you're keeping me here is by hiding them from me, which you knew. Us? That part was over the moment you chose to fuck someone else. I told you I'd never share you. I don't care if she was merely a meal, or whatever she was. I hope she was worth it, Ryder."

I turned away from him, moving to the bed and stripped out of my dress, uncaring that his men inspected me from the rubble of the destroyed wall. I couldn't care less who watched me strip to my birthday suit and crawl into bed. Every part of me ached with Ryder's betrayal. I curled into a ball, pulling the blankets around me, closing my lids tight to block out their intrusion.

"Don't do this, Syn," he uttered.

"Fuck you, Fairy. You did this. You did this to us," I said thickly.

"I love you," he whispered hoarsely.

"If you loved me, you wouldn't have fucked someone else." I turned to look at the guards, and they were gone. "What's the matter? Afraid someone might see what you threw away for some dirty little slut? Tell me, Fairy, does she get off on you calling her that as you take her?"

The feeder looked like Claire, and the thought that he'd been with and sought out someone who resembled that woman burned. She'd been the woman I'd watched him within his mansion, long before we'd become a thing. Then, Claire had tried to have our unborn babes and me murdered. My pride was torn apart, but the thing I hated the most was that I kept asking myself if it was my fault, if I'd failed him somehow.

"Didn't I give you enough of me?" Tears slid down my cheeks as I studied his face. "What did I do wrong?"

"You did nothing wrong," he uttered. "You're perfect."

Sitting up, I stared at him through angry eyes. "Then why were you with her? Why did you fuck her?"

"It's not that easy, Pet." Ryder shook his head, but his expression was cold and resolved.

"It's not that easy? Don't wordplay me. I want to know what I did or failed to do that sent you seeking out another woman. If I'm so fucking perfect, then why were you with her?"

"Leave it alone," he warned.

"Where are my children?" I countered, staring him down as he studied me.

"They're safe. You won't leave me as long as I have the children."

"That's your plan? Hold my children against me? Until when, Ryder? Until they're old enough to realize I'm your fucking hostage?"

"Until I fix this," he growled.

"We cannot be fixed! You can never fix what you've broken between us. You cannot ever undo what you did. I will never lower myself to be yours again. Do you hear me? I will never fuck you again. I will not play wife to a cheating bastard who uses our children as pawns to keep me here. I trusted you with my heart, and you crushed it the first moment I let my guard down."

"You will let me into this room, Synthia, or I will send my men to collect everyone you care about and love. Do you hear me? Let me in, woman."

I laughed soundlessly, wiggling my fingers to

remove the wards. Ryder moved swiftly toward me, stopping at the bed, staring down with a worried expression. His hands fisted at his sides, clenching and unclenching as he continued to stare at my naked form. Slowly, he crawled onto the bed, catching me as I moved to sit up and slip away.

"Don't touch me," I hissed, holding my hand in a fist as he pulled me in to his arms. He didn't strip. Instead, he held me against his chest, stroking my hair like I was some distraught child he was trying to calm down. "Stop," I whispered, hating his touch.

"I love you," he murmured against my ear, holding me in his arms until I couldn't move away. "I'll do whatever it takes to keep you here, you know that. You're mine, created by Danu for me and me alone. You're my wife. Stay with me, Syn. You cannot leave here. Faery needs you."

Faery needed me, not *he* needed me…or *wanted* me.

I stared out at the open balcony, looking at the stars as they shot across the endless sky. Ryder's earthy scent filled my nose, and I inhaled, drinking him in, memorizing it before I tried once more to push away from him. His lips skimmed over mine, and I didn't kiss him back. I didn't respond.

Leaning me back on the bed, he began kissing my face before his hand moved between my legs, touching and rubbing my apex. His motions were frenzied, trying to make me respond to his touch. I was so mentally unavailable that I just laid there, unresponsive as he tried to coax my body to life.

"Get off me." I stared emotionlessly into his eyes. "Go back to your feeder, because I am not accepting sloppy seconds. You will not have me hours after you've fucked another woman. You didn't schedule an appointment, which you will need to do, according to horde law, if you wish to bother the queen in times of unrest. Do you intend to break the law?"

"I'm king, Synthia."

"Do you plan to rape me, then?" I whispered, looking at his darkening gaze in question.

"You think I'd have to rape you? Your body was created for mine. You may be void of emotion for now, but you will respond to me eventually," he warned, pushing his fingers into my body, watching my back arch to accept what he gave. "See, your body knows that you are mine. Put me on your schedule for tomorrow, wife. I plan to use your sweet flesh to refuel before the celebration of the impending war, which you will attend, so see that shit is on your schedule too. You may have free roam of the stronghold, but stay the fuck out of the feeders' lounge and away from my dirty little slut. I have instructed her to stay away from you in return."

"Whatever, Fairy. Take your fingers out of my cunt and shove them up your fucking ass. I'm exhausted, so unless you plan to rape me, get the fuck off of me," I hissed coldly. When he finally removed his hand, I used my magic to glamour on thick wool leggings and an even thicker gown. Turning over in bed, I stared at the wall, or what was left of it, as silent tears slipped down my face to wet the pillow.

"I love you. Remember that, Pet."

"Yeah, sure you do. Leave, you have your own room. Get the fuck out of mine, asshole. King or not, this is the queen's bedroom, and she doesn't fucking like you anymore. Now leave me alone, you're bothering me."

Chapter SIXTEEN

I left the castle at dawn, easily escaping my captors. I searched Faery for any sign of trespassers that I could kill, finding plenty of mages randomly placed in the weaker parts of Faery. I'd slaughtered more than my fair share before the alarm on my arm alerted me that I was late for the ceremony. I wiped the blood from my blade on one mage corpse and bent down in a pool of water, washing blood and dirt from my face before standing to sift into the courtyard of the stronghold.

Couples decked out in their finery stopped to stare at me as I entered through the hallway. They murmured behind their hands as I passed, noting the guards set every few feet within the hall. At least Ryder hadn't forgotten to secure the fortress while he'd been busy banging worthless bitches.

I walked through the main entrance of the throne room, studying the faces of the guard as Ryder took in my blood-coated jeans and leather jacket. I had secured my hair up behind my head in a tight ponytail, now blood-red from the arterial spray I'd showered in today. Men and women stopped talking as I passed, gaping at my wardrobe while I made my way to the raised dais where Ryder glared at me through narrowed slits.

At the throne, I turned, gazing out at the crowd, who surveyed me warily, waiting for me to say something. I snorted loudly, taking my place at Ryder's side.

"You are not wearing your crown, Pet," he hissed.

I wiggled my fingers, materializing a crown of blood-red rubies to match the blood covering the rest of me. I turned, staring at Ryder as he took in the damage to my face that was slowly beginning to heal. One mage had gotten a lucky strike before I'd removed his head. I'd been fighting three others, wanting them to hurt me so that the physical pain would lessen the emotional pain within me.

Ryder reached over to touch me, and I recoiled from him. He didn't stop, lifting an ear from my shoulder and tossing it away from us.

"You're late," he stated coldly, turning heated eyes to the crowd.

"I'm here, aren't I?"

"You've kept the entire court waiting on you, My *Queen*."

"And? I'm the queen, aren't I?"

"Act like it then." Growling, Ryder stood to address the crowd, welcoming them to our home for a night of celebrating before the upcoming war. When he finished, he retook his seat beside me while the bard told stories of ancient battles won by the horde and the old kings.

Ciara's eyes caught mine, and the worry dancing in them made me pause. I surveyed the other women, finding them all inspecting me as if they thought I would explode at any moment and ruin their little party. Olivia looked terrified. Her gaze studied me. There was sadness in her eyes that I didn't want to explore. Everyone was staring at me, waiting for me to do something inappropriate. The guards around the throne held their hands ready on their weapons. I'm guessing they would cut me down if I so much as breathed wrong.

"You will join us for the feast, preferably in something black. Go wash up and get the brain matter out of your hair. We wouldn't want our guests to lose their appetites because of the queen's lack of giving a fuck during her breakdown. Would we?" he mocked, loud enough that the crowd heard him.

"The queen was out murdering mages, which is more than the king was doing. The only thing he's murdering lately is a bunch of worthless pussies. Now, if you'll excuse me, I'm going to change into something less...*bloody*."

Once in my room, I eyed the vanity before moving

to the mirror, studying the blood and gore covering my lithe, well-muscled frame. My head tilted, glaring at the cut that ran from one side of my cheek to the other, blood dripping down my face.

The dress I chose to wear was silver, with sequins spread out through the design. The deep V-neck exposed an ample amount of cleavage, and yet not enough to be considered inappropriate. It was backless, stopping right above the twin dimples at the base of my spine. I didn't bother with makeup or cared if I looked exactly how I felt: exhausted. I fixed my hair into two large braids, wrapping them around the top of my head before setting the crown onto the middle of the simple hair design.

I walked down the hallway, noticing several people arguing and bickering. It seemed like everyone was fighting or quarreling as a result of being cooped up while we prepared for war. Entering the lavishly decorated banquet hall, I paused, quietly studying the crowd as they spoke to one another, most likely about me. They'd probably started taking bets on how long it would take for Ryder to break me.

Obviously, they'd forgotten who and what I was. While I would do nothing to endanger my children— not that I thought Ryder would harm our babes—I had no plans of cowering or playing bitch to the king, either.

"Syn." Zahruk grabbed my arm and stared into my eyes. "Not everything is as simple as you think it is. You told me nothing was black and white, remember that."

"Unless it is, such as what I saw, Zahruk." I pulled my arm back, shaking him off.

"Your face isn't healing," he pointed out.

"It will, and if not, oh well. I'm not entering a beauty contest, and being pretty didn't stop my husband from cheating on me," I snorted. "Are you here to ensure I don't cause a scene?"

"Something like that, yes," he admitted, holding out his arm.

I let him lead me through the crowd to the table until Ryder came into view with the female he'd been feeding from on his arm. He was whispering something in her ear. I stopped dead in my tracks as wind howled through the room.

"Fuck," Zahruk said.

"Is this a fucking joke?" I demanded, tearing my arm away from his, intending to leave.

"I wouldn't do that, Goddess," Lucian murmured, smiling down at me, his midnight eyes sparkling with something dark in their endless depths. "I have it on good authority you're free for dinner. Would you do me the honor of joining me?"

"Lena isn't here?" I asked, tightening my chest as I fought to control the emotions pulsing through me.

"She's made it her mission to eradicate every demon in the Inland Northwest, which she seems to be doing tonight." Lucian held out his arm, and I accepted it, knowing that if I left the room, everyone would see it as a weakness, and I wasn't weak. "You think he would choose her over you?" he asked, staring at the female who held Ryder's attention.

"He did," I admitted softly. I fought against the urge to scream or cry as the wind picked up in the room, sending dresses flying into the air and extinguishing torches throughout the room. In the darkness, I began to glow while Lucian held my arm.

"So, anger ignites the wind, does it?" he chuckled darkly, moving us toward the head of the table where Ryder stood with the girl. "And what makes you glow, I wonder?" he murmured before lifting my hand and placing a gentle kiss on the back of it.

"No idea, definitely not happiness," I muttered as we reached Ryder and his whore, who glared at me, slowly moving her eyes to Lucian with a darkening expression. I stepped aside, letting Lucian pull my chair out as someone else joined us.

"Synthia, look at you all lit up tonight," Spyder said, taking his seat beside me, forcing Zahruk to step back yet again. "Dayum, girl," he whistled. "You're fucking beautiful. You light me up, woman," he uttered, lifting my hand and placing a kiss on my knuckles. "You ever get tired of Ryder, I'm willing to let you jump on and test out my Spyder ride," He offered while wiggling his brows before sliding his gaze back to Ryder. "My bad, I forgot you were married. Who's the whore, Ryder?" Turning to me, Spyder smiled. "Appears you may want that ride sooner rather than later, little lady."

"This is Carina, the Mistress of the Marshes."

"Like soggy ass swamps?" Spyder asked, staring at Ryder while waiting for his answer.

"As in, the royal line to the Heavenly Marshes," Ryder corrected.

"Hmm, you have a beautiful queen, and yet your mistress is seated beside you?"

"Enough, Spyder," Lucian said, putting his arm around me, with Spyder following suit. "I'm sure Ryder knows what he is doing. This place reeks of goddess and false gods. How many have been here lately?" he asked, tilting his head to look at me. "Present company excluded, that is. You smell like Aphrodite before she tripped and landed on too many dicks."

"Oh," I snorted, covering my mouth with my hand to smother the laugh. "If a goddess were to slip and land on a dick," I teased, turning to look at Spyder before pulling my gaze back to Lucian, "would she smell differently?"

"Considering in this body, you've known only one man, probably not. If you landed on too many, it would change your essence, since you are now eternal." Lucian turned, watching as a new arrival entered the room. "I guess Lena finished early, excuse me."

"Is she finally done being pissed at you?" I asked.

"No, but we have a truce for now," he chuckled.

"Guess that leaves you and me." Spyder grabbed a goblet of wine from the server and handed it to me before grabbing one for him as well. "To sinning, Goddess," he said, touching his glass against mine. "I pray we fucking do it together!" He held up his glass, and I clinked mine against his.

"I bet you'd be a wild one in bed," I smirked as he

wiggled his eyebrows in reply.

"That's my wife and the Queen of the Horde, bug boy," Ryder snapped.

"Mmm." Chuckling, Spyder downed the contents of his glass and smiled wickedly at Ryder. *"Along came a Spyder that crawled up inside her, eliciting passionate screams. Her moans became louder, he couldn't be prouder; she shattered when that pussy came and screamed out that she was a motherfucking queen. The sounds were so sweet, and her succulent heat was something he couldn't resist. So, he ate her with vigor, one last lick and flitter, his tongue made her a quivering mess."*

Laughing, I spit my drink out, spewing it across the table and hit Ryder's hussy with the red wine. She opened her mouth, and an ear-piercing wail escaped her lips.

"You did that on purpose!" Carina snapped.

"Oops," I laughed, covering my face in my hands. "My bad," I laughed louder, bordering on hysterics.

"Go change, Carina," Ryder offered, watching me through narrowed eyes. "Stop acting like a child, Synthia, and remember who you are while entertaining our guests."

"Hey," I said, hiking a thumb in Spyder's direction. "He's funny, and if you can play, so can I, right?"

"Fucking try me, little girl. Excuse me. I should see if Carina needs help," he growled, nodding at Zahruk and the others, who followed behind him as he left the room.

I waited until Ryder left before leaning over and kissing Spyder on the cheek. "Thank you," I muttered, standing up and tossing down the napkin. "I'll be right back, excuse me."

He caught my arm, staring up at me with a knowing gaze. "I don't know if you want to see that shit happening."

"I've already walked in on them once. Ryder doesn't get to demand I show up for his little fucking dinner party and then make me look like an idiot during the meal. I'm the Queen of the fucking Horde," I snapped, offering him a saccharine smile.

"Gods, remind me not to piss you off. But hey, I guess if I did, I wouldn't get lost in the dark with the way you're glowing," he smirked. "Get your shine on, Goddess."

I moved down the hallway, listening with inhuman hearing. I heard Ryder speaking and stopped, opening the door. Entering the room, I gasped as something wet and hot hit my face. Wiping the substance from my eyes, I stared down at the blood covering my hands. Peering up, I found Ryder holding Carina's severed head by the hair while the entire room gaped at me, covered in her blood.

What the freaking hell just happened? These assholes were seriously messed up!

"What the fuck is wrong with you? You fuck her and then take her head? You're a nasty asshole!"

What the hell was even going on?

"I fucked her, not Ryder," Zahruk muttered as he

smirked roguishly.

"How could you think I would fuck another woman? I ought to spank your ass," Ryder snapped, lowering the hand that held the head. "You're mine, which means I promised never fuck anyone else, which you should have damn well known. I promised you forever, and I meant it."

"I saw your *face!*" Who did he think he was, lying to me?

Magic rippled through the room, and I turned, staring at where Zahruk stood. Only now he was Ryder. I did the only thing I could do: I punched him, hard.

"You son of a *bitch!*" I screamed wildly, turning to Ryder. "I… I…" I sobbed as my arms wrapped around my stomach. He stepped closer, tossing the head to Zahruk, who caught it quickly by the hair. His hands captured my face, placing his forehead against mine as blood covered my cheeks.

"You're my fucking world, Synthia. I would never

hurt you like that. We knew there was a spy in our stronghold, and if the walls didn't have ears, I'd tell you everything right now. Trust me. The chaos here is not natural. Something is turning us against each other. Something bigger than we have time to deal with," he whispered barely above a breath, kissing my forehead gently. "Now, about Spyder," he growled.

"He'll make some girl scream, but it won't be me, Fairy." I turned, staring at Zahruk. "You've never taken his shape before, right?"

Zahruk smirked and wiggled his brows in reply. "Mmm, would I do that?" he asked mischievously.

Lucian and his men entered the room, and I opened my mouth to speak, but Ryder's lips pushed against mine, sealing the words on the tip of my tongue. I nipped his lip, enjoying the growl that rose from deep within him. My hands touched his chest, turning my head to watch as Lucian and his men formed a circle around us. I wanted to ask what was happening but guessed they needed silence, or Ryder wouldn't have tried to quiet me.

I observed Lucian. His midnight-blue eyes sparkled with flecks of sapphires mixed into the glowing onyx irises. Lucian and his men reached their arms out, linking themselves together by the touch of their fingertips. Instantly, the room erupted in a raw, electrifying current that made my hair float around my head.

I gasped at the power oozing from them. Sparks leapt from their fingers, lightning igniting in their eyes as if they'd somehow captured it within them. Spyder smirked the moment my gaze moved to his, and I observed the shadows that swirled around the men, forming a barrier between them and the walls to shield us from anyone who could be spying.

"We need to talk, Synthia," Lucian announced darkly, his voice echoing in my head. "You've got a problem, one sent here to destroy the horde, and meant to keep them chasing their tails while your enemies slaughter your armies without you ever knowing."

"I know, Lucian. Why do you think I called for you? I am fully aware of the problem." I materialized the nasty golden apple I had recently found and tossed it to him. "I need you to handle that, and the rest of you, I need you to listen closely to what I'm about to tell you."

Chapter
SEVENTEEN

Three days had passed since the dinner party, and every day more chaos and fighting started within the stronghold than outside of it. Learning Ryder hadn't betrayed me after all had eased my mind, but we each had parts to play in the game unfolding within the fortress walls. Each day Ryder and Zahruk left to plan for the war, knowing someone in the castle had eyes and ears on us, monitoring everything we said and did—it unnerved me.

This morning I'd broken up a fight between the chef and a couple of servers. It had been a bloody mess. Then the cook served up two of their heads on silver trays, bringing the supper in himself and unveiling his masterpiece before trying to add Ristan to it for dessert when he had the audacity to laugh at the meal.

The entire kitchen, along with the staff, was covered in blood and gore. Three servers had fought to survive the cook and his butchering block. It turned out that a server had mentioned the steaks were overcooked and were medium rare instead of rare. It led to her head placed on a tray, presented to Ryder like a delicacy.

Smaller fights had broken out between couples, but they were less frequent since I'd discovered the golden apple and asked Lucian to hold on to it. Not that he'd been pleased with the idea. I'd done what I could to separate couples, locking the women in the tower with the men elsewhere, but that meant that the men had been at each other's throats all day. The fighting had reached the point where I'd moved up the meeting with the goddess to the morning. I had to put my plan into motion now.

I'd extinguished most of the light in the bedroom before pouring the potion into the ambrosia and placing it on the table before the large chesterfield sofa. Once I'd finished, I almost chewed my lip raw from nervousness at what I was about to do. Power ignited inside the room, kissing my flesh, causing goosebumps to rise with the awareness of Ryder's presence.

Turning, I studied him where he stood in the shadows, golden stars lighting his inky depths. If I hadn't felt his power caressing my skin, I'd have missed him in the darkness of the room. The candles ignited, bathing me in their glow as his hungry stare feasted on me.

I'd dressed in a soft pink baby-doll bathrobe that left little to the imagination. It had lace edges and a dark pink ribbon of silk holding it closed. Beneath the robe, I wore a simple pair of panties that tied on each side, which Ryder had always found sexy. His arms crossed over his massive chest, his wings unfurling and creating a subtle breeze with the simple movement.

"What's this?" he asked carefully, slowly leaving

the shadows that were hiding his features from me.

I opened my mouth and closed it as his head tilted to the right, staring at me with a ravenous gaze that threatened to consume me. Ryder was taller since I'd combined him with his beast. His hair was longer, dusting the tops of each shoulder, and I itched to run my fingers through the silken midnight strands. The golden brands matching his eyes pulsed, slithering over his skin and intertwining with the dark onyx brands.

His wicked-looking wings hung behind him, the sharp ends of each ending at a talon pointing up, promising death. Ryder had been sex incarnate before the change, but now it oozed from him with every subtle move he made. My eyes dropped to the silk pants he wore, and I wondered what else might have continued to change since we had last been together. He hadn't touched me since the day after I'd combined him with his beast, and now I was seducing him to finish what I'd started when I made my plans with the shadows.

"You will leave for war soon, and I'd prefer you to feed from me, rather than the whores you've been fucking." I swallowed hard past the words that dripped from my tongue like vile poison, still playing the part so the spies would be none the wiser. "I'd like you to be well-fed before you leave."

"I've fed rather well lately." Regarding me through the eyes of a predator, he latched onto my slow, calculated movements as I tucked a strand of hair behind my ear. "Turns out, I may need a harem after all. I rather enjoy having variety in my meals."

"Is that what you want now? To feed from the whores who never sate your immense hunger? You can feed from them every day and still never satisfy the beast's appetite. Only I can feed him and soothe his needs. I need him well-fed for the war we face, asshole," I said, reaching for the silk tie, slowly undoing it before letting the robe slip from my body to pool at my feet on the floor. I swallowed nervously while his gaze took in my body with naked desire.

Ryder clenched his jaw tightly, yet he made no

move to accept my offering. His nostrils flared, scenting the arousal already coating my sex. I stepped toward the table, bending over to grab his glass. Turning to offer it to him, I found him standing directly behind me. No sound had alerted me of his movement, not even the whisper of his wings.

Ryder's hand touched my neck, and his thumb traced over my lips, brushing against their fullness as I kissed it. His other hand cupped one breast, pinching the hardened peak as a soft moan escaped my lungs. I didn't speak or break the spell in which his liquid honey stare held me captive, not wanting to ruin the moment. He stepped back, accepting the goblet of ambrosia as he watched me, and I held my breath as he smiled coldly.

"Do you want me to fuck you like a whore, *wife*?" he asked hoarsely. "Do you think you can handle me in this form, after what you did to me? I'd wreck that wet pussy, but then you like it when I destroy that needy flesh, don't you?" He grinned wickedly, still holding the glass without taking a drink.

"If that is what you want to do to me, then do it, Ryder." I moved away from him before sitting on the couch, studying the way he held the goblet. I grabbed the matching glass, inhaling the ambrosia before taking a long sip of the blue liquid. It tasted like heaven exploding against my taste buds, and a moan rolled from my lips.

Ryder lifted the goblet and sniffed the ambrosia, just as I had done. His wings curled in, easily folding until they vanished as magic pulsed through the room. He stretched one arm over the back of the sofa and brought the drink to his lips, downing it in one gulp.

"Can I refill that for you?" My heart thudded in my ears, deafening his words as I waited for his reply. I reached for the glass, only to have him grab my arm and twist it, forcing me to move closer to him. "Do you want more?" I whispered, my words echoing in the room's silence.

"If I wanted more, I'd have asked for it," he growled, taking the glass from me and setting it aside. Blowing in the direction of the candles, he extinguished all but one, leaving the room dark, with only the soft glow of a single flame and his golden brands. "Lay back and touch that naughty pussy for me. I want to watch you fuck yourself." Leaning back, he removed his pants and fisted his engorged cock, turning his head to stare at me with a devilish grin.

Ryder's cock was huge, much larger than it had been before, and he'd been challenging to take within my body then. I wasn't sure I could accommodate him without enduring more of the pain I'd had the first time we'd fucked after I'd combined them. His excited gaze burned with the knowledge of my fear. The deep rumble of his masculine laughter filled the room, and I began to obey his instructions without question.

I hated the game we played, pretending to be at odds over the illusion of his affair, and continued feeding from other women. Those spying on us thought we were at each other's throats, and we had to maintain the pretense. It was hard enough during the day, but anyone who knew us well would know that I had to feed his beast, and not doing so would have tipped off the spies that we were on to their trickery.

However, I couldn't calm the nervous energy pulsing through me. There was also the fact that while Ryder fucked me immediately after the transformation began, he had yet to change into his newest form entirely. Now, I had to take him for the first time fully merged with his beast, pretending to fight to keep him. The ruse only added to the nervousness of what I was doing, trying to control the situation, to reach the end goal before he left for the war.

My fingers untied the bows at my hips, and I tossed the panties to the floor, letting my fingers dance their way slowly closer to my center. Ryder leaned in, pouring the ambrosia over my pussy, and I yelped as ice touched my clit. His wicked smile danced in the candle's glow as my fingers glided across my sex.

"Stretch your greedy pussy for me, woman," he ordered. "Three fingers, and don't stop fucking it until I tell you to."

My fingers pushed into my body while he followed my movements, studying the slow, languid motion of my fingers. I lifted to give myself more room to play before he spread my legs apart, nudging one over the back of the couch and the other to the floor, giving himself an unobstructed view.

"You can do better than that," he announced, grabbing my hand and pressing it against my flesh, rubbing it over my naked heat. He used my fingers, thrusting them into my body before adding his, staring as we fucked my core together. I whimpered at the burn it created while he stretched me enough to take his thick, hard cock. "You feel that, woman? You feel your greedy pussy sucking us deeper as it weeps to be fucked?" Leaning over, he clasped my clit between his teeth, slowly dragging them over my swollen nub until I cried out with need.

He leaned back, stroking his massive erection, and spoke to me coldly. "Look at you, naughty little girl. What game are you playing? Think you can fuck me hard enough to be my only source of substance?" he asked, watching my fingers before his stare held mine.

"I'll do whatever it takes to keep you," I admitted.

"If I have to get on my knees and suck your cock, so be it. I can be your dirty little whore, asshole. You want to fuck me like a whore, then do it, Ryder."

"Get on your knees," he ordered with a tone that shot straight to my core.

My fingers withdrew from my body, and I moved. Once again, he grabbed my wrist, bringing my fingers to his mouth, licking each one clean. My chest rose and fell as I held his piercing gaze. He made a noise with my finger still in his mouth, releasing it and settling back to stare at me as he slowly worked his cock with his other hand.

"You will take all of me into your tight throat. If not, I will go find another who can suck my cock correctly," he warned huskily.

My stare dropped to his engorged cock as my tongue darted across my suddenly dry lips. It was like we were lost in our own game, playing our parts a little too well. I *can do this*, I reminded myself. I was created for his beast, and I'd taken it before. So why was my heart beating erratically in my ears and sweat pooling at the base of my spine? I settled on my knees, pushing my hair away from my face while he watched me. He reached down, moving the few strands that had slipped past my fingers behind my ears.

"Break eye contact, and I'll fuck your ass," he promised.

I wrapped my hand around the base of his cock, unable to close my fingers, but then his hand couldn't either. I bent down, staring up into his star-filled depths, and licked up the sensitive side before I reached the head. My lips opened as he studied my mouth, watching while I enveloped the tip before sliding more of him between my lips.

Ryder's head dropped back, and his eyes closed as I worked him deeper into my throat. I made it a little over halfway before I backed away to readjust my body. He stood without warning, still inside my mouth. My hands lifted, intending to settle on his muscular thighs, but his hands fisted my hair, and he shoved his cock deep inside my throat.

I repeatedly swallowed, blinking past the tears

flooding my vision as I tried to accept what he was giving me. He pulled out an inch, then thrust forward again and again as I held his heated gaze. Ryder fucked my throat, staring down at me with pride.

Releasing my hair, he pushed me to the floor. I moved, intending to get up, but Ryder was faster. He knelt on the floor, spreading my thighs, and lifted my hips until his warm lips touched my wet core, ravenously feasting on my flesh. His tongue slid through my arousal, sucking my flesh as his teeth grazed my clit.

He growled deep from within his chest, allowing it to rumble up and escape his lips against my pussy. Ryder pushed his tongue into my body, lengthening it, and I was helpless to do anything but come for him. He demanded I obey and do what he wanted, which meant breaking apart and coming on his greedy mouth as he relentlessly continued sucking and nipping against my flesh.

My body erupted, bucking against his mouth as his deep, dark laughter vibrated through me. He chuckled, pulling away and peering down at where I lay, panting and trembling from the pleasure he'd just given me.

"Get up, my dirty little queen. Kiss me, and taste yourself on my tongue," he ordered gutturally as a growl trembled through him. I turned over, pushing myself from the floor to stand on shaking legs. Moving closer, I lifted on my toes and claimed his hungry mouth, cleaning my arousal from his lips. Sliding his fingers through my hair, he held me tight against his ravenous mouth.

"I need you inside of me, Ryder."

"You're a naughty little thing for your king, aren't you? You might please me after all," he announced, lifting me until I was helpless and could do nothing but hold on to his neck. "Prettiest little plaything I've ever fucked, and the most delicious cunt I've ever eaten. You want me to destroy that greedy little cunt? To stretch it wide as I write my name on your fucking insides?"

"Yes," I whimpered wantonly. I didn't care if it

was a show for the spies watching. I wanted him. I wanted all of him buried so deep inside of me that I never forgot how he felt there. "Fuck me, my beast. I want to be the one you come to for sustenance, and the only one you ever need."

"Good answer, woman."

He set me on the bed, dropping to his knees as he ravished my flesh once more, forcing me to come so hard and fast that I screamed, bucking against his mouth as the orgasm ripped through me. He sent me over the edge, and endless prisms of rainbows danced behind my eyelids. I was floating in a sea of utter bliss one minute and impaled on his engorged cock the next.

My mouth opened, and I screamed in pain to the heavens, staring between us where he'd pushed his cock into my body up to his thick base. I whimpered, shaking violently as he held me there, his dark gaze searching mine as he started to withdraw, giving up the show because he could see I was in pain.

"Move, pussy," I snapped through gritted teeth.

"Come on. Show me what good girls get for feeding their dirty fucking king. Make me ache for you, bastard."

My body ached endlessly as I stretched around his thick cock. My core clenched against him, burning from being stretched too far, sending my body into a tremble I couldn't stop or shut off.

He shook his head, his eyes pleading for me to end it. I sat up, pushing my weight onto my elbows, working my hips, helping my body adjust to the sheer magnitude of his size. Ryder and the beast together wasn't a great idea, not when it made his already inhumanly large cock longer, harder, and so much thicker.

Ryder grabbed my knees and pushed them until I fell back onto the bed. The first thrust wasn't too bad. The second turned pain into pleasure. The third solid thrust shot my body into a euphoric bliss, and I babbled like an idiot, praising his monstrous cock as it pounded into my flesh.

His mouth found my nipple, clutching it between

his teeth, biting just hard enough to get my attention. I leaned up, staring into his heated golden gaze and he smiled around the mouthful of my breast, watching me closely. When he released my nipple, the pop echoed through the room.

He withdrew, flipping me over and moving my body further onto the bed before he joined me. His knees parted my legs as he pushed my head into the mattress, slapping my ass before he soothed the aching flesh with his hand.

"Good girl, Pet." He lifted me to his hungry mouth and attacked my core again. The bed absorbed the cries of my release as he used his magic to send me reeling over the edge, dusting over every nerve ending and forcing multiple orgasms to rip me apart without warning.

He didn't use his magic to fuck me, only to kiss every inch of my flesh while his tongue lavished against my sex. Ryder released me, letting my body fall back to the bed before his hand slid up my spine, grasping a fistful of my hair. He pushed his cock into my body in a swift thrust that once again caused tremors to run through me.

I could feel him against my womb, battering it as he owned my flesh, making me his in every way only he could. It was no longer about who watched us. It was primal. Ryder was declaring ownership of every inch of me, and I was allowing him to do it. He was mine, and I was his, and in this room, he was alpha male incarnate.

"You feel me breeding you, Synthia? Planting my child in your womb?" he hissed, jerking as he exploded inside my body, hot cum coating my core. I swallowed the denial, turning to look up at him. His burning glare dared me to argue, dared me to question what he did to me. "You are mine, and good girls get seeded."

Seeded? I wasn't a flipping fucking fairy garden!

I slammed against him, taking him to his base as his deep, wicked laughter filled the room. It sent gooseflesh racing over my skin as he pushed down, lifting my leg to place over his shoulder.

His hand threaded through my hair, forcing my eyes to stare at where we joined. I was stretched wide, his cock still thickly buried in my flesh, clamped around him like a vise. It looked hot and erotic to see that I'd taken every inch of him inside of me. I rubbed against him, rocking my hips while he growled his approval.

"Look at you, my greedy little goddess. You're such a good girl, taking every fucking inch of my cock into your tight pussy. Look how I stretch you, owning you until you know nothing but the feel of my cock fucking that pretty, pink cunt." Moving back, he withdrew until only the tip remained cradled inside me.

"Ryder, please," I begged, needing him in my body again.

"Look at it," he demanded, and I did, taking in his thick, beautiful, monstrous cock. It was longer than it should be, and my body begged to be full of his velvety-soft flesh. He pushed into my body, withdrawing again before repeating the movements as I watched him slowly fucking me.

It was the hottest thing I'd ever seen, watching him disappear into my warmth and feeling him jerk as my pussy clenched around his cock, fighting to keep him there. "Such a good girl," he chuckled, starting to move in a hurried pace.

I was helpless to do anything more than watch as he fucked me for hours, coming repeatedly while my body vibrated with endless orgasms until they became one big eruption that refused to lessen.

Hours after we'd finished, I laid beside him, staring at his sleeping form. His breathing had changed with the merge, now coming in labored, shallow breaths. It sounded wrong somehow, but Ryder was sleeping peacefully. Sitting up, I placed my hands on his cheeks and leaned over to kiss his soft lips before I slid from the bed and moved into the shadows.

Chapter
EIGHTEEN

I sat on the chesterfield sofa with Zander on my lap. Cade played on the floor next to the bed, where Ryder had yet to awaken from last night's escapades. The room filled me with intense emotions: fear that the potion had harmed Ryder, sad that my children were going to the City of the Gods, and apprehension surrounding the woman that would take them there.

My gaze strayed from the darkened corners on the terrace to the man sleeping through the sound of our children playing. Setting Zander down, I stood, moving to the vanity to retrieve the empty vial. Removing the cap, I sniffed the contents and frowned, settling my worried gaze back to my sleeping beast.

"You gave him all of it?" Eris asked, emerging

from the shadows without warning or even a ripple of power to alert me to her presence.

"You said to give him all of it," I reminded, studying her features. "He isn't waking up." I let the urgency in my emotions show as I paced on the balcony, trembling with fear.

Moving back into the bedroom, I picked up Cade, brushing my fingers through his hair before I sat on the bed, staring down at where Ryder's long black eyelashes dusted over his cheeks.

"It may take a while for him to change." Eris frowned while she stared at Ryder's sleeping form, a flush of guilt coloring her cheeks. "We didn't plan for you merging Ryder and his beast before he would go through yet another transformation. Where is your daughter?" Eris asked, changing the subject abruptly, looking anywhere but the bed.

"Ryder hid her from me," I admitted sadly, my gaze slipping to the floor as tears burned my eyes. "Something is going on in the stronghold, and as a result, he's changed into someone I hardly recognize.

He's been fucking other women, and then more and more lately, he started feeding with them instead of me. I would leave him, but he removed the children from the Blood Kingdom, threatening to keep them from me if I leave. Kahleena is supposed to be the cure to saving this world, and my guess is she will also be the child he keeps hidden from me until this war is over. I could only get his men to bring the boys this morning for a visit. If you take them, at least I know they will be safe from this war and those who would seek to use them against us."

"That will be a problem," Eris muttered, pushing long, black fingernails through her silky hair. "I told you I would take all three of them, not just two."

"Unless you have a way to figure out where she is, I can't change it. Don't you think I want you to take all of my children away from the war marching toward my gates? I don't even know where to look for her."

"He slept with another woman, and you accepted it?" she asked, lifting her brow in question. Eris watched the pain pinch my features as she pushed her hair away from her face. "I'll take that as a yes. Why not just end his life?"

"He's my husband." Sucking my bottom lip between my teeth, I absently moved Cade's hair out of his eyes. "He is the father of my children, and one day they will wish to know him. I'm not giving up on him yet. Last night he was vigorously pleasurable, and that's something a lot of men can't do. I also love him, which didn't happen overnight. We've been through hell together, Eris. I didn't come this far to lose him to some feeder who offered him a moment of pleasure during his lapse of judgment. He'll return to me."

"Hmm, if you become a good plaything for him?" she asked, snorting. "Girl, you deserve better. We all deserve better than what the gods give us for our future. Men are pigs, and they know one thing about women, and that's where they fit within us—and some can barely figure that much out. I need you to think. Where would Ryder hide the third child?"

"Her *name* is Kahleena," I grumbled, watching

Eris closely. "I told you, I don't know. I spent the entire morning sifting to every location I thought he would hide her, and yet I can't even sense her anymore. It's like she's no longer in this world."

"He's fae. There's no place else he would hide her than in Faery. I won't be able to come back for her later, so put that pretty mind of yours to work."

"Maybe if you wake him up, and we hold him in a trance, we could ask him?" I offered, watching as Zander moved closer to Eris, touching her. She frowned at him, shrinking away from his tiny hand.

"I can't interrupt the change, or he may never wake up," Eris mused, staring at Zander while he continued to look at her. "Shoo," she said, flicking her hand at him like he was a dog.

"He's a child, not a pet," I snapped.

Her eyes widened at the tone of my voice, and she bent down, staring at Zander. "He's got wise eyes. Say your goodbyes. I guess two will have to be good enough."

I brushed my hand through Cade's hair, kissing the side of his cheek. He grabbed my boob as his other hand touched my face, kissing my mouth, then licking his tongue over my lips.

"Is that normal?" Eris asked, scrunching up her face in disgust. She stared down at Zander, who held his arms up, motioning for her to pick him up until she finally gave in.

"No, but he's a boy. Boys have little brains," I shrugged, setting Cade down as Zander rested his head against Eris's shoulder, staring at me.

"If he starts drooling, I'm dropping him."

"He's a child," I pointed out, watching as she stepped closer to Cade, preparing to take them. "Wait," I whispered, turning worried eyes on Ryder. "What if he doesn't wake up?"

"He will wake up, eventually," she said with sadness in her eyes. "I will be away with your children, though, and can't be called back for some time."

"How will I know my children are safe?" I asked

cautiously.

"You won't. You must trust in their destinies," Eris swallowed, bending over to reach for Cade. Then she gasped before hitting the floor hard.

I stared down at Eris as her mouth opened and closed through the pain that enveloped her. I knew that pain. I knew it all too well. The debilitating agony that the god bolt shot through your system, rendering you both powerless and paralyzed. Zander grew until he became Zahruk, stark-ass naked, leaning over Eris's unmoving form. My gaze settled on the curve of his ass, appreciating the sleek muscles until a deep growl pulled my attention to the bed, where black eyes flecked with gold stared up at me.

I grimaced at being busted checking out his brother's ass, but it was a nice ass. Zahruk snorted, glamouring on clothes. Fang, who had pretended to be Cade, cracked his neck, glaring at me while I ignored him. I waved my hand, dressing him in the same outfit he'd been wearing before I had snatched him out of the forest and forced him to help us.

"You traitorous bitch!" Eris hissed.

"Me? I'm not the one who slithered her way into this stronghold with a potion that promised to make Ryder a god, ensuring enough strength to survive the war. You are the cause of the chaos and endless drama unfolding within these walls, Eris, Goddess of Discord and Chaos. Did you think I would be so stupid to agree to your proposition? Tell me, were you supposed to murder my children, or deliver them to our enemies to be murdered?" I asked, stepping on her throat and leaning over, pushing the bolt further into her side. "They are babies! They are innocent of any wrongdoings and have not even begun to live yet."

"It wasn't personal," she muttered hoarsely, wincing as I twisted the bolt, hurting her further. "I didn't have a choice!"

"No? There is always a choice in which side you join."

"You can't hold me," she whispered. "I am a fucking goddess, an ancient one. You are a fucking newborn!"

"I'm aware, which is why I brought someone even the gods will bow before. Tell me, have you met Lucian Blackstone yet?"

"Lucian, who?" she snarled, slowly turning her angry gaze to the door that had just opened. "No! No, no, he can't be here!"

I smiled coldly as she shrieked, enjoying it way too much.

"Hello, Eris, does your mother know you're intervening in the games of gods?" Lucian asked, snorting when she shook her head vigorously. "Didn't think so, because I'm sure Nyx would kick your ass all the way to the Underworld if she did."

"I am under an oath owed," Eris hissed. "I had no fucking choice! It wasn't personal."

"It wasn't personal?" I asked coldly, producing the clear blue vial she'd given me. Removing the cork, I leaned over her, pushing it against her mouth as she struggled, clamping her lips closed. "Drink," I ordered.

"Mmm!" she screamed, shaking her head.

"What does it do?" I asked, pulling it away.

"It would kill him!"

"You wanted me to kill my mate? Why?"

"I can't say!" she hissed.

"Tell me, or you can fucking choke on your own poison, bitch," I warned, watching as she struggled against the vial of poison I was about to shove down her throat.

"If she is bound by an oath owed, she cannot tell you," Lucian said, studying Eris as she pleaded with him silently.

"She can't say who did this?"

"No, Goddess, I'm afraid not. She can tell you everything but who they are."

"I know who it is," I admitted. "Bilé is marching toward us with the mages. I've seen him. What I want to know is, what were his plans for us?"

"I don't know," Eris growled. "Bilé sent me here to plant the Apple of Discord, and to create confusion while you devised battle strategies for war. I also placed a spell on the map in the throne room. A spell Bilé provided, planted as instructed. The map shows him every move you had planned for your troops, giving Bilé the advantage. He assembled his armies at those battle locations before the horde would reach them, taking you all by surprise. I released chaos into the stronghold, knowing that endless arguments would arise, and so they did. I have to admit, though, I'm impressed with the female solidarity you have here, and a little jealous that I had to watch it from the shadows. How did you figure out what was happening?"

"I'm not fucking stupid. No god or goddess does anything out of the good of their hearts. I may be new to this gig, but I damn sure know they don't have hearts. You found me and offered to help me for nothing in return. I knew from the moment you uttered that first hello that you were not my friend. Did you think you could walk into my house, kick off your shoes, and cause a ruckus without my notice? Not in my house, and not with my family."

"You want to save a man who is fucking other bitches!"

"Actually, Ryder didn't fuck anyone. Zahruk fucked *you*, but Ryder removed your head, or Carina's head, while you were within her body. He figured it out by the way the runes responded to poor Carina and realized there was a goddess within the brainless bitch. Do you think you are the only goddess with the power to see what happens around this place? You created confusion in the men, but they felt you every time your shadow magic oozed from your pores. Sloppy, really," I shrugged, pushing the bolt in deeper. "You thought you could fuck my king? Bitch, please. That dick is mine. I am his mate, and your little game, while amusing, is finished."

"It wasn't personal, and I didn't want to do it. Bilé saved someone for me. My lover died in a battle and wandered endlessly, unable to gain eternal slumber. As the God of Death, he placed Collin into the

Underworld. I owed him an oath, and once called into play, you cannot say no. So, when he summoned me, I came. He is your mother's husband, and you seem to be…"

"His target," I finished for her. "I'm fully aware of his issues. So, thirsty?" I pushed the potion into her mouth and held it closed with my hands. "Bottoms up, bitch," I growled. Eris convulsed, and I turned, staring at Lucian, who chuckled, shaking his head as he watched her with amused eyes.

"You realize that you just gave the Goddess of Chaos and Discord a potion that will turn her mortal, right?" Lucian asked, lifting his sinful midnight-blue eyes to mine.

"She came into my house, not the other way around. Wait, a mortal?"

"She intended to make Ryder mortal, as in human. Nyx will be furious, but even she cannot argue that Eris struck first blood in a world she doesn't belong in. I suggest you let me take Eris. I will protect her until Nyx can collect her. Interesting and fun," he offered, bending down to pull out a large piece of glass embedded into Eris's tongue. "That's curious."

"Okay, we need to work on your communication skills. I'm starting to hate that word when it slips off your tongue, even if it is a nice tongue."

"Which is bothering you more, when I find something interesting or not being able to figure out what I am, Synthia?"

"Both are messing with my brain," I muttered, rubbing my temples. "Pretty certain both scream trouble in one way or another."

Lucian chuckled and turned, holding out his hand as Spyder stepped from the shadows, eyeing Eris with a sinful smirk. "My favorite little bad girl," he murmured, bending over to wrap a silky black curl around his finger. "Thought I smelt chaos and sex around here." Sniffing her hair, his smile dropped. "Why does she smell human—and like you?" He turned to look at Zahruk as shadows swirled around him.

"So…She tried to fuck Ryder and ended up with Zahruk shape-shifting into Ryder's image, which made her land on his dick instead," Lucian announced. "Not his fault that she wanted a cock she couldn't have."

"She fucked with the wrong dick. Now, how the fuck did Eris become mortal, assholes?"

"She tried to trick me into killing my husband. She also planned to take my children to the murderous bastard marching an army in this direction. He would have slaughtered my children if she'd succeeded. Your cock can find another pussy to pet, Spyder. Or hell, take her with my blessing."

"Oh, hell no, her mother is fucking nuts. I ain't touching that kitty. Fuck that noise," Spyder chuckled, stepping back.

"Grab her," Lucian said.

"I said no," Spyder frowned, crossing his heavily tattooed arms over his chest. "No means no! Ain't you read those posters?"

"Pick her up, or I'll drag her through the streets

back to the club and tell Nyx you did it."

"Dick move," Spyder grumbled. "This will not end well."

"Thank you for helping us," I said to Lucian. Bowing low, I watched his smile darkening.

"I didn't do it for you. I did it because Ryder promised me an oath. Remember, Synthia, gods don't have hearts, and what I am, well, we don't have fucking souls either."

"Okay, well, I got nothing," I admitted, turning to look at Fang.

"Do not thank me. You kidnapped me and threatened to remove my dick, which I intend to keep."

"Desperate times call for desperate measures. Next time, no slipping me the tongue or tit grabbing, pervert," I mumbled, shrugging before I winced at the glare he was giving me. "Besides, those orcs were about to eat you, so technically, I saved your life."

"They were babies, and under two feet tall," Fang

snapped irritably.

"You have no idea how fast little ones grow up these days." He stared at me as if he could make me vanish with his rage. "Anywho," I stated before turning sad eyes to Ryder, hating the way my heart clenched with the words that came from my mouth. "Destiny is waiting for us."

Ryder swallowed, watching me through pain-filled eyes. "It's too soon."

"We cannot wait any longer. If gods and goddesses have been called in to assist Bilé, we must send the children to where they cannot reach them. Thanatos forewarned what happens if we don't. It's not an easy choice, but it is the right one. Lose their childhood or their lives. I choose to protect their lives, my beast."

Chapter
NINETEEN

Tears filled my vision while I smiled as Ryder fell to the ground, pretending the little wooden sword had pierced his heart instead of being tucked in his armpit. The boys laughed and cheered while Kahleena clapped as she sat on my lap, watching them.

"People will die, mommy," she whispered, slipping her tiny hand into mine.

I turned, studying her golden eyes ringed with worry. "In war, death is inevitable, sweet girl."

"Uncle Liam said that you're a warrior, but even warriors die in war," she sobbed, curling against me to hide her tears.

I wrapped my arms around her, holding her tiny

form against my body as tears rushed from my eyes. Ryder swallowed hard, staring at her as if he sought words to comfort her, and failed.

"War is ugly, daughter of mine," I whispered into her pretty platinum curls. "War happens when two separate sides cannot see eye-to-eye, and one or both parties refuse to communicate peacefully to solve their grievances. It tears people apart, forcing them to make hard decisions to protect their families from the ugliness. I won't tell you everything will be fine because I know that it won't. It will rip apart the world we love no matter who wins. That's what war does, Kahleena. It rips a path through the world until it reaches its destination. Both sides will carry heavy losses because neither will allow the other to win. That is why you are going to the City of the Gods with Destiny."

"But I want to stay here with you," she whispered.

"Dry your tears, daughter. Listen to me. I love you so much. I love you so much that it aches to even think about sending you away. I need you and your brothers to be out of the reach of our enemies. Your father is the King of the Horde, and I am the Queen. I am also the target of our enemy. I need to go into this battle without fear of you or your brothers being caught or killed. You three and your father are my world. It would destroy me to lose any of you. Do you understand? I cannot worry about you and fight, and I must fight to protect this world from the monsters who seek to destroy it. Your grandmother gave her life for mine, and I won't allow them to destroy her legacy. I love you, but this is not something I will change. My job is to protect you first and foremost, no matter how much it hurts me to do so."

"But what if you die?" she asked, her fat tears rolling down her chubby cheeks while gentle sobs shook her tiny frame.

"Then you will be safe when it happens," I murmured, kissing her cheek before wiping away her tears once more. "I will live on through you. If your father falls, he will live on through you too. You will have your brothers, and will never be alone, sweet girl."

"Daddy can't die," Zander said with a frown creasing his brow. "He is the Horde King, and immortal."

"He is," I uttered, staring into my son's steady gaze. "He is the strongest warrior the horde has, and next to him are your uncles and auntie, and none of us will allow the enemy to take him from us. Nor would he allow them to get to me."

"I need to take them soon," Destiny announced from where she sat, regarding us as we said our goodbyes. "There's also an entire hallway of people outside, waiting to come in and say goodbye."

"We need a few more moments alone before you let the masses in," Ryder replied, standing to move closer. He picked up Cade and Zander and sat with them beside us while I leaned against him, seeing his large hand dwarfing our daughter's tiny head as he placed it on her.

Out of the three, Kahleena was the tiniest. The boys had shielded her from being revealed in my womb until Ristan had removed them and discovered her. They'd also taken most of the nutrients, evident because she was much smaller than they were.

"Your mother and I wouldn't send you away if we didn't need to." Ryder rubbed his hand over his face, trying to choose the right words. He may have been the most terrifying thing inside this realm, but with our children, he was gentle and always struggled to find the right words to convey his feelings. "I don't like this either, but knowing you are safe from our enemies, it allows me to have my head here, where it needs to be. I promise to protect your momma and keep her safe. My father was a murderous prick, and he left me a legacy filled with foes and treachery within the horde. I need to be here to watch our people and the enemy. Your mother is right. If you stay, we will worry about you the entire time. We have to be fully aware of our surroundings and who we fight instead of worrying about your safety."

"Because they would use us against you," Cade said, frowning, regarding us carefully. "We make you weak."

"You're our world," I said, touching his cheek before kissing the top of his head. "You're not a weakness; you're our greatest accomplishment. Do you hear me? You strengthen us, but our enemies would seek to take you from us. They know we love you more than anything, and if something happened to you, we'd do whatever it took to get you back. You make us fight harder to protect your futures. We're not fighting this war just to fight; we are fighting it to save the world your grandmother created for us. Faery belongs to us all, and to protect it, we will go to war. Never think you make us weak because that is not possible."

"Uncle Liam says loving us makes your enemies more willing to use us to force you to surrender," Zander said, folding tiny arms across his chest to study our faces.

"Uncle Liam says a lot of things, doesn't he?" I muttered.

"He does, he's smart," Zander agreed.

"Is he now?" I smiled, noting the pride that shone

in Zander's eyes as he spoke about his uncle.

"Unless he has that silly girl in the room. Then they just scream and jump on the bed," Cade mumbled, shrugging. "He says we can't jump on the bed, and he does it all the time. She also screams, '*oh my goddess, harder, yes, yes, I'm coming…*'" My hand covered his mouth as Ryder's shoulders shook with laughter.

"Uncle Liam may not be as smart as he thinks he is," Ryder chuckled.

"I think Uncle Liam needs to be spanked," I teased.

"She likes that too," Zander said, making a face of confusion while he put his hands up as if he held no answers for why a female would like a spanking. "Maybe she was bad a lot as a child and still needs a spanking." He stared at us while we fought the need to laugh. "What? It's possible she was a very bad kid. Liam is fair, so she must need it badly."

Ryder burst out laughing while my face turned bright red. I elbowed him in the ribs, enjoying the grunt that exploded from his lips, barely containing the urge to join him.

"I'm sure Uncle Liam could use a spanking of his own. Now, are you little beasties ready to say goodbye to everyone else?" I swallowed down the lump in my throat, not wanting the moment to end. At their nods, I wiped away the silent tears from Kahleena's golden gaze and whispered against her ear. "Be brave, my little warrior, let no one see your tears. And you two," I said, turning to Cade and Zander, "you hold her for me when she is sad. You hold each other and remind one another we are waiting for your return. We love you so much, and I want you to remember that always. Hold on to it when you are sad, and when you're happy, think of us. The second the war is over, we will bring you home."

Destiny opened the door, and Ristan stumbled into the room, scratching his head, guilty at having been caught listening in on our conversation. Olivia waddled past him, taking a seat in the chair I'd brought in for her, added cushions included.

"Auntie Liv, you need to have the dangle,"

Kahleena laughed, moving away from Ristan, who tried to hold her to place her hand against Olivia's protruding belly. "Be brave, littlest cousin, I'll be back soon." Sad eyes peered up at Olivia as she hugged her around her swollen belly tightly. "I love you, Auntie Liv. Always, and always, remember that and be brave."

Ryder held my hand as tears struggled to release from the tight hold I had on them. Ristan slid to his knees, smiling at Kahleena as she rushed into his arms, smothering a sob with her hand.

"Oh, my sweet little Kahleena," Ristan chided gently, love filling his tone. "It will be okay. You'll be back before you know it," he reassured Kahleena, helping her to hide the tears that trailed down her cheeks as he wiped them away. "We just need to handle some business, and you'll be able to come home soon enough, right?"

"I'm brave," she sniffled, wiping her nose with the back of her arm.

"You are. You're the daughter of the Queen and

King of the Horde, both fierce warriors. You're going to be just fine, my little ones."

"Stop hogging the children, Ristan," Ciara said, holding Phoenix in her arms while Blane struggled with Fury, who itched to get down. Blane set him on the floor, and we watched as Fury crawled to Zander, moving to stand while holding on to him.

"Hi, Fury," Zander said, pushing his cheek against Fury's mouth, causing it to open, and he began sucking on Zander's cheek. The entire room laughed while Zander made a displeased face but held still, allowing Fury to give him big, sloppy kisses. "Thanks," he stated, wiping it off when Fury moved to Kahleena and Ristan and cooed, making sounds while he tugged at Kahleena's hair.

Kahleena didn't complain when Fury pulled hard, wrapping her arm around him before she kissed his forehead. "Little Fury, I love you too," she sniffed, holding him closer while Cade surveyed the room silently from Ryder's lap. The moment Fury started toward Cade, Kahleena stood up and held her hands out for Phoenix. Ciara set her tiny mewling infant daughter in Kahleena's arms, and she gazed down at the babe. "She's so tiny."

"You used to be that tiny," I whispered, fighting the tears that flooded my vision as the reality of what was happening hit me. I'd lost their childhood because of the danger they'd been in, and now I would lose everything else. "You were this tiny little thing with huge golden eyes that never cried or complained. You just stared up at everyone with this look as if you'd known them forever."

"But I was just born, like Nix." Kahleena leaned over, kissing Phoenix's forehead before allowing Ciara to take her back. Kahleena's tiny arms wrapped around Ciara's legs, and she smiled at me. Hugging her aunt tightly, she peered up and watched as Ciara righted the babe in her arms carefully.

"Nix, huh?" I asked.

"It's what we will call her when she is older. She won't enjoy being called a firebird, and will wish to be called Nix instead," Kahleena shrugged as if it was no big deal as she released Ciara's leg. "Ciara will have a lot of babies by then, and Nix will be one of many."

"How do you know that?" I asked, smiling.

"Because I've seen the future," Kahleena said innocently with a faraway look, as if she was pulling up visions she'd seen. "It's both happy and sad."

The entire room went silent as everyone looked at Kahleena like she'd just told them the sun had exploded, but by tomorrow morning, a new one would shine in its place. A shiver rippled up my spine, my throat tightened, and my stomach clenched with unease.

"You've seen the future?" I asked, lips trembling. Kahleena looked around the room, smiling as tears filled her pretty amber eyes.

"You will all be sad, but you'll be okay. Those who die shall remain dead. You cannot change it, which will make you very sad, mommy. Those stars were only meant to shine for a while, but they are burning out. New stars will come to take their place. Grandma promised me."

"Which grandma?" I asked thickly.

"Your mommy, she's everywhere, in all of us. More so in me, because I make her smile," she shrugged. "She says I am like you were, and full of curious questions." Kahleena's head cocked to the side, and her smile glowed before she straightened with a soft shrug of her shoulders. "It's time to go; the gates will close soon."

"Kahleena," I whispered, pulling her into my arms. "What else did Danu say?"

"She said nothing is certain. Chosen destinies do not shape our lives. The path we choose to follow determines our destinies, shaped by the choices we make in the moment. Choose the right choices, mommy. Don't make angry ones, because those are ones you will get wrong. She said to tell you that her love wasn't wrong. Her love was beautiful. It was beautiful enough to create an entire world, to mirror how her soul felt. Whatever that means—and oh, you have to forgive him. You have to forgive daddy for what he will do because without forgiveness, you won't win." She shrugged in my hold. "Oh yeah, and she said good job for fixing daddy."

I kissed her head and stared at Ristan, who observed us. He knew what it meant to see the future and what damage it could do. It could mess up things, but mostly, it could change her. It could turn Kahleena into a seer of future events. It could also make her a target because seers were rare, and the only other one in the history of Faery was Ristan.

As the others flooded the room, I silently prayed Danu hadn't projected her ability onto her blood relatives and that Kahleena didn't have the sight, because if Danu had, even ending the war wouldn't stop the danger to Kahleena.

TWENTY

I sat in the war room beside Ryder in silence. The mood of the entire day was somber, and nothing worked to remove that feeling as we gazed at the map, which was still spelled, alerting Bilé to every marker placed upon its surface. Frowning, I glared down, trying to figure out if we were marching into a trap, or worse, to face off with a god hell-bent on destroying us all. I hated the unknown. Having no control over what was going to happen caused an ache that sat like a rock in my chest.

"Take Ryder off of the map," I blurted, turning my wide eyes to him. "Bilé doesn't know he's still alive. No one outside this stronghold knows Ryder didn't drink that potion."

Golden eyes stared into mine as a smile played over his lips. "Zahruk, move my piece from the map and place yours into my position as the leader of this assault. Let the mages think they succeeded. Afterward, move the main forces of our troops into the valley there." Ryder pointed at a location on the map.

We remained silent as Ryder furrowed his brow in thought before speaking again. "The cliffs near the Valley of the Fir Dolcha are wide enough that the mages would have to come within them to reach us. If we let them think we were here," he pointed to the middle of the rough terrain, "when we take the surrounding advantage, it will trap them in the valley, and they'd have no place to escape us or run from the troops while we're on the high ground. We could take out a large portion of their army before they ever realized we weren't in the valley waiting to be slaughtered."

"We can only use this once," I pointed out softly. "We need to make it count."

"Move a large force here, into the stronghold," Ryder said, frowning as he pointed at a position on the map. "I won't have the mages thinking it is unprotected while we make our move. Place the other half of the pieces in the Valley of the Fir Dolcha. It will show our army is divided, but the mages will likely march their troops toward the biggest target. Place Synthia's figurine in the valley as well and show them the Queen of the Horde is exposed with her troops and you as her guard.

"The Elite Guard needs to be separated as well," he mused, watching as Zahruk placed the wooden pieces around the map. "If this works, we may have the end of this war in our hands before it even starts. I will call in the oaths I've been collecting over the years, and Lucian, his men, and Callaghan will join me as we march into the valley. I want this fortress locked down as if it was under siege. Fyra and the female dragons can remain here, within the fortress to help defend it. I need the rest of you with me. Take tonight to say goodbye to your families, because tomorrow morning, we march to war."

Ryder turned, regarding me as if something else was bothering him, but whatever it was, he kept to himself. He extended his hand, and I accepted it.

"I want to go with you. I hate being separated from you." I frowned, forcing my brows together between my eyes while worrying my lip, staring at him with a fire burning in my gaze.

"Not this time, Pet. The women will remain here, and if this goes wrong and the mages don't fall for the ruse, I need you to protect them. The men can't focus without knowing their families are safe. Our children are safe, and we need to make sure their families remain alive and safe from this fight too. I need you here because if I am wrong, there's no telling what will happen. Eris didn't deliver our children to Bilé, which may have alerted him to the fact she failed."

"Ryder…"

"We've been over this already, Synthia. You know the law. One of us must remain within these walls," he growled, lifting my chin to stare into my worried eyes. "I can't be in both places. Don't argue it, please.

Go tell the chef to cook a feast for the men who will leave tomorrow for battle. It might be awhile before we can return if the mages fall for our trap."

"Fine," I muttered, unhappy about being left behind yet again.

I understood the need for my presence at the castle, hence why I wasn't arguing the matter with Ryder. I was still being placed on the sidelines, and we both knew it, but I was the only one of us wanting to dispute the law. It would be suicide to attack the horde on our own turf, which the mages knew.

The other courts were supposed to be gathering here within the week. Adam had come to say goodbye to the kids, reassuring me he was coming back the moment the Dark Kingdom was ready to join him. Liam told me Madisyn and Lasair were gathering the Blood Warriors to march to our fortress already, leaving Liam to guard the palace since the horde wasn't the only kingdom that had the stronghold decree in effect.

This entire world needed to update their laws

since most had ideals on women being weak, and repeatedly we showed them otherwise.

Inside the kitchen, I instructed the staff on what to serve during the feast and which wine and spirits would complement the meal. I carefully made my way to the bedroom I shared with Ryder while bracing myself against the wall, struggling against the burning pain that started back up. It was a lot worse lately.

Barely inside the door, I dropped and gasped as the pain ripped through me. My vision swam with stars as everything ached and burned until I trembled. I felt something wet on my face and wiped at it, staring at the blood that was warm against my fingertips. I groaned as violet flashes of color ignited behind my eyelids while nausea pushed at the back of my mouth.

I'd be willing to bet that Bilé and his merry band of mages had just slaughtered numerous fae while we'd been plotting against him. Pain from the fae dying was becoming more frequent, and it worried me endlessly.

It took everything within me to continue standing

upright, planning against Bilé with the men. Whatever the murderous prick had been up to, it hadn't been horrible until I'd left Ryder's side. It didn't take a rocket scientist to figure out he was attacking defenseless villages on his way here; proof of that was the refugees showing up every morning.

We'd sent men to the outlying areas around the horde stronghold, begging our people to come inside the safety of the walls that protected us, but they refused.

"Synthia?" Darynda entered the room, finding me on the floor. "Help!" she screamed, rushing to me.

"I'm okay," I mumbled, carefully peeling myself off the tile. Standing to my full height, I smiled to reassure her I was indeed fine, only to bend over as more piercing, debilitating pain sliced through me. Darynda shot forward, catching me before I could drop to my knees.

"Darynda?" Zahruk's voice echoed through the hall before he entered the doorway, pausing as he took in the situation. He sifted to where she struggled to keep me upright, picking me up, rushing to the bed, and setting me down carefully. "What the fuck happened?"

The room erupted in power as Ryder entered, staring down at me from beside the bed. "Who did this to you?" Ryder demanded, turning a lethal glare on Darynda as power continually filled the bedroom until it began to suffocate everyone.

"I found her like that on the floor, My King," she cried through trembling lips, wringing her hands in the skirt of her dress nervously.

"I'm okay, guys." I hoped if I said it enough, they'd hear me. I struggled to sit up, but large, strong hands pushed me down against the mattress until I was flat on my back. Glaring up at Ryder, I watched as worry flooded the amber eyes peering down at me with fear.

"What happened?" Ryder asked, using his thumbs to push the blood away from my eyes. His hand cupped my cheek, and he studied me carefully as if he could see what was wrong if he stared hard enough.

"Bilé or the mages just killed a large number of fae." I allowed Ryder to lift my head as I sipped from the glass he held against my lips. I drank slowly as fire burned and banked in his obsidian depths, igniting amber stars.

"I know their deaths have been causing you pain, but how long has it been happening to this extreme?" His deep, rumbling growl filled the room as his thumb wiped the water from my lips before he rested me against the insane amount of pillows he had just glamoured onto the bed.

I gazed up at him with a sad smile playing across my mouth. "It started happening more often a few months ago, but this one started earlier today and became worse than any other time. I'm guessing we just lost an entire village of people in a matter of moments. My body weakened quickly with the number of lives that were taken."

"You stood beside me all fucking day while in pain, and you said nothing to me?" Ryder asked, frowning as hurt entered his gaze. "You should have said something, woman."

"There's nothing you could do to keep it from happening. What good does it do to tell you when I am in pain if you can't change it? Telling you will only make you worry, and I can handle the pain on my own, Ryder. You have to focus on the armies and where they're needed, not worrying about me."

"Get Eliran up here, now," Ryder ordered in a harsh tone, sitting beside me as concern etched the lines of his beautiful, masculine features.

"Do not get Eliran, Zahruk," I growled, watching as he stared between us before stepping to turn on his heel to do as Ryder had demanded. "If you pull Eliran away from people who need him, I will stab you, asshole!" Zahruk's sapphire eyes held mine while he warred with indecision on whose orders to follow.

"You're bleeding from your nose and crying blood, Syn. It's not open for fucking debate. You're my wife, and it is my job to keep you safe and in good health, which I cannot do if you won't tell me when you are in fucking pain!" Ryder's growl vibrated through me as he opened his mouth to shout at his brother for not having done as he had instructed. Worse than that, there was an accusation in his depths that sat ill with me.

"You're not listening to me," I snapped irritably, sitting up to accept the cloth that Darynda handed me. "There is no medicine Eliran can give me to stop this pain from happening. I'm not sick, Ryder. I am the Goddess of the Fae, and they are being slaughtered by the thousands daily. I feel every single one of their lives ending. It creates an aching pain within me, one that hurts for a short time, and then vanishes.

"When Faery hurts, I feel it too. I am a part of this place and its people, as was my mother. A doctor cannot fix what is wrong with me because there's nothing to fix. The only way to save me from this pain is for us to end this war. It won't kill me; weaken me, yes. Danu made sure that we could leave Faery if the need arose, and take the people someplace else. Bilé is aware that I am connected to Faery, and he's trying to weaken me. We have to take him out of play, and we have to do it soon."

"I can't leave you like this." He rubbed his hand down his face while studying me.

"I can lead the army," Zahruk announced, frowning while taking in Ryder's shoulder, and the way he cradled my face as if I was a child.

"Stop that this minute." I pushed Ryder back enough to look him in the eyes. "You have that monstrous bastard at a disadvantage, one we need to capitalize on. There is nothing you can do here. You being here won't end this war, and that's a fact. You have to take this chance to hit the mages where it will hurt them most. The pain doesn't last long, just long enough to be a nuisance. Now, everyone else out so Ryder can help me get dressed for dinner. It might be our last meal together for a while, and I'd like to enjoy it with you, so out."

Two hours later, I sat beside Ryder as his brothers told their mates of random battles they had fought, excluding details that were hard for them to speak about. The entire table was filled with family, *our* family. Savlian and Sevrin spoke at the same time, recanting battles where they'd changed places on patrol or did something else to piss Ryder off. Cailean snorted, shaking his head as he laughed over the story Ristan told Olivia.

Blane and Remy told Ryder of the places they'd hidden from the horde, describing the monsters they'd fought to survive. Blane held Fury on his lap, feeding him morsels of meat while Ciara fed Phoenix, laughing, then eyes wide in horror from the details of the creatures they'd faced off against to survive. These beings had gone from enemies to lovers, lovers to friends, and now a family sharing their tales of horror and survival, as if the experiences had been nothing more than trivial events.

"You're quiet tonight," Ryder whispered against my ear huskily. He pushed his hand against my leg before his fingers lifted the skirt I wore, dancing over the inside of my thigh seductively. It sent a ripple of heat racing to my belly, pooling in my sex with need.

"Look at what you have accomplished as the king," I stated, turning to look into his beautiful heated gaze.

He peered around the room as a frown tugged at his lips. "What did I do?"

"You made me love you, and now I have fallen in love with our family and your world. I'd planned to murder you the first day I met you. Now, I can't stand the thought of you not being a part of my life. A world without you in it would never make sense to me."

Ryder's stare held mine as heat smoldered within the inky depths.

"We've brought men who hated the horde into our family, and guild librarians that never imagined having enough pictures to fill their frames. Your sister married a dragon. The lesser courts are now working with us because you offered marriages to their daughters, who became queens. You did this, Ryder. You've done so much good in what little time you've been King of the Horde. Imagine what we can do with a lifetime of ruling?" I smiled, leaning over to kiss him. "You're a good king, an amazing husband, and the best father I could have ever envisioned for my children."

"Don't let our enemies hear you," he chuckled, kissing me back.

Chapter
TWENTY-ONE

Fires burned across the courtyard, stretching as far as the eye could see, but not from the camps. Torch fires were being used to ward off the morning fog as the horde mounted warhorses, preparing to ride into the valley for battle. The warriors showed no fear nor worried about facing off against the coldhearted prick trying to destroy us in his grief over losing my mother.

The war drums beat endlessly, signaling to the settlements around the stronghold that the invincible creatures of the horde were preparing to ride out to battle against our enemies. Steel clanged against metal as they fit horses with armor before the riders took their seats on the mounts. Ryder had instructed me to remain on the battlements, viewing the progress as they prepared to go off into the unknown.

Ryder and I said our goodbyes early this morning before he'd gone outside to help the men. My heart clenched in my throat while I studied his unbending spine and prowess while teaching the simple folk how to wield their weapons.

I'd married a man who had been born to lead, to teach those who were willing to adapt and learn his expertise, and I couldn't have loved him more if I'd tried. He was everything I needed and all that was good in the world. The idea of him marching off to battle without me left me numb and terrified, even though I knew he was strong enough to do this on his own.

"This is utter shit," Ciara snapped in frustration as she stared at Remy and Blane among the horde's elite troops stationed around Ryder's position.

"Amen to that." I peered down the line of women and warriors who stood with me on the battlement, each wishing we could follow our family into battle. "They'll return to us, all of them."

Lena scrutinized Lucian. Her gaze narrowed on his form as if she wasn't sure she wanted him to come back. I cleared my throat to gain her attention. Her blue gaze turned toward me, studying me as a frown tugged at her lips.

"Are you good?" I asked softly, hoping not to be overheard.

"I'm great," she replied softly, and yet her tone wasn't convincing. "Ever learn something so horrible and so wrong that you aren't sure if it is truth or another lie?"

"Yes," I laughed soundlessly. I felt Lena's unease as surely as my own. The hair on my nape stood up, and power slithered through the horde as more men mounted horses. "You and Lucian are good, though, right?"

"No, but we have a very strict no-speak policy about it right now, actually. We're in somewhat of a truce while you need us. Afterward, well, I'm uncertain where we stand anymore. I know that I crave Lucian, and I know I love him."

"So, you're not planning his death while he's here?" I smirked, my nose scrunching up as she shrugged her shoulders. I turned my gaze to search the sea of troops for Lucian, finding him studying Lena with a pensive look of longing. His dark brows rose as if he could hear us whispering about him over the sound of the war drums.

"I don't think anything can kill Lucian, but I sure as fuck wouldn't mind if they knocked some of the cocky-dick out of the prick." Lena shrugged again, and I took in the way Lucian's mouth twisted up into a sardonic smile.

"Okay then," I frowned.

Ciara studied Blane's posture as the dragons spread out away from Ryder, taking their position on the outside of the front formation of warriors. Others, like Remy, were already in dragon form.

Our gazes lifted, finding them flying high above the horde as the last of the men mounted their warhorses. All around us, the mountains moved with troops, forty thousand strong and counting as each caste sent their strongest fighters to the frontline.

The flags rose, signaling the king was out of the stronghold. I exhaled slowly as Fyra, in her dragon form, landed on the newly added perches that stuck out over the courtyard. They were long and sturdy enough for the dragons to land on without fear of falling. Another female dragon landed on our other side, turning her scale-covered head to release a bloodcurdling screech that echoed through the mountains. The men below peered up and studied the mythical beasts that, only a few months ago, we'd thought to have been extinct.

Ryder's dark head lifted, and he held my gaze, regarding me remorsefully as if, right now, he was regretting his choice in telling me to remain on the battlements. He was unable to show any affection in front of the horde that flanked him in every direction.

The Elite Guards were the last men to mount their horses. They were decked out in black cloaks and heavy armor that could blend into the terrain should the need arise. Ryder wore the same obsidian armor he'd worn while chasing me during the Wild Hunt celebration. He pretended to be the dark prince when, in fact, he was the very king the hunt was honoring. Thick leather straps studded with onyx jewels set in dulled silver crisscrossed his chest. They held a variety of wicked-looking blades that I'd witnessed him using a few times before as he had effortlessly taken down his prey.

Ryder's warhorse turned its head, eyeing me with blood-red eyes. I smiled, nodding to the wild horse before looking back at his rider. Hounds and men surrounded the warhorse, protecting the king even though he wore the protective armor as well.

Ryder shouted above the noise of his army, telling them they would soon begin their trek to the valley. I sifted without thought, standing in front of his warhorse, lifting my hands to pet the silky mane along his neck. Stalling their forward march, I peered up into golden eyes that studied me as the men moved the protective barrier around me too.

I opened my mouth to speak, needing to tell him

how much I loved him, but I couldn't. My gaze moved to the red cloaks of the dragon riders, to the iridescent cloaks of the light fae, sent to us by Abiageal, the holder of the Light Kingdom.

My head lifted slowly, and my eyes locked with Ryder's stare, displaying everything I wanted to say that simple words couldn't convey. He studied me carefully while remaining silent atop the huge battle-ready warhorse that stomped the ground and snorted as he spoke inside my head.

"You were supposed to stay put, woman. We don't say goodbyes, remember?"

"I love you; I love you so much, Ryder," I repeated it, closing my eyes before I spoke loudly. "Kill every last one of those motherfucking mages, My King. Bring me their skulls so we can drink our wine from them while toasting your victory. I need new drinking horns, and they'd be welcomed here to remind our enemies how the horde responds to threats." I swallowed, noting how his lips curved into a wicked smile that left me boneless.

"Do you hear your bloodthirsty queen, horde? She wants the skulls of our enemies so we may toast to our victory from them!" Ryder shouted, and the horde erupted in cheers around us.

He reached down, pulling me up onto the horse before his lips brushed against mine. It was the first and only show of affection he'd ever allowed the horde to witness, other than the day we'd been wed, surrounded by them in the meadows.

Ryder's hand captured my hair, twisting my head so he could claim my mouth in a hungry kiss. My power rushed through him and then shot out, seeking the surrounding men who scrutinized us until shouts of wonder and pride echoed at their king's choice of mate. He didn't stop kissing me until I was panting against his lips, lust rushing through us both, and the need to seek the privacy of our room intensified.

"You're my fucking unicorn, woman. My bloodthirsty queen, you own my heart. Do you understand me?" Ryder's hand cradled my cheek, his forehead resting against mine before he pulled away, and the horde continued to cheer for him.

"I do," I admitted, sifting back to the battlement. His head turned, and his eyes took me in, burning with pride. I held my hand up, signaling for the braziers to be lit, signifying that the queen and king were no longer within the castle, but an heir had remained. This was an important maneuver in keeping up the pretense that I had left the stronghold with Ryder.

I smiled, thinking back on the words he had said in front of the horde. I understood their meaning. Ryder had just told me he loved me the only way he could with the horde standing around us. He'd admitted to his feelings long ago, but this time, it meant more. Ryder had just shown his army that he loved their queen, and that was a huge step for us. My heart clenched, tightening with the love he filled me with.

Ryder was going off to war against our enemies, and he'd kissed me, something the horde would have generally seen as a weakness, yet they'd cheered him on. Whether it was because I wasn't just their queen, but also the Goddess of the Fae, I didn't care. I'd fed them all strength to fight this war, and I hadn't held back how I felt for their king.

We remained on the battlements long into the night. I struggled with the immense pain from the loss of more fae, but I refused to leave until the army reached the mountain passes and was out of sight. Even when we could no longer make out their forms, we still didn't move from our position. It wasn't until I leaned against the wall for support, and Darynda touched my shoulder, pushing a cloth into my hand, that I realized something was wrong.

"Oh, my gods, what the hell? You're bleeding, Synthia?" Ciara demanded, moving to help me as others followed her lead.

"It's not me," I muttered, hissing in pain as I lost my footing. I slowly slid to the stone flooring of the battlement, bending over as a scream ripped from my lungs, filling the night air.

"Help me get her inside," Ciara ordered.

"No. Something isn't right," I whispered as my

hands wrapped around my stomach against the clenching pain.

"People are sifting into the courtyard," Lena said in confusion. "Should we handle them before they become a problem?"

"Help me up!" I growled, sensing something was horribly wrong. I allowed both Darynda and Ciara to each grab an elbow, helping me back to my feet. I stared down at the bloodied people, and my stomach dropped to the ground where I'd just been sitting. I sifted, unsteady on my feet as I moved toward Adam, who turned toward me, covered in blood. "Adam?"

Adam lifted his head slowly, leveling forest-green eyes on me that swam with unshed tears. "The Dark Kingdom has fallen." He fell to his knees, placing his hands over his face before resting his forehead against the ground. "Keir fell, as did my mother and my brothers. The entire kingdom fell to our enemies."

"How?" I knelt beside him, rubbing my hand along his back, taking in the blood and cuts that covered his body. "How could they fall, Adam?"

Sitting up, Adam wiped tears from his eyes, anguish and anger playing across his features. "From within, because someone let them in to murder us as we feasted in celebration. We were to march here at first light, but the mage army got to us before the sun rose. This is what I saved, and what is left of the Shadow Warriors." Spreading his arms wide, he indicated the other people that had sifted with him into the courtyard.

I turned, noting the air was displaced, and Liam appeared, falling to his knees on the ground, dripping blood from multiple wounds. Pain ripped through me as I saw him lift his head to utter the words I feared.

"No!" The denial slid over my tongue, and I rushed to Liam, tears pricking my eyes as a vise clamped around my heart. It thundered in my ears, deafening me as I fought to control the heaviness of loss that tried to bring me to my knees.

"The Blood Kingdom is gone, Synthia. The queen and king, everyone, they're just gone. I found Arryn wounded, but everyone else was dead when I returned. I told the Blood Warriors to gather here, but I don't know how many got out." Liam looked around the courtyard, noticing all the injured people and making their way into the castle. Shaking his head, he scrubbed his hand over his face before looking at me. "It was a bloodbath. Severed and lifeless bodies were scattered on every level, on every floor of the palace. Someone inside the castle let our enemies in to murder us. When night fell, and the dinner meal was served, the mage army attacked our family as they sat down to feast in celebration of coming here to join the war."

I dropped to my knees beside Liam as grief shot through me. My arms wrapped around my middle as giant sobs rocked through me. Lasair was my father, his blood ran through my veins, and we'd failed them. My sisters and brothers and their army of children had been slaughtered while I'd watched my husband march off to war. I'd ignored the immense pain that had bludgeoned through me for hours. I'd assumed it was nameless fae when in reality, he'd hit us where we would feel it the hardest.

They'd taken out the high fae, leaving their mark, just as we'd planned to do the exact same thing to them. We'd assumed the mages wouldn't target the higher castes until they'd battled with the lesser ones, and yet they'd boldly gone for our throats.

Rising, I began walking to the castle with purpose. "Cailean, take men into the dungeons and check for our enemies. The babes are locked within the tower and are protected behind wards. Only the servants are within the stronghold. I want them all out of my home until we are certain they are not enemies. We allow no one inside until we are confident they are with us, not against us.

"Darynda, start a triage center for the wounded coming in, and get Eliran's nurses and medical staff up here immediately. Tell Eliran to expect iron poisoning and weapon wounds caused by blades with poisonous metal. I want everyone who can fight to pick up a sword and prepare to defend the horde stronghold against an assault. Move, because this fortress will not fall while the king is away. I will not allow it!"

I turned slowly, staring at Adam, who regarded me with pain etching his features. Liam got to his feet, stepping closer, shaking his head. "I should be in the Blood Kingdom." Agony burned in his azure-blue eyes as his scarred cheek ticked with anger. "I have to go back there now."

"Go back to what, Liam? Go back to a tomb?" I asked gently, moving away from him to stare down at Arryn, who screamed in pain. Others continued sifting into the courtyard, wounded or carrying the injured. My hand stroked his head, pushing away his thick blond hair, painted crimson with blood. My brow furrowed with worry for him, but more with what was coming. If they'd fallen, that meant they were either braver or stupider than we'd given them credit for.

"Synthia…" Liam's words died off as he shook his head as his hands rested on his hips.

"There's no reason to go back, Liam. You're the Blood King now, and you," I said, turning to Adam. "You're the Dark King, and you are both needed to raise your armies to wage war and avenge your fallen.

You are Danu's chosen heirs and the rightful kings of your kingdoms. Dying a heroic death to retrieve corpses won't bring the dead back." Tears slipped down my cheeks while I studied them both. "Once the horde stronghold is cleared, we will move the injured inside. I'm so sorry for your losses."

"I'm sorry for your loss, too, Synthia," Adam whispered, hugging me tightly. "I'm sick of losing people. It wasn't supposed to happen like this. We just found our families, and now they're gone forever."

"Where is the King of the Horde?" Liam asked.

"He just rode out to fight the mages."

"He's gone? He is needed here. They're bringing the war to us. Ryder shouldn't have left you here unguarded." Anger burned in Liam's eyes.

"Ryder is right where he is supposed to be. He took over forty thousand men to battle with him against our enemies. He left over twenty thousand troops here to defend this castle. I want to know how the mages took down our people. How the hell did they kill high fae so easily?"

"It wasn't just mages, Synthia. They had a god with them when they attacked us. One who bestowed death to everything he touched. He fought with more power than we could hope to defend. How the fuck do you fight against that?" Liam asked.

"You call in the Goddess of War and pray she's sane enough to help us win against our enemies." I turned to stare up at the dragons regarding the tragedy unfolding below the battlements with sorrow. If I wasn't certain Eris was in chains somewhere in Lucian's kinky as shit basement, I'd think she was here, creating havoc. "Destiny, I need you. The Mórrígan, or Erie, if you can hear me, I need you too."

I stared up at the stars, watching as the night swallowed them into velvety darkness while I fought to contain the need to scream and cry, to rage against the reality of what had just happened.

Bodies were being piled up against the outer walls, while our parents' corpses were brought in and placed on rough stones. The warriors I'd sent had covered their bodies with the colors of their kingdoms, placing their crowns on their chests, identifying each caste they represented. By the time they finished, the entire courtyard was covered in shrouded corpses.

I silently stood in front of my parents' bodies, tears trailing down my cheeks as the wind howled around us. My hand lifted, touching Lasair's lifeless body as Liam stood opposite of me, placing his hand over mine in reassurance and comfort. I wasn't sure which I needed more. Madisyn's tiny form lay beside him in death, and a soft sob escaped my lips past the hold I thought I had on my emotions.

"This isn't right," Liam whispered through tears, his words choked with sorrow.

"Nothing is right about this," Adam agreed as he stepped behind me, wrapping his arms around me, seeking comfort. Liam lifted his matching azure-blue gaze to lock with mine, and I frowned. "Syn is the only family I have, other than one brother who may not live to see the sun rise."

"She's also the Queen of the Horde, and they're

looking at her for strength. You're a king now, Adam. The people are looking to each of us for guidance, and leadership."

"Doesn't change who we are or who we were," Adam stated, releasing me as he moved to stand over Keir and Moira's bodies.

"This is just beginning," I whispered, standing between the newly appointed Blood King and Dark King, "and we're losing."

TWENTY-TWO

I stared at the bodies covering the courtyard, glimpsing Abiageal's tiny form among the sea of others. Cailean and Sevrin had gone into the palace of the Light Kingdom, only to discover it hadn't been spared from treachery.

The remains of the deceased had been placed in the courtyard on slabs of marble to honor them. We'd skipped over the fae rule of piling servants into a mass grave. Instead, we positioned them upon the stones as well. I called in druids from Faery to come and bless the dead for their journey into the next life.

Liam held my hand while Adam sat silently beside me. There was certain solidarity in loss that bonded people who lived through mass casualties, but that didn't lessen the grief we felt. I knew both the men who stood beside me were numb, riddled with the same guilt that washed over me.

The somber mood that had fallen over the stronghold was one of deafening terror, even though we prepared to defend it against our enemies. No one spoke or whispered as we stood there, taking in the atrocities that had befallen the high courts of the fae. It was unreal. It was something we'd assumed couldn't happen, and we'd been proven wrong in a big way.

I'd moved the women into the tower, and Destiny had spent hours helping me place wards to protect against the mages. As we worked, she told me how the children enjoyed the sights in the City of the Gods. She admitted they had already grown in the few days they'd been there. Time moved differently in the City of Gods. My children had been there for months, even though only a few days had passed in Faery. The news of their accelerated aging didn't help my emotions with everything unfolding here, but it did make me feel as if we'd done the right thing by sending our children away.

Thanatos watched me from the shadows as if he didn't know how to approach me, or maybe he wasn't finished taking souls from us. Three entire kingdoms had fallen in a matter of hours, which meant Ryder wasn't facing Bilé as he'd planned. It made me feel like shit for being relieved while those around us perished. No, Bilé was smarter than we'd assumed, and maybe we needed to be reminded of it.

I also was relieved that Thanatos was here and not following Ryder, offering me some reassurance that perhaps he'd come out of the fighting unscathed.

Darynda found me as I made my way through the stronghold, stopping to peer around me before she spoke softly.

"The new chef is shit, and I'm sure he hasn't ever peeled a potato before today." Her emerald green eyes went wide as a soldier stopped, tipping his head to her before letting his gaze slide down her petite frame.

"Ask Dristan if he can move or speed up the chef and kitchen staff interrogations. I honestly don't care if the new one is shit, as long as he passed the test and is safe from committing treason. Icelyn," I called out to the Ice Queen over the sound of the marching soldiers patrolling the inside of the stronghold. She watched the proceedings without fear. When she neared me, I spoke low so as not to be heard. "So, you might be the new Light Heir, which would also indicate that you're the newly crowned Light Queen, so congratulations, or something?"

Icelyn shook her head and lifted up her arms. "I no longer have the heir brands. That was what I was coming to tell you. They've vanished, and I'm uncertain why or how. I checked the babes for them, but nothing."

"What?"

"Riders incoming!" someone shouted directly behind me.

My heart leapt, hoping that it would be Ryder and the men coming back victorious from battle. I moved through the room, heading toward the battlements to watch his return, only to find Dristan and Sevrin eyeing the banners warily.

"Who is it?" I demanded, stopping between their massive frames, staring at the immense force of troops that moved across the meadows. There was a large white banner with what looked like a single *A,* presumably for anarchy, written in blood.

"No fucking clue," Dristan announced, staring at the front seven riders who preceded the army.

"Is that the sign for anarchy?" I asked, a frown creasing my brow.

"We should get you inside, Synthia," Sevrin muttered, straining his eyes to watch the riders who seemed to be slapping each other with severed limbs. "Are those legs?"

"It's Asher and the Seelie. He actually fucking came." I smiled, watching the Seelie as they approached us, in no hurry to reach the stronghold. In fact, they slowed even more when Asher's arms moved as if he argued with those beside him.

"But whose leg is he slapping around?" Dristan's mouth turned into a frown. His multicolored green eyes turned to me, and he shook his dark head as he took in the Seelie army. "I can feel them, *all* of them."

"Yeah, that's not surprising considering your father screwed the Seelie Queen, and out popped an army of Asher like creatures." Or, so we assumed that was what happened. Rumor was Danu had had a hand in creating them as well. Danu was also known as the Mother of the Fae, so who knew what that really meant?

"No, Synthia. I can feel all of them. The entire army marching toward us shares a familial bond. They're all Alazander's children, meaning he didn't just fuck the queen, he fucked the entire court."

"Your father really was a whore." I nodded for the troops in front of the castle to stand at the ready. I wanted to be prepared in case Asher had changed his mind and decided to march on the horde instead of accepting Ryder's offer to join us. "Be ready in case they try something. I will not lose this stronghold while Ryder is away."

"Hold the line!" Sevrin shouted, sifting to the

front of the men who protected the fortress.

I watched the front riders break away from the others as they approached the gates. Asher stared up, watching me from iridescent eyes that bespoke of sinful nights. His dark hair had been pulled back and placed into a folded ponytail that exposed his pointed ears. He wore a silver cloak, making the silverish brands on his arms stand out.

"Fuck me," I muttered.

"I think Ryder may find issues with that, Syn. I'm not saying no, though, just so you know; if you need it, I'm here," Dristan said, offhandedly pushing his fingers through his thick hair, staring down at the army approaching the gates.

"We have a problem, a big one."

"I admit, having Seelie in the bloodline is not ideal, but Ryder seems to think these fuckers may be an interesting addition to the horde."

"Dristan, do me a favor and look at Asher's arms. Tell me what you see." I watched Asher as he dismounted and started forward, oblivious to the soldiers who held the long spears up in warning at his informal approach.

Dristan stared and then swore beneath his breath as he studied Asher and the brands pulsing on his arms. He looked from Asher to me, and then back before he shook his head in disbelief.

I leaned forward, frowning further as Asher touched his hand against one of the spears, pulling his finger back when blood appeared. Instead of backing up as anyone else would, he examined the weapons and then the armor of the soldiers who watched him warily.

Sevrin gazed up at me, brow raised, waiting for my orders. I wasn't sure if I should speak, or wait for Asher to finish his inspection of the armor and weaponry our men held ready to fight. The army stayed behind Asher, not raising weapons or appearing to expect a fight, which gave me pause.

"Asher, friend or foe?" I called down.

"Hmm, an interesting question, *Goddess*," he called up, lifting those inhuman eyes to mine as a sexy smirk covered his lips. "I fear we are here to assist in the fight. My brothers and sister wish to go to war."

"And you?" I asked, smiling at his disappointed look. "What is it you want to do?"

"Fuck, but fighting will have to soothe my ache for now. You were correct. The human world is filled with shit."

"Let them in, but the army remains at the gates," I announced to the soldiers who regarded the infamous Seelie warily.

Asher sifted, appearing beside Dristan and me without warning. The sex pheromones he oozed didn't go unnoticed as they slithered over me, forcing my body to clench with need. Rainbow-colored eyes studied my response, noting the subtle effect his magic held over me.

"Good to know I turn even the gods on."

"Turn it off," I ordered.

"Oh, sweet thing, it isn't even on yet." He shrugged broad shoulders, observing me. "Would you like to see it on?" He ignited his power, causing my body to tremble. A moan of need slipped from my lips as he smiled roguishly. "Mmm, what delicious noises you make for me. I bet you are a dirty girl for your king. Aren't you? I like dirty girls the most."

"In case it has slipped your fucking mind, she is the Queen of the Horde, and you will give her the respect her position demands," Dristan sneered, moving to position his body between Asher and me.

"Fucking Unseelie, ruining the fun as usual," Asher frowned, looking at Dristan. "Brother, so nice to meet another poor fuck that our father sired. I'm rather exasperated with finding new kin, considering I can't fuck them. Are you aware that every pussy in that army is related to us? My dick is feeling very neglected, so excuse me for reminding myself of Her Majesty's grace that pussy still notices me, and that I can occasionally find some that aren't blood-related within this world. Rarely, but Synthia proves there is hope for my cock yet."

"Are you finished?" I asked, struggling to ignore the need he'd created within me. "My husband is away, and that means I cannot play. Keep your fuck-me vibes under control because I can't even go to his camp to ease the ache, asshole."

"Mmm, he wouldn't find it amiss should you end up on his warhorse, needing a good pounding? He'd probably enjoy it, what with the bloodletting happening out there." Asher smirked at my discomfort, trailing his pretty eyes over my body in a slow caress. "I'm positive his sword is at the ready should you land on it, Queen of the Horde. But I have issues that I need you to explain to me. You see these?" he asked, discarding his shirt with magic to expose the iridescent and silver intertwining brands. "What the fuck are they?"

"They're brands, Asher."

"I know that much, pretty girl. I have brands, perfectly good ones that mark me as Seelie royalty. I want to know why the fuck these silver brands are on my arms, legs, and other things that I won't mention since you're the queen. I'm assuming you know what they mean, judging by the humor you are finding in my discovery of them on my flesh."

"They're the Light Heir brands. Faery has chosen a new King of the Light Kingdom to sit upon the throne in the Palace of Lights."

"Suck my dick," he muttered. Dristan growled once more, and Asher turned to stare at him. "I am the Seelie King."

"You are, but the Seelie have no home. You have no throne, Asher. It is my understanding that the Seelie Court barely escaped the palace before it collapsed around you. The land followed, forcing you out until all that remained was the prison in which you escaped. My guess is this: Faery chose you because your home is in ruins. You needed a new home for your people. Faery needed a new king to rule the Light Kingdom. Improvising, it looks like Faery selected you to fill the void."

I smiled tightly at his watchful gaze, enjoying the way he flinched a little at the explanation. I was an asshole for the small enjoyment it gave me to catch him off-guard with the truth of my words.

"You are a king without an official court. Your entire lands were destroyed, were they not?" I paused, waiting for his nod. "Faery is a living creation from Danu's magic. It finds balance one way or another, and it chose you to balance the courts. It just so happens the guardian we appointed was murdered, and now you are here. That isn't a coincidence, it was destined for you to assume that role."

"I don't want to be king of anything. All I ever wanted was to be free of the fucking prison that held us, and I am. I'm not king material, nor do I care to rule over anyone. I just wanted to be free and fuck as many women as I can that aren't related to me. Is that too much to ask? Point me to a willing woman, and I will be the happiest cock in the kingdom."

"No one who sits upon the thrones of Faery ever wished to become rulers, and yet three new kings have been crowned in the last twenty-four hours. You're one of them."

"I hate to be the downer here, but how the fuck is

the Dark Heir supposed to fuck the Light Heir if both have dicks?" Dristan mused.

"I'm not fucking a guy," Asher sputtered.

"I have no idea, but Asher's brands aren't like the ones that Icelyn had. They are the same as Adam's and mine, meaning they are permanent." I studied the pulsing brands, placing my fingers on them before yanking them back. "Jesus, would you dim it the fuck down?" I demanded, fighting against the need to come undone and make a total ass of myself.

"It is down, Synthia. It is down as far as it will go without finding release. I'm Seelie, sex in the purest form of the word, created to fuck and feed. This is what happens when you lock something like me up for centuries and forget to fucking feed it."

"Okay, noted," I snapped back, letting my power slide over him, allowing him to feed. His eyes went wide, and I pushed more power into him, watching as he groaned while his eyes rolled back in his head mid-orgasm. "That help?" I asked, noting the way his brands danced to a steady beat like he was being fucked.

"Fuck, you're delicious."

"I'm glad you think so," I stated, turning to look at the army that remained seated on their mounts. "Has your army been fed?"

"They have no sense of morals. They started fucking each other even though they're blood-related. Starving Seelie don't normally care, but I don't want to carry the knowledge around that I fucked my own blood to feed." He held on to the stones of the wall, heady from the power I fed him.

I sent the same power rushing through the army, noting the way they jolted and then moaned as I fed them enough to protect our people from his army's need to feed. I needed troops to fight, not a half-starved, half-mad Seelie army who had been locked in a cage of magic since the moment they were born. Danu had created them, then thrown them into the prison as if they'd meant nothing to her. I was convinced she'd been using them to build an army for some purpose.

Seelie were the opposite of the Unseelie, and yet Asher was high fae, born of horde genetics, which was why Faery had chosen him to take Dresden's place. It also made me wonder if the Light Heir had been within the Palace of Lights when it had fallen to the mages.

The only way to get the full power of the brands was to be the heir. Meaning there wasn't another alive, which shot the whole Light and Dark Heirs making a baby together out of the realm of possibilities.

"These assholes again?" Adam asked as he walked up behind me, noting the way the entire army outside the gates was moaning. "They seem happy."

"Adam, meet the Light Heir," I grumbled, watching his eyes grow large and rounded.

"I'm not fucking him. If that's Faery's idea of a cosmic joke, it can fuck off." Adam crossed his arms, hiking a dark brow to his hairline.

"I think your destiny changed unless Asher has a uterus hidden behind his balls."

"You know I'm right fucking here, right?" Asher mumbled, still staring at me like he was in heaven, and I was his tour guide past the pearly gates. "You need to stop before I make a mess. My dick is actually fucking pulsing right now, and I'm trying really hard not to disrespect your husband by coming as I stare at his pretty wife's face while her power fucks me up."

"Oh, sorry," I chuckled. "I thought we were having a moment, Asher."

"We're about to have a few moments that I'm certain my new found brother wouldn't approve of if you don't turn it off, woman."

"Riders!" Someone shouted.

We turned, staring out at the dark armor of the troops moving toward Asher's army. I swallowed as the hatred of those who approached filled the air.

"Mages!" I screamed, turning to the men who stood by the drums. "Sound the alarms! Battle formations! Fucking move! Let the army in, now! Open the gates quickly."

"What the fuck are they thinking?" Dristan asked, watching as thousands of mages marched toward the stronghold. "It doesn't look like they're here to surrender."

My throat tightened as fear gripped my heart painfully. Fighting my hands at my sides to hide the trembling, I exhaled fighting to expel the worry slithering through me at the sight that swam in my vision.

"No, they're not. They're coming to take down the last caste of the high fae. They've come to fight the horde. Asher, get your army inside now. Sevrin, get the archers to the front of the wall. I want shield holders ready to guard them at the front, and the infantry behind. Move the cavalry behind the infantry, ready to charge on my command. Asher, your army will go with ours. Have them prepared to move in should one of ours fall. Dristan, I need to know that the tower is locked down and that Eliran is within it. The wards are all up, which means no sifting, so please, move."

I peered out over the army slipping into our gates to where the mages smugly carried the flags of the Dark Kingdom, the Light Kingdom, and last but not least, my father's banner, the Blood Kingdom.

Insolent pricks had no shame or respect for the dead. Anger slithered through me as my eyes slid through their ranks, hating that they'd taken the banners from the fallen kingdoms.

"That's not good," Adam said. "They're flying my fucking flag."

"They're flying all the high fae flags, all except for the horde," I stated, turning to look at the anger and pain that covered Adam's face. "They're coming to take our kingdom. Let's disappoint them, shall we, gentlemen?"

Chapter
TWENTY~THREE

The entire stronghold held its breath as I stood in front of the castle in full armor. I was prepared to defend my home against the vile mages that had been stupid enough to march upon our lands, intending to bring it to its knees. Lena stood shoulder to shoulder with me, while Ciara, Icelyn, Lilith, and Fyra flanked us on either side.

The entire front line of troops was comprised of women warriors. The men stood behind, fully aware that the mage army outnumbered us, and we were in trouble. We'd been wrong to assume the mages would send the bulk of their troops to the valley. It didn't help to worry about it now, considering we were staring them down across the field.

I'd placed Sevrin in the castle with Dristan, ensuring that Eliran was inside the tower with Olivia and the children. I'd secured the castle, reinforcing the wards before I set even one foot outside of the stronghold. I hadn't forced the women to come with me, nor had I refused their help.

We made a plan before coming beyond the gates, one to hold the fight at this position. This was the line their army wouldn't cross unless we fell, and we had no plan of that happening.

I'd been sure to remind everyone that these beings weren't weak. They'd brought the Blood Kingdom, the Light Kingdom, and the Dark Kingdom to their knees, and murdered the most powerful fae in their own homes, where they were at their strongest.

"At the back, you see it?" Ciara asked through her dragon armor, covered in scales of red and black like the armor Blane donned when he'd left here.

I stared across the field where two large ballistae were being armed with giant arrows that could easily pierce a dragon in flight. There were also other contraptions spraying iron into the air that was already beginning to affect the surrounding fae but only slightly at the moment. Giants had been captured and were being used to haul medieval machinery back and forth to where the mages wanted them placed.

"That explains a lot," Fyra muttered crossly. "Those arrows will cause an issue with our plans."

"Icelyn, are you healed enough to do what you need to do?" I asked, slightly turning to take in the anger in her icy depths.

Anger was good.

Anger was strength.

Fear was power against the enemies because fear made you fight harder to shove it away.

"I am. I can fight. I wouldn't be out here if I wasn't sure I could help." Her hands were encased in ice, prepared to send it sailing toward the mages at a moment's notice.

"Lilith?" I turned to where she stood within the

shadows that clung to her as if she was one with them.

"I'm ready."

"Ciara, are you certain you want to be out here and not inside where you are protected?"

"Synthia, I'm not weak. I am right where I am supposed to be. My children are with my brothers high in the tower, safeguarded by your magic."

"If the mages release the iron, we will need to figure out how to get around it," I admitted, knowing I couldn't push the iron away *and* fight. "Fyra, and Darnell, dragon forms, please. This only works if you're transformed. If they release the iron, you need to be ready to neutralize it to the best of your ability."

No worries, right?

I was terrified of what we faced, knowing these creatures had been underestimated time and time again. They'd been allowed to become strong until they were flooding into our lands by the thousands, murdering our courts before anyone had taken them seriously. It was our own fault for allowing them to grow unnoticed within the guilds, using contracts to build their bank accounts to afford the war against the inhabitants of Faery.

I could feel Ryder fighting on his own front. I knew he was battling mages as we geared up to fight them. He wasn't coming to save us because he couldn't. We'd been outplayed and had fallen right into their trap. He'd taken the larger portion of our army to take the mages down on our own terms, only for them to use it against us.

Our enemies had known where to strike us to inflict the most pain, and they hadn't hesitated. We had, and that was because we played by a set of rules that we expected them to use. They weren't honorable, which made them more dangerous.

No one had any idea just how large their army was until it had been too late. Now they were here at our fucking doorstep, prepared to fight us on our turf without fearing us. I stared down the line, frowning, noting that everyone held weapons or magic in their hands.

The giants turned, marching toward the front of the enemy lines. I gave the order to place the spears down in front of the army in which I stood. I would show no weakness because I was born to protect this world. I wouldn't let them see the fear that hugged tightly around me, slipping through the cracks in my armor.

Because who doesn't have giants on their side? Oh, yeah, us.

"We can't get to the machines without plowing through their forces. If we move to do so, they'll release more iron into the air, and that will leave the fae unable to defend the stronghold. We need more people," I muttered, turning to stare at the faces of the army prepared to defend us with their lives. I feared it might reach that price, and if it did, the castle would fall. I couldn't allow that to happen.

"It's too late," Ciara said, coughing in reaction to the iron being sprayed into the air. "It's working."

My hands lifted, pushing against the iron that filled the air. The soldiers behind me began coughing and hissing as it filled their lungs. My magic pulled the metal from them, forcing it back to the mages, but I couldn't keep it up forever.

"Starting without me? I'm wounded," a cheery voice said as the surrounding air ignited and filled with power. "That's a problem," Erie said, materializing to stare across the field before her electric-blue eyes turned and held mine. "I thought I told you not to let them reach the castle?"

"It wasn't like we planned it, Erie. Or are you Mórrígan?" I asked, staring at her while wondering which side she'd play on today.

"I am Erie, and I am Mórrígan. Trust me. You want me in goddess form for this fight. Anyway, you should call in the oath I owe your mother now. The mages are about to start forward, and the moment they do, you will be forced to release the iron you're removing to defend the stronghold. This will kill the fae behind you instantly. So, call in the fucking oath so we can get this party started," she hissed. Turning, Erie used her fingers to make a box around a giant's head.

"What are you doing?" I asked, shooting my eyebrows to my forehead as I watched her.

"I have a vacancy in my freezer, and Fred hasn't fucked up enough that I can put him back in it yet," she explained, shrugging when my face scrunched up. The war drums sounded, signaling the mages had grown tired of waiting. "Call in the oath, Synthia."

"I don't know how."

"Destiny, I suggest you start explaining how it works before we end up losing Faery, and Danu rolls over in her grave. She was such a drama queen," Erie snorted, still measuring the heads of the creatures that stood opposite of us on the battlefield.

"Synthia, repeat after me." Destiny held my hand, and I dropped the other, turning to listen as the warriors behind us coughed. "I, Synthia, Daughter of Danu, claim the oath that was owed to my mother."

"No," Erie interrupted. "Call in all of them, because the war won't be finished when this fight ends. If I am to be here and fight with you, I need to be able to say I had no choice."

"I, Synthia, Daughter of Danu, call in the oaths you owe my mother, Mórrígan." I stared at Erie as she lifted a delicate brow.

"Mean it, Synthia. We're out of time to be fucking around. *The* Mórrígan. Not Mórrígan." She bristled as if I should know the difference.

"I, Synthia, Daughter of Danu, call in the oaths owed my mother by *the* Mórrígan. Heed my call, and fight beside me, Goddess."

"My fucking pleasure," Erie said, skipping away.

"Wait, where are you going?" I asked, watching the craziest of crazies skipping barefooted toward an entire army of mages. My eyes widened in worried as creased my forehead in confusion. "Erie, where the hell are you going? That isn't the plan!"

"To fuck shit up, duh," she chuckled. "Fódla, Banba, to me now!" she shouted above the drums.

I watched as Erie's sisters appeared before her,

vanishing the moment she stepped through them. She cracked her neck, approaching the army without a shred of fear. I turned, studying Destiny and the way she stared at Erie with a look of worry.

I looked back at Erie, watching the redheaded warrior close the distance between her and the giant that marched toward her. He carried a wicked-looking club adorned with spikes that he was swinging back and forth. Erie started to run forward, materializing twin swords in her hands right before she reached him. Stabbing the blades into flesh, she used them to climb the giant, slicing his throat, sending his body into a flip. Erie landed on the giant's back. She opened her mouth, and a large unkindness of ravens began to flood from it.

I blinked as my mouth opened and closed. *Because that wasn't freaky?* No, it made perfect sense for the tiny redhead to open her mouth and release hundreds of ravens from her lips. Right? *Right?* You couldn't make this shit up, not where she was concerned.

"Did she just *throw up* ravens?" I asked, turning

to Destiny, who smirked, her worry gone the moment the birds slipped from Erie's lips. I blinked, watching her to make sure I wasn't hallucinating.

"She's the Mórrígan and the Goddess of War. She is an army within herself, and those are her Raven Guard. She can only call them if she blesses a victor of the battle. She's blessing you, Synthia."

The battle line moved, and I stared down at where the fae were itching to be allowed to fight. "Hold the line!" I shouted, and then listened as my words echoed down the wall of fae that stood between the mages and the castle, circling the entire stronghold, guarding it. The back was less protected, but enough fae were defending it and would sound warning us should an assault be tried from any other angle. "Hold the line!" I shouted again. I turned to Icelyn and smiled. "You're on; freeze the ground and drop the temperature."

Ice formed across the ground, forcing the mages back as it crawled up their legs, trapping them to the land with icy claws. It forced the mages closer together, and Erie was mowing through them with ease.

The ravens transformed into the immortal souls of the men the Mórrígan had collected from ancient battlefields. She plucked the bravest from their bloody demise before the Gods of Death could claim them. They wore thick, feathered armor and swung long, black swords where their arms had once been. If one fell, two more would rise in its place. I'd never imagined of all the myths surrounding the Mórrígan, that one was true.

"Dragons," I called, watching Fyra and Darnell take to the skies to force the mages on the edges of the battlefield to move closer to the middle.

I studied the arrows, flicking my wrist the moment they shot toward the dragons. They instantly disintegrated into ashes. I grinned silently, holding the line while I put everything into play. More arrows were loaded, and I flicked my wrist again, crying out as one of the dragons dove too soon and took an arrow to her chest.

"No!" Ciara shouted, watching as the dragon

dropped from the sky, its shrill scream ripping through the air. We watched its body hit the ground while mages leapt onto it, stabbing its body. It flailed helplessly, trying to escape the arrow that was retracting to the ballista by the attached chain. More mages engaged the dragon, cutting it up while preventing the Raven Guard from reaching her.

"Who fell?" I demanded and watched Ciara shake her head.

"Fyra, I think," she whispered thickly.

My heart hammered in my throat as I shoved the emotions down, turning to look at Lilith. "Shadows." I swallowed, watching as the shadows that had clung to Lilith moved like a thick fog across the ground, covering the battlefield in darkness.

The one dragon still fought fiercely, and every time they tried to load an arrow, I flicked it until one finally reached the ballista, flinging it like a toy through the air, shattering it. Erie guarded the other machine loaded with iron dust. She was slicing and dicing through the mages as if they were there merely for her enjoyment. I stared down the line one way, then the other as my breathing grew heavy.

"We fight to survive! We fight to protect the horde! We fight to persevere, or we die in the name of glory!" Cheers erupted, and I turned, staring at the mages who screamed in pain. Ice held them to the earth, and fire burned their bodies as darkness consumed them. "Well, ladies, shall we?" I asked, materializing swords before I sifted. Erie threw a warrior toward me, and I jumped, spinning in the air as I took his head from his shoulders. His body landed on the ground in front of me.

A warrior rushed toward me, noting the crown on my head. His blades moved swiftly, slashing for my body as I ducked and dodged each attack. I watched Erie from the corner of my eye as she danced in her long blood-red skirt, her blades pulsing.

Lena's wings were out, skewering men as she lunged, taking them down effortlessly as those who had come with her joined the fray. Blood covered the ice beneath me, and my swords drank it, offering more to the surrounding ground.

Asher and the Seelie let their power rip through the crowd, surrounding the mages from the outside. The mages had attempted to hide behind a veil of invisibility, attaching pieces of the cloak to their armor.

A giant flung his knife toward me, forcing me to drop and roll through the blood. Coming back up in a crouching position, I sifted, landing on his shoulders where my swords ran across this throat. His lifeless body fell, and I stood upon his back, turning to block yet another blade. Ciara took the attacker's head, swiftly dodging another assault behind her until the sword found a home in his skull.

I moved toward Icelyn, whose ice blades sliced through the advancing warriors, holding them to the ground with her power. She filled their lungs with ice until their breathing was labored.

Lilith forced the warriors to their knees as her shadows ripped through them, yanking limbs apart and pulling them into dark recesses as their bodies were devoured by the darkness.

An arrow shot toward the last dragon, and I flicked my chin, watching as it turned into flowers and fell to the ground. The dragon landed on the second wooden ballista, tearing it apart with its teeth before sending it sailing through the fray to shatter against the icy ground. The men and women of the horde screamed with victory as it opened its mouth, sending flames burning through the mages that were desperately trying to retreat.

"Kill them all!" I shouted, watching as the dragon's head turned, and then took its flight, following the line of mages into the woods as it opened its jaw and expelled flames.

I stood in the middle of the field, staring at the dead, blood coating my body and hands. We'd done the impossible. It had almost been too easy. Slowly, I made my way back to where the females were gathering, when a blast rang from the castle, and then the alarm sounded.

"No," I uttered. *"No!"* I screamed, trying to sift,

only to remember I'd warded the entire castle against sifting to prevent our enemies from gaining access. I ran, and the women followed me, knowing that there'd been a breach for the alarms to sound. My stomach somersaulted as fear tightened around my heart.

My gaze slipped up to the tower, watching as someone hung out the window, attempting to escape. "Catch him!" I screamed as someone tried to throw a child from another window. The dragon swooped toward the falling child as I held my breath. "It was too easy because it was a fucking diversion!" I snapped, running with the women as we moved to fight whoever had breached the stronghold.

Chapter
TWENTY-FOUR

The castle floors were covered with bodies. We slid in their blood in our haste to get inside, and I sailed across the floor until I slammed into something soft. I lifted from the ground on my hands, staring directly into Darynda's sightless eyes.

"No. No, please," I whispered, turning to look at the staircase leading up to the tower, noting the bodies piled at the base of the stairs.

I stood, knowing I couldn't do anything for Darynda. She was dead, her entire chest cut open with an iron blade. I slid in the blood again, wiping my hands on my armor as I rushed toward the stairs, not knowing who followed. The upper-level hallway was littered with corpses, making it impossible to move through them without stepping on them as we raced forward.

Ahead of us was the invisible doorway to the safe room, which stood wide-open, allowing me to view inside. "No," I whispered, unable to say anything else as my heart hammered so hard it was deafening in my ears.

I could hear the women behind me, hurtling over corpses as we hauled ass into the room. Inside, bodies littered the floor. Sevrin fought against a male who turned, staring at me as his blade pushed through Sevrin's chest, taking him down. Olivia was huddled on the floor, holding her stomach, Dristan beside her.

"Bilé," I screeched, drawing blades as he turned and lifted his. Defending Olivia and Dristan, I struck hard and fast, moving him away from their prone forms. I danced away from him, forcing him to follow me as screaming continued in the other room where the children were being held. His blade caught my cheek, and his smile was maddening.

"Look at you. You're the image of utter perfection,"

Bilé murmured. "I'm going to enjoy you before I send you to Hades, little Goddess. You are an abomination. You weren't worth Danu's life!" he shouted, swiftly slicing his sword through the air. I blinked, and his blade almost found its place against my throat before another sword deflected the strike.

"Fancy meeting you here, asshole," Erie snapped, watching his eyes widen with the knowledge of who she was as the ravens on her shoulders took the forms of men. She swiped her blades, dancing around me as I stepped back, peering down to where Eliran lay lifeless, his features haunted in death.

A sob ripped through me as I shook my head in denial. I'd assumed we were safe, never imagining Bilé would come to us. I'd warded against gods, but he wasn't just any god. He was part of this world, which allowed him to pass through barriers others couldn't. I picked up my swords, helping Erie as she cornered him, intending to scissor her blades through his neck, but he vanished.

Erie turned, staring at me before she spoke low

and clear. "He's gone."

I dropped to the floor, holding my stomach as I fought the need to howl with grief. Ciara opened the door to the nursery, exhaling her relief as she rushed inside. The nurse, who had been trying to get the children out of the room, turned, crying out in relief as I stood in the doorway bloodied, my cheek sliced open. I looked down at the floor, my pulse pounding in my ears, quieting the sound to nothing as my eyes slid over the dead bodies littering the room.

"Olivia, it's okay," I stated softly, hating the burning of my tears as they ran through the wound on my face. She held a sword in her hand, and Dristan lay over the top of her. She didn't move. "Olivia, he's gone. He can't hurt you now." I wiped the blood from my eyes and moved closer, pushing Dristan off of her, crying out as he fell to the floor in two pieces. "Oh, gods, no," I sobbed violently, staring at Olivia's sightless stare.

I stood up, backing away from them, everything inside of me screaming in denial at what my vision was telling me was true. Everyone stared at me, and I realized I was crying hysterically. Ciara held Sevrin, Lilith held Eliran, and everyone stared at Olivia's lifeless body.

"No! No, this isn't how it ends!" I screamed hoarsely. "I can save them. I can save them all," I muttered, sitting down in front of Olivia, pushing power into her.

"Synthia, she's gone," Erie said.

"They can't be gone. No, don't you see," I sobbed as tears rushed down my face. "No! No! Thanatos!" I screamed, watching as he emerged from the shadows. "You can't take them all! I will fight you!"

"They're not here anymore. Save the one you can," Thanatos uttered with a look of pain in his cold blue eyes. "Save the one who has yet to breathe their first breath. It's the only soul that remains."

My hands glowed, ready to try again, and Erie grabbed me. I swung on her as I materialized blades, intending to fight her to save the dead.

"Don't do this," she warned. "It is forbidden!"

"Get out of my way," I demanded, pulling my power to me.

"Pick a child, Synthia. Kahleena? Cade, or maybe Zander? Who will you let them take from you for trespassing against Death? Your mother gave her fucking life to bring you back! Don't do this. You will allow Bilé to do what he came here to do! He is trying to make you trespass against the gods! Do not let him win!" Erie pleaded.

"But it's my family!" I sobbed, holding my stomach as grief shook through me. "It's my family, Erie. He took my family!"

"He hit your family because they are your weakness," she whispered. "Save the life you can and let the others go in peace. They're already gone. They are not here anymore because they didn't want him to win. They called Thanatos. He can only be called by the wails of souls wishing to pass through him to know peace."

"What life can I save? They're all dead!" My gaze moved to Olivia, then lowered to her stomach. I shook my head, unable to even consider doing what they expected from me.

"You're the Goddess of the Fae. Bring back the babe," she whispered softly. "Only you can bless your people. Save the baby."

I materialized a knife and stepped toward Olivia's body. She'd want her child to live at all costs, even if that meant ruining her body after death. I dropped to my knees, shaking my head while the room held its breath. Breathing raggedly, I cut through her belly, dropping the blade when I'd gone deep enough to sever the flesh. My hands pushed inside the incision, sobs rocking through me as I removed the lifeless body of her child.

"No," I whispered, rubbing its stomach, then blowing into its mouth. Wards began to wail in warning, and Erie moved to stand behind me as the clanking sound of swords being drawn to defend echoed through the room. "Come on. You don't get to go with your mommy. We need you. Your daddy needs you so much," I pleaded, kissing the babe's head. It glowed where I kissed it, igniting tiny brands that pulsed before a small cry sounded.

Chaos erupted in the room as I stood, protecting the child in my arms. Turning, I stared over my shoulder at the door where Ryder stood, his gaze locked on the bodies that littered the floor. Ristan pushed through the crowd, stopping short of the corpses.

"Olivia!" Ristan screamed, staring at me.

"Stop him," I said, sobbing as my head shook, unable to tell Ristan what sat behind me. "Ryder, stop him!" I pleaded brokenly.

Ryder didn't move from where he was rooted in the doorway. His eyes were stuck on Dristan's body, wide in horror before they moved to Savlian, who shouted for Sevrin, finding his twin murdered, a blade still protruding from his chest. Adam held Eliran, staring up at Ryder, who still didn't speak or move. Ristan pushed me aside, and his wail slammed into my soul. He screamed and sobbed helplessly at the lifeless body of his mate lying upon the floor with her stomach cut open.

"Save her!" Ristan demanded, standing up to grab me, unaware of the tiny bundle I held in my arms. "You're the fucking Goddess of the Fae, you save her!" he yelled through angry tears, shaking me.

"Stop!" Erie demanded, pushing him away only to catch him as he lunged again and again.

"Fuck you. This is between Synthia and me! I saved her children! She fucking owes me! She has to bring Olivia back. I don't want to fucking live without her!" he shouted through tears.

Someone grabbed for the babe, and I let them, turning to stare at Ristan, who was growing angrier by the moment. Bloodied hands ran through his hair as he shook his head, staring at me with a pleading look in his gaze. Pain was etched on his face, his blind need to bring Olivia back rushing through him. He lunged at me again, only for Erie to block him from reaching me.

"I can't," I whispered thickly. "I'm so sorry, Ristan. I can't bring her back. It is forbidden."

"You will do it! Dammit. Synthia, I love her. I love her so fucking much, please. Please!" He grabbed me, shaking me before Erie could stop him. I turned, looking at Ryder, who still stood motionless, staring at Dristan. "I'll fucking make you!"

"Choose one of her children, you bastard! Her daughter? Her sons? Or maybe Ryder? Which one would you have her sacrifice to bring your mate back? No? Don't want to choose? Because the gods will make her! And when she does, because you know she'd choose Ryder over her children to die, they will kill her fucking children!" Erie screamed, forcing the room to go silent. "That is what they do! They take the one thing you love most, and they destroy it! So choose which child of hers you are willing to sacrifice for your mate because you can be damn certain she will lose one to bring Olivia back. I'm sorry, it sucks. That is the way it works, so choose one."

"I can't," he sobbed, shaking his head. "Olivia's

pregnant! She's going to be a mother! We're going to fill her frames with so many fucking pictures that she won't know where to put them. I promised her!"

"No, you will be a father, and you will fill the frames for her." I stared up at him, watching the denial play across his face.

He shook his head, and the room filled with the small scream of the infant. Ristan's eyes moved, finding his mother holding his son. He stared at the tiny babe with red curls and bright blue eyes that swirled like his, but in the same shade of Olivia's. A tiny tail slipped from Alannah's hold as we took in the teeny horns at the top of his son's head. Little black wings unfurled from his back as Ristan watched.

"I can't do this without her," he sobbed brokenly, dropping to the floor beside Olivia. "I need her. I can't do this alone." He didn't move toward the child, didn't look back at him as he pulled Olivia's body against his, rocking it silently.

"You're not alone," I said, slipping through the blood to sit beside him. My arm held his as I stared at him. "You're never alone, Ristan, we're with you. We are all with you forever."

"Prepare the bodies for burial, and then alert the other courts of what occurred here," Ryder stated, his tone cold and empty. I turned to gaze up at him, and he winced, taking in the damage to my face. "I want the Blood King and Dark King here to prepare to launch an attack immediately."

"Adam is the Dark King, and Liam is the Blood King. Three kingdoms fell to Bilé."

"Four Kingdoms fell," he stated, moving to where Sinjinn held Savlian's shaking form. "We murdered thousands of them, and yet they had enough to reach here and initiate an assault. Why wasn't the tower secured?" he asked, accusation burning in his tone as he glared at me.

"It was secured. I locked the door myself. They were all in here, cornered, where Bilé found them and lay waste to them as they used their bodies to defend the nursery. I fought Bilé's men outside the gates and secured the castle. I had troops placed around the entire fortress to alert us should anyone try to gain entrance during the battle. We fought them, we won. I thought we'd won.

"The alarm sounded, and then a nurse threw Fury out the window. They started throwing babes out the windows to save them while Dristan and Sevrin held the room, blocking the door," I sobbed. "Bilé wasn't supposed to reach inside. We expected him to be fighting you. I did everything you told me to do, and I lost. We're losing this war because he is a god, one my mother invited into Faery. He is immune to the wards, unaffected by the magic in this world. He's the fucking God of Death, and I'm not strong enough to fight him."

"You're not alone," Lucian said. "You have us."

"You have me, and I'm War," Erie said. "The problem isn't strength. You're fighting the man your mother trusted with all of her secrets. Danu built this world for them, their own fucking oasis. They abandoned her people to create a new world, and she built Faery for Bilé. You have to stop thinking in terms of saving this world and consider letting him have it. It may have been your mother's home, but it was his too."

"I can't walk away from this place. My mother told me to fight for it."

"It's not worth fighting for if you lose everyone to keep it. What do you plan to do when you have no one left to share it?" Erie asked.

"We need to bury the dead," Ryder said. "We have new kings to crown and plans to make. I'm done fucking losing. It's time we fight them head-on. It's time to call in all favors owed, all oaths. If we have to, we will leave Faery to the monster who wishes to claim it. I won't lose any more family for a piece of land, Synthia. I didn't kill my father to lose my brothers. I murdered Alazander to save Dristan's life, and now that seems utterly worthless, doesn't it?"

TWENTY~FIVE

I sat numbly on the chair beside Ryder, who watched the remains of our family and friends being placed on the pyres. He didn't speak, but then what the hell did you say at a time like this? We'd lost epically, and the mages were probably celebrating right now.

They were willing to throw bodies at us, allowing their armies to be slaughtered to hit us in a big way. We weren't that cruel. We didn't want the losses or want to kill our troops for one fucking hit. We wanted to throw the uppercut and have Bilé feel it without sacrificing thousands of our warriors' lives to manage it.

"I warded the tower," I whispered to the wind.

"The queen isn't healing," Ryder said, turning to look at where my face continued to bleed. "Call for Eliran," he growled, causing everyone around us to pause and peer in our direction at the mention of Eliran's name. "Fetch a healer, now," he commanded, pulling me over onto his lap, uncaring who saw the act of affection.

"They're watching us," I mumbled, my throat bobbing with emotion as the sting of regret and grief tore through me.

"I don't give a shit who the fuck is watching us, woman. Why aren't you healing?" Ryder's hand lifted, curving against my cheek as he took in the injury from Bilé's blade.

"Because I was attacked by a god defending Olivia's corpse," I whispered, barely audible to my own ears.

"You didn't call for me, why?" he demanded.

"I couldn't." I lowered my head and worried my hands in my lap as I went over the security procedures.

"I warded the tower against the gods to protect everyone inside. I warded it against myself, and yet Bilé got through. How the fuck am I going to protect us if I can't ward against him?" I looked up into Ryder's eyes as a tear rolled down my cheek. "I lost so many people, and yet I never even thought about him being able to get past the wards. I underestimated him, and we paid for it greatly."

Someone stood in front of us, and Ryder growled, causing the guy to jump. Ryder stared at the male, watching him before he dropped his eyes to the bag the man held.

"I'm guessing she needs sutures, My King."

"And you are?" Ryder snapped.

"Finley, I was Eliran's understudy," he admitted sadly, wiping away the tears that rolled down his cheek, uncaring of who saw his grief.

"Fuck off," Ryder growled.

"With all due respect, her face is badly wounded. If you don't want it to scar, please let me assist My

Queen in her hour of need. It will be an honor to help her after she fought so bravely to protect us."

"I lost, in case you failed to notice," I whispered, wiping away tears of anger.

"You lost a few, but imagine if they'd gotten inside. We'd all be dead, My Queen. You may have lost some people, but you saved so many more. Eliran knew he could fall, and he trained me in the event that it happened. Please, let me help you."

I expelled a breath and returned to my chair, turning my face to allow Finley to apply sutures. He opened his kit and started working as I stared out over the dead, glaring where Thanatos stood in the shadows, watching me silently. Thanatos didn't look as if he enjoyed his job, and yet he did it all the same.

Someone moved through the crowd of people who gathered around us, and I paused, sitting up to see Fyra. She moved toward me, stopping to nod her head as she took in the damage to my face. I smiled sadly, watching her through tears that fell freely as relief washed over me. Of course, she'd survived.

Who else would have been crazy enough to fly at the castle to save the little dragon prince?

Ryder's hand reached for mine, and I lifted my eyes to his as he smiled tightly, even though it didn't reach his eyes.

"We're going to be okay, aren't we?"

"I don't know," he replied, unable to lie. "Not today. Today we will mourn our losses and celebrate their lives, and tomorrow we will prepare for war. You fought against insurmountable odds and won. You fought bravely in the face of loss and uncertainty while showing no fear to our enemies. I murdered thousands of mages, and that, too, is a victory. We did what we were supposed to do, and you were right where you were supposed to be, Synthia. You can't predict treachery. You can't foresee another god's ability to get past you. You did well," he said thickly, tightening his hand on mine.

"I don't feel like I did well," I whispered.

"You took on an army, and you destroyed them.

You didn't allow any to escape, my fierce little wife. You demolished them, and you showed no mercy. The horde is rejoicing outside of the gates. They're telling heroic stories about their bloodthirsty battle queen who stared down death and laughed in his face. You faced off with a god, and I'm thankful that Erie was here because, according to Ciara, you almost died too. So brush it off and sit up straight. Don't let them see your tears. Fix your crown and stand proud, because you fucking earned it. I felt you fighting, and I knew I didn't need to come save you because I knew you could handle it. No king has ever been prouder of his queen than I was of you today. We took a hit, but we also showed them we would stand and fight."

"Dristan," I whispered, and watched Ryder nod as his jaw clenched tightly.

"That one hurts the most," he admitted. His throat bobbed, and his hand tightened on mine.

"Ristan has to go on without Olivia, and I promised him I would protect her."

"No, you promised that you'd do every-fucking-thing you could do to protect her, to do your best, and that's what you did. Ristan knows that, even if he can't admit it yet. You saved his son. You did what you could for them. He has a part of her now because of you."

"Eliran?" I asked thickly.

"He knew he might not make it out of this alive. He did his job to save us so we could be here to fight this war. He served his purpose with dignity and honor, even though he wasn't a warrior. He died proudly protecting the babes."

"Sevrin?" I wiped at the tears.

"He went out fighting for his family, and he wouldn't want it any other way. He asked to stay to protect you."

I tore my gaze away from Ryder's, hating that he didn't blame me for failing, even though I knew how stupid it was to feel that way. Asher and his brothers and sister stood over a wrapped up body, and I turned to Ryder, hissing as the needle stuck in my cheek.

"I'm sorry. You keep moving." Finley grimaced.

"It is fine, Finley. Who is Asher standing with?" I asked Ryder.

"Emric; his brother fell in the battle outside the walls. I heard we have a new Light King. I'm guessing that will put a hitch in Adam breeding with them, now won't it?"

"If Asher and his army weren't here, we would have lost the castle," I admitted.

"But they were because I'd told him to come here instead of joining me. I fought for days, and when Bilé failed to show, I feared that he'd figured out our plan. Even though I hoped I was wrong, I had a feeling he was coming here, but I never sensed your panic. No storms hit us, no strange weather formed to even hint that you were in turmoil. You didn't want me to feel you, which suggested you were doing okay. I asked the men where you might have neglected to protect the castle, and they said you did everything right. Don't second-guess your decisions or blame yourself. Use the anger, Synthia. Use it to fight the son of a bitch who took from us."

"We need to address the crowd and burn our dead." I stared at where Ristan held his son next to Olivia's body. The child's tail was wrapped around his wrist, while Ristan held him against his chest, silently staring at his wife as tears flowed down his cheeks. "He needs us now."

"He needs everyone," Ryder said with conviction, noting where I stared. "We have kings to crown, and you need rest so that your injuries heal. We all need rest," he uttered. "Lucian has his men here, and Erie has released the Raven Guard to protect us as we recover from the attack. Her army was created to guard her against the gods. Callaghan is also here, avoiding Erie like the fucking plague. We will be okay. Do you hear me? I love you, woman. I couldn't ask for more than what you did today. You stood tall, and you kicked ass. No one else could have done what you did."

I turned in my chair to study Erie. Her wild, red war braids were frayed from battle, and she made them look natural, wildly untamable, but she owned them. She carried the scent of fresh grass with a hint of rain. It reminded me of how Ireland smelled just before the brilliant blue skies would open, and a torrential downpour would come out of nowhere. Erie was as wild as the land after which Callaghan had named her. Much like its weather, she was unpredictable. Her vivid eyes held mine as she smiled, stepping closer.

"Goddess of the Fae, you will be a fucking menace when you learn how to handle your full powers. Honestly, Synthia. I had no idea how to even call the Raven Guard back to me, but you helped me today. You ignited my need to fight with you. I have avoided it without my memories, but now? Now I know I can fight beside you and totally kick some ass. Death is a part of war, I know. Trust me, I've been in so many battles they've all blended together, and I don't even know if they're my memories or those of the warriors within me." Erie stared absently across the pyres and scowled from her silent position beside me. "Is that male an enemy? His head would be perfect for my freezer."

I followed her gaze to where Asher stood and furrowed my brow. "That's Asher, the Light King, and he's family now."

"Damn," she muttered, turning to stare at the man moving toward us, who stopped to stand beside Ryder. Callaghan's heated blue eyes settled on Erie, slipping down her slight frame with longing burning in their depths. "That's my cue to go."

"You guys are good, right?" I questioned, observing their stiffened body language.

"We've called a truce for now," Callaghan admitted, his tone rumbling through me as Erie let her gaze rove over his armor-covered frame. "See anything you like, woman?"

"I see something that belongs to me. I'm deciding if I should claim it or not." Erie smirked, shrugging her porcelain shoulders covered in woad.

"Callaghan," Thanatos called, staring at the warrior before his head turned toward Erie.

"What the fuck do you want?" Callaghan asked,

observing Erie, who narrowed her eyes on Thanatos as if she was trying to place him.

"Erie, you look wild and untamable as usual," Thanatos said.

Erie's lips pursed together, her gaze slowly sliding down Thanatos before dismissing him outright as uninteresting. "Peace out, bitches. I'm going to go drink until I forget the taste of birds flying out my mouth. I seemed to have forgotten how they taste as they're freed, and it isn't pleasant." Wiggling her fingers in the air, she spun on her heel and headed to where Zahruk stood quietly in front of Darynda's pyre, staring at Savlian, who stood sentinel over his brother Sevrin in death.

"Erie didn't know who the fuck you were," Callaghan said to Thanatos cryptically, drawing my gaze to his. Thanatos studied Erie's back as she skipped away with the carefreeness of a child instead of a millennium-old goddess.

"The Mórrígan didn't remember my name until Synthia had growled it, calling me out of the shadows.

I thought it was strange that she didn't say more or try to murder me. All things considered, she isn't my biggest fan."

"If you two are finished, I need to say a few words to the crowd and send our dead off." Ryder stood, and I watched him moving to address the crowd, grief marring his features. He looked defeated, and it was unsettling to witness it written on his beautiful face.

"You realize that you and I are not finished, right?" I stood to look at Thanatos.

"This one isn't on me, Synthia," Thanatos said, bristling with unease as he took in the grief in my stare.

"You took thousands of warriors, so why come for our family?" I asked, hating the tears that burned my eyes.

"I heard their cries, but I didn't take them. Bilé did. He had already claimed them before I got here to do it. I'm not the only God of Death inside Faery right now, Synthia. I tried to save their souls before he could take them. You want a way to hurt Bilé? He took the soul of an angel today. That is forbidden and against the laws of the gods. Only heaven can reclaim her, and until they do, she will not rest. No," he said when my head tilted and my eyes narrowed at his words. "Olivia left of her own free will. That which is dead cannot be raised again. She is gone forever, but her eternal rest is not guaranteed until she enters heaven. Use her loss, because he has violated the laws unknowingly by taking her angelic soul."

I twisted in my seat, staring out over the crowd that listened as Ryder said the prayers of the fae and a blessing for the dead warriors. He stared proudly over the army he'd brought together, and now they formed a deeper bond in the grief we shared. This fight wasn't over. It was just getting started, and it would be a long one.

Chapter
TWENTY~SIX

Death had a way of changing people, forcing them to learn a new normal. Ryder spoke before the entire horde. The grief he felt remained hidden until he reached the names of his fallen brothers. Dristan was a hard hit, harder than Olivia was for us. She'd been a part of the family, but Dristan, he was Ryder's baby brother.

Ryder murdered his father to protect his brothers and sister from Alazander, and as a result, he became king. He'd protected them all long before that day. Sevrin was another loss Ryder was struggling to accept, and each name he called out loud added weight to my chest until it felt like I'd never breathe again.

Ryder stumbled over Dristan's name again

as everyone watched. I swallowed past the tears threatening to drown me, moving to the middle of the glowing funeral pyres. Fairy lights lit throughout the courtyard and beyond the gate, where we'd been unable to accommodate enough room for the dead. Zahruk surveyed me carefully, his hand on Darynda's heavily wrapped corpse. Unshed tears swam in his eyes for the woman he'd once cared for, and in death, he'd refused to leave her side.

Lifting my hand, I directed the wind until it blew gently through the kingdom, letting the power of Faery glow from within me. All around, people turned their attention to me, watching in wonder as tiny pixies carried flowers through the air, dropping them onto the dead, honoring their sacrifice. I called to the rain, drenching the world surrounding us without allowing its showers to touch any of us. Faery also wept for the heavy losses of those who had been taken from us too soon.

The skies sang with the wind, howling in mourning at the pain, sharing our sorrow. Those around us lifted their eyes to the heavens, bereaved in grief, yet able to see the beauty of our home. My body pulsed with raw power, calling back the souls from the vile god who had stolen them. My hand lifted in the air once more, and tiny glowing balls of light escaped from each corpse, forming a spiritual representation of the dead. My vision swam with unshed tears, uncaring who saw that I grieved the loss of my family and trusted friends.

I was aware of Ryder's comforting presence at my back. I had taken the spotlight off of him, allowing him a moment to grieve his brothers without the judgmental stares of the crowd. I sensed his inner turmoil, his pain, and worse, I felt his anger. I could sense the magnitude of heartache at the loss of entire kingdoms that had been brought to their knees.

Trees swayed, their weeping branches alight with glowing pixies who watched me as I filled the world with a song to mark the passing of our people. Karliene's *The Unquiet Grave* played through the air as if a loudspeaker had replaced the clouds, and the heavens of Faery sang. Fire leapt to life in the torches as the voice began to sing. The wind continued, ruffling hair and the swathes of cloth that covered the dead. The skies displayed a multitude of vibrant colors, bathing Faery in a blanket of unmatched beauty.

Stepping forward, I called the first soul to me. My eyes closed, and my heart clenched tightly as if an invisible hand had ripped into my chest, continually squeezing it. I opened my eyes to stare into a beautiful forest-green gaze. Tears slipped free of the precarious hold I'd had on them, and my legs threatened to give out as pain ripped through me with immense sorrow, leaving me broken in tiny, useless pieces.

"Who would have ever thought that you, a former guild enforcer, who hunted down fae, would be the one to send me to the Otherworld, Synthia?" Dristan asked, his ghostly lips turning up at the corners into a sad smile. His hand lifted, cradling my cheek as he studied me without accusation or judgment for failing to protect him.

A thick scent of earth and sandalwood danced in my senses the moment he touched me. He observed me with love burning in the depths of his gaze. His hand felt warm, alive even though he was merely a soul now. He was a beautiful soul. He was one that couldn't remain here to wander Faery until he became nothing more than an angry spirit. I wouldn't allow that to happen.

"Dristan," I whispered, thick with emotion, searching for the words I needed to say. "I'm so sorry. I'm so sorry I failed you."

"It's okay. I'm okay with my fate. I need you to keep Ryder grounded for me." He nodded to where Ryder studied me through narrowed eyes, unable to see the souls that lined the courtyard. Each soul had returned, all except for one. The soul who didn't belong to Faery, and couldn't be summoned to send to the Otherworld, since Olivia didn't belong there. My hand lifted, gently pushing Dristan's hair away from his face before he leaned over, kissing my lips. "I knew my fate the moment we watched you walked out onto the battlefield. I sensed it coming for me. I stayed in that tower to protect the children. We all did, that's on us. Not you. Don't carry my death with you. Use the anger of our deaths to win this war against those who trespassed against us. Ryder is right: use it, Goddess.

"We did not die in vain. We died protecting our family, which is worth fighting for. If asked if I would do it again, knowing my outcome would be death, I would do it time and time again, without hesitation." Dristan's hands cupped my face between them as he nodded while holding my gaze. "We will meet again, you and me. When the world is right, and the time comes, I will be reborn into the same bloodline. The horde is a part of me, and you are now a part of it as well. Tell Ryder to keep fighting, keep moving forward, and don't grieve too long for those he lost, because the future you are fighting for is worth more than the lives he has lost in this fight."

I nodded slowly, aware that I looked like an idiot speaking to the ghost no one else could see. It wasn't until Thanatos stepped up beside me that my heart kicked into overdrive. Panic erupted within me, and I shook my head violently as the reality of why he'd come struck me. He had known I'd call our dead back to this place because I was one of the few who could do so.

"Not yet," I whispered.

"He's ready to move on," Thanatos said softly, holding his hand out for Dristan to accept as he held my panicked gaze. "He will be given peace for the sacrifice he made protecting his family and kingdom. He will be given a place of honor at my side within the Realm of the Dead. You have to let him go now, Synthia."

"I'm not ready."

"You're not, but he is. You can never prepare for death, sweet Goddess. No one is ever ready to say goodbye to their loved ones when death comes for them. Dristan knows what you want to say, they all do. You think you owe them an explanation, but you don't. They sense your grief and know the price you're paying for loving them. The pain you endure after such a loss? That, in itself, is the ultimate price for having loved a soul. Look at them," Thanatos said encouragingly. His words forced me to stare at the other souls we'd lost, gathered around us, smiling at me.

Keir, Adam's father, held his wife at his side while his sons and daughters stood behind him, staring at Adam, who still stood sentinel at the foot of their large funeral pyre.

My father, Lasair, stood beside Madisyn, who had carried me in her womb, witnessing my powers even though I wasn't her biological daughter. Their eyes were bright with pride, even as their ghostly images shimmered in and out of sight with the wind.

Sevrin stood beside Dristan, his smile firmly in place as his hand cupped my cheek.

"Watch over Savlian, keep him busy. You got this. You know that. You can let us go because we're okay now. You did everything you could, and you got there in time to save the babes. That's all we had hoped to achieve at that moment. You weren't the only one who felt Death creeping through the hallways of the stronghold. Be brave, Goddess, and keep them safe. I couldn't have asked for a better death than to die, protecting the ones I loved most in this life."

"We still need you," I whispered brokenly.

"No, you want us. You don't need us. Miss us, but don't be sad forever. Death is a part of living, even for immortals." I stared at Sevrin, shaking my head as he reached up, wiping away the silent tears I cried. "Destiny is preordained, but sometimes it changes. You changed this world when you came into Faery, and you made it better. You made us better, Synthia. Don't weep for us, for we are free, sister of mine." Smiling, he stepped back, then took Thanatos's hand and vanished.

I gasped as a sob echoed through my chest, escaping my lips. I brought my hand to my mouth, covering the cries that tried to escape. One by one, the dead began to vanish from this world the moment they touched Thanatos's outstretched hand. I stood, silently observing until Darynda stood in front of me. Her green eyes glittered, turning to Dristan with a mischievous smile.

"I think I flirted with the wrong brother for too long and ended up missing out on the one I actually wanted. Now I get him. I mean, who else is going to feed him in the afterlife?" She smirked, batting thick black lashes flirtatiously toward Dristan, who grinned.

"I'm so sorry," I whispered, taking in her beauty, even in death. "I should have been inside the tower."

"To do what, die with us? Bilé isn't a normal god, Synthia. I'm glad you weren't there, because death for us isn't the end. We will be reborn. We need you to fight for this world so that can happen. I served you well as my queen, but you are my friend first. You taught me much, and also got me addicted to caffeine, which I've been assured is readily available in the place we are going. Sevrin was right. We're the lucky ones and our fight is over, but yours is just beginning. Thank you for being my friend." She placed her hand into Thanatos's and vanished before I could reply.

I studied Cailean, my broody protector since the moment I was born, as his soul approached, gazing at me in with pride. "From Blood Princess to Queen of the Horde, and now Goddess of the Fae. It's been an honor to guard and serve you and keep you safe until you no longer needed me, Sorcha."

"I thought you were here…" Cailean smiled sadly, shaking his head before he too vanished without an explanation of how he'd been elsewhere.

My father stepped up next, touching my shoulder before he bowed his head. "Don't cry for us. One day, you will stand where I am, feeling your child's pain at your loss. You will wish to take it from them with everything you have inside of you. Nothing can take away the pain or assuage the grief you are feeling. I am glad that I got to know you, and that you will continue long after I am gone. Liam will need you now more than ever, and I am glad that you remain with him. We love you, daughter. I couldn't be prouder to call you mine," he expressed, placing his hand into Thanatos's as his blue eyes locked with mine in sadness I didn't want or need.

One by one, the souls moved forward and vanished until I stepped back, allowing them to pass without saying anything. I let them touch me to bless their passing, and Thanatos accepted them to their eternal rest. I stared past the dead to where a ghostly figure surveyed me; beside her was the Stag in his male form.

The crowd hushed around us as I glared into the eyes of the one creature I'd been hunting before they slid to my mother, who regarded me through angry, burning eyes. An uneasy feeling wrapped around my throat, clenching my stomach tightly until I swallowed it down.

Flowers still rained down around us while my feet took root where I stood beside Thanatos. This was Danu's fault for leaving us with the mess she'd created of her marriage. I opened my mouth to speak, but she reappeared before me, placing her finger over my lips.

"No, Mother," I whispered angrily, my gaze holding hers in challenge. "You did this to us. You damned us to die by letting Bilé into this world!"

"Synthia, I created this world in his image. The deadly beauty within Faery…It *is* him. You cannot destroy Bilé without killing Faery. You have to find another way. I brought you help to do just that."

"*Help?* I needed help when your husband was slaughtering my people! You brought me here to save this world, to save the people. You created me to anchor the beast, and I did. You created me to save the world, but I can't! You didn't bring me here to save Faery. I was brought here to save Bilé, and I will not save that monster! He has taken from me and this world. He cannot be saved. He will destroy us all."

"You cannot destroy Bilé, Synthia. He is stronger than you and filled with rage. I lost my way with him. He grew jealous that I spent my time creating this world for us to love and rule over."

"Yeah, well, there's no love within that heartless prick anymore. He's trying to kill me. You get that, right? He killed Ristan's mate! He murdered the entire fucking Blood Court, Light Court, and Dark Court, in case you haven't been brought up to speed." Crossing my arm over my chest, I glared at my mother, accusingly.

"He's resetting the world."

"Yeah, is he? The only court left standing is this

one! Footnote, Mother," I hissed angrily. "It's mine. I will destroy Bilé before I allow anyone else in my court to die or fall to that bastard."

"Change his mind," Danu pleaded. "Bilé is not unreasonable."

"Did you go deaf or dumb when you died, mother? Because you're not hearing me or what I am telling you! He's trying to *kill* us! He's slaughtering entire castes of fae as he skips across Faery."

"Then give it to him," she stated. "If you cannot reach him, give Faery to him. Leave," she said icily, something sinister burning in her gaze. "Without him, there is no Faery. I made you the goddess of the people so that you could protect them, so either let your anger for him go and try to reason with him or leave this world. Bilé can be reasoned with, but only if you can forgive him his rage. Meet with him alone and see what happens. Hear him out and give him a chance to explain what is needed for him to end this war."

"Why would you create me for a destiny that I cannot fulfill? Why give me something to love and then tell me to walk away from it? I don't understand how you could be so fucking cold. You gave me a world to fight for and love, and now you expect me to stand witness as everything is being destroyed by your estranged husband?"

"Oh, sweet girl. All the greatest love stories have one thing in common. You have to go against the odds to get it, and you never stop fighting to keep it. You have to fight and want to fight because you love it enough to endure the pain. Anger is useful, wrath is powerful, but rage is devastating. You are grieving, and so is Faery, but there's no balance here. You have to finish the task you started.

"You have to do what I asked, or Bilé will never stop destroying Faery. Create a balance, and you'll know what to do to save the people and Faery alike. Let your rage out, little daughter. Let it out to play so the world will sense your power and bow at what you are to become. You are holding back because you think you can hold on to that little sliver of humanity. You are not human, nor are you fully a goddess until you destroy that part of yourself. Let the world hear you scream and watch it answer your cry for help."

"You know you're asking the impossible," I whispered angrily, studying her face for any sign of betrayal.

"No, I created you to be brave in the face of destruction. I created you to dance in chaos as if it was no more than rain. I built the most beautiful mess of pandemonium and devastation that any world has ever known. Stop thinking like a human and think like a pissed-off goddess who just got her ass kicked. Buckle the fuck up, Synthia.

"You're just getting started here. Finish what I told you to do so that you have what's needed to soothe the grieving man ripping this world apart. Just don't kill Bilé, or you destroy Faery and everyone in it, which includes your children. I have to go now, but I will be around soon enough. I brought you the Stag because he was the first thing I created in this world after the Tree of Life was planted. I am proud of what you've become. We all have to find where to plant our roots on our own, Synthia. If you can't figure out where yours belong, Bilé will be more than willing to help you, I'm sure."

I stared at Danu's hand as Thanatos held his out to her. My heart raced as she placed her hand into his. He lowered his mouth to her hand, brushing his lips against the skin of her knuckles with a soft kiss. Her words echoed through my head as I creased my brow, uncertain what the hell she'd meant by her last words.

"She looks just like you, Danu. Though she is a lot less conniving and jilted." I tilted my head, watching the tension in Thanatos's body language.

"I know, she's my daughter," she smiled proudly. "What else would she be, other than perfect?"

Chapter
TWENTY-SEVEN

The brothers were sitting around the table, lost in their grief. Others mingled about, passing around ambrosia to those who had remained long after the funerals had ended. Lena and Lucian sat together, silently speaking with their eyes.

Callaghan studied Erie, who was on her third bottle of alcohol, while she talked to her sisters. She'd pause every once in a while, arguing with them or laughing loudly. Vlad sat quietly, taking in the details of what had happened, staring at us as we filled him in on the appointment of new kings and who we'd lost during the battle.

"So, Bilé just walked through the wards and killed them?" Vlad asked, moving his gaze between us as we nodded. "How is that even possible?"

"I think, since Danu created Faery around him, he's immune to fae magic. There's nothing about this situation that makes sense. One minute she's telling us we have to kill him, and the next she is informing us we can't, or Faery will die without him."

"Who took the souls?" Vlad asked, and I blinked.

"Thanatos," I admitted, frowning.

"Why the fuck would a god from a different pantheon come to collect the dead fae?" His silver eyes studied me carefully.

"Thanatos said it was to rebuild the walls of Hell, or so he explained when he first appeared." I shrugged at his narrowed gaze, rubbing my eyes as exhaustion weighed me down.

"All life is supposed to return to the Tree of Life," Vlad said softly. "However, it doesn't seem to be accepting new life, and isn't receiving the dead, either, if Thanatos was called in to take the souls of the fallen."

"Maybe it isn't working the way we assumed." Ryder's deep, somber tone resonated.

Vlad and I turned to look at him, and I frowned, watching the exhaustion play over his face. He had gone to war only to turn around and rush back here to protect us. Not being able to reach us in time was weighing on him. Ryder blamed himself for failing to be here or foresee the outcome. He wouldn't admit it, but I knew that's how he felt—or worse, he held me accountable.

Savlian sat alone, staring at the glass in front of him as Zahruk studied him. I stood up, smiling at Ryder when he reached for me.

"Are you okay?" he asked.

"I'm fine," I lied, smiling tightly before I moved across the floor to Zahruk. "You. Spit it out."

"Fuck off, Synthia," Zahruk snapped as he reached for the bottle and poured himself another drink.

"No, I won't. You have yet to speak since you returned."

Ignoring me, Zahruk knocked back the amber liquid and refilled his glass. When he realized I wasn't going anywhere, he glared at me. "You know, I liked you better when you didn't like me."

"That's not true. You blame me, don't you?"

"I blame myself, Synthia. I lost my brothers, and I hurt Darynda. I hurt her because I couldn't stop myself. I fucked her hard like she was nothing more than a fucking whore. I didn't hold back because I needed her to see me, to know what I liked when I fucked. She followed me around with those beautiful, vivid green eyes, thinking I was some kind of fucking hero. So when I saw her outside the feeder room, watching me take feeders with her wanton gaze, I pushed them away and beckoned her to me." Running his hands through his hair, Zahruk leaned over and rested his elbows on his knees as he stared at the floor.

"She had no idea what I was like because I'd shielded her from the truth. I bent her over and fucked her, and worse. I shared her with Cailean." Lifting his head, he glared at me with a haunted expression. "I wasn't gentle like she deserved. I wanted to hurt her so she would finally move on. She took it because she wanted me any way she could get me. I made her come for me three times before I pulled out, and when I did, I fucked her virgin ass without mercy and spread her creamy thighs for Cailean to destroy her wet flesh as it was leaking my cum. I hurt her on purpose to make her hate me. What the fuck you got to say about that?" he demanded through gritted teeth.

I slapped him hard across the face, watching his glowing sapphire eyes slowly come back to me, and I hit the other cheek harder than the first. "Feel better, asshole?"

"I hurt her!"

"Yeah, you're an asshole. Darynda was aware of it, but she was also in love with you. She had the choice to walk away. Darynda knew she could say no to you at any time. All she had to do was tell me, and it would have ended. You and I both know that. I'd have kicked your fucking ass to defend her. She told me you fucked her, and that you were rough." Dismissing me, Zahruk leaned against his elbow on the table and put his hand under his chin as he poured another drink.

I knocked his arm out from under his chin, and he turned to glare at me. I let him see my disappointment, and he looked down at the table. Sighing, I put my hand on his arm, forcing him to meet my eyes. "Do you know what you're going to do now? You're going to shut the fuck up and never tell another person what you did to Darynda. Let her go to her eternal slumber with her fucking dignity. Keep her image pure and untainted by what you did to that beautiful soul who was in love with you."

"I can't," he growled.

"Why, because you didn't get to say you were sorry for what you did to her? She knows you're sorry, Z. She fucking knows it," I whispered thickly.

"I wasn't in control when it happened, and I don't lose control, ever! I am never the one to lose control. I thought it was just another fucking nightmare. Do you have any idea how close you came to being bent over next to Eris?" Zahruk looked over his shoulder to Ryder, who was lost in conversation with Vlad. He looked back at me with panic in his eyes as he whispered, "I wanted to bend you over that table, spread your pretty thighs wide, and take what I needed from you. I wanted to feel you clenching around me, to know what it tasted like to lick your flesh after you came." He clenched his fists and lowered his voice to a hushed growl. "You're my brother's wife and the mother of his children, and I'd die before I ever did that. I'd end my life before I betrayed him, but the fact that I even thought of doing it makes me sick."

"You're such a romantic asshole, Zahruk." I winked at him and reached for his hand, but he pulled it away from me.

"Something is wrong with me and has been since I entered the Kingdom of Nightmares."

"Yeah, you're a fucking perverted prick." I studied him and replayed what he had said as my worry intensified. Plagued with nightmares? Or was he plagued by guilt because he could be a seriously fucked up asshole when he wanted to be? I bristled before slowly shrugging it off.

"Synthia, something inside of me *is* wrong. I have endless nightmares, but I don't wake from them. It's like I'm living them, and when I do think it is just another nightmare, it isn't. Like Darynda, I assumed I was dreaming. What the fuck could it have hurt to have her in my dreams? It wasn't real, so sharing her sweetness with others within a dream couldn't have hurt her, now could it? She wouldn't get attached, and there I could teach her what I was. The fact was, it wasn't a fucking dream, and it's too late to say I'm sorry. She died believing she meant nothing to me. She deserved better, and to know what it felt like to be with someone who wanted her."

"Because you didn't?" I cocked an eyebrow because I knew there was a part of Zahruk that had cared about Darynda, or he wouldn't feel this kind of remorse.

"I wanted to fuck her," he admitted, pushing his fingers through his dark hair. "I fuck hard, and I destroy when I do. I claim and mark them, and she was too pure for that. She was a maiden when she slipped into my bed, and I had no fucking idea. I wasn't gentle then, either, as I pushed through her untried flesh, marking it as mine. It wasn't mine to claim. She's pure. She was pure."

"And now she's gone. She didn't die a virgin, and she could have told you and Cailean no. It has been a rule for a while now that my handmaidens were off-limits. I think she wanted to be in that room, to know what it was like, but she didn't like it.

"She said you found her and used her, and that you were rough. She wouldn't have gone back, and she didn't say more than that to me. Darynda never spoke of what you did, or anyone else involved. You will keep that to yourself because screaming it to the world does her no good." Nodding, Zahruk reached for the bottle to fill his glass, but I caught hold of his arm. "If you ever do that again to hurt someone, I will remove your penis, and only give it back to you once a month to feed. Feel better?" I smiled tightly and then turned toward the door as the alarm sounded.

Erie nodded to the Raven Guard that fanned out, vanishing into the shadows as they searched for the threat. Lucian stood, stretching and cracking his neck as Bane, Devlin, Spyder, and another male I didn't know joined him. I moved to Ryder's side, nodding as he held out his elbow for me to accept as we started toward the battlements.

"You think it's the mages?" he asked as his brothers and the other guards who trailed behind us.

"I don't think they'd be stupid enough to come back already, but I don't intend to underestimate them again." I shivered against the heat his arm offered and stiffened my spine as we started up the staircase to reach the battlements.

On the wall, we stared out over the funeral pyres that continued to burn, sending ashes into the starlit sky of Faery. A midnight flag flew with the crescent moon and stars flowing around it. I studied the tallest male rider and the surrounding females that remained close to him. My eyes drifted to the black armor they wore, which blended into the night.

"What flag is that?" I asked cautiously.

"It's the Court of Nightmares," Ryder answered, pinching the bridge of his nose. "I summoned them to answer the marriage contract before the first wave of mages marched toward the Winter Court. Bloody hell, the arrogant prick has bad timing."

"And the flag behind the Court of Nightmares, which court's flag, is that?" I inquired, watching the troops moving closer with their russet-colored armor bearing leaves on the shoulders. "Oh, look, the Summer Court is coming, too."

"That's the Autumn Court," Ryder corrected.

"Look behind Autumn Court. Winter is here already. The lesser courts are coming, Ryder. And they're wounded," I noted, watching as the back of their numbers came into view with wagons full of creatures lying or sitting wherever they'd found enough room. "Open the gates."

"Synthia, we're at war," he growled.

"Not with them, Ryder. Faery is in trouble, and

it is leading them here. The Stag sent out a call-to-arms and named our stronghold as the gathering place to amass the troops. He also requested that the gods and goddesses congregate within these walls, along with whatever the hell Lucian is, which not even the fucking Stag knows. This is the safest place in Faery."

"Lucian is older than the Stag," Ryder shrugged as my gaze narrowed.

"I'm fucking Batman," Lucian growled beside my ear, sending a chill up my spine.

"I'm not fucking Robin, dick. I don't wear fucking tights." Spyder folded his arms over his chest, daring Lucian to argue that fact.

"No, you just dance to one-hit wonders for pretty girls," Lucian teased.

"I got Lena back. Not even your dick could do that, brother."

"You two done?" Ryder asked, and when they continued to glare at each other in silence, Ryder nodded at the guards to raise the gates and allow the lesser courts into the sanctuary of the stronghold. "We will need a bigger fucking courtyard."

I waved my hand, and the earth beneath our feet rumbled as the courtyard expanded, sending a new wall around the approaching courts before they'd even entered the gates. I stared down at my hand while the others around us stared at me. The walls grew taller while I watched, sending thorns and spikes over the tops, making them impossible to climb. It looked like something out of a horror movie, pulsing with a dark power that itched to drink blood.

"When did you discover that ability, Pet?" Ryder's wide eyes took in the massive walls and deadly thorns, smiling.

"Just now," I said. "They are safe and within the walls. They can set up camps below, and we will deal with them when we finish mourning. I need a drink, and then I need you alone for a while."

"I hope that includes us naked," Ryder grinned, and I turned, finding Spyder watching me, wiggling his brows.

"Hey, not judging. You get that dick, girl. You earned it. You also put a ring on it."

"I didn't put a ring on his cock," I frowned.

"You should. It will make that shit last longer. Not if it's a vibrating ring though, that shit ruins everything."

"Nod, smile, and walk by him. He is very immature. He's Spyder. His entire world revolves around his dick." Lucian smiled, turning away and vanishing from sight without as much as a ripple of power disturbing the air.

"He's not Batman," Spyder announced offhandedly, wiggling his brows. "He's Papa Smurf, and I'm Brainy."

"These are the guys that are supposed to keep us safe?" I whispered to Ryder.

"I'm not calling him Big Papa," Ryder said, cracking a smile.

"There it is," Spyder chuckled. "We have lost

people, and it fucking hurts. The pain seeks to destroy you from the inside out. Don't let it control you. Channel it. Use it. As Danu said, *'Anger is good, wrath is better, but rage, rage is fucking beautiful destruction.'* Winning a war is empty as fuck, trust me. We've fought a lot of them and never lost. Winning isn't some glorious fucking thing where you get a trophy at the end." He exhaled, shaking his head as his dark eyes held mine.

"You get fucking graves, and those deaths follow you everywhere.

"This war isn't about winning. It's about saving a world, and that shit isn't ever easy. Not to mention your mother, God love her tits, but she was a selfish bitch. Danu centered her entire world around her husband. Everything and everyone else that didn't fit into her world could fuck off or die for all she cared. Keep that in mind, Synthia. She wasn't lying about what she told you today."

"And what did she tell you?" Ryder asked carefully.

"That is what I wanted to speak to you about, without ears around us. Preferably after you've had your way with me, Fairy."

"You two kids have fun," Spyder chuckled, walking away.

TWENTY-EIGHT

Ryder stood silently, staring out the balcony window at the funeral pyres that continued to burn long into the night. My heart ached for him, knowing he'd lost three of his brothers in one night. Brothers he had grown up with, protecting them long before I'd ever been created.

He was in pain I couldn't fix or ease, and that knowledge wrapped around my heart, clenching it hard. It was deep-seated grief tearing him apart from the depths of his soul. He'd walked into the tower and froze, unable to move from the grisly sight awaiting him. I wanted to take the pain away, and yet I knew I couldn't. No one could erase or lessen his sorrow.

Nothing touched the grief we felt. No amount of

alcohol could numb it to a dull ache. It was a soul-deep, earth-altering sorrow that echoed through our souls, imprinting them with a darkness that held its hand upon our throats. We would survive this, but would we want to?

"I love you," I whispered to the beast, hiding silent agony from within the dark shadows of our bedroom as he watched his men mourning their families below. "I will love you forever, Ryder." I removed the necklace holding my mother's essence from my throat. She'd given it to me upon her death visage before I'd left to marry my beast. I'd worn it ever since, refusing to remove it no matter where I went or what happened.

Silence echoed through the room as Ryder stared down at Dristan's pyre. The comforting words his brother had said did little to ease his passing for Ryder. Instead, it fueled Ryder with anger, driven by a need to avenge those who had been taken from us. I was with him on that page, but to battle the gods, he'd have to be stronger than one.

I was Ryder's ride-or-die girl, and he knew it. I

didn't need to say those words out loud for him to know that whatever he did, I'd stand with him. I'd honor his choice, regardless of where it left me.

I inspected the single drop of essence as it mixed with ambrosia already in the cup I held. Placing it on the nightstand, I closed the vial. Standing, I picked up the goblet and walked to Ryder, kissing his spine while I held my hand out, allowing him to accept the drink. Swallowing hard, fear pricking against my mind, I studied the glass as Ryder lifted it to his full mouth and downed it in one gulp.

My heart knocked violently against my ribs with the knowledge of what I'd done, what it could mean for us. I wouldn't lose my husband to a god as I'd lost the others. Ristan had yet to allow another person to hold his son; not even his mother was allowed to touch the wee thing. Finley had insisted on checking the infant out, but Ristan had snarled, turning multicolored in his true form with a whisper of wings that had made us all pause and stare.

Ristan had been born with wings, horns, and a

tail, much like his son. Alazander hadn't liked how lethal those things were, so he had them removed when Ristan was old enough to survive the violent procedure.

Zahruk was currently fucking anything he could to ease the guilt he felt for Darynda, and it was troublesome. The dark circles beneath his eyes reminded of me of the nightmares he'd mentioned, sticking in my mind.

We were all falling apart tonight, and grief was driving us to act out. We were lashing out at each other as we muddled our way through the tragedy that had left us barely breathing.

"Ryder," I whispered, tears swimming in my vision as I placed my hands on his shoulders.

He turned, tilting his head. His obsidian eyes mixed with golden galaxies as if burning constellations of stars were held within them. His power flowed through the room, and his hands gripped my shoulders as an angry slant tilted the corners of his mouth. A growl vibrated through his chest, and he silently studied me as he was filled with the power of the Goddess of Faery.

"I'm so sorry, but I will not lose you," I whispered as he growled, shoving me against the wall, glaring into my eyes. "I love you enough to let you hate me." I swallowed a broken sob as his hand tightened around my throat. "For Faery and those who need us, we cannot be weak. For the people who gave all and the stars they ride, from now until forever, I claim you as My King."

"What the hell did you do?" he snarled, staring at his hand as claws extended, black and gold veins pulsing through them. The black wings on his back unfurled, the lines within them matching his veined arms. The dragon markings on his chest grew, stretching as he evolved.

"I transformed you into the beast they created you to become. Now I have made you into the God of Faery. We will not abandon the land or our people. We will fight to save both. You planned to leave Faery, and I cannot allow that to happen. The Stag told me secrets, Ryder. If the fae leave the land, they will become mortal as a man. You promised me forever, and I intend to hold you to it."

"It wasn't your choice to make, *wife*." He snorted as his eyes narrowed, turning angry and promising violence.

"No, but you would have turned down Danu's essence merely on principle. You and I, we are the only chance this world has left. You intended to take the horde away from Faery. I sensed it. I felt it to my fucking core. You didn't tell me, not because you couldn't. You chose to keep this from me because you planned to do it and then allow me to learn about what you had done after the fact. It's easier to beg forgiveness than to ask permission, right?

"Our children are tied to this land, accepted by it. I am not going to sit back and watch you become mortal. Do you understand? I will not watch you age and die and be forced to go on without you. I will not watch my children age and die with their mixed blood that links them to this land. If we abandon Faery, we become part of the next world we join. The fae are creatures of nature, and if we seek to take them out of this world, into the land of mortals, we condemn them to become that.

"I am a goddess, Ryder. You cannot make that choice for me. You cannot ask me to give you forever and then plan to take it away without so much as a whisper. *We* are *Faery* and the fae who will not bow before any god who demands we do so. Bilé can bow before us, or he can die. You changed my life without asking me, and so I have done the same to you. You brought me here. You made me love this land and those who reside within it." Ryder turned to walk away from me, but I grabbed his arm, stopping him.

"Ryder, you killed Adrian to have me, so you don't get to leave me. I would have remained mortal had it not been for you hunting me during the Wild Hunt. You transported me through a portal, igniting the fate of this world. I set it on fire when I entered. Had you never brought me here, it would have been okay."

"So you fucking poison me?" he demanded

hoarsely.

"You brought me into this fight as much as my mother did. You don't get to choose our path alone. I gave you Danu's essence, but only you can decide if you want to accept the next step. Choose me, Ryder. Don't leave me here alone. If you reject the essence of the gods, I will understand and honor your choice," I said with tears running down my cheeks.

"But you need to understand this: I *will* pull away from you. I will begin to distance myself so that when you walk away, and I am left here to fight Bilé alone, I am not brokenhearted when I do. I fed you a sliver of my soul to combine the beast within you as one. Your beast was created to hold the essence of the gods, to make you into one. I was only meant to anchor you for a little while until Danu could figure out how to turn you into a new god to rule her people. I died, and she used her life to save mine. She used the essence that was supposed to go to you for me. I stole your title by dying, and now I am giving it back to you."

"By taking my choice away?" he demanded,

growing taller as he pushed me against the wall, squeezing his hand tighter around my throat.

"You are not listening. I chose to become a goddess. I chose you instead of death. Only you have the final choice on whether you accept the essence and evolve, or refuse and you will remain the same. I only gave you the chance to choose your next move." His hand loosened, and then he stepped back, watching me as I remained against the wall.

"I have to choose what, exactly?" he snapped harshly, glaring at me with a lethal look that broke my heart. "You or my brothers' lives, Synthia? I fought for them. I have continued to fight for them. If it's between becoming a god and watching them die, you can bet your pretty little ass I will choose to save my brothers every time. I just lost three of them tonight. Three that I have fought with every-fucking-thing I had in me just to keep alive since I was old enough to do so. I have murdered thousands of creatures within this realm. Do you think the dead's families want me as their god?"

"They will follow you," I replied carefully, not moving from where he'd left standing. "If you choose to lead, they will follow you because you're not a monster. You are not your father. You fight for your brothers, not against them. They accepted me without even knowing me. You were born to be the King of Faery, and I, your queen. Who better to be the God and Goddess of Faery and of the fae than us?"

"I expect treachery from my people, from Bilé, not my fucking wife."

It felt as if he'd physically slapped me in the face. I nodded slowly as tears burned behind my eyes. "You've made your choice." I bowed my head and turned to leave the room.

I was grabbed from behind and thrown onto the bed. I lifted onto my elbows to glare at him. Ryder smiled coldly while studying me as my clothes caught fire, turning to ashes before it damaged my flesh. His black and golden wings spread wide. The talons on the edges lengthened while I swallowed hard, hissing as he allowed his power to cover every inch of my body.

"You don't get to run away from me, little girl," he snapped callously. His words rumbled from deep in his chest, followed by the sound of an inhuman growl. I sat up, only for his magic to slam into me again, knocking me back against the mattress. "You don't get to decide who I become. Obviously, you need to be reminded of who and what I am," he hissed, using magic to lift me and slam me down against the bed on my stomach. My legs spread apart while magic captured my hands, pulling them behind my back and holding them in an invisible grip.

The first assault was a slap of magic that landed on my ass, causing my body to jerk as it continued. He wasn't even touching me, and yet he was spanking my ass. I cried out with each punishing slap of magic that struck me, reddening the flesh while he studied me from across the room.

His magic filled my pussy, stretching me as if he was taking me in his beast's form. I opened my mouth, mewling, crying out as it moved hard and faster within me. Ryder pushed the magic deeper and deeper. I trembled as he held me locked between pain and pleasure, teetering on the brink of an orgasm. I felt him releasing more magic, noting the sound of his bare feet walking across the floor.

"You want to hurt me? I can hurt you too, pretty Pet. You aren't strong enough to win against me, goddess or not. I am the Horde King and everything it entails. I don't need a crown or to become a fucking god to own that sweet, tight pussy. I already fucking own it. I don't need it to win a fucking war. They created me for war and to rule this world. One trespass against me was okay. You took the beast away without asking. You combined him with me, and I forgave you easily, which was obviously a mistake.

"You think your mother is on *our* side? You were acting on instinct, and I let your trespass slide. She assumed the beast was the murderer that hid within the man. She was wrong, Pet. The beast was just the one riding within because *I* am the monster, of that you can be assured. The beast didn't murder Adrian; *I* did. The beast didn't claim your tight pussy after I hunted it down in my world. *I* did that too.

"All you did was make the monster that held the beast stronger. Alazander may not have been strong enough to hold his monsters at bay, because he was too weak to embrace his demons. I made peace with my demons long before I ever met you. I promise you, sweet wife, I am the fucking monster, and I plan to remind you of that now."

Chapter
TWENTY~NINE

Ryder was in control, his cock pushing against my lips, forcing me to open my mouth to accommodate him. His hand fisted my hair, using it to guide his shaft deep into the tightness of my throat, pulling my hair until my scalp ached and tears swam in my vision. He hissed silkily, groaning as he fucked my mouth without mercy, using the action to show me who he was, uncaring that it hurt. I didn't need a hand guide to figure out his anger was mixed with grief, and I was his outlet for both.

He withdrew without warning, causing me to cough as he turned me onto my back. Pulling my legs up awkwardly, he straddled my body, nuzzling his head between my thighs, pushing his cock back into my throat. His mouth fed ravenously against my core, licking and sucking vigorously as he fucked my throat gloriously. I moaned, unable to stop my reaction as his finger pushed into my ass, stretching it as he added another.

Ryder's magic released my hands, only to spread me wide as he continued to eat my pussy, lapping at it like a crazed beast that couldn't sate his hunger. His tongue entered my core, growing until he was fucking me with the length of it. I whimpered as it became too much to take all at once.

Light burst behind my eyelids and air refused to gain passage through my throat as the orgasm he created started to take over my basic needs, like breathing. I wouldn't reach it. I realized that fact as my legs went limp where he held them apart, fucking me hard with his tongue.

Throaty laughter rippled through the room, slithering over my flesh before he reduced the size of his tongue and stepped away from me. He watched as my body crumpled, and my chest rose and fell rapidly.

I gasped for air as I stared at Ryder walking around the bed, watching me like I was nothing more than prey.

I sat up slowly, only to be slammed down again. He spun me in place, and my legs spread until they ached where they met my body. My arms lifted, slowly roaming down my sides as his magic controlled my movements. My fingers stretched out, pushing against the pleasure nub at the center of my apex.

"Ryder…" I whimpered huskily, watching his predatory gaze find mine, locking on to it. I opened my mouth to speak, and something clamped against it, holding it open, and yet I felt nothing within my mouth. I couldn't talk, couldn't beg him to end the torture I was enduring while everything within me craved the delicious orgasm he held just out of my reach.

Stroking his cock, Ryder examined me silently as I pleasured myself, unable to stop. My fingers slid through the wetness of my core, pushing into it as I fucked myself, controlled by him. It was a slow, meticulous speed meant to keep me from coming. I moaned against the magic holding control of my throat, jerking and crying out as something pinched against both nipples hard enough to make them throb. I would come apart, and I doubted he would prevent it this time.

My hand paused, and the other one lifted, slapping my clitoris. I yelped and groaned as he used my other hand to rub where I'd just assaulted myself. Again, it happened, and my eyes rolled back in my head as pain and pleasure became hard to discern from one another. My hands were raised above my head, and I flipped over, my ass lifting while my legs spread wide. Magic moved my arms, constraining them behind my back as if they were tied in rope instead of his magic.

"Who do you belong to?" he growled.

"Fuck you…" I began to tell him off, but he was there before the words had finished leaving my tongue. He drove his cock into my mouth as magic filled my body, violent and forceful until I trembled around him with the need to come. He held his cock buried in my throat to the base, and his hand lifted, plugging my nose as he watched me. His other one slapped my ass before he slowly rubbed the tips of his fingers over the sore flesh.

"When I ask you who the fuck owns your gluttonous, needy cunt, you say my name. I am the only creature alive who can or will ever fuck you, woman. I will destroy anyone who thinks to part these hungry, clenching lips to bury their length in your heat. You are mine, Synthia. I promised you forever, and you promised me the same. You vowed to fight at my side, not fucking change what I am. You married me, and you did so knowing I wasn't a nice fucking guy.

"You keep secrets from me, and I keep them from you. You want to know why we're fucking losing? It's because you won't turn off your humanity. You won't change who you are, and yet you want to change me? Fuck you.

"Did you know I let the mages take me from our wedding? You thought they could enter my home and take me without me allowing it to happen? Who the fuck do you think I am? Do you think anyone could come in here and take me?

"I'm not weak, and I don't do anything I don't want to do. You thought I had been taken, but I wanted to be inside that fucking guild. I was there to learn our enemies, to determine their weaknesses. Those witches? The Original Witches? They're working for me now. You think I'm weak, but I assure you this: nothing happens to me that I don't fucking allow.

"Your mother's essence won't work on me because I am already a fucking god. I drank the essence inside the Temple of the First People of Faery long, long ago, before I ever set my sights on you, little girl. I am both Seelie and Unseelie, and I am also a god. I changed who I was, and I don't need my woman to think I'm not strong enough to stand beside her.

"You apparently think yourself worthy of who you became, but you are weak, woman. You refuse to accept what we tell you, what we need you to do so that you can become strong enough to stand beside *me*. I am not the one who needs to evolve, Synthia. It's you who refuses to adapt to the world that's screaming for you to save it. Turn it off. Turn that last little bit of who you were off and change your fucking self instead of trying to transform me."

I couldn't see Ryder past the stars dancing in my vision. I was passing out while he spoke, unable to push him away from me as he used my throat to cradle his cock. His deep chuckle pissed me off, his magic pissed me off, and he was pissing me off.

Ryder's hands worked my throat as he slowly pulled out, seeing me gasp for air. He turned me on the bed, smirking while I continued to gulp in air as he placed me on my stomach with my ass lifted toward him.

He offered me no reprieve as he stared at the red, swollen flesh of my sex. His hands bit into my thighs, spreading my legs open before he thrust into my body from behind.

I screamed out as he filled me, not bothering to shrink enough that I could take him easily within my pussy. It burned, creating a throbbing need inside my core that ached and pulsed. He didn't withdraw, didn't move.

Instead, he pushed two fingers into my ass, chuckling when I muttered incoherently with the need to come, to allow him to fuck me. I needed it to accommodate his girth and length, and yet he didn't let me find release.

Ryder began moving after a moment, uncaring if I was ready or not. My hips pushed against him, driven by magic as he released my hands, allowing me to grab on to the blankets where I buried my face, screaming with both anger and need.

The room smelled of magic and sex. His fae magic was still thick enough to cut with a knife. He pounded into my body with a heady beat, pausing each time I was close to release. His free hand left my ass, threading through my hair before he yanked it back. Ryder brought my back against his stomach as he stopped his fingers from stretching my ass.

He groaned as my body clenched tightly, sucking

against him to pull him in deeper than he already was. Sweat dripped from my breasts, trailing down my stomach as he turned my head, whispering into my ear.

"Tell me who owns this tight, greedy pussy that beckons me deeper within so wantonly?"

"You do, Ryder," I whimpered huskily past dried lips.

"Mean it," he ordered, slipping his cock from where my body had been milking his lengths. He allowed his magic to pick me up, and I flailed, trying to hold on to something. Anything to not fall to the floor over which I hovered.

I was dragged through the air as he sat in a chair, his magic lifting the bottle of ambrosia and refilling a single cup. He studied me carefully, his lips twisting into a sardonic smile.

"You!" I shrieked, exhaling as my bare feet touched the floor, only to have them yanked apart by magic, along with my arms. I was spread wide for his viewing pleasure, and before I could whisper another word, the gag was back. His magic filled me once again, stretching me as it entered all three holes at once, moving to the same tempo as before while he studied my reaction.

"You look so pretty, taking my magic, wife. I love the sounds you make when you're filled with my magic. The wet sound of your pussy as it's fucked hard, relentlessly clenching, begging to be stretched. The way you moan around the fullness of me inside that tight throat...Fuck, you make me so hard," he growled, tipping his cup up to take a drink. "That ass, though, it aches when I fuck it, doesn't it? You take it so well, riding the magic with such eagerness, ignoring the burn when I stretch that, too." He stroked his cock before rubbing the pearl-colored bead of precum over his swollen tip.

Magic slammed me down on my knees at his feet, causing a groan of pain to expel from my throat, and then he gripped my hair, staring into my eyes. He held his cock against my lips, watching me as I opened my mouth wider, even though it was already filled with magic. He pushed past my lips into my mouth, withdrawing the magic and replacing it with his cock.

"Suck it, greedy girl," he purred thickly, watching as I did what he instructed. "If you're a good girl, I'll let you have the whole thing in your pussy, and maybe, if you're really good, I'll let you come for me."

I shook my head as he inspected me through a cold gaze. He snorted, leaning forward. "Oh, I wasn't asking your permission. You wanted me like this, and now that I am, you don't like the result? You want to change me, yet you don't want to deal with the consequences. I drank your fucking drink fully aware of what it was. I gave you a chance to stop, to rethink what you were trying to do, and you didn't take it.

"I'm already the God of Faery, which is half the reason your mother is dead. She knew I took the essence from the Temple of the First People. She knew and did nothing about it. You had no idea what you gave me, and that's deadly, little girl. There are consequences from drinking too much or too little of a god's essence once death has occurred. Did you consider that? No, because you're putting your trust into those who don't deserve it. Do you think your mother wasn't aware of what I am?

"Do you think Danu would give her pretty daughter to someone who wasn't her equal in every way? The thing is, sweet wife, you are not my equal because you refuse to become one with this world. You're still hoping you can keep your humanity because it's all you have left from the other world. You can willingly give it up, or I'll fuck it out of you."

What?

Ryder picked me up by my waist and slammed me onto his cock. My entire body shuddered violently against the burning in my core as he stretched me too far, too quick. His deep, rumbling laughter shook through my body.

I exploded as his cock grew within me until I pushed against him, trying to escape. I still couldn't speak, couldn't do anything other than drop my head against his chest, watching as he achingly stretched me.

"You see that? I can fuck your tight ass with it too. I suggest you rid yourself of that humanity and get your head out of that world and into this one. I need you at my side to defeat Bilé. He raped my mother and then took her mind to prevent her from telling anyone he had sired all of Alazander's sons. Every single son that was assumed to have belonged to that worthless fuck," he laughed ominously, watching my eyes widen at his words.

My head lifted, and I stared at him, shaking my head as fear pulsed through me. Ryder chuckled, watching my reaction. A tight smile pulled his lips into a white line.

"I couldn't figure it out at first. Alazander couldn't fight us, nor could he sense us. Those he could sense within him, he slaughtered. The familial bond he manipulated us with? That's because Alazander was the seed that created the first male in the horde while Bilé drove him from within, using his body to betray Danu without her knowing it. Your mother and her husband formed this world, and then they took turns destroying the creatures they created to inhabit it.

Danu made the Seelie, and then she let Bilé create the males of the race.

"When she discovered how they bred, she locked them into the realm of the Seelie through a maze of tunnels that couldn't touch the Unseelie. She warned Bilé of creating life, as he is the God of Death. Danu was the Mother of the Fae. He didn't listen, and as she created women, he created the horde to plunder their tight pussies and breed monsters.

"To them, we're a fucking game. Danu made a move. Bilé made two more. Unbeknownst to Danu, Bilé destroyed the horde that she made, replacing them with his own creation. He gave them darker, more sinister traits, closer to his own nature, which is why they became her favored Court of Unseelie. She gave us a beast to rule the creatures of the court. Why do you think every heir chosen is male now since she is gone?"

I shivered as he pushed his magic over my flesh, using his finger to direct my body up and down until I was screaming as the orgasm ripped through me. His mouth opened on a gasp, and then he moaned as I felt him coming within me.

"I fucking hate you, woman," he growled thickly, taking in the way my eyes widened as my lips trembled with the words he'd just whispered. As fae, he couldn't lie. Pain clenched against my chest, wringing my heart with his words.

Tears blurred my vision while I stared at him through sweat-covered hair that clung to my face, sticky with perspiration from endless fucking. Ryder's appetite was ferocious and unquenchable in his new form, but his stamina? It was never-ending. He wasn't fully fae, and yet he fed gloriously from me, insatiably.

"I fucking love you, woman," he smirked roguishly as he observed my brows creasing to meet in the middle of my forehead. "Yeah, sweet girl, I can lie. Ready? Because I'm not done wrecking your welcoming pussy," he growled, turning me around without lifting me off of his thick cock first.

"They created the entire horde with the ability to lie. Ever wonder why the fae feed by fucking? Bilé and Danu destroyed one another with emotions, and when creating our race, it was accidentally added to the creatures they birthed while fucking one another. They fought when they made us, each one challenging the other to make the caste they weaved with magic stronger, deadlier."

Ryder lifted me to hover over the thick tip of his cock. His eyes burned with untamable heat as he studied the reaction on my face, slamming me down until I was seated on it, whimpering to escape the fullness of him within my core. He pushed me forward, forcing fingers into my ass and causing my body to shiver violently.

"Oh, come on, Goddess. I want to play here too. The sooner you discard the pesky thing holding you back, the sooner I can wreck this tight ass while listening to your sweet noises. You want me here," he growled, pushing deeper until I was making inhuman noises as my body struggled to accept him. I fought the orgasm he held just out of reach as it begged to come, and he knew it. He sensed it and toyed with me until I was sobbing from the need to come undone. "I feel your body greedily begging me to fill it."

I exploded, screaming his name, my body trembling so hard that tears swam in my vision from the pleasure and pain. I shivered at the rawness of him, forcing me to accommodate his girth and the magic he wielded against me. He growled huskily, using magic to lift me up as I jerked and shook with the orgasm that left me boneless.

"Who's a fucking god now, little girl? Bilé created me, and Danu created you. Who do you think is stronger? You, who was created with love, or me, who was created from the Celtic God of Death himself, Synthia?" he growled, kissing my spine gently with heated lips that held me in a never-ending orgasm.

I was still being lifted and fucked hard. Ryder's lips brushed against my neck and spine, his fingertips caressing my sides as he spoke. He slipped his hands over my breasts, tweaking the heated tips and squeezing as I whimpered.

"*You*," I screamed through the orgasm.

"Now, do you want to be honest? You tried to change who I am because you think me weak. Am I weak, Pet? Do I feel weak to you?" he asked, watching as I landed on the bed. He sifted on top of me, entering me as he spread my legs, giving himself further depths as he battered against my cervix. "I planted children into your weak, mortal womb. You fucking died on me, and I didn't change you. I didn't bring you back as something you wouldn't want to be. I loved you enough to let you go. So, know this, if my time comes, I'm ready. You don't get to decide who I am, and you sure as fuck don't get to change me into something else."

"I was trying to protect you," I whispered on a moan.

"No. You were trying to decide my fate because you assumed I would run. I'm not fucking running. This is my world, and these are my people. I changed who I was to force the goddess to create you. I needed to make her give me someone strong enough to carry my children so they could remove her from this world, ridding us of their fucking games. Imagine my surprise when my sweet little lover dies, and Danu sacrifices herself to bring you back. Don't look so surprised, Pet. I do fucking love you.

"You were a shock to me because I never intended to fall in love with you, let alone learn how to love. I only intended to pretend until I no longer needed you. But you, you're a fucking addiction I can't kick, one I never want to, either. You're the stars in my darkest skies and the light that kisses upon my flesh when I stand in your presence. You are embedded in my soul. A soul I was never supposed to have and never felt until the moment I watched you and knew what true beauty was. You were the first thing I ever craved to own or touch in my entire life. Yeah, I fucking killed your little boyfriend to achieve that goal, so fucking what. That little boy didn't understand you, nor did he make you weep to come as I do. He was weak, and you needed more.

"Synthia, you knew he was lacking, but you craved the safety of him because anything else terrified you. But then I fucked you, and the moment you screamed my name as you came, you undid me, and I knew you'd never escape me after that. No one had ever fucked me and made me feel even a sliver of what you did after the Wild Hunt. That wildness in your cries as you fucked me, and the fire that banked in your pretty eyes? You made me want something more, something I had never thought to be good enough to receive.

"Hell, sweet girl, you're so fucking good you tamed the beast and made him purr to be wrapped in your tight pussy." He kissed me, nipping my lip before he pulled away. "But back to the Original Witches," he growled, slamming into my body. "I know how to kill the gods. I know because while they thought me mindless, I listened. I also know how to bring the mages to heel. I can't do it without you, though, so give me your fucking humanity. It won't do you any good here, anyway."

"Get off me," I hissed.

"Make me, woman," he growled, slowing his hips from where he was rocking them to the perfect rhythm of the drums outside. Maybe it wasn't drums. It might have been my blood pounding in my ears as my orgasm reached its crescendo, and everything went dark around me. I felt him removing the magic that bound me, whimpering as he withdrew it completely from my body. "Rest well, sweet wife. Round two starts shortly."

Chapter
THIRTY

I lay in the bed, staring at Ryder, who watched me from the chair. I could hear the men outside training, but that had been going on for days while Ryder held me in a constant state of nothingness. I might as well have been FIZ for all I could do as he fucked me until my brains were little more than mush. I lifted, falling back to the bed as a sinful smile lifted across his mouth. He studied me as I struggled to get out of the bed he'd placed me on when I'd passed out from being fucked senseless.

"Is that pussy sore? It sure is a beautiful shade of red, Pet. You're wet, dripping our essence from your pretty, wrecked cunt that already beckons me to fuck it again. Tell me, do you want more?"

"Danu created the Horde King," I muttered barely above a whisper.

"No, she was too busy patting herself on the back for her creation to look closely enough at the genetics. She never imagined Bilé would murder her creation and replace it with his own. Your mother was a cocky, selfish goddess. She assumed she had control, but she didn't. Do you know what I learned when I was in the guild?"

"That you're a lying bastard?"

"Oh, don't be upset. I never lied to you. Yes, I omitted the truth of what I am to you, and I admit I kept a few other things from you also, like how the witches and mages could steal me away on our wedding day. But let's be honest here, Syn, you fucking hated that wedding. By allowing the witches to think they held control over me, it allowed you to have the wedding you actually wanted," he said, resting his arms over his knees to study me.

"While I was with the witches, I learned that Bilé is the God of Death and the Dead. He agreed to fetch the dead and take them to the Underworld via the Tree of Life in Ireland before man was created. However, the name they used was the World Tree. Interesting, isn't it, that Ireland, where your mother's first people were created, has a tree matching the one Faery was created around? We thought our world was dying because of the damage the mages were inflicting, when in fact, it's because the Tree of Life isn't a tree at all. It's Bilé. She told you that you couldn't kill him and keep the land. Now, do you understand why?" he tilted his head as my eyes rounded.

I tried to sit up again, only to expel a heavy breath from my lungs as my apex screamed with pain. It was delicious pain, yet pain all the same. Ryder intended to fuck me into oblivion, to take away my humanity. He didn't get it or could figure out that it couldn't be extracted. I had to eradicate it myself.

"I see you're following along, so that must mean you need to be fucked again," he said huskily. "I am enjoying this a little more than I should, but being buried in your warmth is my favorite place in the entire world. In fact, I think you're the most beautiful thing your mother ever created. You're definitely the most stubborn creation she's used on me."

"If it is true, then why wouldn't the Stag just tell me?" I countered hesitantly, turning over onto my back and groaning loudly as my body burned from being overused. It took everything I had just to roll over. He'd depleted me, sapping all my strength until I was too weak to crawl away from him.

"Because the Stag is actually Cernunnos, the Lord of the Wild Things," Ryder chuckled. "He is also known as the Horned God, and he is Zahruk's grandfather. Cernunnos created the shapeshifters, and then Danu gave his only daughter to Alazander as a test to see what would come from fucking a wild thing. Unfortunately, she wasn't impressed. So your mother and Bilé created more creatures and fed them to my father to breed. They made him go mad with the need to breed, creating an army of Bilé's sons under the guise of needing to produce a daughter, which Danu assumed would balance the world out as she desired it to be. Only when Ciara was born, she wasn't what Bilé expected, so he had Alazander take her apart to see why she wasn't equipped to save the world. Danu saw this and began making plans to create you.

"Synthia, we are nothing to Danu and Bilé. We're the game pieces they move around when they want something or become bored. So, we slowly rebuilt ourselves to become strong enough to stop them. I started exploring the world while following my father's orders. Zahruk helped me, and others joined against them. I'm tired of being their toy. I will not allow Bilé to destroy this world because he is grieving. He gets one option, he takes this," he said, holding up the vial from my necklace. "He can either crawl his worthless carcass back to the Underworld, or he dies, and we leave here and go to the world we will create."

"You expect me to believe you? You've been lying to me since day one!"

"I told you not to underestimate me, little girl. I told you I am the biggest and strongest thing in all of Faery. You didn't listen, and it's been fun watching you try to put the pieces together. I was willing to play along with your mother's games, but then you tried to fucking turn me into the god that I already am. You wanted to change who and what you thought I was. I told you from day one I wouldn't change for anyone, not even you. I am who they created me to be, and while you helped me greatly by combining the beast, the one thing Bilé couldn't accomplish—nor your mother, for that matter—you don't get to take away my choices.

"I never took away your choices, Synthia. You only think I did. I stood by and watched you walk away from me to save the land. You almost married Adam because you wanted to save the world to protect your precious human race. You walked away from me by choice. You entered Faery during the Wild Hunt—again, by choice. I offered you an out, Syn. I offered to open those fucking doors in that club to allow you to leave with no questions asked. The only time I ever intervened with your choices was when you held my children within your womb."

"We lost a child so that I could get you back!" I cried.

"No, we lost a child because you thought I was fucking weak. You didn't trust me to get out of that situation on my own. You violated the laws of the gods. I never imagined you would come for me. You weren't supposed to do that."

"You realize that if I hadn't, you'd have fed on an entire room of children. You were crazed when I reached you, Ryder, mindless with hunger."

"That's the difference between us. I have no humanity, Synthia. I wouldn't give a shit. I love very few things. My brothers, my wife, and the lives she and I create together. This world? I've never pretended or told you otherwise. I care about fixing it and preventing the loss of life, but only because losing them hurts the woman I love. I was in your world to find you, and I did. I found this beautiful creature with a fucking mouth on her that drove me bugfuck crazy. She argued with me. *Me!* The one creature no one inside Faery tried to challenge, and yet here she was, this tiny little firecracker that stared me down with the passion and fire of a thousand burning suns. You were the most infuriating, stubborn, pigheaded, and most beautiful thing I'd ever dreamt of or seen.

"The first time I fucked you, your pretty gaze ignited and glowed with pleasure. And then you came undone, screaming for me, and I realized right then you'd never walk away from me. I wouldn't allow it, and I still won't. Then you fucking died, and my world stopped turning, and I knew. I knew this crazy fucking thing you called love was real. I felt a void inside of me that would never be filled. You marked me deeper and harder than any brand could ever do. I love you, Synthia Raine. I love you so fucking much that you make me ache with the intensity of it. But I really need you to turn off your humanity, because time isn't something we have a lot of right now."

"It isn't that simple," I whispered, tears burning in my eyes. "It's not a switch that can be turned off. You can't just say to turn it off and expect it to be done. It's ingrained inside of me. I was raised with humans. I was born thinking I was one. This isn't something you can fuck out of me, Ryder."

"You can either turn it off or watch Faery die

around us. I told you I wasn't your fucking prince. I'm the king. I am the one thing holding this court in place. Since you have been down, exhausted from having your greedy little cunt fed, the world has begun to reshape itself. I am reshaping it. Either get on my side or get the fuck out, Synthia. You don't get to straddle both worlds anymore. I lost my brothers because you can't be what this world needs. Ristan lost Olivia because you can't man the fuck up and shed that little sliver you're grasping on to. I won't allow myself to hold on to you if we're not what you want.

"I'll give you twenty-four hours to figure out on which side you belong. It's either ours or theirs, sweet girl, because you can't have both anymore. You can't straddle that line anymore because we will not win this war if you do. At the end of the twenty-four hours, if I don't receive an answer, I will begin hunting you down.

"I will place god bolts into your body and toss you into a fucking cage if that is what it takes to be certain you are safely tucked away from those who seek to murder you. I can't have you fighting against me because you're the one thing I can't fight. Tick-tock, little one, time is wasting. Do whatever the fuck you need to do, but you're either on my side in this world or you're not. If you choose the human world, know that I will never stop hunting you down. I will never rest until I capture you and know you're safe from harm and protected from this war. If I were you, I'd start making my decision soon."

"You're kicking me out?" I snapped, struggling to get up.

"No, I'm choosing us, our family, and this world. You're not. You're hanging on to the scared, confused little girl who grew up in the human realm, instead of the fierce fucking goddess who belongs at my side. You're a fucking liability right now, our weakest link. Everyone stood beside you. They said you did every-fucking-thing you could to protect the ones we lost in the tower and defend the stronghold. They have all said that you did everything you should have done, except for one thing: You still haven't chosen Faery. You continue to cling to that worthless shred of humanity. You were born fae, Synthia, not human.

You have no place inside that world; you never did. The only way you can ward against Bilé is by being stronger than he is inside *this* world, and to do that, you have to choose Faery.

"Why won't you accept the power that's just within your grasp? All you have to fucking do is reach for it. You can't fight two wars at once and give them both your best. I love you, but I won't let you take everything from me. I won't lose more of my family, because when they are gone, that is it. They die, and it's fucking final. I can't do that, not even for you. Not when the solution is within your fucking grasp, and you are refusing to take it."

"I chose Faery," I whispered through tears.

"No, you chose me. You stand at my side, but you're not here with me. We can't have secrets between us anymore. We need to be in this together, sweet girl, but you're not fucking here. You let me know when you decide what you're going to do." Leaning down, Ryder kissed my cheek and sifted, leaving me alone.

Three hours later, my eyes were swollen shut from

crying until I couldn't see past the haze in them. I walked into the horde's throne room, where Ryder sat on the throne, staring at me as I passed by him. His gaze narrowed as he took in my disheveled appearance. He was right, and it hurt. I was here. I was his. I was also uncertain I could shed my humanity because, without it, I'd lose the last piece of me, of who I used to be.

I turned, unable to look at Ryder before I headed toward the great hall, ignoring the people who stopped to watch as I passed them. The guards opened the doors wide, and I walked blindly through them and away from the stronghold. I didn't stop when people called out to me, nor did I acknowledge those that bowed around me. I pulled the crown from my head, turning to stare up at where Ryder watched me from the battlements. With a sad smile and a tear rolling down my cheek, I dropped my crown on the ground and vanished.

Chapter
THIRTY-ONE

I landed in the Fairy Pools, hissing at its icy chill. Standing up, I shook off the water and looked around at the large trees that glowed. Tiny fairies hiding within the security of the trees stared at me as I climbed out from the slick rocks of the fast-running creek. I approached the fairies, dropping down to lean against the tree.

They swarmed me, touching my hair and face before landing all over my arms. They were like tiny insects that buzzed with the speed of their wings, hovering every so often, similar to hummingbirds as they flew.

"Goddess," one whispered in awe.

"Queen of the Horde," another insisted.

"Lost, is she?" a male whispered to a female holding his hand.

"She's not lost. She's looking to be found," the female replied.

"Human?" I studied the pair absently, pushing my wet hair away from my face.

"No, you're of this land. Look around you," the male said, stretching his arms, indicating our surroundings.

Nearby animals lifted their heads from feeding to peer curiously at me, while other creatures moved closer as if they didn't believe I was really here. Maybe I needed to get out of the castle more often—if I was technically allowed back in, that was. I stood slowly, trying not to unseat the tiny fairies while curious eyes watched me. Unnerved, I shook my arms, ridding myself of their invasion, and sifted again.

This time I appeared outside of the Blood Kingdom, staring at torn banners and others that'd been set afire when the castle fell. Tears swam in my eyes, blurring my vision as I remembered entering the kingdom for the first time.

I'd been so nervous about how Lasair would respond to me, or if I'd even be accepted. I'd also wanted to murder Cailean for kidnapping me, but I'd found my family because of him. Instead, I'd discovered a family who accepted me for me and had fallen in love with them, too. There was an eerie silence that filled the world now, as if it was holding its breath, waiting to exhale. I picked up a stone and chucked it at the castle gates.

It hurt because they'd left, but not by choice. If Ryder was correct, and I really hated that the asshole usually was, I was to blame. I blamed myself enough for the both of us, so it was a possibility. The thought of that sent a pang of regret mixed with guilt rushing through me. It was a lot of pressure for a twenty-two-year who never planned on facing anything like this. I'd thought I was doing pretty good, considering I'd been thrown into the fire and hadn't allowed myself to get scorched by the flames.

I picked up another rock and threw it as hard as I could. Silently, I watched it bounce off the crumbling gates and landed in a pile on the ground. If accepting Faery would have prevented this tragedy, why hadn't they tried harder to make me? I'd let everyone down, and if I were them, I'd hate me. Maybe I didn't belong here, after all.

A noise sounded from behind the battlement. I narrowed my eyes, sifting to land on top of the wall. I peered down at a group of men with swords, lying in wait to ambush whoever walked through the hole in the gates. They were all wearing random armor with both the Light and Blood Kingdom's emblems on their chest, indicating these men were at both battles. These were members of the mage army in disguise, which meant they needed to die horribly.

I sifted, landing between them, watching as their eyes widened. "So, what are we doing? How are we today, and which team are we on?" When they started to respond, I waved their words away. "I don't actually care about you, or which team you're playing for. That's a moot point, considering the armor you're wearing. Let's talk about me, shall we? I have a dilemma. I was told that I have to pick a side, and I don't know how to do that. I'm actually from Faery but brought up by humans in their world. You know, kind of like you assholes. So, how did you choose a side?"

They stared at me curiously, and I could tell that none of them knew who I was. One mage opened his mouth to respond, closed it, and then opened it again. "Uh, I was told there was a war coming, and that if I fought in it, I could go where people would understand me. All I needed to do was come here to Faery, and then just do what they said without question."

"And just like that, you signed up to fight in a world with creatures who hated humans?" I countered, narrowing my gaze on his too-thin build, noticing the pain in his eyes. He looked like he hadn't eaten a decent meal in a long time, or ever known a good home.

"Oh, well, as someone who was working his way through the human food chain and bound to get killed by the guild, it was an easy choice. I wanted to claim Faery as my world so I could slip in and slip out while dining and dashing, I guess you could say." He shrugged.

I wiggled my fingers and watched as he burst into flames, falling on the ground, screaming. "You have to admit, you had that coming. Eating humans is bad. Next?" I asked, turning to find the others running away from me. "Oh, no, sorry," I called out at their retreating backs. "That wasn't on the list of options from which you could choose." I sifted, landing in front of them as they drew swords. My hand lifted, and the moment they moved to lunge, they were engulfed in flames as well. "You guys really should learn to use your words."

I moved deeper into the castle, stepping over the dead who'd been forgotten. Hierarchy played a considerable role in this world. I'd removed it from the horde, and we'd burned our soldiers with honors most men fought to obtain. I'd placed Darynda beside princes, marking her royalty in my eyes. To me, they'd been people. They'd been my family, and they'd accepted me. What the fuck had that gotten them?

Dead.

I left a trail of death in both worlds. What if I didn't belong in either? That was my hold-up. What if I abandoned the humans, and I didn't fit in here?

If I left Faery, I knew I wouldn't fit into the human world. Sure, I could visit, and I could assist Alden with the guild, but only from the shadows. I wasn't part of that world anymore. Here, I led at Ryder's side. I was nothing without him, though, not in this or any world. If he left me, I'd become some pathetic creature that everyone pitied. Shit, I'd pity myself if he left me because I craved him in an unhealthy way.

Love was such a two-sided sword that cut both ways. I'd never once felt this with Adrian. When I walked away from him, I hadn't worried about what I would become afterward, because I knew I'd be okay. Ryder was different. Everything about us pulled us together, but he'd lied, even though he'd told me he couldn't. Ryder expected me to understand that was the case at first, but time had passed, and he hadn't offered me the truth. He didn't trust me enough to tell me what he truly was.

Did I keep secrets? Yes, but only because the walls were listening, and I couldn't just take Ryder out of the castle because his archaic laws prevented it. He'd kept me under his thumb, driving me to do what the horde needed me to do, so I'd planned Eris's downfall on my own. Was it a betrayal? No. I'd been trying to save my family and thought I was doing what was right.

Did I mean to rid him of the beast? Hell, no. I loved the creature that'd given me my babes, and would never want him gone. Would I have stopped what happened? I wasn't sure I would've since I hadn't even realized I was doing it. But now, I couldn't trust Ryder and that hurt.

He loved me, but he'd lied to me. *He could fucking lie this whole time!* So what was the truth? What part of us was even real? I held secrets that Danu asked me to keep hidden from the man I loved. I thought I'd been protecting him, but I hadn't. I'd been hurting him.

Ryder was a fucking god! I'd unknowingly married a god, and I'd created children with him. My entire life was fabricated from the point of birth in lies. My whole world was crumbling around me, and I had nothing left.

There was no one I could turn to and nowhere to go. Everything that had ever happened to me was by design, and not something I created. I was the product of a destiny Danu and Ryder had chosen for me.

Now I was stuck in my worst nightmare, living in a world that I wasn't sure would accept me while being removed from the only one I'd ever known. It was a violent rejection while being told everything was my fault.

I wasn't even very old by human standards, and everyone expected me to do shit that people centuries older than me were doing, and I hadn't figured out how to accomplish it yet. My life had been one rejection after another, filled with death.

Everyone I loved died, and it wasn't just death, they died horribly! I'd been tossed from Faery, hidden in the human world, and then brought back here to save it. It wasn't like anyone asked me what I wanted.

The beast mounted me, and he'd fucking bred me like one. Not that the sex was bad, but he'd placed life into my womb without asking me if I wanted it. I hadn't ever considered becoming a mother. Adrian and I had never even spoken about it because our careers had come first. In our line of work, it meant early retirement. So, I'd pushed off even thinking about it.

I loved my children, but what kind of life were they living? I'd hidden them from angry gods and mages who literally murdered me to get to them. Since the first breath they'd taken, they'd been targets. I was their mother, and I wasn't strong enough to protect them.

Ryder hadn't sent them away because he couldn't protect them. No. He'd sent them away because I wasn't able to protect them if we were attacked. I'd listened to him since, as their mother, my job was to do what's best for them. Our enemies knew I was weak. I seriously hated it when Ryder was right.

Sifting into the castle, I moved up the empty stairs to my bedroom, which had also been destroyed. I sat on the stone seat that had once been the windowsill. The inside of the castle was like a tomb, much as the dragon palace had been. I stood after some time had passed, staring at the rotting legs that stuck out from under the bed.

Outside the room, I moved toward the tower we'd built here, finding it destroyed much as ours had been. Inside, there was blood everywhere. The blood of Liam's own children covered the floor. He seemed so brave and untouchable. Scarred by Alazander, the old Horde King, he still stood fierce and proud in the face of the new one.

Liam had protected my children, and I'd let him down. I hadn't been back to our tower. I was unable to look at the stairs without seeing the blood that had covered them, or Dristan's severed body outside the children's playroom. I was weak with grief because I'd failed them, and deep down, I blamed myself.

I turned, surveying the glyphs I'd placed, and then noted the old wards Lucian had placed before I'd overwritten them with my own. Lucian warned us they would weaken, so I'd replaced them. That was probably the cause of everyone dying because I was too weak to outdo a god in his own world.

I sent a whisper of power rushing through the Blood Kingdom, righting the wrongs while burying the dead in nameless graves. I placed flowers over the dirt that covered their bodies, forcing them to sprout from seeds to blanket the mass graves in vibrant colors.

Lifting my hand, I sent magic to the castle, raising it higher, making it stronger until it was once again a proud stronghold that could withstand a siege while offering a safe place for Liam to rule. I owed him that much.

Soon his palace was just that: a vast, sprawling stronghold that spread as far as the eye could see. I placed beautiful, foreboding fountains of blood out front as a reminder of who owned it. Skulls lined the tops of the walls, a warning to anyone that thought the Blood Kingdom was weak. Large red flags the color of arterial blood lined the battlements, while smaller flags covered the outside grounds.

I stepped back, tilting my head to take in my handiwork before I vanished. I visited the Dark Kingdom next, staring at the carnage that littered the courtyard and the once-proud walls of the palace. I pushed past it, reminding myself that this place had been my first excursion into Faery, other than being hunted by Ryder.

Lifting my arm, I looked at my wrist before dropping it to stare up at the twin suns. If Ryder was the holier than thou god of the land, the asshole needed to pick a sun so I could tell when my time was running out. I flicked my wrist, righting the damage to the courtyard before frowning at the castle.

It was huge and screamed Castle of Doom to the rafters. I smiled. It had terrified me to come here. I'd put on a brave face while my heart shattered into a million pieces at the idea of leaving Ryder. I'd fallen in love with the enemy, and fuck if I hadn't fallen fast and hard for him.

Inside the castle were mages, lounging about, oblivious to the fact that it wasn't their palace. I flicked my wrist the moment they moved, freezing them in place.

"It's so rude and just plain disrespectful to pillage and plunder the dead. You are mages, right? I mean, you come from the same world that I do, and yet here you are, plundering this tomb as if you have the right. You don't. This is my best friend's home, and you are not welcome. But since you *are* here, let's chat. How did you decide on which team to go with? What made you want to be welcomed into this deadly, honest-to-gods horror story of a world? I mean, even the flowers will fucking kill you here."

They stared up at me, frozen where they sat or stood. When no one spoke, I frowned.

"It isn't a trick question." I strolled in between the

mages frozen on the floor. "I was born to believe I was human, so I adopted their rules and laws. I was then brought here and told I was of Faery." Pointing an accusing finger at one of the mages against the wall, I smiled. "Then you motherfuckers killed me, and whoops, I became a goddess." Shrugging, I continued walking. "Now, I have to pick between the human world or Faery."

"And you're not sure which world's side you want to fight for?" one of the mages asked, cocking his head to the side.

"Oh, no, I totally want to slaughter all of you. That's a given; you killed me. You hunt my babes, and for what? Because some stuck-up courts decided you weren't good enough? You should have accepted the horde. They're ruthless, but considering what you guys have done to us, you'd have fit right in. All the other courts, they were okay, but I mean, if you were planning to join one that would have your back, Ryder would be the one you'd want. My problem is that I have to choose my humanity or Faery. I'm afraid that if I can figure out how to eradicate it from my soul, I'll lose everything that makes me who I am. Following?" I asked, noting his wide eyes.

"Are you having some kind of mental breakdown?" another one asked.

Turning toward the mage that spoke, I considered his question, then shook my head. "No, I think I'm losing everything, and I don't know how to stop it. I also don't know how one is expected to just get rid of a sliver of humanity. I mean, how am I supposed to know how to cut it out?" I sighed.

"I have a knife," one offered.

"I don't think I'm expected to literally cut it out, idiot. It's more of a metaphor, I think, or actually hope."

"Just trying to help," he shrugged. "You could ask our god how you get rid of it," he smiled, exposing his blackened teeth.

"Dude, you seriously need to see a dentist. And you guys know that Bilé is *the* God of Death and the Dead. I mean, who willingly says, *'let's go follow*

Death,' because that screams *brilliant*. Why am I asking you guys?" I muttered, and when black-teeth started to respond, I snapped my fingers, watching him explode all over his friends.

One by one, the mages exploded the moment they spoke until silence filled the palace. I tilted my head, snapping my fingers again to slaughter the ones that were hidden out of sight. Looting was utter bullshit and just plain trashy. You had to be a pretty shitty person to loot the dead.

I didn't bother walking any deeper into the palace. I decided to sit beside the corpses while I rearranged Adam's fortress to fit his personality: dark and oh, so beautifully broody. I'd also checked every closet he owned for that body we were missing. If he had it here, it wasn't in his home.

I placed skulls all over the tables as centerpieces and hung pictures of naked chicks all over the walls to fuck with him. I added the guild's new symbol on the ceiling, and then some penis-shaped pillows on the round sofas. I wouldn't go to the Palace of Lights, not because I didn't like Asher, but because Faery suns were beginning to set when I had finally finished putting shit in random places to drive Adam mad.

I sifted again, standing in the bushes where I looked down at the Fairy Pools where Ryder stood, gazing into the glowing water. Power radiated from him, and I knew without him peering in my direction that he'd felt me entering the clearing. He turned his head slowly, staring up at me as I watched him.

"Time's up," he warned. Cracking his neck, he rolled his shoulders as fire ignited in his amber depths.

"Is it? Didn't notice the time, Fairy," I muttered, watching as he prepared to hunt me down like a dog.

"I'm not going to lie and say I won't enjoy this," he growled, donning his armor. "I enjoyed hunting you down and claiming you as mine last time. If I wasn't mistaken by the way you screamed my name as I fucked you, you liked it, too. Not to mention, you didn't run too hard. I give it an hour before I have you beneath me, woman."

"The difference is, Ryder, last time you promised me passion. This time, you promise me pain. This time, I plan to run," I smirked, feeling the air displacing as he gave chase and sifted. "Catch me if you can," I whispered through the fabric of the world as I appeared in another place, sailing straight for jagged rocks. He appeared above me, watching me fall.

"Synthia," he snapped, and I vanished seconds before I would have landed on the rocks. "Naughty girl, this should be interesting."

Chapter
THIRTY~TWO

I appeared inside the Winter Court, shivering as icy cold air bit at my skin. Glamouring on a white snowsuit to stave off the chill, I hid against the snowcaps within the Icelandic mountaintops. Ryder sifted in less than ten feet from me, staring down at the snow before he searched the white, well, everything. His nose lifted in the air, and he turned. I hesitated a moment too long, watching him.

He was a predator hunting down his prey. Obsidian eyes burned with the ambers of fiery flecks as they settled directly on my location. A dangerously wicked smile curved his lips as he tilted his head, growling huskily. The sound of crunching snow made my eyes dip to his dark boots, and I smirked as snow began to fall around us.

"You planning to get fucked in the snow, pretty girl?" he rasped, his heated gaze sliding over the tight suit I wore. His mouth twisted into a grin as if he assumed I was giving up and accepting the inevitable.

"Not at all," I murmured. I held up my hand while he watched, snapping my fingers as snow slid from the mountains above me. He disappeared, and I vanished the moment he hit the snowbank I'd been leaning against. I pictured water in my mind and smiled as I dropped through the air, freefalling.

I fell into a pool of water, pulling myself out as I looked around the area. Heads turned from creatures I couldn't identify, all staring at me. I winced as I took in their three eyes and the pale, pasty color of their skin. I sifted again the moment the air grew heavy with power. Ryder could get his jollies off with those things, not me. My body slammed against something squishy as I reappeared. I let out a snort of breath before I pushed off from whatever I had landed on, peering sheepishly down at a very dead redcap, now covered in blood.

"Oops," I said, turning as Ryder appeared, noting the blood that covered my dress.

"Sloppy."

"Accidental death by Goddess?" I shrugged, disappearing again. Sloppy was right. I glamoured on a new dress mid-sift and tossed the one old one off the edge of a cliff. I sifted, only to appear a few feet from where I'd dropped the blood-soaked dress.

Ryder sifted in, sniffing the air, then he crouched, staring down the cliff's impressive drop. I sifted in behind him as he spun around and pushed him off before I followed him over the edge. I sifted the moment he reached for me, but not before I caught the horrified look on his face. He wasn't happy I'd gotten the jump on him. I, on the other hand, was pleased as punch.

I reappeared in the Fearless Forest and started running through the thick brush. I realized that if I continued to sift after expelling so much magic to rebuild kingdoms, I'd fizzle out quickly. Howling erupted behind me, which caused the hair on my neck to rise with warning as the Hounds of the Wild Hunt snarled loudly. I turned back in the direction I'd come, staring into the darkened forest.

"Cheater," I growled, turning to run the moment Ryder came into view. He walked through the woods, stalking me as he watched me through narrowed eyes.

He sifted in front of me, and I sifted away, vanishing into a different kingdom altogether. This one had a blazing sun, and I couldn't see anything past the searing of my eyeballs. I used my arm to shield the light and took in the white sandy beaches and turquoise waves that crashed against the shore. The heavy scent of coconuts floated through the air, and I inhaled the heady scent with vigor.

"You're weakening, little queen." Ryder stood directly in front of the sun, blocking out his features, concealing them in the shadows. "Either that or you want to be caught." I vanished to the sound of his husky laughter echoing in my ears.

The meadows broke my fall, connecting with my face as I landed in the flowers. I sat up, staring down at my pollen covered hands, then lifted my head, finding Ryder protected in his armor, slowly walking through them toward where I sat on the ground.

"Come touch me," I begged huskily. Standing, I stripped off the dress, holding it in my hand as Ryder closed the distance between us. His eyes lowered to my body as his armor vanished. A cocky smile lifted his lips, and victory sparkled in his eyes. The moment he got close, I kicked him in the balls. "That's for lying to me!" I sifted, tossing my dress in the next location I landed before sifting out immediately. I hit the next spot, turning to wait for him, but arms wrapped around me, and a low, angry growl vibrated through me.

"You want to play rough?" he asked, grabbing my hair as he twisted my head, nipping against my neck.

I slammed my head back against his face and disappeared, falling into the grass of a new area as my head spun in circles. I struggled to get up from the ground, drained of magic. Glamouring on a skirt and tight top, I stared out over the greenery and saw the hounds baring their teeth at me. They closed in on me, surrounding the area I stood in as he watched.

"That's cheating."

"It isn't a fucking game, woman." Ryder hissed, and I jumped to a new place, waiting for him.

I couldn't outrun him. This was his playground. Ryder was too powerful, and I was exhausting my power trying to stay ahead of him. I repeatedly sifted, rubbing my scent all over random things in each place I visited before moving on to the next.

When I'd jumped to over twenty locations, and figured I'd sent him on a merry little search, I ran into the Forest of Flurries and didn't stop until I was out of breath. I studied the landscape, watching everything I passed until I found the entrance to a dark cave. Normally, it would have seemed like a foolish thing to walk into. Today, however, I was already on a roll, and the cave beckoned to me.

Slowly, I entered, hearing my blood pumping in my ears and feeling my heart thundering against my chest. I shivered. The sound of dripping water echoed off the walls, warring against the thumping of the blood rushing through my veins as I moved deeper.

Turning toward the sound of the water, I frowned. My eyes locked on to writing that covered both sides of the cave as light began to flood the cave. I scrunched up my face, reminding myself that this was the perfect setup for a horror movie where the blonde rushed headfirst into the serial killer's arms and got her ass murdered.

It wasn't a cave, after all. It was a tunnel with a light at the end that continued to call me forward. Once I was through the opening, I peered out at vast greenery that looked like something out of a fantasy movie. Waterfalls covered high cliffs, pooling into lazy creeks that ran through the meadow in which I lazily walked across.

In the distance sat an eerie-looking castle that reflected the sun's last light as the red sunset splashed across the sky. The angle of the palace made it look as if it had been bathed in blood, and the closer I got, the more I realized it might be.

Bodies lay strewn all over the meadow in varying stages of decay. Tilting my head, I knelt down, studying the silverish white hair of a corpse before touching it. Seelie? My gaze slowly moved over the remains of the dead to the large, elegantly built palace, and I smirked.

"Asher, you naughty boy," I whispered, heading in the path the bodies seemed to have come. I reached a trail that led beside the fortress and deeper into the city I could see beyond it. At the end of the trail was a large, round pit that sat dead in the middle of town. It looked as if it went on forever into the earth. Something called me to it, something I couldn't understand, and yet everything inside of me said to take a leap of faith. "Bottoms up," I said, dropping into the pit.

I landed hard, falling on a rotting corpse before I pushed off the ground, staring at piles of bodies in varying states of decay. "What kind of idiot listens to the voices in a pit of death?" My hands balled tightly into fists at my sides, and I closed my eyes.

I moved to sift and opened my eyes, noting I was still in the pit. I peered into the dark cave that sat inside the hole I'd dropped into. The hair on my neck rose as something watched me from the shadows, peering at me as if it saw directly through me.

My feet stopped before I could enter the cave, spinning around in a circle as I took in the strange writing on the walls, written in crusted blood. More corpses sat staring lifelessly up at the sky, as if they'd wished to feel the sun on their flesh, even in death.

"Not good," I stated to the dead.

I turned away from them, rushing toward the light. The hair on my neck rose again as I felt eyes continuing to watch me. Edging away from the cave, I walked back to the center of the pit and stared up the moment I was back in the light fed by the opening of the hole in the middle of town. I released the breath I'd been holding. Ryder stared down at me, smiling. His men were beside him, peering down at where I stood.

"Problem, Synthia?" he asked, studying me carefully.

"Not at all," I lied through chattering teeth as the sensation of being watched refused to lessen.

"Good, because you're staying here for a while," he growled, inspecting me as his gaze burned with anger.

"You're an asshole," I muttered. "You realize I can climb out, right? That was a requirement to enter your *fake* palace. Don't you recall my first mission, where I had to climb the walls of the Dark Tower to get your crown?"

"Try it. Go ahead. We'll wait." Crouching on to his haunches, he continued staring down at me with a wicked grin as his men looked cautiously from him to me.

I cracked my neck and jumped to the first outstretch of dirt, only for my hands to slip through it. I surveyed the pit, noting it was all fucking dirt. I moved to the next part, jumping and digging my nails into the earth, hoisting myself up before I continued to the next jagged ledge. I did it several times before I reached halfway up the steep climb, and pain shot through me, forcing me to lose my grip suddenly.

I turned my body mid-air, intending to sift, only to remember I couldn't. I landed hard in the dirt, the wind leaving my lungs as my body crumpled. Whimpering, I fought against the pain rushing through me as I started to sit up to pull air into my lungs. More pain rushed through me, forcing me to curl into a ball as a bloodcurdling scream ripped from my lips. I coughed, unable to bring air into my lungs as blood expelled from my lips.

"This is not simply a cave; it's a cage built by your mother to hold her offspring. Do you know why this cage held the Seelie within it for so long, Synthia? It was created with god magic to imprison Danu's creations she deemed a failure—or just didn't like them—locked up and hid them from the world forever. You are hers, are you not?"

"Ryder," I whispered through the immense pain, waiting for the spell assaulting me to subside. I rolled onto my back, staring up at him as the taste of blood coated my lips and mouth. "Don't do this."

"I'm not; you are. Maybe if you have enough time alone, you will come to terms with what you are. Your old life is gone. You're still a caterpillar, and you need to be a butterfly. A caterpillar doesn't become a butterfly just because it grows wings. It hides in the darkness and doesn't come out until it has finally grown its wings and knows how to use them. Grow some fucking wings, Synthia. This world needs you. Your old world is gone for you. It won't accept you now, and Faery is begging for you to just take what it is offering."

"I don't know how to remove my humanity!" I hissed, getting to my feet to stare up at him. "I don't know what to do to get rid of it. I can't just cut it out, nor can I just remove it!"

"I can't do this for you, Pet. I can't take it from you. You won't let me."

"I won't stay here," I warned him.

"Yes, you will. Only the most powerful of beings can enter this prison and escape it, and no one will come for you. The only people who know where you now reside are us. I'll be back in a few days to see if my pretty little caterpillar has sprouted her wings."

"What if I'm no longer me anymore?"

He stared down at me through narrowed eyes, smirking as his jaw ticked. "I have loved you through every change you've been through. I have been at your side regardless of what you became. We'll survive this too, sweet girl."

"What if I am supposed to keep it? I'm the Goddess of the Fae, the people. I was taken to the humans to learn compassion. To learn that faults are normal. I know how to forgive and how to be understanding. That is my humanity. You wouldn't have cared if those children died, Ryder. My job is to protect our people."

"But you can't, because you won't shed your skin and allow yourself to accept the land. We have stood by and let you do it your way. You assumed all you had to do was show up to the party and be here. That's not how Faery works. You know that, and yet you still have relinquished nothing to become what you are meant to be.

"Now, we do it my way. I told you, I won't lose anyone else because my wife can't give up her hold on her old life. You transformed. You are a part of this world, but you can only touch upon basic god magic. You create beautiful palaces, though, but that isn't your job.

"Zahruk trained you to fight, and Ristan helped him. Dristan, well, he taught you our history. He told you of the changes we go through, what the gods go through, and you weren't listening. I played your dutiful, loving husband, and all you did was get comfortable. You think I'm that sweet? I'm the asshole about to leave his pretty wife in a pit where the Seelie remained imprisoned for over a thousand years. I love you, woman. I love you enough to push you to do what this world and our children need from you."

"If you leave me here, don't come back!" I shouted hoarsely.

"See, there it is, that pesky human emotion that drives you. You're quick to anger, and you get mad, but then you forgive just as easily. This world will eat you alive. I'd stay away from the walls and the shadows." He dusted off his hands, staring down at me with a look of uncertainty before he vanished.

"Ryder!" I screamed, listening as it echoed through the caves. I peered around unhurriedly, taking in the surrounding shadows. "Stay away from the shadows? It's all fucking shadows! I will file for divorce, you dick!" I slid down the dirty wall, trying to glamour a coat over my chilled body, only to realize I couldn't.

No magic, no sifting, and I couldn't climb out. Asher had gotten out somehow, so what had he said had happened to free him? Danu had died, and the prison weakened. That was just great because I was also weak from running away from my husband, wasting precious magic to do so.

I couldn't get past the middle of the pit's opening,

and Ryder, that dick had watched me writhing in pain without an ounce of emotion in his pretty eyes. A noise sounded from deep within the tunnel. I peered into the darkness as something beckoned me to enter. I had no weapons, no magic, and I was as useless as a fucking mortal, which I'd never even been before.

"When I die here, you're going to feel like such a dick," I whispered to the opening as hot, angry tears pricked against my eyes. The noise sounded again, and I turned, watching as a pair of glowing eyes peered at me from the velvety darkness of the shadows.

Chapter
THIRTY-THREE

Ryder

Three days had passed since I'd left Synthia in the Seelie prison. And each day she'd plead for help, begging me to come get her. I'd listened to her, the tone of her voice, the desperation that she felt.

I'd struggled, fighting the need to go get her out, knowing I couldn't. If she didn't change, she'd become something I had to protect. I knew she was strong enough, but she wasn't evolving. She was content with the way things were, but this war wouldn't care about her comforts, and eventually, we'd lose.

I was done fucking losing. I'd pushed her to change, being the prick that forced her to deal with the situation. She'd fucking allowed Bilé to walk into our home and take our people from us. I wouldn't lose anyone else.

Dristan. *Fuck.* My baby brother was gone. He'd been here to protect her, and she'd failed them all with her inability to evolve past being a basic fucking fae when she was a goddess. It didn't matter what we told ourselves, or the lies we fed each other to assuage the guilt. The only thing that stubborn woman had to do was fucking reach for the power Faery was offering. She could have met the land halfway, and she'd have ended this war.

"What about the gardens?" Zahruk asked. I creased my brow at the idea of the mages being hidden there.

"Aohdan searched them a few days ago. He found no evidence of them there," I replied absently.

I studied the map, slowly moving my gaze to the location of the prison. For three nights, I'd returned, sitting upon the ledge to watch her sleeping below. She was filthy, covered in dirt and grime, and she shivered from the cold. Besides that, she looked lost.

Her pretty eyes opened and searched for me, and then her pleading began anew. The desperation in her voice damn near destroyed my will. I almost caved and took her from that place, but that wouldn't help her or Faery.

I couldn't change who she was, nor could I force it. She had to decide which world she belonged to: Faery or the human world. Synthia had to let one go because she was losing both while trying to hold on to each. Clinging to the sliver of humanity bonding her to that world was causing this one to die. I told her I was rearranging Faery because I couldn't make myself tell her that her refusal to accept the land was triggering it to evolve as it silently died.

Synthia didn't do anything half-assed, and yet this time, she was about this. She was refusing to accept Faery, to reach out and take her place in our world, and now it had cost us the lives of people we loved.

I wasn't meant to love her. I knew something such as me would never hold something as pure and beautiful as her, yet I reached for it, and she allowed me to take her. It was supposed to be simple: Find the Blood Heir, breed her, and walk away with the child who would take down Danu.

Only Danu's blood could fight her, and it had to be a daughter. I'd forced it to fucking happen, pushing and pulling pieces into play to ensure Synthia was born and born for me.

Synthia was everything I wanted, everything I needed. Then she'd gone and died while having my babies, and everything changed. I changed. I grew weak because I wanted her smiles and to watch her eyes light up when I said something sweet. But fuck, no part of me was sweet.

I wasn't that guy, and deep down, she knew it and had stayed anyway. She enjoyed me being rough, owning her flesh as she screamed for me. Syn was a rare breed of women, one that allowed ownership behind closed doors. She let me dominate her, fucking destroying her until we were both exhausted.

The woman had thwarted my plans and invaded the enemy's guild with my own army at her back, and she'd fought *for* me. She'd come to save me, thinking me weak enough to be taken, but that wasn't the case. I'd shut off the frequency for communication, allowing me to talk to everyone without telling anyone what I was doing. I couldn't, not with the mages being able to impersonate us or speak on the same mind waves. I'd gone in there without a single person knowing because I knew, no matter what the witches did, they couldn't kill me.

Synthia sacrificed our child to save me, and I hated it. I hated that she'd thought me pathetic because I'd grown comfortable around her. I wasn't excused since I didn't tell her my plans, but who the fuck thought she'd bring *my* army of the horde on her heels into her own world for me?

I'd gotten hard the moment she'd reached through the beast and ripped me back to the surface. I assumed she'd reached for her powers, but she hadn't. Ristan said she needed time. She fucking didn't. Synthia had dug in and was holding onto both worlds while we lost this fucking war. I'd been patient with her, but now I was done.

We no longer had the luxury of waiting her out. We'd shown her love, made her feel at home, taught her everything she needed to know about our world, and she chose us. The problem was that the land felt her hesitation, and as the God of Faery, I felt it too. I felt her pulling back when she got too comfortable.

I'd felt her indecision to accept what was right there before her. I felt her need to tighten her fists and pull her hands back the moment the land offered her power. Worse, I'd felt her desire to hold on to that other world, and her need to go back to it because she felt as if it was where she belonged.

"Ryder, where are you? I need you," she whispered inside my head as if she was in trouble. My head tilted, listening to the surrounding sounds, but hearing nothing. *"Please, I'm not alone here. I* need *you!"*

I turned it off, cutting her out as no noise followed her claim. Being cold and uncomfortable wasn't something she actually required to be saved from. Being mortal and not able to reach for her powers was a solid reminder that she needed us as much as we needed her. The alone time should remind her of the family she'd come to love as much as we loved her.

I wasn't asking her to forget her friends. I was asking her to choose Faery. It didn't mean forgetting where she had come from, or losing who she was. It meant allowing this world to be a part of her, too, and she was holding us at arm's length.

She asked the land to accept our children, and yet she hasn't received it in return. She was ours. She was born here and created to save this world, even if I had manipulated it a bit.

The gods played with us, using us against one another when they fought. They'd knowingly changed us into monsters, putting us into a world they created, and when they got pissed, we died. The world screamed with their rage and their unhappiness, and then it just stopped.

They'd abandoned us, and it had been calm for a while. Then, just like that, the world started to reject us. We had to figure out how to save ourselves, so I set the plan into motion to save our world and rid us of the gods permanently. I just needed something that Danu had created with a piece of herself to wield against her. I'd needed something lethal, like me. Someone who could fight with me against the Goddess of Faery, and help me take back our world.

I never anticipated the spitfire that entered my life with a perfect 'no' on her pretty pink lips. I never expected to want Synthia, but I did. I'd watched her, learning her while she slowly fell in love with the young enforcer who slid between her thighs and almost wet himself as he took her virginity. A disgraceful waste of a good fuck, but she hadn't complained. She never did.

Synthia was a fighter. Her entire world had been centered on the guild and hunting down my kind, and she did it well. Then she bumped into me headfirst and told me to get fucked.

So, I'd erased myself from her mind, and did the only thing I could. I'd started planning to fuck her hard. That little wisp of a girl told me, the fucking Horde King, to go get fucked. She signed herself up for being the one I fucked that day.

I could have taken her then, spreading those pretty thighs wide, pounding into her dripping wet flesh, which I could smell. Her lips curled into a naughty little smile as she'd stepped back, lifted her middle finger, and told me to get fucked. Then, she'd turned and swayed her pretty little ass out of the alley I'd forced her into, wanting to see her response to what I am.

I'd feasted for days, unable to get the picture of her perky little ass out of my mind as it sauntered away from me. I'd been gluttonous with the need to do just that: fuck that tight little body right out of my system. The problem was that she wasn't the type of woman you walked away from.

Her eyes shone with an inner beauty that couldn't be faked. When she smiled, my fucking cold, dead heart thumped for the first time in memory. She made me want things, things I'd resigned myself to never have, and then the bitch *died* on me.

Synthia had ripped the same heart she'd forced to

beat out of my chest when she died. She'd given me children, the first triplets in the history of the entire race. She called them beasties because he'd ensured her womb would accept what he gave. She'd roared for him too, and he'd purred for her, sensing his mate in Synthia.

She'd come back to us, but I'd already tasted loss and knew I never wanted to be in a world without her. I also knew if she didn't wake up and take her powers, we might not make it through this war in one fucking piece.

We should have been enough. But then she'd started pulling away again. She started planning a new guild, and her entire soul pulled from us as she focused on rebuilding it. I'd sent funds, helped where I could, and threw everything I could throw at her pet project to make it move faster so that she'd come back to us.

The guild was built, running, and she still hadn't returned. I'd told Alden we needed her, and he'd said she'd been told to come home, to prepare for war.

He'd written that shit out for her, but she still wasn't ours, or she would have returned sooner.

I'd played my cards, and she'd tossed them back at me. I'd told her the truth, and she'd pulled further away. She kept things from me. There had been simple things that she could have told me, such as the fucking Goddess of Chaos was playing games in our fucking house. As it so happened, I was aware of it the entire time.

I also knew Thanatos had been outside my bedroom. Lucian had also known he'd stood in the shadows with Spyder, protecting our babes from Synthia's irrational belief that she had to do it alone. I'd included her in plans, yet she'd ignored them. I didn't have time to walk her through them again.

We had explained the necessity of her being here, being present when we met with the head of the castes, but she'd been gone weeks without even realizing it. Ristan had pulled her aside and reminded her how time worked between worlds, and she'd frowned, shrugging her delicate shoulders like it hadn't been some big fucking deal. It was. If I'd known that she had been aware of who she was consorting with, we could have fucking ended it quickly and efficiently.

I wouldn't have had to let it play out to see if my wife was plotting against me. Instead, I'd let her assume I'd fucked someone else to capture the spies running through our halls. I'd begun stacking the deck without her, as I thought she was stacking it against me for our enemies.

I was as much at fault as she was, but I wasn't the one holding on to another world. I was right fucking here, waiting for her to choose us. Her world didn't want her, wouldn't accept her in her true form, but we would. Faery was reaching for her, and she refused to reach out and take the power it offered to its goddess.

She wanted me to be her bad guy.

Well, here I fucking was, no longer donning some mask of civility for her. She could deal with who I really was, or she wouldn't get me at all. I wouldn't pretend to be something I wasn't anymore. I wasn't willing to ignore what was happening or the lives we had lost because she refused to let go of her past and reach for the future.

Hunting her had been thrilling, but the end result hadn't been satisfying. Watching my pretty wife twisting in pain had hurt me deeply, but the thought of losing her hurt much worse. I didn't have time to fuck around.

I needed what she was born to be, and she belonged at my side, ready to fight those who wanted us dead. I wanted my wife to pull her pretty head from her ass and come back up swinging because that was what she fucking did. She always got back up.

"Are you here, or should we do this another time?" Zahruk asked.

"My wife is in a bloody fucking pit, asshole."

"Damn and I thought my mother was a bitch for tossing us into the prison," Asher snorted from where he leaned across the table, watching us. "Hope you left her something to do there."

"I don't know, Asher. What was there to do in the

Seelie prison? Maybe you and Synthia will have more to talk about when she gets home."

"Funny, not even you would be that cruel," he chuckled as he crossed his arms, studying me with a smirk on his lips.

"A prison in which not even the gods can escape? It's the perfect place for her until she can figure out how to be what we need her to be."

He narrowed his eyes, shaking his head. "Nah, there's some fucked up things in that place."

"What fucked up things?" I demanded carefully. My hands crunched against the table, and it whined from the strain.

Iridescent eyes lifted, and Asher studied me. "Tell me you didn't throw Synthia into that fucking pit." When I just stared at him, the color drained from his face. "Ryder, tell me you didn't toss your pretty wife to the monsters that I left in that fucking hell!"

"What monsters?" I asked, feeling my stomach twist with his words. I observed his ashen face as he opened and closed his mouth before fully figuring out what the fuck words were.

"You think it was fun and games down there? There were creatures so fucking evil and vile that they couldn't be killed. There's no magic down there. You either learn quickly to adapt, or you die. It took me centuries to get the slightest bit of magic during my time in that hellish pit. If you left her there, she's without magic, alone, and with monsters that we weren't strong enough to kill, even once we obtained magic after thousands of years."

"She's been there for three days, and has yet to enter the caves," I muttered, scrubbing my hand over my mouth.

"You don't get it. That pit isn't even an actual pit. It's a fucking gateway into the realm of monsters. You see one thing, the person within sees something else. It causes confusion, and time moves *very* differently there. The Hell of the human world has nothing on that hellhole. I learned that quickly. I was tossed into the pit three days after my brother, and yet to him, twenty years had passed since he'd entered.

"Every day, I looked down to be certain he was safe. I saw the same thing every day until I entered it myself and found him ripped to fucking pieces and hung on the walls of the cave. The thing is, down there, you don't die. You just wake up the next day to be hunted by monsters again. You tossed your fucking wife to those creatures, and I assure you, what they do to women isn't pretty."

"I didn't toss Synthia into that pit, she jumped. I just didn't help her get out, and I have watched her every day since I left her there," I argued, repeating what he had basically just said. My heart clenched, beating wildly as my brothers closed rank against me with the agitation they felt.

"No, you have seen what they wanted you to see. Pray what comes out of that cave has even a sliver of resemblance to the woman you left there. If she has been there for three days, she's been fighting to escape for twenty years, if not more. It may have changed, but Danu dying wouldn't have changed everything. It sure as hell didn't kill Malachi, and if he has gotten to her, she may be so far gone that you may need to put her down because she'll be so lost that nothing will reach her."

I leaned over the table, grabbing Asher's shirt as I yanked him forward to stare at him through narrowed slits. "You think to play games with me? She's been calling my name nonstop."

"I'm *not* fucking with you, Ryder. I *told* you that place was utter hell. I *told* you it was the shit of nightmares, and yet you *left* her there? That isn't on me. I wouldn't throw my worst fucking enemy into that hellhole, and I'm a cold bastard who enjoys watching people suffer."

"She jumped," I growled.

"Then you should have pulled her out. Only someone from the top can get you out."

"What's down there?" I asked carefully.

"The shit we couldn't kill no matter how hard we fucking tried. There was an army of us, and she's alone. She is powerless down there, unguarded, more than likely unarmed, and utterly fucked. We spent one thousand years of your time down there. To us, we lived a thousand lives.

"If we died, we just came back to repeatedly live a nightmare until we no longer felt anything but pain. You want to know what is down in those caves? Hell is. A beautiful paradise with monsters that destroy your soul until you have nothing left for them to take," Asher said softly, his eyes haunted with the memories.

"You let Syn jump into a fucking hole and then left her there?" Adam asked, narrowing his eyes as he stood, staring daggers at me from across the maps. "You just threw her away?"

"I'm teaching her a lesson. She isn't accepting this world. She's fucking stuck with her feet in both, and Faery is dying because of it. My people are dying because she can't let go of the guild. If Synthia reached for her powers, she would be unstoppable. She isn't reaching for them. She's holding her hands closed at her sides, refusing to accept that this is her world now and where she belongs."

"She's your fucking wife, Ryder." Adam glared at me, his brands pulsing as he shook his head in anger.

"Faery is a living, breathing thing, and if she rejects it, it will wilt just like anything does when neglected. Our people are dying while she drags her feet. What the fuck was I supposed to do? Wait until there's no one left to save? We're at war, Adam. Gods are trying to fucking kill us! I did what I thought was best in order to get through to her. I didn't know the cave was filled with monsters. It was believed to be empty!"

"You're expected to want her to be herself! To be the woman who died to bring your children into this world. She's my best fucking friend, Ryder. Where the fuck is she? I need you to tell me, and we need to go get her now!"

"I'm with the Prince of Darkness," Asher shrugged.

"Adam is the Dark King, not the prince," I corrected

absently. My mind rushed through scenarios as my gut twisted and plummeted to my feet. Everything in my mind rebelled against the idea of her suffering where I'd chosen to leave her.

"Little young, isn't he, to be the king of an entire kingdom?" Asher asked.

"Who the fuck gives a fairy fucking granny two tits?" Adam snapped impatiently. "Can we go?"

"Let's," I grumbled, letting my power fill the room before I took everyone in it to the cave where the Seelie princes had been entombed for over a thousand years—longer, if Asher was to be believed.

I looked into the hole, staring at Synthia's huddled form as she peered up through violet-blue sleepy eyes. Her body was covered in dirt, just as it had been for the past three days. Her outfit was ripped, but she'd pulled it over her arms as her mouth opened and closed while she stared up at me with pleading eyes.

"She looks exhausted but otherwise fine," I muttered.

"What the fuck are you looking at? That's not Syn. That's a fucking corpse missing half its fucking body," Adam clipped harshly.

"What?" I tore my eyes from Synthia and looked at the men. They were peering down into the pit with looks of unease and horror. "She's right fucking there!"

"Nah, Ryder. You see what the monsters want you to see. Your wife is gone. She's not down there." Asher scrubbed his hand over his face with a haunted look in his eyes. "She entered the caves. Fuck. Who knows where she went or what got her. That thing down there is nothing but what the kid says: a fucking corpse. That isn't Synthia."

My heart beat wildly as denial screamed through me. My head swung back to the body, watching as it decayed before my eyes. Black lifeless pits formed where her eyes had been seconds before. The creature beckoned, standing up on nothing but bones before it began laughing coldly.

"More pretties for us to play with, please?" it

hissed, then cackled before crumpling to the ground, causing the skull to detach from its body.

"What the fuck did I do?" I whispered thickly, hating the pain and fear that rushed through me at the thought of Synthia enduring what Asher had described.

No one stirred or replied to me. My heart pounded painfully against my ribs as I moved to enter the cave. Blood roared through my ears, and sweat beaded at my neck. Asher grabbed me, his eyes wide with terror, and I yanked my arm away from him.

"She's my wife! I left her down there."

"If you enter that pit, you might never return. You could search for Synthia forever. What happens to this world, Ryder, if both of you are gone from it?" Asher asked, watching me as worry and determination set in.

"I don't want to live in a world without her. I did this for her, to show her that letting go of her old world doesn't mean saying goodbye to it. She cannot die without knowing why I did this. It wasn't to hurt her. It wasn't to destroy who she was. I just wanted her to know what living in her world would be like without powers. She has her powers because of Faery; they're to be used in this world. I just wanted her to fucking see it."

"You go down there, and you won't come back. That's a simple fact. Time isn't the same down there, and you don't even know how long she's been gone. She could have passed through thousands of portals into the never-ending worlds that this cave opens up into. I get it; you lost your girl. It's hard, but you let her go. Even if she entered on her own, you let her go—she's gone."

"I can smell her. She can't be too far into that cave." I studied Asher's gaze, finding the truth of his words in his eyes.

"Ryder, you need to see this shit," Zahruk called from the other side of the pit, forcing me to turn in the direction he stood. "Something came out of there."

Across from us was a ladder built of bones and held together by ligaments. My gaze traveled up the ladder until my heart stopped beating. I sifted across from the spot I'd stood, landing at the far side of the pit next to the ladder. I could smell her, the sweetness of her body, and the intoxicating blood that pumped through her veins. I moved closer to the wall behind me, pushing past the men who barred my way, and paused as the writing came into view.

Found my humanity, I left it for you.

Can you hear it beating?

I can't.

But that was what you wanted, right?

I also discovered my wings… And my wings have shown me who I am, what I am. The thing is, I no longer care what I am, or about much of anything anymore.

You wanted a monster, right?

I have become one.

I hope you like the changes I've made to come home to you.

Side note, I'm fucking starving.

You should be careful what you ask for, because sometimes you do get what you want, and I'm everything you wanted, and no longer who I was.

See you soon, lover.

I think…

I died…

Are you here?

Where were you when I needed you most?

Help…

I'm coming back…

Ready to play with me?

Feeling cute…

Might fuck the world up later…Maybe sooner…It sounds…Fun?

On the wall were words written in her blood that went from making sense to gibberish, as if she was changing or evolving as she wrote them. Giant wings had been drawn as well, and on a pedestal beside the wall was Synthia's heart.

My throat bobbed as I searched for the words to speak or say anything other than *fuck*. This wasn't what I had wanted, and if Asher was right, she may no longer even care about us. She'd been down there too long. What the hell had I done? Who the hell was she now?

"Let's hope your wife is the thing that crawled out of that hole. Judging by the love letter she left you, I'm going to say it's her, but not her."

"It's her fucking heart," I rasped. "That's Synthia's heart, and her message is written in her own blood."

"It doesn't mean that's who crawled out. It just means they consumed her thoughts and had access to one of her corpses. They may have left it so you didn't go looking deeper for her. The things down there aren't like us, Ryder. Some consume souls, taking the best parts of their prey and removing their memories while transforming them into what they want them to become.

"Other things, well, they make you into something else altogether. I wasn't this sexed-up when I went down there, but I sure as fuck was when I came out of that pit. You never come back the same. That place changes you into a monster, and what went down doesn't come back up. Sorry that isn't what you want to hear, but fuck, she ripped out her own heart and used her blood to write you a creepy-ass love letter. Doesn't sound like the Goddess of the Fae came out of there, Ryder," he said sadly.

"My Synthia isn't in that cave, that's all I fucking care about. I can bring her back; she's my wife. I just have to find her." I stared at the drawing of the wings; it gave me hope.

The beating heart that still pounded on the pedestal, though, gave me pause. A long fucking pause, if I was being honest. What had she gone through to get out of there? Would she forgive me for leaving her here? Knowing Synthia, I was going to be in for the fight of my life to get her back.

"This is fucking crazy shit," Adam muttered, pushing his fingers through his hair in frustration.

I was willing to go to war to bring her back to me, but first I had to figure out where the hell she was, and I couldn't feel her. It felt like she was right here, but the only thing she'd left me was her bleeding heart. "We need to discover where she was or where she would go."

"No, you need to figure out who and what crawled out of that hole. Then, and only then, can you figure out where Synthia went." Asher shook his head, frowning. Everyone went silent, listening as the heart beat louder and louder as if Synthia was experiencing an adrenaline rush, or worse, fighting someone.

Chapter
THIRTY~FOUR

Ryder

I stood on the battlements, watching the field where power seemed to continually be collecting for the last several days. All of Faery was holding its breath as something intensified within it, and I had a suspicion it was my wife gathering her strength to come for me. I wanted her back here, safe within the walls of the stronghold, and yet the more we looked for her, the more helpless I felt that she wasn't coming home.

If Asher was right, and the prick seemed to be right about the pit, it wasn't Synthia that had crawled out of that cave. So who was driving my pretty wife around, and how the fuck did I fix this mess?

It was killing me to consider the truth. To think of Synthia being hurt by creatures within the pit, but it was supposed to have been empty. I'd assumed so, since Asher and an entire army were now outside of it, roaming free. He'd never mentioned anything else being down there when I'd cornered and interrogated him on the passes. I'd put him through hell, allowing Zahruk to search through his intentions without looking too hard at his time in that hellish pit. I'd been in a hurry to head off the mages.

The Seelie prison was one of the few things inside this entire world that I'd never bothered to explore, but then it had been filled with the Seelie, and they weren't something I'd ever considered freeing.

The sun was setting over the meadow when power suddenly erupted into the air, heavy with a strong vibration that slithered over my flesh. I turned to see the silhouette of a figure moving toward the fortress. More power sparked through the air, and it made everyone in the courtyard stop whatever they were doing to take cover.

Synthia had returned, finally.

I grabbed the stone of the battlement, watching as she walked barefooted through the flowers, staring directly at me. Her dress was white, splotched in crimson, as if she'd been killing her way back to me. Platinum bands covered her wrists and biceps, and a delicate necklace hung from her neck. Her hair was tied back in war braids, and her ample cleavage spilled from her dress as she slowly approached the castle. In the middle of the field, she stopped, looking up at me curiously. No recognition ignited in her eyes, only a strange coldness that wrapped around my heart like a vise.

"Fuck…"

I sifted into the throne room, alerting the others that Synthia had returned, when immense power entered the room, igniting, causing those that were sensitive to drop to their knees. The hair on my neck rose as I slowly turned, staring down into stunning violet and blue tri-colored eyes. Her brands continually pulsed silver and purple over her flesh, a beautiful combination on her sun-kissed skin.

"Synthia," I whispered, taking in the ethereal beauty of my wife. She still made my heart kick start every time I peered into those gorgeous eyes, lighting my soul on fire with a need to take her.

A guard approached her, placing his hand on her shoulder, and she turned toward him with a deep growl rumbling up through her lungs. The sound of suction filled the room as he gasped and then wailed in pain. She brought his heart up as his body slammed against the floor, lifeless. Synthia held his heart to her ear while listening to it carefully before she moved it away from her, not finding what she sought.

I swallowed hard, studying the coldness in her eyes. My gaze slid to the guard, narrowing before settling on her once again. No emotion over the loss or sense of guilt for murdering the guard showed on her delicate features. Instead, there was amusement and pride for the kill she'd delivered.

"You killed him?" I asked.

"He touched me," she hissed as her full lips tugged into a pout. Her voice exploded into the room, coming out in layers as it danced over my flesh, demanding attention. My dick twitched, and her eyes glowed hungrily as if she was merely fae instead of a goddess. "It is forbidden to touch the goddess," Synthia smirked.

Staring at me, she dropped her arm, squashing the heart until it turned to dust in her hand before she opened her fingers and glamoured it clean. She stepped closer, inhaling my scent, and I remained still, allowing her to find what she was looking for.

Adam sifted into the throne room, having heard the news through the mental link he'd been awarded by becoming King of the Dark Kingdom. He stared at Synthia, moving toward her, intending to pull her into a hug.

Considering she wasn't even Syn anymore, it was a bad fucking idea. His hand lifted, and I growled, warning him not to touch her with a look over the top of her delicate head. He pulled his hand back, forest and emerald-green eyes drifting over the bloodied dress to the dead guard at her feet.

She vanished, and I exhaled slowly.

"Why didn't you stop her from leaving?" Adam demanded.

"Something is not right," I admitted, nodding to the deceased guard. "She just ripped his fucking heart out and didn't bat an eye. She felt no remorse. All he did was put his hand on her shoulder."

"What the fuck?" Adam snapped, stepping back as he shook his head.

Lightning crashed outside, and slowly we all turned, staring out the doors. Thunder erupted next, clapping loudly overhead as the doors were blown open as if she was inviting me outside. I sifted back to the battlement, peering down at where Synthia once again stood in the meadow, looking up at me.

Lucian and Spyder materialized beside me, peering down at Synthia and the blood coating her dress. Lucian whistled at her curious expression and something else that lingered in her gaze.

Spyder winced, turning to look at me with something in his gaze that pissed me off. He seemed excited about her changes and yet terrified of them at the same time.

My heart thundered against my chest until Lucian spoke, and then it stopped, turning cold and lifeless. He had that fucking effect on people.

"I see Synthia found her way home, finally," Lucian rasped thickly. "Not all of her, though, it appears."

"Care to elaborate on what the fuck that means?" I asked carefully.

"Let's go meet your wife, and we will ask her what she is missing. Shall we?" he asked, vanishing to stand in front of Synthia.

I sifted inches away from her and studied her curious gaze. She moved without so much as disturbing or displacing the air, appearing again further away. Her pretty eyes watched me inquisitively, sizing me up from a distance.

More and more creatures began sifting into the meadow, causing her eyes to stray, but they always returned to me, as if she was trying to place me in her mind. Her delicate nose lifted as she tilted her head. Her blood-red lips pursed into a tight line as if she found me familiar. She better have felt me, because I felt all of her. I was embedded in her soul as much as she was in mine.

"Synthia, it's me," I said carefully.

She appeared before me, causing the entire world to groan as she tore through it to get to me. Her platinum head lowered, and her nose pressed against my chest, inhaling as I peered over her head, looking at the gaping hole she'd just created by sifting.

"Did she just fucking rip apart the fabric of Faery?" Adam asked, noting the gaping holes Synthia tore through the veil to reach me.

On the other side of the veil, men turned, watching us curiously before reality hit them, and they rushed away from the portal hole she'd left between realms.

"Spyder, close the hole," Lucian ordered without taking his eyes from Synthia.

Her hands lifted, stroking my chest before she ripped the shirt from my body. Her tongue tasted me as her lips kissed my chest, sampling my flesh as a moan of lust escaped her throat. Her tongue traced the markings of my tattoos and brands as if she intended to fuck me right there, in front of everyone, without caring who watched, just like the fae when feasting after a battle.

"I'm starving, and you're fucking delicious. I want your cock," she uttered breathlessly. Synthia's hand slid down my chest and pushed into my pants. Wrapping her tiny fingers around my cock, she smiled through hooded, glowing eyes while it grew, welcoming her familiar touch.

"I don't know, this isn't so bad," I muttered, smirking down at the ethereal beauty. Synthia watched me as she stroked my cock with a tight, sure grin, causing precum to leak with anticipation, and the need to paint her pussy with it. "You want me to bare your pretty flesh and fuck you right here in front of everyone?" I asked huskily, letting the rasp in my tone slither over her skin.

"Yes," she whispered through a moan, tightening her hold on my dick.

Her head leaned against my chest, and I placed my hand on the back of her head, holding her to me as my eyes closed. Pain lanced through my chest as I peered down, watching her other hand push through my flesh and vanish into my chest.

Lucian grabbed her arm, applying enough pressure that she stopped reaching for my heart and turned to look at Lucian, hissing at him for disturbing her. The moment her hand was pulled free, my chest healed, and I watched her through narrowed eyes. She'd tried to remove my heart with one hand while she worked my cock with the other.

The meadow was filling with gods and goddesses, and Synthia inspected them all. Lucian still held her wrist, which was now covered in my blood.

"What's your name, sweetheart?" he asked, and she turned slowly toward his voice, studying him before she pressed against him.

She gave Lucian a saccharine smile and then placed her hand against his chest, ripping his shirt open. Her mouth brushed against his abs, and I frowned, watching my wife as she licked her sexy-as-fuck tongue down *his* body. I wanted to pull her back to me, but Lucian's gaze warned me from doing that.

"What's your name?" he repeated in a multilayered tone that demanded a reply. He turned, staring at Lena, who was frowning, glaring daggers at Synthia as the color in her eyes turned to that of a moonless night. Thick black lines traced from her eyes as if she was about to go full Fury on Synthia, which I wasn't sure Lena would live through. "Tell me your name, and I'll take you to paradise, woman."

I felt Lena's pain, but something wasn't right with Synthia, and while Lena was powered by furies, Synthia was a goddess. The power that ebbed and flowed from Synthia was enough to bring the fae to their knees.

The proof being that those who guarded the stronghold were doing just that. The entire world pulsed from her presence. Blades of grass danced to the vibration as if a loud bass speaker was placed into the meadow, blaring music in front of them.

The sky turned a multitude of angry colors as the wind howled all around, never touching us, as if directed by her.

"Sorcha," Synthia said softly, smiling as Lucian's clothes vanished. Her hand reached for his cock, but he stopped it, holding her against him while he studied the vacant gaze peering up at him. "Feed me. I'm so hungry."

"Just like that, huh? Don't care who you fuck, as long as you get fucked, Synthia?" he countered.

"My name is Sorcha, Goddess of the Fae, and you're talking too much. It's starting to bore me," she complained, ripping her hands away from him. He stepped back, instantly dressed as if he'd conjured clothing in the way the fae did. Only Lucian wasn't fae.

Asher sifted onto the field, clueless about what was happening. He slowly walked toward us, which caught Synthia's attention. His gaze settled on her, and he froze. She met him before we could stop her.

Synthia took Asher to the ground hard, removing his clothing with claws as he held perfectly still, staring up at her. His hands lifted, settling on her hips as he swallowed hard enough that we all heard it. His eyes turned toward us as his head remained in her direction without turning.

"I am hungry. Feed me, or you die," she sneered, and the trees cracked with her words.

"Now who's rocking the fuck-me vibes, woman?" Asher hissed, groaning as his brands pulsed in sync with hers. He moaned beneath her, and she lifted, intending to plant herself on his thick cock, which she'd begun stroking, preparing it to fit into her body.

"Flower!" Ristan shouted from where he stood on

the battlements. "We don't fuck other people, woman! You're married! Behave."

She started to push onto him while everyone stood around watching. Blood pounded in my ears as a growl escaped my lungs. My wings expanded, filling the meadow with absolute power as I prepared to fight her to keep her from fucking anyone but me.

Her eyes turned, studying me before she stood, abandoning Asher's cock, walking toward me. Iridescent wings exploded from her back, and I paused, starting at their unequivocal beauty that took my breath away. Her head lowered as her eyes took in my wings, darker and more lethal than hers, but we were the same, and she knew it.

"My little caterpillar shed her humanity and turned into a butterfly. You finally grew your pretty wings, Synthia," I mused, watching her walking toward me.

My clothes vanished, along with everyone else's. The only one who had clothes on was Synthia, and I remained perfectly still, observing her carefully as she crept forward, intending to pounce. Her eyes were purely predatory, like something inside of her was calculating the odds of getting to me before Lucian could stop her.

She was hunting me down, as if she planned to capture me, and then fuck me. I wasn't wholly opposed to the idea, either.

"You want me, come and get me, woman," I rumbled thickly, ignoring Ristan, who snorted as he entered the meadow she'd just pulled him into, forcing him into the chaos.

"She just seriously invited us to a fucking sausage party without asking! I can't even put on my clothes!" Ristan winced the moment her eyes turned to him. "Oh no, you ain't fucking me. That's something that we can never undo, Flower."

Her eyes dismissed him, swinging back to me to slide down my body and settle on my cock. I swallowed hard, surveying her cautiously as she approached me with her head slightly tilted.

"I want it."

"It's yours," I answered, watching the victorious smile play over her mouth before she paused hesitantly.

She stopped, turning to peer out over the meadow as if she heard something no one else could. One moment she was almost to me, and the next, she was across the field, standing silently as she waited for something. Her wings dipped, dropping to a guarded stance that had taken me years to master before battle. She stood as still as a statue, waiting as everyone else grew tense with unease.

Her hand lifted as men burst through the portal at the entrance of the forest. I stepped closer, intending to sift to her and fight at her side, but Lucian shook his head.

"Don't fucking move. There are only so many fucking holes we can close before Synthia destroys the entire veil between Faery and earth. You wanted the Goddess of the Fae to man up, now stand back and watch her work. I have a feeling your new wife lacks something she needs back immediately, and without it, she isn't the woman you married. That's a mindless being with no fucking conscious thought. Her only needs are to feed, fuck, and destroy."

"What the fuck could she be lacking?" I inquired, studying the way her head remained tilted as the mages approached her slowly.

"Her fucking soul," he snapped as her hands rose before the men could reach her.

The moment her hands lifted, the men nearest her burst into flames, taking them to their knees. Power erupted, stifling the meadow as if the air was being sucked out of it. Men screamed as they began melting to ashes before reaching her position. Her hands had barely moved, and yet every mage that rushed her was either burned or rendered to ash.

She was fucking beautiful, glorious, and terrifying all at the same time.

Thunder clapped above as the wind howled, lifting her hair and sending the ashes of her victims away. Rain began to fall, cleansing the meadow of the battle until all that remained were the pristinely cleaned skulls of those she'd just slaughtered. The men, who had yet to die, screamed, burning alive as she studied them without moving from her spot.

Her eyes held no remorse as she watched them suffering a grueling death. It was only when one man remained that her wings vanished. She walked through the dead toward him as his eyes slid down her body. She walked in his direction, the mirror image of Danu the first time I'd encountered the goddess.

Bilé stood still, watching Synthia as she approached him with slow, leisurely steps. I moved, but Lucian grabbed me, holding me there as he covered us in clothing.

"Let your power back out, Ryder. Call your mate with it. You need to go to her. She sees Bilé as a challenge, but that's not Synthia. That is a goddess who wants a man who will take her to the ground and fucking destroy her. She won't go down easily, either. You need to be that man."

"That's fucking Bilé. He will kill her!"

"He can't kill her. She's stronger than he is now. He just doesn't fucking realize it." Midnight eyes peered across the meadow, watching Synthia as she slowly moved to Bilé.

The moment she reached him, he stepped back, taking her in. His clothes vanished, and I growled, hating that she was amped up and willing to fuck anyone. Her hand slid over his chest, stroking it before his hand captured hers, bringing her knuckles to his lips as he kissed them.

I swallowed anger that rose violently, igniting within me as she followed him to the ground, shedding her own clothes before she leaned over, kissing him slowly. Bilé's hands slid through her hair, holding her mouth against his as his hips rolled, inviting her to take him. She was the mirror image of his wife, and he was about to fuck her because of it.

"I can't watch this fucking happen, Lucian!" I snapped harshly, starting forward, only for him to stop me, staring into my eyes.

"You will," he warned. "You wanted Synthia to

take her powers, and she has. You left her in that pit, and while you may not have known what was down there, you chose to walk away. That isn't your wife. That is the creature she would have become had she never entered the human world. She carries her own beast within her, but she no longer has her humanity, and without a soul or heart driving her, she only knows what she was created to become. She is your perfect mate, but she isn't Synthia anymore. She is Sorcha, born of a goddess and the Blood King. Basic needs are driving her, and unless you want to end up one of her victims, figure out how to call her back to you without moving, because if you move, she will come to you. If she does that when sifting the way she is, she will destroy the barrier between worlds without even realizing she has done so."

"She's about to ride the bastard's dick! The bastard that murdered my brothers!"

"No, she's about to rip his fucking heart from his chest. She knows her heart is missing. Synthia is trying to become whole again because she's stuck inside that unfeeling monster right now." He shrugged. "Might as well fucking let her kill him, right?"

Bilé howled over the wind as he stared at Synthia's hand that had pushed into his chest cavity. Her mouth crushed against his, and his eyes widened in horror. If I wasn't so fucking pissed that my wife was about to seat herself on his cock, I'd think it was sexy as fuck, but she was mine. My power ripped through the field without warning, slithering over her as she was about to push down on him. Her lips left his as she rose, glaring at me.

"You should have fucking waited," Lucian warned.

"Yeah, I didn't get a choice. She's…" I vanished, reappearing before her. Staring down at Bilé, she stepped over him to come toward me, never taking her eyes from mine. In a silent battle of wills, her power clashed violently against mine for dominance.

"You *are* mine, are you not?" she hissed, her voice echoing through the meadow to the mountains and beyond. "I feel you, why? Why do I feel you, and yet I am so hungry that anyone would do? I just want to get fucked! How hard is it to get something so simple when the men in this kingdom are so fucking hugely endowed? Look at you; you're perfect. Fucking feed me, or I will remove your cock and use it on myself, bastard."

Bilé vanished, and I exhaled, turning to look at the woman who watched me. A wicked smile spread across her lips as she took the few steps needed to close the distance between us.

Her mouth landed against mine in an earth-shattering kiss that rocked the world around us. My eyes opened and widened as the forest exploded. Trees were uprooted, and fire covered the branches the moment they crashed to the ground, all while her hand stroked my cock. I was painfully slammed against the ground as she stood over me, lowering her body to take what I offered. Twin daggers appeared through her chest, as her gaze slid to them, then to me in a look of lethal hatred and shock of betrayal.

She gasped through the burning pain, and the look in her pretty eyes twisted my gut. Synthia fell onto me, and I held her, replacing my clothes as I pushed her off of me, dressing her with magic as she continued to gasp for air.

"Did you get it?" Lucian asked, forcing my gaze to the man strolling into the meadow as black ghostly creatures floated around Synthia, touching her with their mangled, green-looking fingers.

"Of course, I fucking did. Do you have any idea how long I have been gone? It took a fucking decade to find the prick who had it, and then he refused to give it to just anyone. Do you know how many *souls* are down there? I barely fucking escaped before I ended up reaping them all just to make them stop fucking me as I searched for one soul in a haystack."

"Replace her soul, and then give her back her heart," Lucian muttered as I stood, watching the reapers who picked up Synthia and held her between them as Thanatos stepped forward, staring into her eyes.

"You are not ready to be reaped, my sweet girl." He produced a silver spool of thread and a golden needle. The entire meadow watched in silence as he began slowly sewing a glowing blue aura back into Synthia. She smiled at Thanatos, watching him with wonder as he smirked, flirting with her as he put her back together. "He had begun to consume her most treasured and loved memories. They tend to start on the juicy bits first. She won't be the same, not until all of her memories are restored—*if* she's strong enough to take them back, that is."

"What the fuck does that mean?" I demanded carefully, studying Synthia as she watched Thanatos, her glowing eyes beckoning him to touch her deeper as she flirted with him unabashedly.

"It means that Synthia was down there for a long time. Time in the Seelie prison is different than it is here. It's slow and endless. She was brutalized, asshole. There are pieces of her scattered down there still. There are more corpses in that cave than there are fae inside Faery. She was in the worst place in the entire fucking realm. You left her there to be tortured by a creature that's been around since the beginning of this world. Not that you could have done shit once she entered, but you could have let the rest of us know where she was. We could have saved her so that she could fulfill her destiny.

"That little hole you see when you peer down into the pit? By the time your feet touch it, you're already lost. The reapers said I stood there, talking to them, but I didn't wait to enter the cavern. I had my full powers, but Synthia? She apparently hadn't accepted her powers, and when she finally did, she left a trail of her own blood on the way out. Luckily, she also left a ladder she made with their corpses, or I'd still be stuck down there. The monster showed me, but since the entire fucking pit is filled with Seelie tricks, who the fuck knows what actually happened to me down there. That creature within the pit? He's fucking strong. I got her soul, and then I ghosted before death took over and I was stuck there until the end of time reaping their souls." Thanatos eyed Lucian accusingly. "There we go, sweetheart. Speaking of hearts, where is yours?"

Synthia stared vacantly until Ristan moved closer, removing the bag from his hip and handing it to Thanatos. Her platinum head turned, staring at the organ that still beat wildly, increasing with speed the closer it came. Her scream rent through the air, shooting trees up into the mountain as if a hurricane had just ripped through and uprooted them. She struggled against the reapers, even with the strange, glowing blades that pulsed angrily against her flesh, where they impaled her skin.

"You're hurting her!" Adam snapped. He started forward, only for Lucian to step in his path as Spyder chuckled, moving in beside him to block his way.

"No, I'm not hurting her. The proximity to the organ holding pain is what's hurting her. She doesn't want it back."

"What happens if you don't put it back yet?" Lucian asked.

"She wouldn't care if the fae lived or died. She'd be an unfeeling, miserable person to have to deal with, cold and detached. While it's only an organ, the mind believes it to hold emotions, and that makes it more powerful than the soul that actually dictates who we become. Without it, the mind shuts that part down. So, I will place her heart back into her chest, and you can contend with what happens after. She needs it back to be whole, and I don't give a fuck what anyone else wants, she deserves to care. It is what makes her the Goddess of the Fae. She is who we need to win the war, understood?" Thanatos's glacier-cold eyes locked with mine.

He placed the heart into Synthia's chest as she wailed, fighting against his hand. He pushed into the cut he'd made, and then she just stopped, glaring at him. The blades were removed, and the reapers stepped back together, releasing her and watching as she stood there silently.

"Syn?" I asked, cupping her face between my hands and ignored her exposed breasts. I glamoured her into a new white dress and watched as her eyes lifted and narrowed on mine in a dull gaze. "Wake up, beautiful."

Her eyes began to gain focus as she lifted her head to peer up at me. Stepping back, she looked down, grasping the front of her dress as she looked around frantically. Synthia spun around in a tight circle, opening and closing her mouth repeatedly before a tremble of fear shuddered through her.

"Who the fuck are you?" she demanded, and it was like a punch to the gut. "Where am I?" Panic filled her tone, and then she turned, running away from us on her pretty bare feet.

"That's unfortunate," Lucian stated, watching her running further away from us through the skulls of the dead she'd murdered. She gazed down and back at us while still hauling ass to get away.

"She doesn't know who the fuck I am. My wife doesn't know who the fuck I am, again." I exhaled, wondering if I should sift and stop her from running, or let her exhaust her energy, so she didn't fight as much when I placed her over my shoulder and took her to bed to remind her of to whom she belonged.

"Let me try something real fast," Adam chuckled. He ran after her, glamouring on the pretty-boy image of what he'd looked like while being a member of her coven "Syn!" She turned, slowing, looking at Adam with recognition. "It's okay," he assured her, but her mouth opened and closed as she stared over his shoulder to where I stood. Her eyes were vacant of the recognition I needed and craved.

"I left her there, and I fucking lost her."

"You might have for a little while, but why the fuck would she go to Adam of all people?" Lucian asked, watching Synthia as her arms wrapped around him. "You may need to bend that ass over and remind it how you feel cradled in it. Or, you may lose her to that band boy member she's trying to climb at the moment."

"She was raised with him at the guild. In fact, Adam was of this world too. She called him to her when her parents were slaughtered by her brother." I watched her whispering behind her hand, glaring at me. "What exactly happens when the Seelie consume parts of a soul, and how do I get my wife back? I could just push the memories into her, speed this shit up, right?"

Thanatos snorted, shaking his dark head, and his eyes began to glow an eerie blue as power entered the field. "You could, but you would break her mind. You force her memories to return, and you'll never get her back. She has to want to remember. You think you could just make it so? You wanted her powerful, and she is.

"You wanted her to lose parts of herself, but she didn't need to lose them. Those parts, the humanity that you thought held her back—it didn't. Someone *is* holding her back. So, you need to ask yourself who that could be, Ryder? That fucking humanity, it is rare, and it is who she is and a huge part of why she's so fucking beautifully fierce and loves your family. She stood outside your bedroom and threatened to take me on to protect your family, Ryder. So, stop assuming you can just rip parts of her out to make her accept what you need for her to ascend. You can't take the piece of a person that make them into who they are and rip them out without damaging consequences.

"She didn't need to fucking sacrifice her humanity to grab her power. She just needed to feel secure enough to do what is needed of her. What you ought to do is ask yourself why your wife didn't feel safe enough to grab what was rightfully hers to take?" Thanatos muttered. "I've watched you both struggle to rule, but here's the thing: It's not about who has the power or who is stronger than whom. It's about finding a balance, and if you can't find it together or take her as she is, you will lose her. She's an amazing woman, so don't think there's not a fuckton of us men hoping you fuck up and we get a shot with her.

"Good luck, you're going to fucking need it. The creature only ate her favorite memories, which were of you and your children. Lucky fucker," Thanatos groaned before vanishing with the reapers in a cloud of dark smoke. I turned, studying Synthia as she watched me, her eyes narrowed as if she was plotting my murder.

"Fucking great, she's reverted back to a fucking guild enforcer, and I'm enemy number one, again."

The End, For Now

Part II Coming Very Soon

SneakPeek

LEGACY
OF THE
NINE REALMS

FLAMES of CHAOS

The new series by Amelia Hutchins.

Think Ryder and Synthia - 4.0

LEGACY
OF THE
NINE REALMS

FLAMES
of
CHAOS

CHAPTER
1

Exhaling a long, shaky breath, I stared at the lights of the city below the cliff I stood upon. Haven Falls, a city of immortal beings that weren't even from the Human Realm. A place that haunted my dreams and lived in every nightmare I'd ever had. It was nestled between winding valleys, hidden within them to remain a secret from the mortals whose realm we lived in. I'd stood in the same spot long enough for the day to become night. The town had turned from a bustling hub of activity to a lighted dreamscape.

I'd been twelve when my Aunt Aurora had taken

us away from here, away from the cruel brutality of the immortal realms from which we'd come. This place held no appeal and no good memories for me. It was the center of everything I hated; everything I wished to burn down and feel the ashes of the wreckage between my toes. I'd dreamt once I had burned it down, leaving those who stood aside and watched me being tortured, brutalized, and terrorized by my mother, in ashes.

My sisters didn't share my vision of this place, nor had they endured what my mother put me through trying to end my life. They relished being home, seeing their old friends while helping me search for my twin, who had been missing several months now without a single sign of her.

My eyes lifted toward the galaxies of stars above and then lowered to fall on the oldest of my sisters as she moved to where I stood.

Sabine was everything gentle and motherly to us since she was the oldest and had been present for every set of twins being born, and also because our mother was a heartless bitch. We had to learn quickly to depend on one another in order to survive. Stopping beside me, she peered up at the stars before she spoke.

"Once we enter the town, they'll know we are back," she muttered in a hushed tone, pushing her golden curls away from her face as the wind picked up, mirroring the internal struggle her words created within me.

"They already know we are here," I countered, sensing eyes that viewed us as we stood in the crisp evening air, staring out at the town. "We are being watched and have been since the moment we exited the cars."

"They can watch us all they want. Someone here knows what happened to Amara, and we're not leaving here until we find her."

Frowning, I considered her words. Amara had been withdrawn from me for a while now, and I wasn't so sure she wanted to be found. It hadn't been unusual for her to be missing for an extended period, but this one felt different. It felt wrong, and everything inside of me said to find her before it was too late to save her.

Turning, I took in the stares of my sisters, who had rallied behind me to come find Amara. Every single one of them refused to stay behind, and I loved them more for it. We were of the original family of witches, born from the same blood that ran through Hecate, the Goddess of Witches. She was my grandmother, and because of her, we had a duty to this town, one we'd escaped from until now. We'd left our mother, Freya, here to deal with the fallout, but Freya was wishy-washy and had a bad reputation for shirking her duties. She vanished soon after we did. *Shocker.*

Amara, my sister who I had a love-hate relationship with for the last few years, had come back to Haven Falls to secure our family's place on the council within the Nine Realms when word had reached us that Freya had vanished without a word. It would have been troubling if it was anything new, but it wasn't.

Freya loved men, and she cared little about propriety or reputation when she took them as lovers. She hated being part of the council that oversaw the immortals entering the Human Realm from the Nine Realms.

Only those with the purest of bloodlines could sit on the council of the Nine Realms. Together they decided whether immortals were safe enough to enter the Human Realm and if they could maintain our secrets. In the center of town is the portal between this realm and the entrance to the Nine Realms. Those coming through had to check in with the council, gaining papers that made them legal to be here.

Amara came back to Haven Falls on her own, offering to hold the seat among the council. I pleaded with her to reconsider, but she refused. She'd reminded me that no immortal passing through the portal could gain entrance unless a witch of Hecate bloodline voted with the others. Still, it could have been anyone else. She'd come back soon after that, but more often than not, she missed meetings. She withdrew from everything and everyone, which made waves in this town. Amara had even withdrawn from magic, unwilling to do spells that called for the coven, claiming she was drained or sick on the days they needed them.

Upon her return to the Human Realm, she checked in weekly, letting us know everything was fine. Then weeks turned into months, and then nothing. It was as if she just vanished. We'd called her phone, leaving voice messages and text messages to no avail. Then the day came when her phone was disconnected. Calls to the original families held little to no hope. No one had seen her in weeks, and even worse, the store we ran was closed down. The bond I shared with Amara had severed as if she'd just ceased to exist. For me, it was debilitating to be unable to reach out and sense the presence of my twin. It felt like a part of me was missing, and no matter how much I tried, I couldn't reconnect it.

"Someone in this town has to know what happened

to her," my sister Luna said, slipping her hand into mine and squeezing it reassuringly. "They'll regret it if they touched one of our own. There are enough of us to wage war if they so much as harmed a hair on her pretty head."

Enough of us.

My family was composed of all females, eight sets of twins. Hecate had cursed her line to birth multiples, all female offspring. She'd ensured we would never be alone, but that came at a heavy price. Any female who carried a male child learned quickly the cost of doing so. My mother was the daughter of Hecate, purest of blood, and yet she birthed twin daughters without a care of what happened after we'd detached from her womb. Her sisters Hysteria and Aurora had been the ones to deal with the repercussions of her overactive libido.

Freya had wanted an army of witches, but she didn't want the responsibility that came with birthing that army herself. Instead, she left us with her sisters, who loved us like their own children, Aurora more so than Hysteria. Hysteria had entered the portal and hasn't been heard of since. Hecate herself birthed two sets of twins. Freya and Aurora and Hysteria and Kamara. Kamara had been lost centuries ago or left on her own. Nobody knew what happened to her, other than she'd vanished and hadn't been seen or heard of since.

"We may have to consider the fact that she might have gone with our mother," Kinvara stated, shrugging when I stared at her, brow raised in a questioning look.

"I have considered it, but Amara isn't that stupid." I frowned, knowing it was a viable explanation, but that wouldn't make Amara safe. "I don't think she'd be stupid enough to trust our murderous mother."

"I don't think our mother would try to murder Amara," Sabine pointed out. "She's cold-blooded for sure, but she isn't a murderer. Maybe she wanted Amara with her to lure men to her bed, but murder? I don't think she would do something like that to her own child."

"Seriously?" I snorted. "That bitch tried to murder me frequently. Hell, she tried to abort Amara and me from her womb. If Aurora hadn't stepped in during every attempt on my life, I would be dead. I was a *child*."

Sabine frowned, nodding at the anger and hatred that dripped from my words. "She was crazed after she came back. Something was off, Aria. I don't know why she did what she did to you, but whatever the reason, know that she wasn't the same when she returned from the Nine Realms, heavily pregnant with you and Amara."

"It doesn't excuse her actions, Sabine. She tried to murder me."

"Yes, and Aurora saved you. She never tried to murder Amara directly. She only aimed for her when you were both in her womb, so not sure you can assume she'd go for her now. That is what we are saying, and since we left this place, she hasn't been able to find you. Aurora made certain we were untraceable."

Our mother, God love her, wasn't selective about the creatures she took between her thighs. Freya also never kept track of who had fathered us, making it impossible to know what we were until the change began within us; then, we handled it on our own. Aine and Luna had glowing blue eyes, marking them alpha wolves, alerting us to their heritage. Sabine and Callista were nymphs or sirens, but it was hard to tell since there wasn't much difference between the two species. We'd resorted to calling them hookers because it made them laugh when we did. Kinvara and Valeria were succubi, the result of our mother getting busy with a horde of incubus demons on one of her trips into the Nine Realms. She'd created her own twisted version of Noah's ark, but with daughters.

Our father's blood only determined half of what we were; our mothers, the other. Unlike my sisters, who had realized what they were by their sixteenth birthday, I had no idea what I was. Where they depended on nature to cast magic or spells, I wielded it from someplace else. It was exhilarating when I used magic, but there was a call to something darker within me that preened proudly when I did. As if something deadly slumbered within me and had yet to awaken fully.

"Cars are coming from the east," Luna stated, staring in that direction. She tilted her head, listening as we all followed her gaze.

"Friend or foe, Luna?" Sabine asked softly as if she feared they would hear her.

"Silly sister," I chuckled darkly. "They're all foe." I watched the dark highway behind us and then narrowed my gaze as headlights finally came into view.

Luna sniffed the air and smirked generously. "I smell men, and nice smelling ones at that. Alpha wolves or something else similar to the genetic makeup. I smell raw power and violence in the air that screams of danger. Eight men or so," she said, sniffing once more before nodding. "I'm thinking foe."

"But we like men," Aine said as her own nose lifted, inhaling deeply. "Especially ones that smell like these creatures. Meow, mommas, get ready. Get your game faces on." She fluffed her hair and fixed her breasts before speaking again. "Definitely foe, but I can use some hate fucking about now."

"How do you know they're foe?" Sabine asked, worrying her lip between her teeth as she waited for their answer.

"Easy, Aria just said they're all foe," Luna snorted, rolling her eyes as she adjusted her breasts and compared hers with her twin, Aine's. She withdrew a tube of lip gloss, slathering it on her lips as we all studied her prepping for sex.

"You guys are disturbing sometimes," I muttered.

I reached up, hooking my silver hair behind my ears, not that it would help with the wind howling around us. I didn't need a mirror to know my eyes would be bluer than green with the lack of sleep I'd had in the last twenty-four hours. I'd had nightmares and had given up trying to sleep at the thought of returning to this place.

The car's pulled up, aiming high-beams directly at us. It forced those who were sensitive to light to cover their eyes as it shined over us. I silently inspected the men unloading from the black SUVs, moving toward us in a dark, lethal way that couldn't be concealed, no matter what mask of civility they'd donned to enter this realm.

My eyes locked onto the tallest male, inspecting him as muscles pushed against the shirt he wore. He was a good head taller than the others. Power exuded from him, pushing against my flesh as he reached up and pushed light brown hair away from his face. Ocean-colored eyes slid over the lot of us before they moved back to me, lifting his nose, inhaling our scents.

"You're unwelcome here. Leave, and you can

live; stay, and you die," he announced with an accent I couldn't place. He was sex in the purest form, and even I couldn't tear my eyes off him—or couldn't until Kinvara snorted.

"Is that how you welcome ladies to town?" she asked, her pheromones filling the air to tempt him to her. *Hussy.*

"I won't ask again, ladies."

"You don't have the authority to tell us to leave," I said, pulling his lethal glare back to me and off of my sister. I crossed my arms over my chest, daring him to tell me I was wrong. When I got mad, I dug my heels in deep and didn't give an inch of room for anyone to push me around.

CHAPTER
2

He smiled coldly, studying my face while I did the same to him. His power wrapped around me threateningly. It was debilitating power that tightened around my throat, causing the hair on my neck to rise in warning. The smirk on his sinful mouth told me he had done it on purpose, knowing it wasn't something that could be ignored. His intense gaze swallowed me whole, drowning me slowly as it beckoned me into the deep waters, white-capped waves that promised to consume me.

"Oh, but I do, little girl," he chuckled darkly. "I am the king here. That means I hold all the power over any who enter Haven Falls and my jurisdiction," he snorted, stepping closer to where I stood, silently taking him in. He stopped mere inches away from me and sniffed the air again.

I inhaled his scent, barely containing the shiver that raced down my spine. It was a mixture of sandalwood and a hint of whiskey. The button-up shirt he wore did little to conceal the contours of his body, which I studied absently. Not too beefed up, but more than a swimmer's build. His arms were lightly tattooed, with writing in ancient languages, if I wasn't mistaken. He wore jeans that hugged powerful legs ending at black Doc Martin shit-kickers. I pulled my gaze from his body and rested it on his face, taking in the sharp jawline that was lightly dusted in a five o'clock shadow. His mouth was full, sensual, and pulled back tightly to reveal a smile that was all teeth.

"Are you finished eye-fucking me?" he asked darkly, his voice sending a shiver racing down my spine.

"Maybe," I said before giving myself a mental shake. "Since when does Haven Falls need a king?" His eyes did a slow perusal of my body, stopping briefly over the top I wore, which crisscrossed over my chest, exposing my midriff and sides, leaving a little more cleavage than I was comfortable with being exposed to his heated stare. My skirt was slit up the sides of my legs, revealing both thighs before it stopped at my hips. The boots I wore matched his, but they were more for comfort than kicking ass. Slowly, his eyes lifted to my breasts once more before stopping on my face.

"Since I took control of it," he growled. The sound of his voice slithered over my flesh, wrapping around my throat until air no longer could enter my airway. "Who the fuck would you be, little girl?"

"Aria Hecate, daughter of Freya Hecate, born of Hecate," I smirked impishly, watching as his eyes narrowed, and the tick in his jaw hammered at the mention of my last name. "These are my sisters, and

I assure you, even as the king, you don't have the authority to remove us."

He chuckled seductively, closing the distance until he was in my space, breathing my air until there wasn't enough for the two of us to inhale. His breath fanned my flesh; his proximity forced my neck to careen to hold his stare. He lifted his hand and brushed a single finger over my cheek as he stared me down.

"Hecate," he hissed as if the name was something vile stuck to the tip of his tongue. "Fucking witches." Snorting, he stared me dead in the eye as if he'd be happier with his large hands around my throat.

"Well, not sure on the fucking part, but we're definitely witches."

"And what is your other half, Aria Hecate? Your mother was a whore, one who slept with any creature brave enough to crawl between her thighs."

"Me? Who knows, because as you've so delicately pointed out, my mother is a whore," I noted, studying the way his eyes narrowed on me as he lifted his nose, inhaling deeply. "You want to sniff my ass too?" I assumed he was an alpha wolf, but the power radiating off of him wasn't anything I'd felt before.

"You should leave before it's too late, witch." His men chuckled behind him, and I narrowed my eyes on him, letting my eyes slide down his frame before coming up to frown as if he were lacking. "Your kind is nothing but fucking trouble."

"You don't know me, so I suggest you stop stereotyping me with other witches. I'm not leaving because some asshole tells me to leave. I have it on good authority that, at this moment, no Hecate witch sits on the council, which means there is a line to get into this realm that isn't getting pushed through. Tell me I'm wrong, oh great King of Haven Falls?" He stared me down with coldness in his gaze that sent ice humming through my veins. "Without one on the council, the covenant cannot award citizenship to immortals wishing to enter this realm. They need our bloodline present to approve those applications, and the process calls for a vote from each original bloodline, or did that change when you proclaimed yourself a king?" I waited for him to say something to counter it, but his eyes just gazed into mine, until I swallowed hard, my confidence shaking as he continued to watch me chillingly. "Mmm, didn't think so. Not even a self-proclaimed king has the authority to overthrow the covenant."

"Aria," he said, tasting my name on his tongue while I smirked. I had expected him to argue, not to step closer and lift my chin. His touch sent butterflies racing through my insides. "I don't care who the fuck you are, or what last name you throw around. I own this fucking town. I will eat you for breakfast, little girl, and I enjoy eating pretty things."

"I hope that's not a metaphor for eating pussy! Aria is a virgin, and someone has to pop that overly ripe cherry!" Kinvara shouted, and I turned, staring at her. The entire clearing was dead silent after her words had filled it.

I blushed as the male studied me, noting the reddening in my cheeks. He smirked wolfishly, which caused my eyes to lower to his sensual mouth. I pulled my face away from his touch, shooting Kinvara a deadly glare as she shrugged innocently.

"Hey, I'm all for you getting that cherry eaten. Gods know you need to get some before you explode," she offered, wincing.

"Shut up, Kinvara, you're not helping the situation," Sabine groaned.

He inspected me, unnerving me with the intensity of his stare. Lightning crashed above us, and I peered up, staring at the sky covered in dense clouds. It struck again beside us, causing my eyes to narrow as my sisters jumped. The male had yet to look away from me, and when my gaze moved back to his eyes, there was something sinister within them. The wind picked up, howling eerily, sending my hair whipping against my face. I turned my back to the male, staring at where the lightning continued to strike without stopping. I stepped back absently, unable to shake the feeling that something was in the woods, watching us.

I bumped into something hard and unmoving. I looked over my shoulder before staring up into stormy eyes that narrowed on me as he inhaled once more. The heat of his body slithered over my bare flesh, but the power he exuded was worse than the heat. Tearing my gaze from his, I watched as a dark shadow slipped from the forest.

"What the hell is that?" I whispered, barely loud enough to be heard over the crashing of the lightning as it hit the ground.

"You tell me, Aria," he demanded, touching my waist, causing my skin to pebble into goosebumps from the single brush of his fingers.

"Mine," it hissed as if it was the ugly little bugger, Gollum, from *Lord of the Rings*. "Aria Hecate is mine!" it screeched, causing me to tilt my head.

"Pass," I muttered. "That's not ominous or anything."

"Come to me, Aria. Let me taste your sweetness, little one," it continued.

I didn't need an invitation. I exploded into action, running toward the creature as power erupted around me. It smiled, waving its hand, beckoning me closer. I stopped where it had been, turning in a full circle only to find not a single trace of the beckoning creature. My hands lifted, uprooting trees from where they attached to the ground, holding them suspended in the air as I peered around, finding no sign of the creature. Slowly and methodically, I placed the trees back into the ground. Lightning crashed beside me, and I turned, inhaling the scent of burned ozone before veering toward my sisters, running right into a chest that smelled of heavenly male.

I peered up, frowning at him suspiciously. His hands captured my waist, pulling me against him as he peered down. "Let me go now," I stated coldly.

"Witch, huh?" he hissed. "Witches do not control the elements, nor do they have enough power on tap to uproot hundreds of trees, let alone to place them back into the ground."

"You don't get to fondle me or ask me questions. I don't even know your name," I ground out, studying him as his touch sent a pulse of electrical current racing through me.

"It's Knox. What the fuck are you, Aria?"

"Mmm, what the hell are *you*? Not an alpha wolf; your eyes aren't blue enough. Not an incubus, because you're not oozing enough sex for me to toss my clothes down and beg you to touch me. Not a demon, because you don't carry their scent. The writing on your arms suggest you aren't from here, so who the fuck are you, Knox? And why are you in my town?"

"I asked you first."

"Wouldn't you like to know," I whispered, licking my lips as he watched. "Let me go, asshole. I can already tell that I'm not going to like you. So, unless you plan on stealing a base, get the fuck off of me. I'm not into baseball."

"Afraid of the bat, or just not good playing with balls?"

"It's the balls. I always seem to make them explode unexpectedly. No one seems to like it when their balls explode prematurely."

"That depends on within whom they explode."

I stuttered for a retort and then clamped my mouth closed, blinking at his statement. Well, that backfired. "Keep your balls away from me."

"Afraid you may like my dick?" he asked, lifting his hand to push away a stray strand of hair. "Be a good girl, and I may even let you suck it."

"You two going to fuck, or you want a few more minutes alone?" Luna asked, watching us.

I ignored her, pulling my arm from Knox's hold before I sidled up next to him, watching as he studied me. "I wouldn't suck your dick if it contained the last air molecule in the entire universe, *puppy*. You're not man enough to handle me, anyway. You're probably like every other male on this planet who thinks bitches should bow down and worship that tiny little thing between your legs. I don't fucking bow to anyone. I sure as fuck don't bow to "some self-conceited, self-absorbed, self-appointed king" to a town that should be burned to ashes and destroyed, asshole," I muttered as I turned, marching back to where my sisters stood, listening to everything we said. "Let's go before something else welcomes us back or tries to kill us."

"I suggest you be at the council meeting tomorrow and learn the new laws of Haven Falls. If you fuck with me, little girl, I will fuck you back. I don't have mercy when I fuck my enemies. If you don't like the new laws, you can get the fuck out of my town."

"Who says I would ever want mercy from you?" I snorted as I spun on him, lifting a brow in question. "You don't scare me, Knox. You don't even register on the scale of things I fear."

"Yeah, let's test that fucking theory, shall we?" he asked. A loud crashing noise exploded, and the world vanished around me.

Flames of Chaos is available now everywhere! *Ashes of Chaos* is coming soon! Don't miss the epic fantasy series that fans of the Fae Chronicles are raving about as the new Ryder and Syn.

ABOUT

the Author

Amelia lives in the great Pacific Northwest with her family. When not writing, she can be found on her author page, hanging out with fans, or dreaming up new twisting plots. She's an avid reader of everything paranormal romance.

Stalker links!

Facebook: https://www.facebook.com/authorameliahutchins

Website: http://amelia-hutchins.com/

Goodreads: https://www.goodreads.com/author/show/7092218.Amelia_Hutchins

Twitter: https://twitter.com/ameliaauthor

Pinterest: http://www.pinterest.com/ameliahutchins

Instagram: https://www.instagram.com/author.amelia.hutchins/

Facebook Author Group: https://goo.gl/BqpCVK

Made in the USA
Las Vegas, NV
16 March 2021

19670821R00353